The shaman stepped back, hands pressed over Balkis' body, and finished the incantation.

In desperation, Balkis thought the words, mind flinging them like darts even as the room began to blur around her:

"Abort this spell; its gist ignore!
Regain the world, this earthen shore!
From this realm I'll never stray
And never shall be torn away!"

The room turned to mist, vertigo seized her, she felt herself whirling through a void that was not of her world—but distant and fading, she heard the shaman's howl of rage and knew that, even unspoken, her spell had frustrated his, though not canceled it completely. She sailed through emptiness to a destination unknown both to herself and the shaman who launched her—unknown, but of her world . . .

By Christopher Stasheff
Published by The Ballantine Publishing Group

A Wizard in Rhyme:
HER MAJESTY'S WIZARD
THE OATHBOUND WIZARD
THE WITCH DOCTOR
THE SECULAR WIZARD
MY SON, THE WIZARD
THE HAUNTED WIZARD
THE CRUSADING WIZARD
THE FELINE WIZARD

Starship Troupers:
A COMPANY OF STARS
WE OPEN ON VENUS
A SLIGHT DETOUR

The Star Stone:
THE SHAMAN
THE SAGE

THE FELINE WIZARD

Book VIII in *A Wizard in Rhyme*

Christopher Stasheff

A Del Rey® Book
THE BALLANTINE PUBLISHING GROUP
NEW YORK

A Del Rey® Book
Published by The Ballantine Publishing Group
 Published in the United States by The Ballantine Publishing Group, a division of Random House, Inc., New York, and simultaneously in Canada by Random House of Canada Limited, Toronto.

www.randomhouse.com/delrey/

ISBN 0-345-39245-0

Manufactured in the United States of America

First Edition: June 2000

10 9 8 7 6 5 4 3 2

AUTHOR'S NOTE

Though I have taken great liberties and embroidered considerably, most of the wonders Balkis and Anthony encounter on their trip north, such as the giant ants, the Grand Feminie, the magical oasis, and the curing stone, are taken from later versions of the Prester John letter and from works claiming to describe his empire. I have even taken a new name for Prester John's capital city—an older name for one of the great cities on the trade route. I have, of course, invented events to tie them all together. I hope the reader will enjoy the result.

CHAPTER 1

The royal children were pestering Matt and Alisande when the call came.

"Mama, *need* another kitty!" Princess Alice said, pouting.

"She has the right of it, Mama," Prince Kaprin maintained with the magisterial weight of his six years. "Balkis was a great deal of fun, but she went away!"

"Good cuddle, too." Alice was still pouting.

The family was gathered in the solar for a few precious minutes before the queen began her arduous day. Breakfast leftovers cluttered the sideboard, and the table bore the scraps of a good breakfast. Both the notion of a well-balanced meal and the china on which it was served were the suggestions of the Lady Jimena Mantrell, the royal grandmother. She had imported them from her own universe with her husband, who sat back watching his grandchildren fondly and his daughter-in-law the queen with admiration. Jimena glanced at her son, the Lord Wizard and Prince Consort, and was pleased to see that his attention was all for his family.

It was just a quiet family morning, only the two children, one mother, one father, two grandparents, one governess, one nursemaid, a butler, and two guards at the door. There had been a footman and two servers, but they had disappeared back into the kitchen.

The richly grained wood of the table, the chairs, and the sideboard glowed with the light of the morning sun streaming in through the tall clerestory windows. It brought out the highlights in the Oriental carpet and made the figures on the tapestries seem to quiver with life. The fire on the hearth had died to coals—both fireplace and chimney were the Lord

Wizard's addition from his own universe, and his father had contrived to add a fire screen when the little prince started crawling.

"There's nothing quite like a cat curled up and purring to give a room a feeling of contentment," Matt admitted.

Queen Alisande sighed. "I will readily admit that another cat would be a pleasant companion, but we could never find one like Balkis."

That was an understatement. Balkis, after all, had been a human teenager with the uncanny knack of changing herself into a cat whenever she wanted. She had entered the castle under false pretenses, presenting herself as a mouser and playmate. Actually, she had come to eavesdrop on Matt and learn his magic; she already knew a great deal, but had been hungry for more.

"Want Balkis back!" Alice progressed from pouting to a trembling chin.

Alisande sighed and gathered the three-year-old into her lap. "You know she could not stay with us, dear heart. She was a veritable princess of a cat, and had to go back to her people in their need."

In fact, Balkis had helped Matt free her enslaved people—but she hadn't known they were her people until after she and Matt helped Prester John lead them in reconquering Maracanda from the barbarians who had overrun it. Then they discovered that Prester John was her uncle, and that Fortune had led her home. Matt had dropped by Fortune's cave to thank her on the way back to Merovence. Balkis, under the circumstances, had decided to stay in Maracanda and reclaim her mother's title: Princess of the Eastern Gate.

"Her people needed her," Matt explained.

"So did I!" Alice's trembling chin firmed, lower lip jutting.

"I know that no other kitty could ever be Balkis," Kaprin said, with an air of precocious wisdom, "but we could have another for playmate."

That, of course, was the rub—that royal children were notoriously short on playmates. Alisande winced, remembering the loneliness of her own childhood, and Matt tried to hide his smile as her shoulders slumped in capitulation.

A loud pop saved her from having to answer.

Actually, it was more of a small bang than a loud pop. Alice cried out and hid her face in her mother's bosom. Kaprin shouted and ducked behind Alisande. The sentries' halberds flashed down to guard. Alisande and Matt both tensed to fight, his hand going to his dagger, her left arm tightening around little Alice as her right hand dropped to the dirk sheathed in her kirtle. Her gaze was already on the source of the noise.

So was Matt's. They saw a scroll suspended in midair, spinning around and around for a moment before it fell to the floor.

Three Days Earlier and Thousands of Miles Away

The King of the Gilded Earth ladled soup into Prester John's bowl, as he did on the first day of each week. Five other kings and one queen took turns with him, a different one on each day. They did not serve Prince Tashih, Princess Balkis, or the clergy, of course; that office was left to mere dukes and counts, who took the duty in rotation—sixty-two dukes and 365 counts, a different nobleman-server for each day of the year. Other aristocrats were assigned to other duties.

The talk passed about, lively and spiced with wit, an archbishop replying to the observations of a protopapas with quotations from Aristotle and Confucius while the prince countered the witticisms of a patriarch with sallies of his own. Amidst the good cheer, though, Balkis sat wan and dispirited, poking at her food with her chopsticks but not really eating.

If the others noticed, they said nothing. Prester John asked with kind concern, "What troubles you, my dear?"

Balkis looked up, startled, then gave him an apologetic smile. "Nothing, truly, Uncle. I am only a little cast down by thoughts of ho—of Allustria."

Prince Tashih looked up, but Prester John's concern only deepened. "We must lift your spirits, then. Perhaps coming to know the people of this land would make you feel more at home."

Balkis looked out over the sea of courtiers. "I have met many, and they do seem to be kind and generous people."

"I speak not of these gilded nobles alone, but also of the common folk. There are differences among them, though—each district has its own customs and styles. Perhaps a journey would cheer you, a tour of the provinces—with a full entourage and armed escort, of course. It would help you come to know the land of your birth."

Balkis gave her great-uncle a gentle smile, touched by his concern. "I am truly quite happy here in my native land, Majesty—I have had no other home since my foster parents died."

"But tonight you are not happy," he objected.

Balkis stirred impatiently. "Oh, there will always be homesickness for my grand and awe-inspiring Allustrian forest, Uncle—but I have no home there now, and do have here. I daresay I shall grow out of this melancholy in time."

Prester John frowned with concern, but said no more about his proposed tour. His son did, though, after dinner in his own suite, to a dozen dandified sycophants and their languid ladies. "A tour of the provinces indeed!" he stormed. "Why should she need to come to know this land in such detail if she is not destined to rule?"

A courtier, quick to read the prince's mood, agreed. "If not all, at least part."

A lady shuddered. "Divide the land? Then both halves would be weak, and prey to the barbarians."

Her shudder passed through the whole cortege. They had all had experience of the barbarians' rule.

"Who is this chit anyway, to come among us so suddenly?" another courtier asked in disgust. He had spent years ingratiating himself with Prince Tashih and was appalled at the notion of his investment going to waste.

"We all know that well enough," a lady sighed. "She is the daughter of Prester John's sister, who managed to send her baby into freedom before she died. Now the lass has come back to claim her mother's title."

"And half the prince's inheritance, to boot," a man said grimly.

Prince Tashih winced but waved a hand in dismissal of the notion. "I am sure my father will do what is right, and is best for the empire."

"Or what he thinks is best," said another courtier darkly. He thought that the road to success lay in putting into words the feelings the prince longed to articulate but would not, out of loyalty to his father. "Agreed, the young lady is charming—she might well charm him into giving her anything she wishes—but could she rule well or wisely?"

"She has shown no sign of a wish to rule." The prince strove to disprove the very suspicion he had himself planted.

"If she does not," said the first courtier, "why does your father wish her to come to know the land?"

The prince turned away in agitation, unable to refute his own point without seeming foolish.

Two of the younger courtiers, who had not been with the prince long enough to gain much preference, exchanged a significant glance. Sikander gave a small, secret smile, and Corundel's rouged lips smiled back.

When the courtiers left the prince's apartments, Sikander and Corundel lagged behind until they were sure they would not be overheard. Then Sikander said, "I do not think the prince would be overly distressed if the princess were to disappear."

"I think he would be inclined to favor those who aided her escape," Corundel agreed.

"But what if she does not wish to escape?" Sikander asked.

Corundel tossed her head. "Then she must be made to see the advantage of it."

"You are as clever as you are beautiful," Sikander replied. "How, though, are we to convince her to resume her travels?"

"I have a powder with which to spice her wine," Corundel said. "The apothecary who sold it to me is a Polovtsi shaman, and I think he may not be as loyal to the Christian and Muslim gods as one would expect of a good citizen of Maracanda."

"Nor of the Buddha, nor Confucius either?" Sikander smiled. "If he is a barbarian, perhaps his true sympathies lie with our recent conquerors."

"They might." Corundel's lips curved in a malicious smile.

"Surely he would know a barbarian sorcerer whose renunciation of Ahriman might not be as complete as he pretended."

She, like so many of the court ladies, resented the beautiful, vivacious young princess who had suddenly appeared in their midst and captivated all the young men with her grace, charm, and innocence—but she knew quite well that those who appear suddenly can disappear just as suddenly, and she had great trust in the fickleness of men.

The room was silent, everyone staring at the scroll. It seemed harmless enough, just a rolled sheet of parchment bound by a ribbon and fastened with a large blob of wax sculpted into an ornate bas-relief by the sender's seal.

Grandpa Ramon broke the silence. "Special delivery, I think."

"It would seem so," said Grandma Jimena. "There must be dire need if it requires the magic expended to send this letter, my son."

"Yeah, there sure must," Matt agreed.

No one moved, all staring at the scroll where it lay, no one particularly interested in picking it up, the sentries and the governess through fear of its magic, the wizards—Matt, his mother and father—through wariness of the news it must hold.

Finally Alisande asked, "Will you be so good as to lift that scroll, husband?"

"I suppose I should." Matt leaned forward and picked up the scroll. He stared in surprise. "Addressed to me!" He held it up for them to see, and sure enough, there was his name in very ornate brush-stroke calligraphy.

"Then I think you may open it," Alisande said, with a touch of impatience.

"Huh? Oh, yeah!" Matt untied the ribbon, broke the seal, and unrolled the parchment. His eyes grew rounder as he read.

"May I know?" Alisande's voice had a definite edge now.

"A letter from Prester John." Matt exchanged a significant glance with Alisande.

"Ay di mi!" Alisande sighed. "The world presses in again! Sometimes I envy the burghers' wives, who need have no fear that affairs of state will descend upon them while they are enjoying quiet moments with their families."

The children understood these preliminaries—they had heard their like many times before. Kaprin sighed philosophically, kissed his mother, hugged his father and grandparents, and went to the governess. Alice readied another pout, but Alisande cajoled her. "Come now, sweeting, you know I would not send you back to the nursery without strong need. There now, your mother is a queen, and may not always do as she wishes."

The younger sentry visibly restrained a look of astonishment—he was new at this duty.

"Don't like it!" the three-year-old stated, but she slipped off her mother's lap anyway.

"There's my darling!" Alisande leaned forward to kiss the crown of her head, then turned her toward the governess and gave her a pat to start her. "Perhaps a story, Lady Lenore?"

"I have just the one!" The governess reached down for the children's hands. "Come, Highnesses—tonight we shall learn why people live so much longer than animals."

"A wonder tale!" Kaprin cried, his enthusiasm definitely forced—but it was contagious, and Alice was bombarding Lady Lenore with questions as they left the room.

Alisande reached out for Matt's hand as she watched them go, then dropped her gaze to the parchment. "Read."

Matt sighed and took it up. " 'From Prester John, King in Maracanda, Lord of the land of . . .' How about I skip all his titles, okay?"

"I am surprised he spent the ink to send them," Ramon said dryly.

"It is a necessary protocol, I fear, and wastes a good deal of parchment," Alisande said. "He addresses himself to you, my husband?"

Matt nodded. " 'To his most noble highness, Matthew Lord Mantrell . . .' I'll just skip to the message. 'We regret to inform you that your former ward, our niece Balkis, Princess of the Eastern Gate, is no longer at our court.' "

"She has run away?" Jimena stared.

"Not voluntarily," Matt said grimly. " 'On arising this

morning, we learned that she had been spirited away in the night. We hold the immediate malefactor in our prison, but know not the whereabouts of the man to whom he handed over the princess. We would slay him out of hand, but we are in hope that by your magic you may be able to wrest from his mind some indications of Princess Balkis' fate, as our own magic, and our jailers, have failed to do. We enjoin you to beg leave of your sovereign lady Alisande, Queen of Merovence, and come to aid us with all speed.' " He looked up as he rerolled the parchment. "The rest is courtly protocol. Um, sovereign lady—"

"Go," Alisande said instantly. Then tears filled her eyes and she reached out for his hand. "But O My Husband, take care!"

Ramon stood. "Perhaps his mother and I should go with him."

"Oh, I don't think there's any need for that," Matt said. "It's just a missing persons case, after all, not an attacking army."

"Yet by your tales, my son," Jimena said darkly, "even your minor troubles sometimes herald war."

"If there is any sign of it, summon aid at once!" Alisande commanded, still holding his hand. "Fetch Balkis quickly, husband, and come back to me!"

"I will," Matt promised. "It shouldn't be that hard a problem for a wizard. After all, it's only a kit-napping."

One of Balkis' ladies-in-waiting wished to keep a moonlight tryst with a handsome young courtier and found Corundel to be very sympathetic, offering to take her place for the evening—so that night, the princess' bedtime cup of heated rice wine was something more than it seemed. When Balkis had fallen into a sleep far deeper than usual, Sikander stole into her bedchamber, threw her cloak over her and wrapped the blankets around her, and carried her out into the hallway. With Corundel pacing ahead to keep watch, he carried the sleeping princess down a flight of stairs, out a door, through the shadows along the walls of the palace, and across the lawn to a man who waited astride a horse. There, he handed up the sleeping princess. The rider gave the courtier a nod of thanks, but as he turned his mount away, his lips curved with a smile of contempt.

Back into the palace Sikander went, where he told Corundel, "She is persuaded."

"And has begun her journey? Good!" Corundel's eyes shone. "What manner of man is her carrier?"

"Neither a Mongol nor a Turk—that much I could tell." Sikander shrugged. "Nothing more, though. He might be a Polovtsi or Kazakh, or of any of the other tribes of the western steppes." He turned away eagerly. "Let us tell the prince that he has one less concern."

"No, wait!" Corundel caught his arm. "Let the palace find her gone and take alarm. Then, when he cannot suppress his glee, let us tell him privately, so his gratitude may be all the sharper."

"Brilliant as ever." Sikander turned to beam upon her. "Still, let us celebrate by ourselves, sweet Corundel."

So they did, with wine and laughter—but in the midst of their merrymaking, Corundel could not rid herself of the thought that a man who would kidnap a princess could not be trusted in any way. Sikander, for his part, realized that a lady who would drug her mistress' wine must be naturally treacherous.

Such being their natures, the knowledge added spice to their evening.

Prester John lived half a world away, so Matt wasn't about to walk. He recited a spell to contact an old friend, then set off down the road from the capital. He had gone about three miles before a dragon pounced on him.

Of course, this dragon was the old friend. Matt looked up at the boom of wings cupping air for a landing and grinned. "Long time no see, Firebreather!"

"Long indeed, Softskin!" Stegoman settled beside Matt, folding his wings. "What emergency urges you to summon me from my life of indolence?"

"Indolence, my foot!" Matt scoffed. "What's all these stories I hear about a dragon scouring the countryside looking for troops of bandits to chase?"

"Mere popular fictions intended to lend color and excitement to an otherwise boring and lackluster existence," Stegoman said airily. "Where shall we wander, Matthew?"

"You remember that little cat I was traveling with last year?"

"The one who was a princess in disguise? She stayed in Central Asia, did she not?"

"Sure did, but now she's gone and gotten herself kidnapped."

"Well, we cannot have her lost in the wilds of the steppes, can we?" Stegoman lowered his neck, the triangular plates along his spine forming a convenient stairway. "Climb aboard, Matthew!"

CHAPTER 2

Even as the dragon flies, it was a three-day journey. The first night, Matt bought a bullock from a farmer for Stegoman. Apparently he paid more than the beast was worth, for the dragon complained that Matt had given him a bum steer—old, tough, and no longer good for anything but leather. The second night, though, the dragon was able to hunt and bagged an elk.

They were on the same latitude as the Holland of Matt's universe, and as they flew over the broad, flat plains of Russia, Matt realized that Prester John's realm had to be at the southern edge of the Siberia of his own world and wondered how it could be anything but a frozen wasteland, let alone so warm and fertile as the land he had seen when he visited. He had come up from the south then, flying in the arms of a genie princess, so he hadn't been able to see much, but the glimpses he had gained made it seem quite natural to go from the heat of India and the dryness of Afghanistan into the moderate climate of Maracanda, Prester John's capital city. Coming from the west, though, he was far more aware of the steppes, and when Stegoman gave him a culinary review on a dinner of raw musk ox, Matt realized they had come into tundra.

The next day, though, they flew over a lake that was so huge Matt thought it was a sea until the far shore came in sight. When they were finally over dry land again, he could see the eastern horizon glitter with a sheen that could only be another vast lake. Between the two bodies of water, the land fairly glowed with the green of rich farms and was tidy with the neatness of fields diligently tended. The same climactic shift that had kept the England of this universe joined to the rest of Europe had also created a lush realm in the very heart of the Asian plains.

A climactic shift, or enchantment. Matt looked down at Prester John's kingdom and wondered how much magic had gone into the creation of this realm. If it had, then magic must also sustain it, and what would happen if there were no Prester John, no heir to the title, to keep that magic flowing? Matt did not doubt that Prester John prized Balkis because she was his long-lost niece, but he began to wonder if it was also because she was a powerful wizard, only in her teens, with the promise of learning even more.

Looking off toward the north, Matt saw the green fade into the tan of steppeland again. Looking southward, though, he saw the richness of field and orchard die away in the desert into which Prester John had fled to escape the horde. He thought he saw more greenery beyond, but it was so dim with distance that he couldn't be sure.

Then alabaster towers appeared on the eastern horizon. Half an hour later they were flying over the steeples and minarets of Maracanda.

Matt had better sense than to try to land in the middle of the city—people were already crowding into the streets and squares, pointing up at dragon and rider and exclaiming in excitement and fear; he could hear the buzz of talk even a hundred feet up. "Better land outside the walls, Stegoman."

"That would seem prudent," the dragon agreed, and circled outside the wall to land in the center of a grove a quarter mile away. As Matt climbed down, Stegoman said sternly, "None of this creeping off in the night to spare me danger, now!"

"Not a bit," Matt promised. "If we march and I have to ride with them, I'll let you know."

"March?" Stegoman reared back his head. "Would this Prester John truly take an army to search for a missing child?"

"Doesn't seem likely," Matt admitted, "though the rumors about him make you think he never goes anywhere without a few thousand troops. But we've met before, and I think I can talk him into letting me go alone."

"Not alone!"

"Present company excepted, of course. I'll call you when I

leave. In the meantime, take a well-earned rest. Lie around a little. Have a cow."

The drug was not as effective as it might have been; a creature so saturated with magic as Balkis could not be held unconscious for long. She regained awareness with the jolting of a horse beneath her, saw the buildings of Maracanda passing stark against a starry sky, and wondered what manner of dream this was.

Then the horse stopped. A man slid from its back, pulled her down into his arms and carried her through a darkened doorway into a darker house. Balkis would have screamed, would have clawed at her captor's face, but though her mind was aware and her eyes open, a strange lassitude gripped her; she was too weak to move even a finger. Fear stabbed; she would have recited a spell to defend herself, but not even her lips would move.

The rider bore her down a narrow corridor past doorways closed by thick, richly decorated blankets, then through one final portal that held an actual wooden door, quite thick. She saw a ceiling of tree-trunk beams, stone walls darkened by dampness and lit by the glow of a brazier, and a rack of shelves containing clay jars and wooden boxes. The acrid reek of the place assaulted her nostrils—brimstone, saltpeter, smoke, and mold. Her stomach knotted as she recognized it for a sorcerer's workroom.

Her fear accelerated to panic as an old face loomed into her vision, a wrinkled and wind-burned face squinting down at her and nodding with satisfaction. He wore the headdress of a barbarian shaman. He spoke; Balkis recognized the language as Khitan and, thanks to the silent translation spell the Lord Wizard had taught her, understood it as well.

"Yes, that is she," the old man said. "That is one of the pair who can prevent the gur-khan from rising again. Without her, Maracanda will lie open to him when he has reunited his forces."

"Kill her, then?" the rider asked.

Panic lent Balkis strength; she managed to crook her fingers; her lips trembled—but nothing more.

"Would that we could." The shaman's eyes burned. "She aided his defeat, after all! But Prester John has mighty magic and can learn quickly if she has died, though he may not be able to discover who killed her, or where. No, we must send her away, send her so far away that she can never come back!"

Balkis' panic ebbed; anger replaced it. She used its energy to try to make her mouth move. She strained, fought to shape the words, but her lips only quivered.

"Lay her on the stone." The shaman gestured to his work-table. The rider laid her down while the shaman turned to throw incense on the coals in the brazier. An acrid aroma filled the room as the shaman set a variety of fetishes about the princess, chanting a spell.

> "Go you east by my fell power,
> To the land where peach trees flower,
> Where's never grief and never care,
> No leaving or departing there!"

Panic surged again as Balkis realized that wherever the shaman meant to send her would be as good as a prison—a very pleasant prison perhaps, but a prison nonetheless. She labored with all her strength to make her recalcitrant lips and tongue obey.

The shaman stepped back, hands passing over Balkis' body, and finished the incantation.

> "Far to the east, far from this world
> Where never known is mortal strife.
> Let this lass at once be hurled,
> Returning never in her life!"

In desperation, Balkis thought the words, mind flinging them like darts even as the room began to blur about her:

> "Abort this spell; its gist ignore!
> Regain the world, this earthen shore!
> From this realm I'll never stray . . ."

She floundered, beset by her old handicap—the final line! She had always had great difficulty ending a spell—why, she did not know.

"Why" did not matter—only the spell did! What rhymed with "stray?" What syllables could precede it, produce it?

At the last instant her mind found the words and hurled them after the rest.

"And never shall be torn away!"

The room turned to mist, vertigo seized her, she felt herself whirling through a void that was not of her world—but distant and fading, she heard the shaman's howl of rage, and knew that, even unspoken, her spell had frustrated his, though not cancelled it completely. She sailed through emptiness to a destination unknown both to herself and to the shaman who had launched her—unknown, but of her world.

The guards at the gates of the city had trouble believing this unprepossessing person in stout traveling clothes could really be an emissary from a foreign queen, let alone a lord. But those garments were outlandish, as were the round brown eyes and the pale skin, so his claim seemed possible, if unlikely.

"You have no entourage," the older guard pointed out, "no phalanx of soldiers to guard you, no minor lords in attendance."

"I prefer to travel light," Matt explained. "You learn more that way. Take my advice, boys, pass the buck. Call the captain of the guard."

The captain came out, and Matt showed him Prester John's letter. The two guards recognized the seal and turned pale. The captain stared, then flicked a glance from Matt to the letter, then back again, clearly unable to believe that this merchant-without-a-caravan could really be a lord. Nonetheless, he decided to get out of the middle and pass Matt along to *his* boss. He gave him a chariot ride and an honor guard of half a dozen soldiers. Matt rode the jolting vehicle over the ocher cobbles, very much aware that the guards could seize him as well as protect him.

The guards turned him over to the chamberlain, and the

man stared in amazement, recognizing Matt from his last visit. Then he recovered his poise, clearly resolving not to make the mistake he had made then, when he treated Matt and his party as common travelers. He bowed and said, "I am amazed that you could come so quickly, Lord Mantrell."

"Your king's letter made it seem urgent," Matt said, "and I had air transport available."

The chamberlain stared. "That dragon who flew over the city . . . was that . . ."

"Me on its back? Yes, but I didn't want to take a chance on landing in the plaza in front of the palace. Your sentries take their duties very seriously, and it never pays to underestimate a crossbow."

The chamberlain smiled, pleased at the compliment to his fellow citizens. "Will you follow, my lord?" He turned to snap a phrase to a page, and the boy stared at Matt, then took off running.

Possibly as a result, Matt only waited a few minutes in the antechamber before the chamberlain ushered him into Prester John's private study.

"Lord Wizard!" Prester John advanced, arms wide in welcome. "How good of you to come—and how quickly!"

"Glad to be back." Matt bowed, then straightened to survey the man closely. Prester John had lost weight; beneath the black beard, his cheeks had grown gaunt. His eyes were shadowed and haunted, and his golden skin had faded to parchment. He was taking the loss of his newfound niece very hard indeed. "Of course I'm glad to help any way I can," Matt assured him. "Any progress in finding Balkis?"

"Come and see." Prester John turned to the window in a whirl of gorgeous robes.

Matt stepped up and looked down through an elaborately carved screen at a courtyard full of soldiers milling about. He stared. "Is this your idea of a search party?"

"Of course," Prester John said, surprised. "Her rank merits nothing less. Balkis is Princess of the Eastern Gate, Lord Wizard."

"Well, yes, but a smaller force might be less noticeable and find her faster. Has there been any word of her? Maybe a beggar delivering a discreet note demanding that you surrender half your kingdom if you want to see her again?"

Prester John stared at him in horror. "No, not a word. Are such things common?"

"I've heard of them happening," Matt said in as neutral a tone as he could manage.

Old anger seeped through, though, making Prester John frown with concern. "Of course! Your own children were stolen last year."

Matt nodded. "And Balkis helped me find them, if you recall, so it's time to return the favor—but if there's no word of her, we also have no clues, no hints as to where she might be."

"None, save the man who spirited her away—but even he had no notion where the man to whom he gave her might have taken her." Prester John glared out at the army in the courtyard, his face dark with dread. "I very much fear she may be already dead, Lord Wizard."

Matt could see the grief welling up beneath the scowl. Alarmed, he said, "I very much doubt that, Your Majesty. Remember, she's a cat whenever she wants to be, and cats have nine lives. I suspect that a cat who is also a human wizard would have nine times nine."

Prester John turned to him with the ghost of a smile. "Eighty-one lives? Perhaps—if she transformed herself to a cat in time."

"Not much that could stop her," Matt assured him, then turned away toward the comfortable-looking chairs in the corner. "But I need to know everything that happened. How about you sit down and tell me about it?"

"Perhaps I have been pacing too long," the king admitted. He proved it by pacing over to the corner and sitting with a sigh. "Yes, that is welcome." He frowned at the still-standing wizard. "But you too must sit, Lord Wizard!"

"In the presence of a sovereign? Perish the thought!"

"You are not my subject, but the emissary of my fellow sovereign, the Queen of Merovence, and her consort! Come, sit!"

Matt bowed and sat. The chair was a welcome rest. "Now tell me how it all happened. Right from the top."

Prester John frowned. "The 'top'?"

"The beginning," Matt explained. "How long did it take Balkis to get used to Maracanda?"

"At once, and not at all," Prester John sighed. He gazed off into space, seeing the events as he spoke of them. "My niece loved the palace and the people instantly, and they rejoiced in her presence. Still, there were moments of melancholy . . ."

Prester John's voice trailed off. Matt tried to be reassuring. "That's normal enough in a teenager far from her own land, Your Majesty. There's bound to be the occasional bout of homesickness."

Prester John's smile was tight with irony. "But this is her own land, though she never knew it till you brought her here. Still, I cannot be surprised that she thinks of your Frankish land of Allustria as her home, since she grew up there."

Matt didn't think the Germanic people of Allustria would have appreciated being called "Frankish," but they'd had to suffer it during the Crusades of his own universe, too. "She would kind of miss the dense forest and the hundred-year-old oaks—and the mountains."

"She did indeed, and she yearned for—" Prester John broke off abruptly with a guilty glance at Matt, who smiled covertly.

Matt had been aware of Balkis' crush on him. He found himself hoping that wherever she'd been taken, she would find a gentle, handsome young man. "I hope you made sure she wasn't lonely."

"I did indeed," the king averred. "I surrounded her with young men and women of noble birth and set my own son Tashih to entertaining her when I could not. But if I could be with her, I was."

His eyes shone with the memory, with besotted fondness, and Matt, watching closely, saw that Balkis hadn't just been the great-niece returned to him by Fortune—she'd been the daughter he had never had, too. "Did the other young folk like her, or belittle her as subtly as they could?"

"Ah, they adored her. You would expect as much of the young men, for she is very beautiful. However, the women made her one of them instantly." He shrugged. "Who would not? She is not only beautiful, but also witty, spirited, and gentle. The older people were as entranced as the young, and she soon became the darling of all my courtiers."

Matt frowned. "That kind of instant popularity is bound to make someone jealous."

Prester John looked up, startled, then turned away, abashed.

"Someone did get jealous?" Matt asked, his voice low.

"My son Tashih," the king admitted, "he who is to become Prester John after me. Oh, he never spoke of it, but I could see it in his eyes when he watched her in the center of a knot of young men and women, chatting and laughing."

Matt dreaded the next question, but it had to be asked. "Just how jealous do you think he is?"

Prester John leaned back and closed his eyes with a weary sigh. "He might perhaps have worried that Balkis could gather a strong enough following to displace him when I die, Lord Wizard. I do not believe that is true, but it is possible."

He said it as though Matt had pulled it out of him with pincers, and the wizard felt himself tense at the thought. He knew enough of palace intrigues to believe that the crown prince might very well have wished to rid himself of a potential competitor. It wouldn't have been the first such abduction.

He couldn't say that to Prester John, of course. "But there was no real sign that he might take action?"

"Not truly, no." Prester John looked down at his knees, frowning. "Matters came to a head at dinner one evening a few days ago. It was no state banquet, but our daily informal affair—only my three thousand regular courtiers, and a few casual guests—say a thousand . . ."

Matt's head reeled with the numbers. He wondered if Prester John used his dining room as a parade ground when he wanted to drill his troops in bad weather. "I seem to remember such an affair. Each courtier finds a small bag next to the plate with the money for the next day's expenses, right?"

"It is the most unobtrusive way to deliver their stipends," Prester John said. "Of course, I must not care only for the wealthy. Twenty-seven thousand of the poor, the lame, and the blind eat in halls throughout the city, as well as widows with children and old-age pensioners."

"Their tables aren't quite as magnificent as your own, though, if I remember rightly," Matt said with a smile.

Prester John returned the smile. "Well, perhaps not."

"Any particular reason why you turned the top of your high table into precious emerald and its legs into amethyst?"

"Of course," Prester John said, surprised. "The magic of the stone prevents anyone sitting there from falling into drunkenness, Lord Wizard. Did you not know?"

"I'll make a note of it," Matt assured him. "Let's see—as I remember, you dine with Prince Tashih at your right hand and the Archbishop of Maracanda at your left."

"Well recalled," Prester John said with a smile. "Now, however, Princess Balkis sits at my left."

"Of course," Matt said, chagrined. "How'd the archbishop take to losing his place?"

"With Christian patience," Prester John said, still with a smile. "He may have hidden indignation at first, but Balkis soon charmed him."

Matt didn't doubt it. Still, he knew that with some men, ambition outweighed personal feelings. He added the archbishop to his list of suspects. "Next to him sits the Patriarch of St. Thomas, then the Protopapas of Samarkand, right?"

"You remember the order well," Prester John said with surprise. "It is so, and on my right, next to the prince, sit twelve more archbishops. The discussion thus engendered is both lively and enlightening."

Matt felt deep sympathy for Balkis, and for the first time wondered whether her disappearance was really a kidnapping. But he smiled bravely and said, "The lively part I can believe, with the heads of three different Christian sects there to argue about which one has a monopoly on truth."

"Oh, I have made them understand the need for tolerance," Prester John said with a satisfied smile. "We do discuss points of doctrine now and then, but for the most part we discuss the ways of the people in each prelate's district, and the strange and wonderful sights to be seen there."

Matt revised his opinion of the dinner table conversation. "How can they do a decent job of managing their dioceses when they're here, so far away?"

"Each of them returns to his dwelling every month in his turn, and another ecclesiastic takes his place."

So Balkis wasn't even hearing about the same old marvels every night. Matt decided she might not have been bored at all. "Doesn't the hum of conversation from the other four thousand diners make it a little hard to hear?"

"They are sufficiently distant, and have the courtesy to keep their voices low. Then, too, the lower tables at which they dine are some of gold and some of amethyst; the columns supporting them are of ivory."

Matt smiled, remembering that gold was an excellent conductor. "So each table holds a spell for muting noise?"

"That, and for restraining any other sort of rude behavior," Prester John acknowledged.

"So if everybody's being so polite, what happened on this one particular evening?"

The king shook his head. "Balkis' sorrow was so deep that she could not hide it."

"Is that all?" Matt asked in surprise.

"It was enough," Prester John answered, and explained. He told Matt of his own ill-conceived idea that Balkis should travel the land and come to know the people, and of Prince Tashih's jealousy, then of the two naive courtiers' foolish attempt to curry favor with Tashih by kidnapping Balkis, and of the aftermath.

CHAPTER 3

In the morning, the ladies came to wake their princess with food and drink—and found her gone. The bedclothes were gone too. They ran to tell the guards, who raised the alarm. Prester John heard it in his study and sent to learn what had happened. When he knew, he rose up in wrath and led the search himself. They looked into every corner of the palace, every nook and cranny, and found nothing. Then the king retired to his workroom to brew fearsome magicks, and Sikander and Corundel began to feel the first brush of apprehension. They attended Prince Tashih in his own apartments and found him pacing in agitation, hurling questions at his courtiers: "Where can she be? How can she have hidden? How could she evade our search?"

"Perhaps she is not in the palace, Highness," one courtier suggested.

The prince stopped dead. "What do you say?"

The man shrugged. "All know that she has her spells of sadness . . ."

"She longs for her home," one of the female courtiers explained, "for the land where she grew up."

"You do not mean that she has slipped from the palace to try to make her way back to the land of the Franks!"

The courtier shrugged. "It is possible."

"She might only have fled for a day or so," another courtier offered. "She may have tired of the court and be seeking respite from her duties."

Prince Tashih shook his head. "She would have left word." But hope gleamed in his eye.

"If she has," Sikander said as casually as he could, "it would be one less concern for Your Highness, would it not?"

The prince swung to stare at Sikander. "How do you mean?"

His glare seemed to pierce Sikander to the soul. His voice faltered. "Why . . . I only meant . . ."

"Surely," said Corundel, "if the princess has fled, she cannot inherit."

The prince gave her an incisive glance. "You know something more of this." He turned back to transfix Sikander with his glare. "Tell!"

"Gladly." Sikander spoke with false heartiness to mask his growing dread. "I bore her forth myself, drugged and sleeping, to the arms of a horseman who bore her far from Your Highness' purview."

"A horseman? What horseman? Where to?"

"Why . . ." Belatedly, Sikander realized that he should not have spoken at all and should speak as little as possible now. "One sent by a barbarian shaman . . . I did not ask where . . ."

"You turned her over to our enemies? Fool!" In two strides Prince Tashih towered over Sikander, grasping his tunic and hauling him to his feet. "Do you seek to bring ruin on us all? Where did you find this shaman? You will know that, at least."

"Why . . . why . . . I did not!" Sikander was horrified at this turn of events. The prince was supposed to thank him, to praise him!

"You did not find him? Then he found you!" Prince Tashih threw Sikander back into his chair. "Idiot! Did you not know that he sought you out to corrupt you? Think what he has gained—a member of the royal house in the hand of a barbarian sorcerer! Do you understand the link between the sovereign, his people, and his land? Do you not see the power you have given the barbarians?"

Sikander fell back, appalled, suddenly filled with self-contempt—but out of that morass rose determination like a shining shield, the resolution to do at least one good thing. He would not betray Corundel! "Highness . . . I did not know . . ."

"And did not ask, nor think!" Sikander turned to his courtiers and jerked his head toward Sikander. "Seize him. Bear him to my father."

Two men pounced on Sikander as the other courtiers broke into an excited buzz of conversation. With a sinking heart, Corundel watched Sikander hustled from the chamber. Should she speak in his defense? But what could be gained other than that she should be punished, too? Surely Prester John would not lessen Sikander's sentence because he'd had an accomplice!

Then fear rose in her, making her tremble. What if Sikander told of her role in the kidnapping? Surely, he had no reason to remain silent. They had never pledged love, only laughed and enjoyed one another's favors, as they had with other young folk of the court—and what if they offered him mercy to tell who had helped him? Why should he not speak? For surely, in his place, she would!

The guard announced them hurriedly, then stepped aside to open the door. The courtiers flung Sikander on the floor, and Prince Tashih stepped forward into his father's workroom, falling to his knees and bowing his head so that his neck was stretched out for a sword's blow. "Your pardon, Father and sovereign! My rash words have brought woe upon this house!"

"What rash words? Why do you kneel like one who cries for mercy?" Prester John demanded in alarm. "And why lies Sikander here upon my floor?"

Prince Tashih poured forth the story, taking more blame upon himself for his jealousy and rash words than he cast upon Sikander. When he was done, Prester John raised him up, eyes shining with pride. "Yes, my son, you were rash and foolish in your jealousy, for never could any other soul stand between yourself and me! Never could Princess Balkis nor anyone else threaten your inheritance, for you are the heir born, as no one else can be, for none can have the mystical link with the land and the people save the child of the monarch. Only you have been trained to be sovereign of this land in my place, and none other can have it. Still, all your kin shall be reservoirs of strength for you in your reign, and Princess Balkis most of all, for she is already a puissant wizard and shall only gain strength as she grows in knowledge and power. There can be no firmer support for the throne than one such as her!"

Still Prince Tashih hung his head. "But to have such a pillar sent into the hands of our enemies . . ."

"That is indeed a grievous threat," Prester John agreed, his voice somber. He turned to Sikander. "And most grievous was the treachery that wrought it! Speak, Sikander, for the shadow of the headsman's scimitar hangs over you! How did you find this shaman?"

"He is the apothecary who supplied the drug." Sikander felt no compunction about betraying the barbarian.

"Is he indeed! And how did you put the drug in the princess' drink?"

Sikander was silent, at a loss. How could he explain that without betraying Corundel? And how had the king known?

Prester John had only guessed—but it had been a reasonable deduction, considering that his niece had shown no signs of being drugged when she left his company to sleep. "You could not have done it yourself, for she had only women about her in her privy chambers. You must have had a confederate, a woman. Tell me her name!"

Sikander raised a stony face and kept silent.

"You shall tell me in the end," Prester John assured him. "It were better if that end were not yours." He turned to the guards. "Take him to a prison cell. Give him a swallow of water every hour, but no food. If he has not spoken by tomorrow's dawn, I shall think of stronger measures."

They hustled Sikander out the door. Prester John said to the two courtiers who had brought Sikander, "You may go. I must have speech with my son."

The prince paled.

The two courtiers bowed and backed away through the doorway. There they turned on their heels and, filling each other's head with wild guesses about Sikander's fate, went quickly to find their companions.

They found them in the courtiers' common room, a chamber high-ceilinged and spacious, floored with Persian carpets and walled by frescoes. Some nobles were in chairs, others were among the islands of cushions on the floor, all talking breathlessly of the events of the morning. When they saw the two men approach, all rose and fell upon them, demanding news.

"The king sets no blame on Prince Tashih," said the first.

A murmur of surprise passed through the assemblage, although a few had known the king would be very slow to attach any real blame to his son.

Corundel bit her lip and clenched her hands, stifling her own question, hoping someone else would ask it—and several did. "What of Sikander?"

"He confessed," said the second courtier, "but the king knows he had a confederate. Sikander will not tell the name, though."

Corundel almost went limp with relief.

"The king has clapped him in irons and bid the jailers starve him until he tells," said the first, "but I think that if he does not speak by dawn, the king will hand him over to the torturers."

Corundel pressed the back of her hand against her mouth, but not tightly enough—a moan of dread escaped. Another lady turned to her with a look of sympathy. "Aye, you had become close to him, had you not, dear?"

But another lady smiled with malicious delight and crowed, "Close to him indeed, and the fear is for herself, not for him! I think we have found Sikander's confederate!"

Several others of Corundel's rivals cried out with glee and pounced on her, pinioning her arms.

One of the princess' ladies came forward, eyes narrowing. "You served in the princess' bedchamber last night, did you not?"

"That was a favor to Chrynsis!" Corundel protested.

"It was indeed," Chrynsis cried, pushing her way through the throng. "I . . . did not feel well."

"You felt more than well, when I saw you creeping back to your chamber in the dead of night," an older woman said spitefully, "though I doubt not you may be sick of mornings in a month or so."

Chrynsis stared at her, paling. Then her hand flashed out in a slap, but the older lady caught it with a vindictive laugh.

"Take her also, gentlemen! If there were one accomplice, why not two?"

Chrynsis cried out in alarm, but heavy hands fell on her arms and courtiers bundled her away with Corundel.

Prester John, however, knew an innocent and hot-blooded dupe when he saw one. He sent Chrynsis back to her friends, but sent Corundel to a cell, to meditate on the errors of her ways, with no food and little water. Trembling with fear, she told him the name of the shaman, and for that he granted her a bowl of rice a day. In justice, he accorded the same ration to Sikander, now that his secret was known. Then he dispatched Prince Tashih with a guard of twenty soldiers to arrest the apothecary.

"They found the shop closed and locked, and the man fled, of course," he told Matt, shoulders slumping with defeat. "Tashih went there as quickly as he could, but he was too late."

"I suspect it was too late by dawn," Matt said in as reassuring a tone as he could manage. "The sorcerer had struck a blow for his people that more than justified his stay in Maracanda. Why should he stick around?"

"Why, to be caught." Prester John gave him a wry smile. "I thank you, Lord Wizard. Indeed, my niece was gone before any of us wakened, and the sorcerer gone an hour later, belike."

"Likely indeed," Matt agreed, "not that you were about to stop looking, of course."

"Indeed not! I sent for you straightaway, for I knew that you were at least as well acquainted with Balkis as I, having traveled through hazardous realms and faced many perils with her. I know something of battle, Lord Wizard, and of the kinship engendered by undergoing hardships together and standing shoulder-to-shoulder in the face of danger. Then, too, you were her teacher, and I presume that her learning your methods and techniques has engendered in you a magical affinity for her."

"I'd say there's something of a bond there, yes." Matt didn't mention that watching Balkis in spellcasting action had probably given him a greater understanding of the workings of her mind than an endless succession of banquet conversations. "You didn't wait for me before you started hunting, did you?"

"Indeed not! My wizards have searched the ether night and day for a trace of her. I have joined them whenever I could spare the time, but there is no sign of her upon this earth."

Matt nodded, knowing that John was a more powerful wizard than any other in Central Asia. "But you didn't find anything?"

"Not even the most vagrant and fleeting fragrance," Prester John said, chagrined. "While we have searched with magic, though, I have assembled a force of ten thousand men and a dozen wizards, though it has taken two more days to equip them and see them ready to march. Tashih shall lead them through the length and the breadth of the land, wherever the wizards find the slightest hint of Balkis' presence!"

Again Matt bit back the urge to ask if the wizards were any more apt to trace Balkis on the road than here, where she had been cat-napped. However, he did say with as much delicacy as possible, "I am sure Prince Tashih is quite skilled at leadership, Your Majesty, but perhaps it is less than wise to put him in charge of the princess' recovery."

Prester John frowned, storm clouds gathering around him almost visibly, the sheer power of his personality suddenly visible. "He must have an opportunity to prove his loyalty and his willingness to reconcile with her, Lord Wizard!"

"If you say so," Matt sighed. "However, I can't help but wonder if that is the wisest idea, since Sikander seems to have thought Prince Tashih intended the kidnapping. Certainly he stood to gain by Balkis' absence, at least in his own mind."

"In Sikander's, you mean! My apologies, Lord Wizard, but an accusation is not a verdict. I cannot suspect a man who reported the abduction to me as soon as he learned of it."

"I hope you're right," Matt said wearily.

"I trust my son implicitly."

Matt reflected that Caesar would have said the same about Brutus, but also realized the wisdom of keeping his mouth shut. "Still, I might point out that ten thousand men marching down a highway isn't exactly the most subtle of approaches.

Anyone who does know anything about Balkis would be apt to run for cover as soon as he saw them coming."

"There is something in that," Prester John said with a frown, "but surely that is the minimum number necessary to guard a prince."

"He won't find out much, with that kind of ruckus announcing his presence. I must admit, though, that if Prince Tashih is leading a couple of armies through the northern provinces, anyone hiding her in the south is apt to breathe a sigh of relief and stop trying so hard to be invisible—and might not notice a lone traveler nosing around."

Prester John's frown turned meditative. "There is some merit in what you say. You, I assume, would be that lone traveler?"

"Well, almost alone." Matt could see Prester John's overprotective instincts swelling and hastened to reassure him. "I'll take my dragon friend along, of course. He'll stay hidden but near at hand, except when I need to travel from one city to another."

"There could be fewer guards who would be more effective," Prester John admitted.

"Except my own magic spells," Matt reminded him. "I've gotten rather good at crafting passive defenses—they don't hurt anybody unless I'm attacked."

"Then how much pain do they inflict?"

Matt shrugged. "As much as my attacker is trying to inflict on me. Sometimes more, if I'm feeling nasty. Depends on what I set 'em for."

Prester John managed a smile—faltering, but a smile. "Well thought, Lord Wizard. Very well, we will try your style of investigation for a few days. But where will you search, and where shall Prince Tashih march with his army?"

"Give me a few minutes alone with Sikander, then with Corundel," Matt told him. "Then I'll need a quick trip to the apothecary's shop. After that I should have some idea of direction."

The world whirled, a myriad of colors that swirled around her. Balkis had been through this before when Matthew had taken them magically from one place to another, but had never been suffering from being drugged at the time. Nausea churned within her, clambering up farther and farther. She held it down by a frantic effort of will, afraid that in this kaleidoscopic whirlwind it would drown her.

Then the rainbow kaleidoscope stopped whirling, a solid surface steadied beneath her knees, and the malaise would be contained no longer. Balkis was violently sick. Even in the throes of regurgitating, she remembered to lean forward, to keep her robes clean.

The spasm passed, and she sat back on her heels, gasping for air. Now she could look about her, and years of fending for herself as a cat made her put aside her misery long enough to learn her surroundings. She obviously wasn't completely steady yet—the ground still seemed to be tilting.

Then she realized that it really was tilting. She was on a hillside, kneeling in brown frost-covered grass—and those huge four-legged shapes coming to investigate her were cows.

But the smell of her must have been alien to them, for they began lowing to one another in a more and more urgent tone. Her stomach sank as she realized they were egging one another on, working themselves into a herd frenzy to attack the intruder. They were coming faster and faster, and here and there one broke into an ungainly run, then more, then all, charging at her in a thunder of hooves, heads down, horns aimed at this strange and somehow threatening human.

Balkis' every instinct told her to flee, but she knew that in her weakened condition she couldn't possibly outrun a stampede. One thought struggled up through the dizziness of her concussed brain, though—smaller objects were harder to hit. She fought down panic and tried to imagine what these cows would look like if they were six times taller, if the meadow grass about her ankles were up to her shoulders, if the meadow were alive with scents, if she stood on four legs instead of kneeling on two . . .

The old, familiar sensations claimed her, and the cows swelled to become ten times larger, the grass shot up shoulder-high about her, the world became a wonderful symphony of smells, but bleached of most of its color. She knew she had become a cat again—and, wonder of wonders, her headache was gone!

The cows slowed and bawled to one another, confused by the strange human's shrinking away and disappearing—but their momentum carried them to her and beyond. Trotting hooves still flashed around her, and she danced, trying to avoid them, head whipping from side to side as she tried to keep track of each, but there were too many moving too fast, and the lowing and bawling all about her was too confusing. A hoof cracked into her head, making her wobble; then another hoof lifted her high, to carom off the side of another cow, who promptly turned, bawling, to see what had hit her, and trod on Balkis' tail. She yowled. The sound surprised the cows enough so that they pulled back and away from her a little.

Head whirling, Balkis nonetheless recognized opportunity when she saw it. She streaked through the suddenly open space, zigzagged between hooves, and darted into the shelter of a clump of small twisted pines.

The cows ignored her; they milled about, lowing to one another in confusion, trying to find the woman whose appearance had startled them.

Under a pine tree, Balkis curled herself into a fluffy ball of misery. The blow from the hoof had brought her headache back, pounding at the inside of her skull until unconsciousness mercifully claimed her. She didn't even notice the long rip in her side that a sharp-edged hoof had opened, nor the blood flowing from it that began to clot in her fur.

The key groaned in the lock, and Sikander looked up dull-eyed to see the jailer ushering in a man with a face so pale that he wondered what illness had beset him. Then he saw the prominent nose and round eyes, and stared.

The stranger gave him a sardonic smile. "Where I come from, it's rude to stare."

Sikander blinked and tore his gaze away. "Your pardon. It is only that I have never seen a Frank before."

"Only part French," Matt corrected. "The rest is Spanish and Cuban. Mind if I sit down?"

Sikander stiffened with sudden anger. The man was only a commoner! Oh, his buff-and-brown traveling clothes were of stout cloth and excellent cut, but a single glance showed they were certainly not those of a courtier.

The man seemed to read his thoughts. "I'm traveling incognito, but I'm really Matthew Mantrell, Lord Wizard of Merovence and consort to the queen of that land."

Sikander stared, then leaped to his feet. "Sit, certainly, my lord, and forgive my impertinence!"

The stranger sat down on the cell's only stool, then frowned up at Sikander. "I didn't mean to reverse things. Sit down, courtier!"

"You—You do not mind?"

"Hey, it's your cell."

Sikander sat slowly on the edge of the bunk, his mind in a whirl. Had this wizard come out of mercy, or to make him suffer for his wrongs? He could think of no other reason for his presence.

"I need to know everything I can about the night you stole Princess Balkis away," the Lord Wizard explained.

The mention of the princess' name linked with that of the Lord Wizard, and Sikander blurted, "You were her master!"

"Teacher, maybe," Matt qualified. "Traveling companion, certainly—but don't worry, I haven't come to skin you alive. I'll leave that for her to do, when she gets back."

Sikander's heart sank at the thought of confronting an enraged wizard-princess. Then it bounced back up as he realized that for Balkis to seek him out, he would have to be alive when she returned. "Am . . . am I to live?"

CHAPTER 4

"Oh, you'll go on living for a while," Matt said, "at least ten minutes, probably ten days, maybe ten years—possibly even the rest of your life. Exactly how long I can't say—that's up to Prester John. But I have a notion it will have something to do with how helpful you are about finding the princess."

"I shall help! Ask me what you will!"

"Fair enough." Matt grinned. "Now, we know you had help from a lady named Corundel . . ."

Sikander's face closed.

"Don't worry, I'm not trying to trap you," Matt said. "A lady named Chrynsis happened to mention that Corundel had filled in for her on the bedtime committee, and the other courtiers put two and two together."

"Have they indeed!" Sikander's face was still a mask at the thought that Corundel might yet betray him and paint herself as his victim and unwilling dupe. "How interesting. What fable has she told you?"

Matt smiled, amused. If courtiers knew one thing better than any, it was how to lie—but this one wasn't very intelligent. After all, you had to be pretty dumb to commit a kidnapping on spec. "All Corundel told us was the name of the shaman who arranged the kidnapping with you—but for her to know that much, she had to have been in on the whole operation. In fact, she had to have been the one who set the whole thing up."

This last was more a guess than a deduction, but it worked. Sikander said angrily, "It was my idea as much as hers!"

Pride, or a last ditch attempt to shield a lady? Matt gave the man credit for a scrap of gallantry and said, "No point in trying to protect her now. We know the outline of what happened. You might help undo some of your damage, though, if you told us the details."

Sikander deflated with a sigh and started singing like a star tenor. Matt encouraged him with understanding noises and monosyllables, keeping the information flowing. When Sikander ran out of words and sat slumped in dejection, Matt said, "Well, I can't deny that you made a pretty thorough mess of things, but there's a chance we might be able to straighten them out. Did the horseman say anything at all about where the shaman was sending Balkis?"

Sikander shook his head. "He said little but 'thank you' and 'good-bye.' I would guess he was openly a hireling."

"Sure," Matt said. "Why should the shaman risk getting caught with the princess in his own hands? A lot easier to pay somebody else to do the dangerous stuff."

Sikander looked up, startled, wondering if he had been someone else's dupe. Perhaps the prince had wanted Balkis to disappear after all.

Matt rose to go. "Well, thanks for your cooperation. I'll tell the king that you've seen the error of your ways and are trying to help."

Sikander gave him a sardonic smile. "What will that net for me? A quick death instead of a slow one?"

"Well, it should save you from the torture chamber, at least—unless there's something you haven't told me?"

"No!" Sikander declared, sitting bolt-upright.

Matt nodded. "Nothing more to learn, no reason for torture—except simple revenge, of course, and I don't think that's Prester John's style. I'll recommend he keep you alive until we know whether to charge you with murder, or just kidnapping. With any luck, you'll still be alive to face Princess Balkis someday." He turned thoughtful then. "Not sure that I wouldn't prefer the quick death, though . . . Well!" He forced a bright smile. "Let's hope for the best, shall we?"

Then he was gone, and the cell door crashed behind him. Sikander doubled over, head in his hands, and spent half an hour wishing he had never been born.

Corundel was more defiant but had even less to tell; like

Sikander, all she knew was that the horseman had taken Balkis away. When Matt pointed out that she was under sentence of death and that the only questions were when, how, and at the hands of the royal executioner or of Balkis, Corundel caved in and told him that she had opened doors to lead Sikander to the horseman, and that the two of them watched him ride away, then went back into the palace to celebrate. She didn't say that talking to the shaman had been her idea, but she didn't say that Sikander had forced her into being his pawn, either. Matt left the jail with a scrap of respect for each of them, though it was buried under a thick pile of contempt.

He briefly wondered why the guards hadn't noticed the horseman approach, then realized that a sorcerer who could provide the drug and the means of sending Balkis away could no doubt manage a spell of invisibility easily enough.

Matt reported back to Prester John. "The shaman's name is Torbat," he told him, "and his shop is in the northeastern quarter where the Radial Avenue of the Second Hour meets the Twelfth Ring Road."

Prester John, who sat at his desk, was impressed. "You are persuasive."

"Oh, I just recited a little spell before I went into each cell," Matt told him. "I also hinted that you might give them each a quick death instead of a slow and painful one."

John frowned, affronted. "You made no promises in my name, I trust."

"No, just hinted," Matt said, "though I did come out and say my report might influence you into keeping them alive until we could bring Balkis home."

"Why should I be so merciful?" John asked.

"So you would know whether to charge them as accessories to murder or only as kidnappers," Matt said. "Besides, if we do bring Balkis home none the worse for wear, we can just sentence them each to spend half an hour alone with her and see what happens."

Prester John looked surprised, then chuckled. "Yes, that would be appropriate."

"But for now let's concentrate on getting her back."

"Yes, quite so." Prester John frowned. "How shall you search?"

"Well, we know the shaman's name now, not just his address," Matt said. "Sure, it's only his public name, not his private one, so I can't make him break out in boils or drop dead from a heart attack—but it should be enough to bring me to him, wherever he is."

Prester John gazed off into space, correlating the idea with what he knew of barbarian magic, which was substantial. Finally he nodded. "Yes, that should suffice. Let us repair to the workroom, Lord Wizard."

As Balkis, in the form of a cat, slept, small figures stepped forth from burrows under the roots of the pines, stretching and yawning. They wore robes, turbans, and sandals, but their skin was nut-brown. In the Allustria where she had grown up, they would have been called "brownies." They looked around them in surprise.

"What could have waked us at so unseemly an hour, Hurree?" one asked.

Hurree spread his arms, starting to answer, but a white-bearded sprite spoke first. "It was the spirit of the grove. What moves?"

"Nothing, now," said an aged and creaky voice. The air seemed to thicken near one of the pines, then turned into a translucent figure that became more opaque with each step it took until it was solid, showing itself to be a stooped, wrinkled crone, leaning heavily on a knobbly stick. She gave of her life energy to her poor little trees, and though they gave back what little they could, it wasn't very much at all, so she was as stunted and twisted as they, her skin wrinkled and creased as bark. She was robed in garlands of brown needles that rustled as she hobbled forth. "That which moved now sleeps, by my blessing," she told her brownies, "but she is wounded in head and side, and has need of your aid." She pointed with her stick.

The brownies looked, and saw a miserable bundle of fur rippled by the breeze that sifted through the boughs of the pines.

Hurree caught his breath. "That cat is thick with magic!"

The dryad nodded. "Dryad-magic, nixie-magic, brownie-magic—it would seem that magic has rubbed off on her from half the sprites in the world."

Hurree knelt beside the cat, small hand tracing the rent in her side. "How came she here?"

"By more magic, surely," the dryad told him. "I felt the tingling of it, I looked out into the meadow—and lo! There she was, not a cat but a maiden fair, and sick to her stomach, poor thing!"

A brownie-woman parted the veil from her face to ask, "A maiden?"

The dryad nodded. "Even so, Lichi. The cows sensed that feeling of magic, too, and took fright. They moved toward the young woman, lowing to urge one another to defend—but the maiden, looking up, saw them, and lo! In an instant she had changed into a cat!"

Hurree's breath hissed in. "Surely you needed no further proof she was magical!"

"And surely that transformation must have disturbed the cows even more," Lichi exclaimed.

"It did, but the cat was better able to dodge their hooves than the woman would have been," the dryad said.

"Not able enough." Hurree placed a hand lightly on the cat's head, feeling the swelling.

"Well," said the dryad, "the cat is alive, where the woman might have been trampled to death."

"True enough." Lichi joined Hurree, passing her hands over the stiffened fur on the cat's side. She called to another brownie-woman, "Aid me, Alil!"

Alil came to join her magic to Lichi's, mending the wound as two more brownie-men came to rest their hands on Hurree's shoulders, lending him their own magical energy as he healed the head-swelling, both inside and outside Balkis' skull.

The dryad nodded, satisfied. "Find her some of those mice who keep gnawing at the roots of my trees," she said, "and show her where the rocks have caught rainwater. When she is recovered, find her better shelter than this."

"We will, O Wise One," Alil assured her.

"Thank you, little friends." Nodding in satisfaction, the dryad stepped back into a twisted trunk and disappeared.

The brownies gathered around the sleeping cat, each giving a modicum of energy to mend bruised and torn tissue as Balkis' breathing deepened into a healthy and healing sleep.

Matt expected a gloomy, windowless dungeon filled with arcane equipment and bottles of noisome concoctions. Instead he found a wide and airy chamber with tall windows and a worktable against one wall. Fragrant bunches of dried herbs hung over the workbench, and shelves above it did indeed contain bottles, but they held very ordinary things such as pebbles, iron pellets, salt, charcoal, and sulfur. The most exotic item he saw was a silvery liquid that had to be mercury. Oh, the workbench held a rack of vials, different sizes of flasks, an alembic, a crucible, and a mortar and pestle, but Matt knew them all from freshman chemistry.

Of course, none of Prester John's subjects had taken that course. No doubt they found the workroom impressive enough.

The chamber was fragrant with the aroma of sandalwood. Matt looked around for its source and saw a brazier with a feather of smoke rising. He wondered if Prester John had a servant who refueled it periodically to keep the room filled with its scent. Somehow that reminded him of the perpetual fires of Zoroastrian temples, which struck him as a good sign.

In the center of the room was a rectangle of sand, neatly boxed and recessed so that it was level with the floor. Prester John gestured to it, saying, "Stand in the center, Lord Wizard."

When Matt was in place on the sand, Prester John surrounded him with a dozen symbols, inscribed with a polished wooden stick three feet long. It reminded Matt of a magic wand, especially since it had symbols of its own inlaid with ivory and ebony, some of them identical with the ones on the floor.

Prester John went over to the brazier and fanned its smoke, blowing the smell of the incense across the sand-floor while he chanted a verse. Matt didn't recognize the language, but his translation spell gave him the meanings of the words anyway; the emperor was sending him to confront the sorcerer. Matt dropped a hand to the hilt of his sword for reassurance, then reached behind his shoulder to touch the butt of his own magic wand. He never went traveling without it anymore, though he rarely had occasion to use it—he usually went in for broadcast spells, not narrowly focused ones.

Mist rose up from the sand, surrounding him. It thickened, obscuring his view of the workroom, then hiding it completely. Suddenly there was nothing about him but fog. Dizziness struck Matt, then fled as quickly as it had come; he felt a moment's panic before recognizing the difference in the quality of the mist. Instead of the damp, clinging fog of the wetlands in the real world, this was dry, a mist of indeterminacy, the smeared electron shells of quantum physics, the blur of probabilities, of states of existence not yet determined, and Matt knew he was in the Void Between the Worlds.

His alarm abated; he had been here before. He turned about slowly, feeling for the Wind that Blows Between the Worlds to direct him toward Torbat. Prester John had included the sorcerer's name in the spell, and even if it were his public name, there ought to be some sort of direction-finding.

There! Matt felt the faintest of pushes. He took a step forward and felt the force strengthen, pushing him steadily ahead. He strode into the mist, with the Wind that Blows Between the Worlds at his back.

There he was, dimly visible through the mist—Torbat! Prester John's spell had been very accurate, placing Matt only a few dozen yards from the man. He stepped up until he was ten feet away, his steps soundless in the fog, then drew his sword, shouting, "Torbat!"

The shaman spun, eyes wide in shock—and Matt lunged at his right shoulder, trying to disable the man with pain. Torbat was fast, though; he slipped aside and raised a hand, fingers crooked in an odd sign, calling out a verse in his own language, and Matt's sword turned into a snake. "Here, take it!" he shouted, and threw the serpent at Torbat.

Torbat sidestepped again, chanting a different verse, and the snake stiffened, turning back into a sword. That gave Matt time to draw his wand and chant a verse of his own:

"As a pebble in a pond
That's from wind shielded, supercooled,
Sets off a crystallizing chain
And freezes surface and beyond
Into the depths where fluid ruled,
Be thus frozen, naught to gain!"

But he hadn't made it through a couplet when Torbat reached into his sleeve, produced a wand of his own, and swept it in a horizontal arc, shouting a staccato rhyme. Matt felt a blow strike his own wand aside, as though Torbat's stick had actually knocked against his instead of being five feet away. It was enough to ruin his aim; as he finished the final line, an expanding cone of frigid air shot out from the end of his wand, locking the mist of undetermined atoms into lattices of crystal—snowflakes that drifted off into the grayness.

Torbat shouted out another verse, stabbing his wand straight at Matt, who barely had time to riposte, crying,

"Parry spell in terce and quart!
My foe's verses shall abort!"

Torbat's wand spat a line of fire. Matt's wand locked atoms into molecules of air, a stiff, narrow breeze that blew Torbat's fire aside. Matt riposted both physically, with the wand, and verbally:

"Shaman, you who would dethrone
The emperor of this happy land,
For your crime be turned to stone,
And cease your treacherous demand!"

Again Torbat flourished his wand and ruined Matt's aim. Matt hoped there hadn't been anything human and male lurking out in the mist, because if there had been, it would have become a silicate sentient. He made a quick frantic circle with his wand, hoping to bind Torbat's, but the sorcerer swung his stick high with a laugh.

He'd left himself wide open. Matt lunged, crying,

"Give me the avowed, erect and manly foe,
Firm I can meet, perhaps return the blow.
Thrice is he armed that hath his quarrel just,
But four times he who gets his blow in fust!"

He hoped George Canning wouldn't mind his verse being mixed with one of Josh Billings' sayings.

A blow from an unseen hand sent the shaman sprawling on the invisible plane that served as a floor. Matt came after him, glowing with victory—but Torbat jabbed with his wand, calling out his own equivalent of Matt's freezing verse.

Matt slowed as the chill bit. He struggled to hurry, but could feel his feet turning into blocks of ice, his ankles stiffening, the chill rising up his calves as the spell drained the heat from his body . . .

Heat drain! Matt remembered an old friend—well, associate—who would be perfect for this environment. He called out, quickly, before his jaw froze solid,

"Maxwell's Demon, come in aid!
Your friend by heat has been betrayed!
Molecular motion's been transferred,
And Newton's Laws are being blurred!"

With an explosive snap like a carbon arc lighting up, a spark so intense that it hurt the eyes appeared near Matt, humming like a transformer. "What besets you, mortal?"

"A sorcerer who's playing with the Laws of Thermodynamics!" Matt pointed at Torbat. "He's trying to freeze me one minute and burn me the next!"

"Does he dare?" the demon buzzed. It shot over to Torbat, and a ring of fire roared up about the shaman. Torbat cried out and covered his eyes.

"Uh, could you thaw me out now?" Matt asked.

The demon swooped back over to him. "Thaw . . . ? Why, he has gelled you quite, from toe to waist! A moment, mortal." The spark of light swept down over Matt's legs, and he felt them loosen up.

With a sigh of relief, he stumbled, caught himself, and stood straight. "Thanks, Max. I appreciate the break."

"You did not break, but thaw," the demon corrected, "but I cannot criticize your inversion of logic, since that is what I enjoy about your company. Who is this primitive, and why did he plague you?"

"Aieeeee!" Torbat cried, shielding his eyes from the glare as he huddled into a little ball. "I yield me, I surrender! Only quench your blaze before it crisps me quite!"

"Crisps you?" Looking up, Matt saw the ring of fire contracting, moving inexorably closer to the shaman on all sides. "Yeah, that is a problem. Could you douse the fire, Max? I think he'll behave now."

"I shall give him the chance, at least," Maxwell's Demon hummed. As the flames died, it added, "Yet advise him that I understand perversity."

"What . . . why does he say that?" Torbat quivered with superstitious fear.

"Because he knows that people have a way of going back on their word," Matt explained. "Betrayal is perverse—it may get you what you want in the short term, but it works against you in the long term, as people stop trusting one another and, just when they need help the most, discover that they can't depend on anyone—not even for mercy."

Torbat stilled, watching Matt with narrowed eyes. Reluctantly, he nodded. "I shall abide by my plea. What would you have of me?"

"Information," Matt said. "Where did you send the princess you kidnapped?"

"It was not I who kidnapped her . . ."

"No, you just received stolen goods!" Matt found himself getting angry. "I thought you said you'd keep your word."

"Betrayal?" Max's hum rose in pitch with keen interest.

"Yes, I took her from her kidnapper!" Torbat cried. "Yes, I attempted to send her to this Void, beyond it to some other world where she would be happy but never come to trouble us again!"

"Tried?" Matt fastened on the word. "Your spell didn't work?"

Torbat ground his teeth, but admitted, "It did not. She retained some glimmer of consciousness and managed to cast a spell of her own that kept her in this world."

"Where?"

"I know not."

Max's hum shot up in pitch till he was screaming like a band saw as he drifted closer and closer to the cowering shaman.

"In truth I know not!" Torbat cried. "Withhold your familiar! I truly do not know!"

Matt knew the value of panic during an interrogation. "Well, it's not exactly mine to command . . ."

"I know nothing more! I swear by Ahriman!"

"How delightful a paradox," Max keened. "He swears by the Prince of Lies that his words are true!"

"Then I swear by the Thunderer and by the Imperial Dragon! I speak truth—I know nothing more! What more do you want of me? Is it not enough that I must fear Kala Nag? Must I fear you, too?"

Matt stiffened, alert to new information. "Be patient, Max—we have a whole new line of possible paradoxes here. Tell me, Shaman Torbat—who is Kala Nag?"

CHAPTER 5

Torbat looked up in surprise, then turned his head away, watching Matt out of the corner of his eye. "Did you not say this familiar of yours is a demon?"

"The first human who thought of him called him that," Matt snapped. "He got the term wrong—Max is really an elemental, not a demon. But he knows when somebody is lying. Tell the truth—who's this Kala Nag you spoke of?"

Torbat sighed and gave in. "She is the female demon who appeared to chastise me for sending this woman away from Maracanda. There was nothing to trouble her while the child stayed with Prester John, but now she says the chit may meddle in her plans. She appeared to me in a dream and told me she was sending monsters to tear me limb from limb for my foolishness!"

"Oh. So it wasn't fear of Prester John that made you flee? Say, where'd you find this Kala Nag?"

The shaman gazed off into the distance, and Matt had the eerie feeling the man was drawing on the memories of his ancestors, as though they lived in him still. His voice became remote and emotionless. "She was a goddess once, albeit a bloodthirsty one—the hag who rode travelers to weigh them down, who caused the earth to shake and tremble underfoot, who devoured her own offspring. When the gentle Buddha strode into the steppe, she retired hissing, and your Christ obscured her memory. Now, though, she demands attention again! She wakes, she tells all who remember her that she endures, that she will have her sacrifices once more and will bestow power upon those who worship her!"

Matt stared at the man, shaken—he sounded like one of the converted, not a fugitive. "Why did she think Balkis could be a threat?"

"Not the girl alone," the shaman said, his voice still remote, "but another with her. By herself, she is a cipher, meaningless, harmless—and in Maracanda she would be only that, would never find the Other. This I did not know. Fool that I was, I thought only of weakening Prester John by stealing away his wizard-niece. I did not know that Kala Nag was a threat far mightier than any strength the princess could lend Prester John."

Matt felt a chill down his spine—he knew that Prester John and his armies were all that held back the barbarian hordes, that with him armed and ready at their backs, the barbarians dared not ride farther west than their own steppes. "I take it Kala Nag is making progress at winning back the hordes."

"The gur-khan has turned his back on Ahriman, who failed him," the shaman reported, "and makes sacrifice to Kala Nag."

"Then so do all his followers."

Torbat nodded. "All. Certain chieftains among the Polovtsi, among the Kazakhs and the Manchus, the Uzbeks, the Mongols, the Kirghiz, and even some among the Turkomen have begun to worship her again."

Matt shuddered at the thought of the juggernaut that was growing out on the steppe, and wondered how a little girl like Balkis could halt its progress. "That means there aren't going to be very many places for you to hide."

The shaman gave a bleak nod. "Still shall I flee and seek a bolt-hole. The fight is not done until the life is gone."

"Good luck, then," Matt said. He felt so sorry for the man that there was no question of not forgiving him. After all, he might have saved the civilized world by sending Balkis away, though he hadn't intended it. "May the wind be at your back."

The shaman came down out of his trancelike state and stared at him. "You do not seek to punish me?"

"I think that's well in hand," Matt said.

* * *

The mists dissipated and Matt slipped his wand back into its scabbard. Prester John's workroom materialized around him as the fog vanished.

The king stared. "You do not have the sorcerer?"

"Only his information," Matt said. "He was running for his life, and I didn't want to watch his death come upon him."

"What death is that?" Prester John asked, alert for hidden meanings.

"It goes by the name of Kala Nag," Matt said. "Give me a drink and I'll tell you about her."

Prester John had a stock of fruit juice in his workroom, which Matt found refreshing. The carafe sat between them on a small table as he told the king of his encounter with the shaman. When he was done, Prester John asked, "So this barbarian goddess has became a demon?"

"Call her what you like." Matt shrugged. "Goddess or demon, she's devoted to destruction and misery. If people worship her as a goddess, that probably says more about them than it does about her."

"Certainly her behavior would merit the title 'demon' from any civilized person," Prester John agreed. "Still, it is not they whom she gathers, but the barbarians." He frowned in thought. "How can our little Balkis be a bulwark against so terrible a being?"

"Well, she may not be a giant physically, but she has a great heart," Matt reminded him. "Besides, she's only supposed to become a problem if she links up with this 'Other' Torbat mentioned."

Prester John looked up in surprise. "Would that not be yourself?"

"It could," Matt said thoughtfully. "I probably wouldn't have come back to Maracanda if you hadn't called me to help find her—but if that's so, we'd better see about my joining her as soon as I can."

"We must recover her quickly in any case," Prester John said grimly. "You say that Torbat knew where he sent the child, but not where she arrived?"

Matt nodded. "Right. Balkis managed to come up with a

counterspell just as he was launching her." He couldn't help a smile of pride in his apprentice.

Neither could John, though his smile of pride was for his niece, not his student. "She did well and has the courage of her family. Still, we cannot know where she is."

"There is that drawback," Matt admitted.

Prester John nodded thoughtfully. "That is why my earlier spells yielded no hint of Balkis' location—she had traveled through the Void, not been carried for miles drugged on the back of a barbarian pony."

"But now that you know she went through it, you can find her?"

"It may be." Prester John rose to take a yard-wide bowl from a shelf, then lifted a waterskin down from a hook. He carried both to the sand floor, set the bowl on the central disc where Matt had stood, and filled it half full of water.

Then he took a small bottle from his sleeve, shook a few drops into the bowl, and finished filling it. A lovely fragrance wafted to Matt's nostrils. With a shock, he recognized Balkis' scent. Prester John must have taken a sample of her perfume.

He had taken one of her scarves, too—Matt watched him twist it into an arrow and lay it carefully in the bowl, then step back off the sand floor to chant a verse that commanded the silken cylinder to point toward she who had worn it. Matt admired the improvisation—Prester John had used the Law of Contagion, that objects once in contact remained in contact over distance, and the Law of Sympathy, that like will to like, and both strengthened by the same symbols that had oriented him earlier in finding the direction Torbat had gone. Matt stood on tiptoe so he could see down into the bowl. Sure enough, gentle wavelets moved there as the perfume rippled into a pattern pointing toward the distant trace of scent that Balkis wore, and the scarf swung to aim toward the skin that it had touched.

"Almost due southeast, but a little more southerly than easterly." Prester John turned back to Matt with a look of apology. "I regret that is the best I can do, Lord Wizard."

"It's a huge help, Your Majesty. At least I have some idea which way to go now."

But Matt couldn't help wondering how far he would have to travel. Certainly miles, or Balkis would have come back already by herself. Afghanistan? India? Indonesia? Australia? He shuddered at the thought that he might have to go all the way to Antarctica, and hoped Balkis had been wearing a warm nightgown.

The next morning, they attended Mass in Prester John's chapel, bigger than most churches, where 365 abbots took daily turns saying the prayers and administering the sacraments in the Nestorian rite, quite different from the one Matt knew. Then Matt left the city by the southern gate, walked a mile, stepped off the road into a convenient grove, and recited the verse that would call Stegoman. The dragon arrived within minutes. Matt mounted, and together they took off to search for a lost cat.

Balkis awoke as the moon rose, feeling far better than she had before, though still lethargic. Seeing the brownie-woman, weaving pine needles and singing a charm, Balkis came fully alert.

Looking up, the brownie-woman saw Balkis' open eyes and smiled. "Are you healed now, maiden?"

Balkis was startled by the question. How had this wee one known her for human when she was in cat's guise?

"The spirit of this grove saw you transform," the brownie explained, as if Balkis had spoken aloud. "I am Lichi. Have you appetite?"

The question raised a sudden gnawing hunger in Balkis, who nodded. Then, realizing there was no point in hiding her abilities when the brownie already knew she was human, Balkis said, "Most hungry."

The brownie frowned. "What speech is this?"

Balkis had spoken in the tongue of Allustria, where she grew up, and she recognized the language the brownie spoke as very much like one she had learned while traveling with the Lord Wizard. (The thought of him still made her heart leap.) They had stayed a few weeks in a Parsi village, and Balkis had absorbed the language.

She tried it now. "I am most hungry, kind spirit."

"Ah! Those words, I understand." Lichi put aside her weaving and rose. "Come, then."

She led Balkis to a small hole under the roots of one of the stunted pines. Balkis sniffed and caught the scent of mouse as the brownie knelt and cupped her hands around her mouth to call down into the burrow's back door, making a dreadful ghostly noise. Seconds later a mouse shot out, straight into Balkis' claws. When she had finished the morsel, the brownie led her to another burrow, then another.

As Balkis was licking her chops, the sprite asked, "Are you well enough to travel now?"

"I think I am." Balkis took a wobbly step but said gamely, "I shall walk as long as I may."

"Come, then." Lichi turned away.

It was a long walk for a cat whose strength had been depleted by injury. Lichi led the way, other Wee Folk appearing around Balkis as she followed. Several times, Balkis had to stop to rest, and the brownies stroked her, lending magical energy, and their strength revived her. She thanked them and rose to stumble on. During one of these rests she asked Lichi, "Am I in Hind or Persia?"

"Neither," Lichi said with a frown. "You have come into Bactria. Why would you think this was Persia?"

"Because your language is akin to one I learned from some Parsi folk," Balkis explained, "at least, close enough so that I can understand if you speak slowly, though there seem to be many words I do not know."

"Ah." Lichi nodded. "Well, there were Persians who came riding here in conquest, long ago—then Greeks after them, though our mountaineers swallowed them up in time. Then the Persians came again to conquer, but the mountain folk swallowed them, too, over the years. They have left something of their language behind, though. Come, you must see some of our mountain folk."

Lichi led her to a farmstead, though Balkis found it amazing that a house, barn, and storage sheds had been built on such sharply sloping land. Even more surprising, the buildings stood straight, though they were of a style Balkis found most strange—circular and covered with earth, with grass growing on the roofs, yellow now, in winter. There were fenced enclosures near the outbuildings, but all were empty. "The cows, goats, and swine are closed in for the night," Lichi explained, "but there are holes enough for a brownie, or a little cat. Come."

Balkis, tottering with weariness, followed as best she could. She fought down the urge to tell the little woman how queasy she was feeling, how weak, or that the headache had started pounding between her ears again.

However, Lichi seemed to know. She led Balkis through a gap where two boards failed to join near the ground, into the warmth and earthy scents of a barn. "Only a little farther now, sweet kit," she coaxed, and other brownies crowded close to encourage and lend energy by touches. They brought her near a sleeping cow, and Balkis had to fight the urge to shy away as she passed between its hooves. Lichi reached up to pull on a teat, and warm milk splashed in a puddle in front of Balkis. The delicious aroma filled her head and she stretched to lap it up eagerly.

The cow came awake with a startled moo and turned to see who had so rudely awakened her, but Lichi soothed her with strokes on her hock. "There now, O Sweetest of Kine-kind, ye of beautiful eyes! Lend some little of thy milk to a poor starving kit, we beseech thee! Nay, kindest and most gentle of cattle, be not afrighted nor incensed, for such generosity to a poor injured creature will surely see thee reborn as a human babe when thou hast died!"

Mollified more by the tone than the words, the cow turned back to her manger and took a mouthful of hay, suffering a few more pulls upon her teats with good grace. She hadn't really thought about reincarnation, of course. In fact, she hadn't thought about much of anything but food and warmth since her last calf had grown and gone away.

Full of milk, Balkis suddenly felt the weight of her wounds and her long night's walk. She staggered; it took three brownies to hold her up and keep her moving while Lichi led the way again, saying urgently, "Not here, not here! A cow might step on you! The farmer and his sons might see you! Nay, come farther back, sweet kit, and higher, to hide!"

So, with Lichi's gentle urging, Balkis moved up into the haymow, where Lichi tucked her in among the straw. Balkis' eyes fluttered closed, but Lichi said urgently, "The farmer has five sons. His wife died of a fever when the youngest was three years old, and without her to temper them, they have grown into a rough and coarse household indeed! Be sure you wait until they have done their chores and gone out to their day's work before you come to hunt spilled milk. Sleep now, pretty kit—sleep until night falls and the men have gone in to their suppers." Then she stroked Balkis and crooned a lullaby that was in fact a spell, assuring that the maiden would indeed sleep.

By nightfall Stegoman had reached the mountains that formed the southeast corner of Prester John's domain.

"Sun's almost set," Matt pointed out as they coasted through the air. "Time to camp."

"And hunt!' Stegoman said emphatically. "Flying enhances my appetite."

"Must be all that fresh air," Matt opined. "That mountaintop off to the right looks nice and secure."

"That one that seems to be a cup among sawteeth? Aye, the sides are sheer. The mortal would be skilled indeed who could climb it."

"A skilled mountain climber or a skilled magician?"

"Indeed so." The dragon spiraled down, cupped air with his wings, then stretched his legs to touch rock, keeping his wings spread while Matt slid down. "I trust you have wood in your pack and water by your side?"

"Yeah—charcoal and a waterskin. I thought we might be camping in some inhospitable places." Matt took out his supplies as he spoke and began to lay a fire. "Even brought dried beef and hardtack."

Stegoman shuddered. "I will take my beef hot and fresh, thank you."

"If you can find it. If you can't, you should be able to manage dinner on a couple of bucks."

"Deer would be tasty," Stegoman allowed, "but I fear I shall have to make do with mountain goats."

"Not very appetizing," Matt sympathized. "As a meal, that's a sham."

"Or perhaps a chamois?" Stegoman licked his lips. "Well, we shall see what moves. Dine well, wizard." He leaped up atop a tooth of rock, poised a moment, then plunged off. Matt held his breath, though he knew that the air was as natural to the dragon as to any bird. He let it out in a sigh as Stegoman rose over the peak, spiraling on a thermal, up and up to catch the last rays of the setting sun.

Then something else caught those rays, something else winged and saurian. "Look out!' Matt shouted. "Natives!"

Stegoman's head swiveled. He saw the other dragon and turned to face it, hovering and drawing breath, his belly expanding, ready to belch fire.

The local was a little longer than Stegoman and more slender, scales glinting where the sun rays touched it, reddish-brown where he was dark green. Furious, it cried, "Aroint thee, worm! How dare you come within my range?"

"I only seek a night's rest on my route south," Stegoman returned. "If you cannot afford me that, glitterscale, you are selfish indeed."

"Selfish or not, these chamois are mine, and you have no right to take them without the asking!"

"Very well, then," Stegoman said, irked. "May I partake of your mountain goats?"

"No!" the other dragon snapped. "Snake, get thee hence!"

"It would take many hens indeed to make a meal for a dragon." Stegoman's impatience increased. "I would be loath to steal an ox from the farmers nearby."

"Do, and they shall come hunting me! How now, crocodile! Would you give all our kind infamy?"

Stegoman said evenly, "Till now, I had never met a dragon who feared the human folk."

"Fear! Do you think I fear?" The red dragon shot closer, then danced, tilting from side to side a dozen yards from Stegoman's nose.

The green dragon stared, catching his breath—bracing for attack.

"If I fear not an overweening lizard such as yourself," the red dragon demanded, "why should I fear mere soft and feeble folk?"

"Then why should you care if they hunt you?" Stegoman asked reasonably.

"Because there are so many of them," the stranger answered, "and in their cowardice, they may set ambushes or even stake out poisoned steers."

"Hey, now!" Matt called in protest.

The red dragon swung about and stared at Matt, eye gleaming, then said to Stegoman, "I had wondered why you settled, then flew again! How now, serpent—would you pollute my mountains with weak grubs who could never aspire so high by themselves?" Then the dragon dove at Matt.

"Let my friend be!" Stegoman bellowed in real anger, and shot after.

CHAPTER 6

Delighted, the red dragon sheered off at the last second, forcing Stegoman to cup his wings and stall for fear of hitting Matt. However, that also brought him low enough to perch on a tooth of rock again, and the red dragon circled, then stooped on him, claws hooked to catch and tear.

Stegoman stared up, fascinated.

"Go!" Matt couldn't believe his friend was so careless in a fight.

"Not yet . . . not yet . . . now!" Stegoman dove off the peak, and the red dragon had to cup wings and stall for fear of hitting the pointed rocks. A roar of frustration torched them, and Matt dove for cover. He realized Stegoman's tactic now—stalling Red so that he had time to soar high again, without fear of Red pouncing on him before he was in full flight.

Red circled just below him, rising as Stegoman rose, opposite him as they circled higher and higher, each watching for an opening.

A dragon fight was a rare sight, and one Matt didn't particularly care for; his friend might be hurt, and so might Red, who, aside from being touchy and overly territorial, could very well be as good a dragon as Stegoman. Matt dredged up an almost forgotten verse and started adapting.

Red, with folded wings, plummeted twenty feet, then popped them open right under Stegoman. Flame roared up in a fountain. Stegoman hooted with pain as he sideslipped out of the path. Red panned fire-jet, but Stegoman shot upward and wheeled, and Red couldn't keep the fire focused on him. Then Stegoman dove head first, blasting a thirty-foot tongue of flame before him.

Red howled as fire washed burnt umber scales, then darted aside and hovered nose-to-nose with the great green dragon, crying, "You would, would you? Have at thee, worm!" Fire blasted.

So did Stegoman's, and fire fountained high where the two flames met, then winked out as the dragons realized they were wasting their breath. They circled one another, glaring into each other's eyes, fifty feet apart, slipping and sliding on currents of air.

Matt noticed that it had been exclusively a firefight, no claws tearing skin or teeth rending hide. There were those pounces, but even he had seen them coming a mile away. He wondered if this was more a ritual than a fight.

Either way, he didn't like it. Time for a breathing spell.

> "Through thc sky he glided in.
> Red-scale said to armor-skin
> (Hear what slender Red-scale saith!)
> 'Stranger, pause and take a breath' "

Then Matt remembered that taking a breath wasn't necessarily a sign of peace between dragons and hurried on to the next verse.

> "Eye-to-eye and flame-to-flame,
> (Keep the measure, drake!)
> This shall end with none to blame.
> (At thy pleasure, snake!)
>
> Drop to perch and fold your wings.
> (Never chide thee, drake!)
> Accommodation both shall sing.
> (Peace betide thee, snake!)"

Red frowned. "What is that prattling your grub makes?"

"He is no grub, but a mortal man," Stegoman retorted, "and if I know him, he speaks of truce."

"Perhaps he has some reason." Red eyed Stegoman warily. "Shall we perch and talk?"

"There is more profit in that than in wasting flame on hides that will not burn," Stegoman allowed. He half folded his wings, then opened them with a boom as he landed on a split peak off to Matt's right. "My name is Stegoman."

Red dropped down to land on the other half of the mountaintop. "I hight Dimetrolas."

"Let there be peace between us, Dimetrolas. There need be naught else, for I shall be in your mountains only one night."

"Oh, that is ever your way, is it not?" Dimetrolas spat. "To come and go, to pass but a single night, then waft away on the wind and never return?"

Stegoman's eyes flashed as nictating membranes slid over the eyeball, reflecting the setting sun, then withdrew—the dragon equivalent of a blink. "I am a wanderer, aye, and shall be so until I find a reason to stay and ward a mountain."

"How is it you have never found such a reason? Have you too much love for the feel of the wind under your wings?"

Stegoman's jaw lolled open in a dragon grin. "Well I might, for I have had little enough of it."

"Little enough?" Dimetrolas eyed him narrowly. "Yet you must be a hundred years old at least, come into your maturity."

"I am no longer a hatchling," Stegoman admitted—but since it hadn't been an insult, why was he so tense, crouching like a coiled spring?

"You must have wandered for half your life." Dimetrolas too crouched taut, and Matt readied another spell in case the two leaped at one another again.

"I have spent many years among the human kind," Stegoman said by way of explanation. "Their follies amuse me."

"Amuse! Are you not yet old enough to put amusements behind you? Have you a hatchling's mind in a dragon's body, that the work of life holds no appeal for you? Are you not grown, that you have no wish to make a home?"

"Perhaps not," Stegoman said quietly. "I am what I am, and pleased with it."

But Matt caught an undertone of sadness to his friend's speech, an echo of bitterness, and knew the dragon well enough to doubt the truth of his words.

Dimetrolas, though, seemed to sense no such undercurrent.

"Aye, I doubt not you are pleased with yourself, scion of the wild wind! Well, go your way! Be blown where you will, but when your fifth century comes upon you, be mindful of what you have missed." With that, the red dragon dove off the peak.

Matt almost called out in alarm, then caught himself, remembering that dragons were safer in the air than jets. Sure enough, Dimetrolas rose into sight again half a minute later, wings wide-spread, spiraling up to become only a slender curve gilded by sunset, coasting away to the south.

Stegoman watched with a fixed gaze, and the tension in his body seemed to increase, if anything.

Matt decided it was time for a distraction. He cupped his hands around his mouth and called, "Handled like a true diplomat!"

The dragon's head turned slowly, and his eyes appeared to burn. Matt almost backed up a step in fright, but summoned nerve and held himself steady. Then Stegoman relaxed a little, and the burning dimmed to a glow. "A diplomat? An intransigent transient, rather!"

"Okay, so you're a stubborn hobo! How about coming over here so I don't have to yell?"

Stegoman gazed at him a moment, then dove from the peak, his wings booming open. He circled twice and landed beside Matt, who said, "Thanks for sticking up for me."

"Friends are priceless," Stegoman replied. "I have few enough, after all."

"And need all the friends you can get? Too bad Dimetrolas doesn't think that way."

"That may not be the case." Stegoman gazed south where the other dragon was a glowing dot in the sky.

Matt frowned at the cryptic comment, but asked, "What was that business about travel being 'ever your way'? Odd thing to say to someone you don't know."

"It would be," said Stegoman, "if that 'your' meant me myself."

Matt frowned. "What other 'your' could it be?"

"Males," Stegoman said, with a volume of meaning packed into the single word. His gaze was still fixed on the south, his body still tense with leashed energy.

Matt stared as a lot of things became clear, including the tenor of Dimetrolas' remarks, why she had pushed the issue to a fight, why that fight had seemed more a ritual than a battle, and most especially Stegoman's tension—he was highly stimulated, virtually bursting with adrenaline and hormones. "Oh," Matt said. "Dimetrolas is female."

"A fact of which I was instantly aware," Stegoman said dryly.

"And, I take it, a rather pretty one?"

"Absolutely beautiful," Stegoman hissed, eyes burning again.

In spite of himself, Matt backed away a step or two. "Well, then, why didn't you do something about it?" His eyes widened as he remembered the thrust of Dimetrolas' comments. "No. She was basically saying that you should forget it and suffer if you weren't willing to stay for life, wasn't she?"

"Indeed," Stegoman rejoined, "and in all good conscience, I could not pretend that I might."

Matt studied his friend closely. "You could come back, though. When we've found Balkis and retrieved her, you could come back and stay awhile."

Stegoman shook out his wings in irritation. "Could I? What have I to offer a female? I, who have no home and no friends of my own kind, who have been outcast by my own clan and was so long in exile that I cannot stay long in the mountains where I was born for the feeling of strangeness there! What tribe, what house, what people could I give? I have nothing to offer but wandering and loneliness, and estrangement from my own kind!"

Matt gazed at his friend, feeling his heart twist with remembered pain of his own. At last he said, "You could offer a strong male dragon in his prime whose loyalty is proven to border on the fanatical."

"Aye," Stegoman said with a sardonic grimace, "one—and that is not enough for a female. Perhaps there are some such among your kind, Matthew, but female dragons wish to lay eggs and see them hatch, to nurture them and teach them and watch them grow and know them as friends in maturity. That takes other females for company, males to ward them while they lay and brood, a whole clan to ward the hatchlings and shield them from loneliness. No, Matthew, I have nothing to offer, and must not therefore speak with more than civility!" With that, he leaped into the air and dove over the sawtoothed rim of the little plateau. Matt heard the boom of his wings opening, then watched him rise and arrow off toward the north, seeking supper and solace for the wound in his soul that Dimetrolas had unwittingly reopened. He gazed after Stegoman until he saw the dragon, small in the distance, half fold his wings and plunge from the sky. Then Matt turned away to his own campfire to rack his brains for a way to help his friend.

Balkis woke at the sound of cows mooing below her and of a voice answering. She shrank farther into the hay, heart pounding with alarm. Her fur bristled and her claws sprang out. Then the fear lessened, for the voice was a resonant, friendly baritone, addressing the cows fondly. "There now, there's hay for you, Bossy, and for you, Dapple. Come now, Blossom, you'll not have apples again till fall, so you had better eat your fodder!"

Balkis found herself wondering if people called cows by the same names the world over, changing only the language.

A cow lowed with a note of urgency.

"Yes, I know, Sunshine, I know," the voice crooned. "Your udder's so full it hurts, I know, and I shall milk you first, but you must have feed to munch while I do. There now, all, eat and be still while I milk."

The cows quieted. So did Balkis; her fear shrank to wariness, and her claws hid themselves in her fur again. She heard the clatter of a stool and bucket being set while the voice said soothingly, "There now, I'll be gentle with the washing, so swollen is your udder! But you'll feel better quickly, be sure of it."

Then there came the hiss of milk shooting into the bucket. The warm, appetizing aroma drifted upward into Balkis' nostrils, making her mouth water even though she wasn't particularly hungry. She remembered the brownies' caution, though, and stayed hidden. However, cats and curiosity have a long relationship, so she did burrow down, hunt out a knot-hole, and peek.

She caught her breath.

Golden hair, regular features, large blue eyes, broad mouth and broader shoulders—it was a young man in his early twenties, easily the most handsome Balkis had ever seen, and a strange warmth began to spread within her. A cow lowed impatiently, and the young man turned to say, "Yes, I know, I know—as soon as you see Sunshine being milked, you become aware of your own need. Patience, sweet cow—I shall tend to you soon."

Balkis found herself wishing that he would tend to her instead, and beneath her fur felt her face grow warm. He was so gentle, so cheerful! How could this be the rough, coarse boy against whom the wee folk had warned her?

"He is the best of them."

Balkis looked up, startled to hear a voice resonating so closely with her thoughts. It was Lichi who knelt by her.

"He is the youngest," the brownie explained. "The others are quick to put him in his place at every opportunity, and none too gently, either. Nonetheless, he manages to stay cheerful in spite of all temptation to anger and bitterness. They call him . . ."

The sound of the name was quite foreign, but Balkis recognized it as a version of "Anthony." She crouched by the knot-hole, staring down in fascination as the young man went from one cow to another.

"Mark well the spots where the milk spills," Lichi advised, "though I fear most of it will have soaked into the earth before you come."

The milk was the farthest thing from Balkis' thoughts at the moment, though she had to admit that it smelled heavenly.

Anthony was just finishing the last cow when the barn door crashed open and a voice called, "What, sluggard! Are you not done yet? Cease babying those cattle and turn them out to pasture!"

"Yank their teats harder and faster and be done with it!" another harsh voice snapped. "Come on, little fool, turn them out!"

Two young men stepped into sight, muscular under their heavy tunics, heavy-jawed and dark-browed. One had red hair, the other brown.

"Gently, brothers, gently." Anthony's voice took on an ingratiating tone with the ease of long practice. "I am almost done with her, take the other three, if you wish."

Balkis glared at the intruders with indignation. Why should Anthony toady to these swaggerers? Surely not merely because he was the youngest!

"If we wish!" A fourth brother shouldered his way between the other two, just as big, even heavier, dark-haired. "Be sure that we wish it! Be done with that cow *now*!"

"You cannot hurry the milk, Baradur." Anthony's voice still had the conciliatory note, but not the slightest trace of fear.

Baradur's face darkened with anger. "I can hurry it! One side, brat!" He shoved Anthony off the milking stool far harder than he needed and sat down to finish the milking himself. The cow let out a bellow of surprise and pain, but the milk hissed faster. Anthony picked himself up with a look of resignation, and the next brother gave him a shove as he passed. "Work, lazybones! Loose these other three and take them out!" He didn't wait for Anthony to comply with his order but started untying Blossom himself.

"As you say, Kemal," Anthony sighed. He turned to untie Sunshine, but the third brother elbowed him out of the way. "Can you not loosen a rope, fumblefingers? Go muck out the stalls, as befits you!"

Indignation turned to anger, and Balkis found herself thinking, *Stand up for yourself! Tell him to mind his tongue!*

For a moment she thought she must have spoken aloud, for Anthony flushed as he turned away to take up a shovel—only he took up two and tossed the second to the redhead. "Shovel yourself, Philip, and let us see who clears his floor more quickly!"

Philip turned back in time to knock the shovel out of the way with a smile, eyes glinting. "Do you dare tell me what to do, mucksweeper? I shall remind you of your place!"

His fists came up, and the other brothers turned from their work, grinning and stepping in.

Balkis' stomach sank as she realized the nature of the game, and a very nasty one it was—for the older brothers to goad Anthony into talking back, no matter how slightly, whereupon they felt they had the right to slap him down—and slap they did.

Philip struck first, his fist driving at Anthony's belly. Anthony blocked the blow but didn't return it. Even so, Kemal cried, "Oho! The child thinks to strike at his elders!" and stepped in with a roundhouse swing.

Anthony ducked under it, but Baradur caught his shoulder and spun him around, shoving him hard. Anthony staggered back; Philip caught him and held him while Baradur slammed a blow at his chin. Anthony jerked his head aside and the blow landed on Philip's shoulder. The redhead shouted in anger and shoved Anthony far enough away to swing at him with a short, vicious jab. It caught the youngest under the ribs as he was turning; he bent over, gasping. Kemal laughed and swung a blow at his head, but Anthony managed to straighten up, and the punch caught him in the chest. He stumbled back, and Baradur caught him, turned him around, and swung a blow at his chin. Somehow it landed on his shoulder, though. Anthony staggered back, tripped, and fell to the floor.

The barn resounded with the older brothers' laughter. They untied the cows and drove them out, calling, "Clean yourself off, Anthony!"

"You can join us when you've finished mucking out, Anthony."

"Aye, but stand downwind when you come!"

Balkis' anger mounted as she realized the rules of the very unfair game—that Anthony was not allowed to fight back, but it was all right for him to avoid the blows if he could. Balkis felt certain he had faked some of those staggerings so his brothers would feel satisfied enough to leave him alone. As Lichi had said, they were rough and coarse, and Balkis suspected their father was very much like his sons—more, in fact, for they had probably learned their bullying ways by imitating him. At the very least, he had condoned it. All in all, a thoroughly unpleasant family.

With one exception.

* * *

Balkis stayed hidden for a week, gradually regaining her strength through spilled milk and the brownies' petting. By day the barn was all hers to hunt mice and, as she grew stronger, rats. At night the cows, sheep, goats, and pigs kept the barn warm. At sunrise and sunset, though, the brothers and their father drove the livestock in to feed and milk.

The father was the prototype of his sons, though not quite so tall—a redheaded, red-bearded block of muscle. He had grown heavier with age, putting on some fat, especially in the belly. His hair and beard were streaked with gray, and he bellowed his orders in a gravelly voice. If the older brothers joined in criticizing Anthony or bossing him about, their father was sure to support them; as far as he was concerned, there was a chain of command based on age, with himself at the top and Anthony at the bottom.

So when they had finished driving the cows home for the night, it was always Anthony who did the mucking out, apparently doomed to it for life by virtue of being born last. He did the milking, too—in spite of their endless directions about how to do it right, none of the brothers seemed to want such women's work. They preferred to spend their time bullying the animals and repairing the farmstead and fences. Anthony had his share of the chill outdoor work, too, of course.

At night, though, the cold clamped down around the farm. The animals stayed inside, and so, Balkis assumed, did the men. Assuming wasn't enough for her, of course—she was very curious, wanting to see how they fared inside the farmhouse.

That, though, would have to wait for greater energy, and a thaw. Still, by the end of the week she had recovered enough to risk making Anthony's acquaintance—and a risk it was. She was aware that the young man might be passive only because he had no chance of beating his brothers, but that with someone weaker, he might turn out to be as great a bully as any of them. So she waited until she had recovered enough to be sure she could outrun and outclimb him. Then, one evening when the brothers were done driving the livestock in for the night and feeding them, and had left Anthony to his milking with jeers and threats, she plucked up her courage.

As soon as the door closed behind them, a smile of contentment brightened Anthony's face. He began to sing a soft and lilting tune as he milked, and Balkis understood why he was willing to accept the chore—it gave him a few precious minutes alone, away from his brothers' badgering and tormenting.

Balkis almost hated to interrupt such serenity. Nonetheless, she took her chance, climbing down the back wall and threading her way between hooves and heaps of straw. Then, stepping out around a timber, she mewed plaintively.

Anthony looked up in surprise, and his face lit up. "A cat!"

Balkis braced herself for the grasping hand, the tormenting yank on the tail, tensed to rake with claws, to bite and twist and run.

CHAPTER 7

Anthony only held out his hand very slowly and waited.

Balkis' opinion of him soared—here was a man who knew how to make friends with animals! She stepped forward and sniffed his fingers. It was a pleasant smell, warm with the musk of the cow's udder and the scent of milk, but with a masculine aroma beneath that made something quiver inside her. She butted her head against his hand. With a gentle, joyful laugh, he rubbed the top of her head very gently, then went on to massage an ear, asking, "Who are you, kit? How did you come here?"

Balkis decided a change of subject was vital and meowed again, her tone moving from plaintive to demanding.

Anthony laughed with gentle amusement. "Hungry, are you? Well, I think Sunshine can spare a drop or two. Can't you, old girl?" He slapped the cow's side, and Sunshine turned her head as much as her head-ropes would allow, mooing. Then, seeing Balkis, she lowed as though to say, *Oh, it's only her. Why didn't you say so?*

"You see? Sunshine is quite generous." Anthony turned a teat and aimed a squirt of milk right over Balkis' head.

Surprised, she ducked. Anthony rebuked her gently. "You must not waste, you know—and you don't want to have to lap your milk off this dirty floor, do you? Come, stand up and catch it in your mouth."

What would he have said if he'd known she had been drinking off that floor all week? she wondered. Still, Balkis could see his heart was in the right place, and she had drunk from a wineskin often enough. She crouched to show she was ready.

Anthony laughed low with delight, aimed, and let squirt. Balkis sprang up on her hind legs and caught the stream full in her mouth. It stopped, and she dropped down to all fours again, licking her chops.

"Another?" Anthony asked.

Balkis crouched.

Anthony let out a squirt again, making it last as long as Balkis could stand on her hind legs. When she dropped down, licking the last drops off her whiskers, Anthony said, "That should keep you from starving, at least. I've work to do, though. Come close if you wish, but I must be about my milking."

He turned back to his work, but Balkis wasn't willing to surrender his attention so quickly. She stepped up, rubbing against his ankle. "Good cat!" he said, and reached down to stroke her.

Now, that was something entirely different from a little rub between the ears. His hand caressed the length of her back, arousing an intensity of sensation that alarmed her. She shivered with pleasure from nose to tail-tip. He stroked again, and she felt a flush of warmth welling up from the core of her being and spreading through her whole body. In spite of herself, she closed her eyes to concentrate on the pure delight of his touch, and was surprised to realize she was purring. He stroked again and again, and she stood shivering as a vagrant thought drifted into her mind—how would she have reacted to that touch if she had been in human form?

At that, her eyes flew open in alarm—but still she stood quivering, frozen in place by pure pleasure. Anthony stroked again, and her feelings intensified so much that she knew she had gone into heat. In panic, she flowed out from under Anthony's hand and sat down beyond his reach, shuddering with fright but too fascinated to run.

Anthony chuckled. "Had enough, then? Well, come back if you want more. Cats need homes and petting as much as they need milk to keep them from going wild."

Balkis thought that sort of petting was more likely to *make* her go wild. Still, she watched Anthony as he turned back to his work. Gradually, her breathing calmed and her feelings ebbed, leaving her to wonder if she'd really been in heat at all—from what she had seen of cats in that state, it lasted a week or more, or until some tom made it vanish but left the puss pregnant. Then Balkis began to wonder again what kind of sensations she would have felt if Anthony had petted her in her human form. The thought aroused such intense feelings that she ducked away into the darkness to let the panic subside.

From that day on, though, Balkis came out whenever Anthony was alone in the barn, telling herself that with time his touch would cease to be so inflaming. Anthony assumed she came for milk and always gave her a squirt or two, then petted her until she took fright again and retreated. She kept waiting for his touch to cease arousing the wonderful shivering, but it didn't. Still, she watched him as long as he was in the barn, for even the sight of him roused pleasant feelings now—pleasant, but much less alarming than his petting.

For his part, Anthony took to this new friend immediately. He named her Kit and treated her with kindness and affection, bringing her table scraps and as much petting as she would take. He even dangled a string for her to play with. She thought it was silly but found some strange fascination in its twitching and pounced on it anyway. He twitched it out of her claws and jiggled it again. She went along with it to make him happy, then realized she was actually enjoying the game—not for its own sake, but because it gave her a way to play with Anthony.

Spying through a knothole at life in the farmyard, Balkis saw that there was no one for him to talk to except his father and brothers, who didn't want to listen, scoffing at anything he said as the prattling of a fool. With a shock, she realized that, even though a mere cat, she was Anthony's only friend, and found herself wondering if he had ever had any other.

However, she was his secret friend, and had better sense than to run after him in the open, or when the others were about. She could easily imagine how Anthony's brothers would heap scorn on him if they knew he had a pet, or what they might do to any animal about which he cared.

* * *

At the end of the third week, Balkis could contain her curiosity no longer. One cold winter night, she decided to see what was happening in the farmhouse. She told herself that it wasn't a desire to see Anthony at home—it was because the cold pierced even into the barn, and the farmhouse looked so warm and welcoming. She followed the lee side of the barn, then a hedge, a tree, and another hedge, all on the downwind side to avoid the huge snowdrift on the windward side. Even so, the snow was up to her belly, and she moved by leaps, jumping her way to the farmhouse. It was an exhausting way to travel, but the warmth of the firelight shining through cracks in the shutters, and the sounds of laughter and singing in harmony, made her feel the trip had been worth it.

How to get in? The house would surely have a mouse or two, she thought, and if a rodent could find a way in, so could its hunter. She cast about in the snow until she struck one such scent, and not that of a mouse but a rat! She quivered with the excitement of the chase, and with the eagerness to repay Anthony's kindness, at least in a small way.

The scent led Balkis to a gap between the bottom of two boards. It would be a tight fit, but she knew she could manage it—especially if she could gain warmth and company thereby. She crouched down, squirming forward on her belly, until she could thrust her nose into the gap, then pushed a little more, and her head popped through.

Now, if she had guessed wrongly, she would be in a pretty dilemma, with her head caught and unable to push forward—but she wriggled, ignoring the chill on her tummy, and her shoulders followed her head, scraping painfully against the weathered old wood but popping through. Then it was only a matter of wiggling and wriggling until her hindquarters followed. She never could have managed this in human form, she reflected, for her hips would have been too wide. But then, in human form the hole would barely have been large enough for her hand.

She stood after slipping in and whipping her tail after her, and waited for her eyes to adjust to the darkness . . .

There! The rat, half her size, clear in the light that leaked between ill-fitting inner boards, was shrinking back at the sight of a cat, lips writhing wide to bare its scum-yellowed teeth. Balkis' adrenaline flowed, and she was suddenly unaware of chill and exhaustion both. She crouched, tail-tip snapping, waiting her chance.

In despair, the rat sprang at her. Balkis leaped high, letting it pass beneath, then twisted in midair and landed on its back, teeth seizing its neck, hind claws raking. The rat squealed and thrashed, trying to turn on her, but she shook it and struck it against the wood of the wall again and again, until it went limp in her mouth.

The singing and laughter went on, drowning out the sounds of the struggle.

Balkis dropped the limp bundle and sprang back, crouching, tail whipping, watching for any sign of movement. When the rat lay still, she backed away—it might be shamming, after all—then turned and ran light-footed between inner wall and outer. Ordinarily she would have waited for movement and, when she saw any, struck again, then waited and struck and waited some more, until she was sure the rat was really dead and not apt to bite her as she ate it. She wasn't hungry, though—Anthony's last plate of scraps had seen to that—and was eager to catch sight of him in the bosom of his family.

She followed the rat's scent until she found its hole, and peered through. There they were, towering over her, the father in his big chair closest to the hearth, as befit his rank. He was swag-bellied—his silver-streaked ruddy beard nearly touched his belly—and sat with his hands on his knees, nodding in time to the singing. He wore only rough tunic and hose, like his sons, and none too clean, but neither were theirs. His sons sat in a half-circle around the fire, the eldest, Baradur, opposite his father and nearest the flames, which showed his rank. The next eldest brothers, Kemal and Philip, sat next to him on each side, and then still another son, whom Balkis had not seen before and whose name she didn't know. Finally came Anthony, who sat farthest from the fire—the youngest and lowest in rank.

Balkis frowned, displeased at her friend's treatment.

Then their singing broke into chanting, the eldest son calling out while the others fell silent, and she realized that they had only been singing a chorus before. Now Baradur intoned, "Then Rustam raised his steely sword . . ."

Kemal replied, "And swung it down with might and rage . . ."

Anthony's face lit up; he cried, "Against the sorc'rer—"

"No, Anthony!" Baradur snapped.

"Will you never learn?" Kemal said in exasperation.

"But I had a rhyme!"

"You must wait your turn, and well you know it," the father said sternly. "Moti precedes you. Then use your rhyme to add the last line to the verse."

Anthony sighed, and nodded in capitulation.

"Where were we?" the father asked. "Kemal, repeat your line."

Kemal recited, "And swung it down with might and rage . . ."

Philip, the middle brother, frowned, obviously stumped. "See, Anthony! You have made me lose my rhyme!"

"Vary, and quickly," the father instructed.

Philip said, "Swung the great sword Harn with rage . . ."

Moti, clearly the next-to-youngest brother, chimed in: "Swung it at the sorc'rer-lord . . ."

Anthony forced enthusiasm as he added, "And slew the hoary-headed mage!"

"If that is your best rhyme, it was certainly not worth breaking the order," Baradur said in disgust.

Balkis had thought it a rather good rhyme.

"Indeed, Anthony!" Moti snapped. "His white hair had nothing to do with his being a magus, after all!"

"But Moti—"

"And 'mage' is not a proper word," Philip added.

The father nodded. "The proper word is 'magus.' "

"I have a better rhyme to begin the next stanza," Anthony said hopefully.

The chorus of no's was so loud and angry that Balkis shrank back in shock. Anthony did not, and she reflected once more that he must have heard such a chorus often.

"Really, Anthony, will you never leave off trying to go out of turn?" Baradur said in exasperation.

The father nodded. "You are the youngest, so you must speak the last line."

Balkis wondered what would happen if the stanza had six lines, then realized that each had only five because there were five sons. Anthony had been doomed at birth to always come last.

"You shall have your chance to begin a verse when you make up the last stanza, as always," the father said severely.

Anthony sighed. "But there is nothing new to be said by the last verse," he said, and raised a hand to forestall objections. "I know, I know—there is nothing new in the old songs anyway."

Balkis watched his face, and saw the flicker of rebellion, the desire to begin a really new song—which he quickly suppressed.

"Begin the next stanza, mine eldest," the father said with pontifical weight.

Baradur sang, "But from his corpse, the spirit rose . . ."

And they were off again, another round, from Baradur to Kemal, from Kemal to Philip, from Philip to Moti, and from Moti to Anthony. Balkis crouched quivering with anger as she realized that this game must happen every night of the winter months, the family sitting around the fire improvising new versions of the old tales in verse, and that her friend was never to move from his position as last, as no doubt he was last in everything else, too, including orders. Each of the others had a younger to command, but Anthony had no one—except, perhaps, herself. But Anthony hadn't tried to order her about—he seemed to know the difference between a servant and a friend.

She wished his father and brothers did.

They settled into the song, and Balkis found herself caught up in the story. Whenever Anthony's turn came, he was always ready, always had a line that rang with music and internal rhyme or alliteration, and she began to understand why he was so eager to begin a verse or to cast a line in its middle—the poetry came naturally to him, springing to mind unbidden, and he was near to exploding with it. She felt a sharp stab of envy, for although she could memorize the verses of her spells easily, she had a grueling time when it came to making up a new one.

Anthony showed his skill on the last verse, in which he could select the rhyme scheme, link internal rhymes, coordinate alliterations, and actually bring in metaphor, something unheard-of in the earlier stanzas. He gave the epic a pyrotechnic ending, making the final verse a dazzling display of acoustics. Nonetheless, his brothers scoffed.

"Oh, very pretty, Anthony!"

"Can you not manage plain, simple verse?"

"Surely Rustam would have scorned such frills!!"

"Well, what else would you expect of the clean-up boy?" Moti asked, and the others howled with laughter.

Anthony turned red with embarrassment and anger, clamping his lips shut to hold in hot words. Then his shoulders slumped, the flush faded, and he sighed. Once again, anger kindled within Balkis at seeing him so mistreated.

She could not help herself; she had to go to him, try to cheer him. She glanced out the rathole to make sure it was in shadow, unlikely to be seen—and it was indeed; the rat had chosen well. She squeezed her head through, and the rest of her flowed after, heart pounding. Then she skirted the wall, keeping tables and chairs between herself and the older brothers until she had to dare the last two feet of open space between a table and Anthony's stool. She covered the distance in two steps, not so fast as to attract attention, not so slow as to leave her exposed too long. There, she turned once to make sure all of her was under the stool and hidden from enemy eyes, and stretched forward to butt her head against Anthony's calf and twine herself about his ankles as well as she could without being seen.

She felt him stiffen, and hoped it was not with alarm. Her heart hammered—what if he leaped to his feet and kicked the stool over, thinking he had felt a rat?

But Anthony knew animals too well for that. His hand dropped down to swing beside the stool, apparently in weariness and negligence, but Balkis recognized a signal when she saw one, and stepped over to push her head against his palm. Anthony fondled her head, and she quivered with pleasure, fighting down feelings of alarm—a lost kitten was a lost kitten, after all, no matter the species, and Anthony was a friend who needed such reassurance as she could give.

Perhaps not—if he needed reassurance, his fear for her was greater than that need, for when his brother commented on Rustam's bravery in facing an overwhelming enemy, Anthony said, "It may be, Moti, but it also may be that he had more courage than sense. If he had been prudent, he would have known to *go back home where it was safe*."

"Just the kind of thing I might expect a sissy-boy to say," Moti sneered, but Baradur caught the slight emphasis on the last words and frowned. "An odd way to say it, clean-up boy. Have you some hidden meaning?" His glance followed Anthony's hand; too late, Anthony drew it back to his lap. His brother hooted. "What are you hiding there beneath your stool?" He jumped up and came toward Anthony, sidestepping to see around his leg.

Anthony turned with him, looking wounded. "How could you suspect me of concealing anything, brother?"

"Because he does!" Moti made a grab and yanked Balkis out from beneath the stool, banging her head on the seat as she came. The room swam about her as he held her up with a cry of victory.

She clawed and yowled in spite of the nausea. The lad, though, must have tormented cats before, because he kept his hands and wrists beyond her range as he held her up with both hands, crowing, "Look, brothers! Anthony has brought a friend home, a little friend!"

The brothers shouted with delight and crowded in to begin a new and rather sinister game.

CHAPTER 8

"Were you feeding her under the table?" the father demanded, his face darkening.

"And look!" cried Moti. " 'Tis a female! Anthony has found a girlfriend!"

"Aye, Anthony!" chorused Philip and Kemal, and Baradur demanded, "Shall you sleep with her, then?"

"Anthony the cat lover!" Kemal crowed, putting such a leer into the words that he gave them a double meaning.

"She will keep the rats from this house if you let her!" Anthony cried. "Let her go!" He leaped to catch Balkis from Moti's grip, but the lad pivoted, keeping Balkis from Anthony's reach, crowing, "Do you want her, then? Catch as cat can!" He tossed her to Baradur.

Balkis yowled as she flew and tried to turn in midair, but Baradur caught her by the tail. All her weight plunged against his hold, and the pain shot up her backbone. She caterwauled, spitting, front paws spread wide, claws out to catch. Baradur cried, "Ah, the clean-up boy has chosen a spitfire! Beware her claws, my lad!" Then he swung Balkis around his head. "Catch, Moti!"

Anthony barreled into him, knocking Baradur against the wall, and Balkis flew from his grip. She sprinted for the rathole, then dodged and twisted as feet slammed down in her way, hard hands grabbed for her, and hoarse voices shouted. But she made it through the rathole without worse scathe. A hand shot through to catch her tail, but she turned and bit, sinking her teeth into the soft flesh between thumb and forefinger. The hand disappeared like lightning and its owner shouted with pain. "The little bitch! See how she has bitten!"

He had mistaken both Balkis' nature and her species, but she didn't feel obligated to enlighten him, especially since none of the others seemed to think his hurt worth noticing. They were too busy with something else; she heard a great deal of shouting and the sound of blows. She dared a quick peek and saw a pile of fists driving down toward the center. As she watched, one of the brothers went sprawling away, to show her Anthony, face swollen with fury. He spun to lash three quick punches at Philip, who staggered back and fell, then lashed out at Kemal. But Baradur caught Anthony's arms from behind and, shouting triumph, bent him backward and off balance as Kemal began to pelt Anthony with short, vicious jabs.

The two younger brothers lay on the floor, clutching their heads, their moaning testimony to how well Anthony could fight when he was angry and feared for someone other than himself. Balkis looked about, unbelieving, wondering why the father did not stop the beating but only stood by and nodded with grim satisfaction. "You shall remember your place, Anthony," he said, "and never lift a hand against any of your brothers again!" Then he turned to the two on the floor. "On your feet lads—you can't let mere pain keep you idle. Take your turns and your revenge, and teach your younger brother his place."

Teach him again, Balkis thought wildly, *and again and again and again*. She wondered how often Anthony had endured this lesson, and marveled that he still had spirit.

The middle brothers staggered to their feet, faces angry and cruel, and stumbled forward for their revenge as Kemal ceased pummeling Anthony and backed away. But hard though they struck, as Baradur continued to hold them in aim, Anthony only grunted, not crying out with pain or pleas for mercy. That only seemed to anger the brothers further, for they struck and struck again in fury.

Balkis retired from the rathole shaking with fright and anger. No one would hear her speak—they were far too intent on their beating. She had better sense than to turn into a nubile young woman in the company of such brutes, but surely her magic could save her friend!

"Let their blows upon them turn,
Each receiving what he earns
By striking at his younger sib.
Let him . . ."

She ran dry. The rhyme wouldn't come. She searched frantically—she knew what she wanted to say, but she couldn't find the right combination of words, the imperative, the meter and the rhyme! And, of course, the harder she strove, the more her mind blocked. In despair, she searched among the verses she knew . . .

Too late. The beating was done, and the father held the door open while the brothers rushed Anthony through it and pitched him headlong into the snow. Then the father stepped full into the doorway, standing silhouetted against the light, and thundered, "Get you gone and sleep with wild beasts, where so rude a child belongs! Any boy who forgets his place so far as you have done does not deserve to sleep with his family!" He stepped back to slam the door.

Balkis couldn't believe her ears. Had the man no fear for his son, no care? Anthony was beaten and hurting, and could die for all he knew. Did he not love his son?

The answer came unbidden: of course he loved Anthony—but he loved his authority, too.

She dashed between the walls, frantic with fear for her friend. She squeezed between the boards to run cat-foot around the house to where Anthony lay groaning in the snow. Fear shot through her, for she saw the snow stained with blood by his mouth. How could his older siblings have been so villainous?

But as she crouched beside him, she felt helpless, at a loss. What could a cat do for a grown man?

She would have to become human again, of course. There was little enough to fear from his brothers—they were inside, crowing about their victory and laughing at one another's insults to Anthony—and toasting their success with ale, no doubt. Anger spurred Balkis, and the barnyard swam about her, everything becoming smaller as she grew into a woman. Then she was kneeling over an Anthony dramatically smaller than he had seemed. He was curled around the pain in his belly, groaning, and Balkis felt panic. Luckily the kidnapper had wrapped her in her own cloak when he stole her from the palace, and she whipped it off to drape around Anthony now. She shivered as the wind bit into her, but her gown was made of wool and would keep her long enough to reach the barn. "There, now," she said, "that should keep you warm a little while. Come, rise, for I cannot carry you, and we must get you into the shelter of the barn as quickly as we can!"

Anthony looked up at the sound of a strange human voice—then, pain or not, he stiffened and caught his breath, staring at her.

In her mind, Balkis cursed impatiently. Was a woman so strange a sight as that?

Yes. To a boy raised with only a father and four brothers, she was a very strange sight indeed.

Well, he would have to get used to it. Balkis bent low, tucking the cape beneath him and lugging at him. "Come, on your feet! Surely they have not crippled you!"

But Anthony only stared at her, wide-eyed and awed, and asked, "Who . . . who are you?"

"My name is Balkis, and I am come to keep you from freezing to death! Will you not rise?"

This time, Anthony allowed himself to be chivied into standing, but as soon as he did, one knee buckled. Balkis stepped in so he leaned on her shoulder, and he was heavy, very heavy. He blinked, staring down at her, and there was still awe and reverence in his eyes as he asked, "How did you come here?"

"On my own four feet, of course," Balkis snapped. Then honesty compelled her to add, "With some help from the Wee Folk, that is."

"Wee Folk?" Anthony managed to lift his weight off her, his stare turning into superstitious fear. "But surely I would have seen you, surely one of us would have seen you!" Then he frowned. "But how can you have four feet?"

"When I turn into a cat," Balkis said, exasperated, and pulled him toward the barn. "Come, if you can stand, surely you can walk."

Anthony tried, but he stumbled, and she had to prop him up

again. He stared at her in wonder. "Turn into a cat? No one can turn into a cat!"

"Oh, stand on your own two feet!" Balkis said.

He managed it, and she thought of his calf being at the height of her head, thought of the house as being a vast, towering structure, thought of the snow as brushing her belly—and sure enough, everything swelled into gigantic proportions as she felt her gown wrapping tightly about her, turning into fur.

Anthony cried out and stumbled away, then managed to stop, tottering.

Balkis turned back into a human faster than she ever had and ran to prop him up. "You helped me when I needed to recover," she said, "helped me with friendship and sweet milk. Now let me return the favor. Come to the barn."

Anthony hobbled with her, staring down, caught between superstition, awe, and some other emotion that made Balkis look away in discomfort as that strange warmth spread through her again. "Stop staring like a trout!" That made her wonder if she had hooked him, and she pushed the thought from her mind in irritation.

"So you were my friend Kit?" Anthony whispered.

"I was and am, and fool that I was to try to comfort you for the insults your brothers gave you! If I had not, they would not have beaten you!"

"Oh, they would have," Anthony sighed. "If not today, then tomorrow or the next day—and if not about you, then because I soured the milk or broke the scansion of a line or spoke out of turn." He smiled with pride. "At least you gave me cause to fight back for once."

Balkis stared at him in amazement. Fighting back had brought him a worse beating, and he was proud of it? She burst out, "Why do you stay here?" then turned away, instantly ashamed. "No, forget I asked that. It is none of my business."

"You were nearly torn to catkins for seeking to comfort me," Anthony said grimly. "I think you have some right to know."

"Later." They had come to the barn, and Balkis pulled the latchstring, then hauled the door wide enough for the two of them to hobble through. "Hold yourself up," she directed, and turned back to pull the door shut. When the latch fell, she turned to give Anthony her shoulder again. "Can you climb to the haymow?"

"I think so," Anthony said, and he managed it, albeit slowly and with much help from her. There, he collapsed into the hay, and she ran down the ladder to fetch a water bucket from a cow, then back up to wet her handkerchief and clean his cuts.

"Sleep if you can," she urged, and began to sing a soothing tune that was really a spell, one that would send him into a healing sleep.

But Anthony stopped her before she had sung even one line. "Your answer."

"Answer? What answer?"

"As to why I stay here." He closed his eyes, lying back in the straw and looking suddenly older and very, very weary. "Because I have nowhere else to go—and because, rough or not, these men are my family. How should I live without them?"

"A far sight better than you do now," Balkis said tartly. "Sleep, lad, and let your body heal." She began to sing again, and Anthony's eyes closed. It occurred to her that she could very easily weave another spell into the lullaby, one that would make him fall in love with her when he woke . . .

No! The lullaby faltered as she realized what she'd been thinking, shocked at herself. Why would she want him to love her, after all? And if he did, what good would there be if she knew it to be only the work of a charm? *Wait,* she told herself sternly, wait for real love.

Something within her asked, *But what if this is it?* She ignored it, though, and managed to sing on while Anthony's breathing deepened and steadied as sleep claimed him. Then she cleaned the last of his cuts, laid her handkerchief out to dry, and crawled under her cloak, cuddling up to him—for warmth, she told herself. But she couldn't resist reaching out to press the huge bulge of muscle in his arm, the swelling and hardness of his chest, then pulled her hand back as something within her responded with a gush of heat that frightened her. She closed her eyes and willed herself to sleep—but her attention was still taken by the man who lay so closely beside her, and sleep was a long time in coming.

* * *

Balkis woke to see rough homespun an inch from her nose, and stared at it, wondering what it was and where it had come from. She followed it up to the swelling of a man's chest, and the evening before came back in a rush. She lifted her head slowly so as not to wake Anthony—but found him gazing down at her. She went tense with alarm, but his gaze held only tenderness and awe, admiration that bordered on desire but held to the line. Nonetheless, it stirred the warmth within her again, the still strange but delightful and alarming feeling.

Below them, the cows lowed.

Grateful for the interruption, Balkis said, "Should you not milk your kine?"

"They can wait a while yet," Anthony said. "Only the left hand of dawn is in the sky, and the sun will not rise for an hour."

"Why do you stare so?" she demanded, voice sharpened by her alarm at the stirring within her. "Have you never seen a woman?"

"Rarely," he said frankly. "Only when we go to town to trade—after the harvest and again after the thaw. But never have I seen one so lovely as you."

His blunt tone, devoid of even the awareness of flattery, made Balkis' heart flutter, but she managed a cynical smile. "If you had seen more lasses, you would not find me beautiful."

"Oh, I would," Anthony said softly. "Be sure that I would."

She stared into his eyes and saw such complete and total honesty there that she had to look away, reminding herself that Anthony could have served as a model of naiveté. "Surely your brothers will come to see to the livestock soon."

"Not until the sun is well risen," Anthony said. "In the cold months, only I must stir early."

Balkis turned to him in outrage, then forced a smile. "No wonder you dare not leave. How should they manage without you?"

Anthony turned toward the barn door, startled and almost alarmed. Balkis' heart sank—she had not thought he would take her seriously. She answered her own question. "On the other hand, each of them had to learn to milk before you were old enough, did they not?"

"They did," Anthony confirmed. "Still, it is so long since they have done it . . ."

"I am sure it is something one's hands never forget."

Anthony turned to her with a sad smile. "Have you ever milked a cow, then?"

"I have." Balkis remembered milking her foster parents' sweet Dapple. "I am certain I could do it again in a minute." She sat up. "In fact, I shall do it for you—you must be feeling very poorly."

"No!" Anthony protested. "You must not sully such pretty hands! Besides, I am quite well." He levered himself up—then bounced to his feet. He flexed his arms, staring at them in amazement. "I do feel well! How can this be? That was the worst beating that ever they've given me, and I've never healed so quickly before!" Then he remembered Balkis' shape-changing and stared at her in awe.

"I do have some small magicks at my command," Balkis admitted. "The song I sang you last night held a spell for quick healing."

The awe was still there, but submerged under a mischievous grin. "Well then, surely you know that I am quite well enough to milk!"

"Oh, very well." Balkis started toward the ladder. "I shall only help you, then."

"No!" Anthony cried in alarm. "What if my brothers should find you?"

His alarm touched her deeply, which made her sound cynical again. "Only a minute ago you assured me they would not."

"Well . . . yes . . . but that is while we are here in the loft," Anthony said, "and you have time to become a cat again." The thought alarmed him. "They might come hunting you to torment you!"

"Are you saying I should be gone?" Balkis asked, her voice level.

Anthony looked away. "I do not wish it—but you should. For your safety."

"Then so should you," she said quietly.

CHAPTER 9

"I?" Anthony turned to Balkis in alarm—but not, she saw, in surprise. "They are my family!"

"Family!" Balkis scoffed. "What manner of family love is this, to scorn you and mock you and beat you and rejoice at your humiliation?"

"There is a better side to them," Anthony said, but he did not meet her eyes.

"If there is," she told him, "I have not seen it. You are no youth in his teens, but a man grown and able to make your own way in the world—and they have cast you out into the snow! Truly, Anthony, there is no reason why one so good-hearted as yourself should stay to be degraded and beaten by your own family."

"But . . . where else should I go?" His gaze wandered. "I know nothing but farming, after all—surely not enough to make my way in a strange world."

"I do," Balkis told him. "I began my life with a caravan and took up my travels again only two years ago, when my foster parents died."

"Truly?" Anthony asked, wide-eyed. "But how could such journeying have been safe for so young a maiden?"

"It was not," Balkis admitted, "but it was safe enough for a cat."

This time Anthony's grin came slowly. "Of course! You need only appear as a woman when you wish it!"

"Which is not often, when I travel," Balkis said, "only with someone I trust." Her gaze met his, and the feeling of contact, of mind meeting mind, shook her so that she looked away quickly.

"You honor me," Anthony said softly.

"You have been a kind friend," Balkis said, still studying the hay.

"Yes. I never pulled your tail."

"And you had better not!" Balkis fixed him with a glare, but his grin was infectious, and she felt her lip quirk into a smile, then laughed. He joined her, and they leaned together, laughing. Then Balkis looked up at him, her expression serious. "I must journey again," she said. "I must go home. I would feel much safer with a companion."

Anthony met her gaze again, and his grin faded into the slightest of smiles. "Still you honor me, beautiful maiden."

Balkis looked away uncomfortably. "I trust you, as I said—you have a good heart. You have defended me—now I will defend you, and helping one another, we might well come unscathed to the land of Prester John."

"Prester John!" Anthony breathed. "Is his kingdom your homeland?"

She saw the wonder and longing in his face, and said, "It is the land of my birth, yes." Later she might explain that she had grown up far to the west, in Allustria, but that could wait. "I know not the way, though—I was sent here by magic."

"Magic! You have sorcerous enemies, then?"

"It would seem so," Balkis admitted, "though I had not thought I had offended anyone." *No one but the gur-khan and his chief priest,* said a small voice within her mind, but she ignored it—surely the men of the horde would have slain her, not exiled her. "Travel with me," she urged, "and I shall find a way for you to cope with whatever trials we meet. When our journey is done, you shall see the land of Prester John."

"The enchanted kingdom!" Anthony said, staring off into space at his own dreams. Then he came back to earth and frowned. "I could not leave my father and brothers to worry, though."

"Then leave them a note," Balkis suggested.

"A note?" Anthony said in surprise. "But I am only a peasant! I cannot write!"

"I can." Balkis felt a surge of annoyance. Really, did the boy know nothing?

Only what mattered: how to be kind and gentle—and how to defend a friend.

"If you could write a note for me," Anthony said slowly, "Father could take it to the priest to read . . ."

"Then let us do so." Balkis looked about her. "Charcoal will do for the writing, and a clean board will serve for parchment."

"I shall fetch them." Once decided, Anthony had no hesitation. He descended the ladder, found charcoal at the forge and scrubbed a board clean, then dictated the letter. He choked over the words, and Balkis feared he would change his mind and stay, but when the message was written, Anthony fetched a coil of rope and two waterskins, then led her out to the smokehouse and gathered a dozen sausages. Balkis changed into a cat and leaped up to his shoulder, and equipped only with food, water, and rope, they set off down the hillside.

Anthony hesitated only as the sun rose before them. "The cows . . ."

"Your brothers will milk them when they come looking for you," Balkis meowed at him. *Or for me,* she thought.

Anthony looked up at her in surprise. "You can talk in that form, then?"

"Try to stop me," Balkis retorted. "Have you heard anyone say where the land of Prester John lies?"

"North," Anthony answered.

"North let us go, then."

Anthony nodded, turning so that the sun was on his right, and set off diagonally across the hillside. Balkis looked back, wary that his brothers might try to track him and make him come back. She murmured a verse in Allustrian and a small whirlwind blew up, following them and obliterating their tracks with blown snow.

Satisfied, Balkis turned and looked forward again. For a moment her conscience hurt—it was good for her to have a road companion, but was this leave-taking good for Anthony?

Then she remembered the beating, and it firmed her resolve—this couldn't be worse, surely. If Anthony had been a boy in his teens, not yet ready to face the world on his own, it might have been different—but he was a man who would have already married and left home if there had been more women in his country. He was ready to go out into the world on his own, past ready—and if he didn't like Prester John's country, he could always come home. In fact, she could make sure he had a horse and a mounted escort—and money enough to set his father and brothers in *his* power for a change. She relished the thought as Anthony finished traversing the hill and struck a set of icy ruts that served as a road leading northward. "We have begun our journey, Kit!" he said, exulting. "I mean, Balkis."

"We have begun indeed, son of men," she agreed, "and begun well."

The road stretched out before them, all the way home to Maracanda.

The road may have led toward the north, but it also led downward. Toward evening it rose again for a mile to a ridge that fell away to a valley floor. As they descended, the road slanting toward the stream below, Balkis noticed that the drifts by the roadside scarcely came to Anthony's knees, and saw dripping icicles on the bare branches whenever they passed a stand of birches.

As they strode lower, though, the sun hid behind the peak at the western end of the valley and the dripping lessened, then stopped as the air chilled, leaving the icicles frozen again. It was the mountains' height that had brought them snow, Balkis realized, and the lower they went, the warmer it would be, as she expected from a southern climate. "When we come out of the mountains to the plains," she asked, "will there still be snow?"

"I doubt it," Anthony said. "The flatlands are always oven-hot when we visit them in the summer, and they must be warm enough for crops to grow even now." He made a face. "The air is thick with heat and moisture, though. It will be painful to breathe."

Balkis hid a smile. She didn't doubt Anthony's words—for a man raised to breathing the thin, dry air of the mountains, the lowland air must indeed seem like soup.

The ground leveled about them, and they were so far below

the ridge that the land lay in twilight. Suddenly a partridge burst from cover almost beneath Anthony's nose.

"Good hunting!" Balkis cried, and leaped down off Anthony's shoulder.

"Good indeed," he said, and she heard a hissing. She looked up to see a circular blur above his raised hand; then his arm whipped down and the partridge gave one raucous cry and fell out of the sky.

Shaken, Balkis stared up at her gentle Anthony as he wrapped the strings of the sling around its leather pouch and tucked it back in his belt. "I think we shall have fresh meat for dinner," he said, "not merely boiled jerky."

"It would seem so," Balkis replied. "Do you always carry that with you?"

"Of course," Anthony said. "You never know when dinner will spring up before your eyes. Do not people carry slings in your homeland?"

"Not in the cities," Balkis said, "but we find our dinners in the marketplace there."

"Ah." Anthony nodded, understanding, and went to fetch the partridge.

Balkis decided that perhaps he didn't need quite so much help as she had thought.

They ate in companionable silence. Balkis changed back into a woman for the occasion, reasoning that her larger stomach could hold more food, which would sustain her longer. She told herself it had nothing to do with Anthony's admiring glances—but she did relish them. She was beginning to enjoy the strange, warm sensation those looks raised in her. Besides, the feeling was less intense in human form.

As she wiped her fingers on a tuft of dead grass, Anthony said, "Shall we play the old game, then?"

"What?" Balkis stared at him, trying to decide whether or not to feel insulted.

"The game," Anthony explained. "You saw us at it last night, did you not? I have played at telling the old tales in verse as long as I can remember."

"Oh! The old tales," Balkis said, relieved. "It is not a game with which I am familiar, Anthony. Besides, I may not know your tales."

"How diverting!" Anthony exclaimed. "A new tale! Make up whatever comes to your mind, then."

"I—I do not know if I can." But Balkis realized what a rare treat this must be for him, to start not only the verse but also the whole saga, with no one to object. She couldn't disappoint him. "I shall try, though . . ."

"And you shall succeed!" Anthony assured her. "Here, I shall begin it." He stared into the fire; his face became blank, then his eyes began to glow as he intoned, "Rustam woke and . . . No, he sprang from his bed . . . No, the meter is off with that . . . Rustam op'd his eyes and . . . Drat!" He broke off with an embarrassed laugh. "I have never begun the lay before! Once it is under way, I have no difficulty with the middle lines and certainly not with the last—now and again, even a first line will come to me—but the first line of a whole saga? Your pardon, for this will take some time."

Balkis' heart ached for Anthony, frustrated when he finally had the chance to begin. If she could start him, though, he would be able to keep the tale going, at least. "Let me try, then." Balkis was quite sure of herself with beginnings and middles. "What does Rustam do?"

"Why, he wakes, says his morning prayer to the sun, and equips himself for the hunt," Anthony said, as though it should have been obvious. Then he reddened and gave an embarrassed laugh. "Your pardon; already I have forgotten that you said you do not know the tale."

Balkis' resentment faded as quickly as it had come; she appreciated his understanding of his own gaffe. She did hope, though, that he wouldn't be asking her pardon every time she turned around. "It is enough to know how the lay begins. Let me see, now . . . Rustam woke and blessed the dawn . . ."

"See! You are quite able!" Anthony said, his enthusiasm restored. "Prayed to dawn and took his bow . . ."

Bow? What next? Then Balkis remembered what one did to prepare a bow. "Bent the stave with easy brawn . . ."

"Dawn and brawn! Good!" Anthony approved, then added, "Strung it and chose well his arrow . . . Finish the verse now."

Balkis' heart sank at the prospect of finding the end-line. Arrow? What went with an arrow? And rhymed with "brawn"? Balkis stammered, "He shot at . . . I mean, he pulled the feathers . . . Confound it, Anthony, for confounded I am! I have never been able to end a verse!"

"I can, be sure," Anthony said with a wry smile and chanted, "Slung his quiver and upon . . . There, now, begin a new verse."

New verse? Knowing only that Rustam had "upon"ed something? Upon? Upon what? Was Anthony mad? But Balkis remembered that she did not have to make this line rhyme; she could end it with whatever word she chose, and the rhyming would be Anthony's problem. With a wicked grin, she said, "Out upon . . . the grass he . . . he stepped . . ."

"To seek the spoor and stalk a doe!" Anthony cried. "You see? It is easy!"

Easy for you, Balkis thought, but she returned his smile, caught up in his enthusiasm. Then she remembered that she had to rhyme her own first line. Stepped? What rhymed with "stepped"?

Leapt! "A stream he found, and o'er it leapt . . ."

"Long he sought . . ." Anthony said, diving into the second verse.

Balkis kept up with him as well as she could, which was quite well on the first and middle lines—but the final rhyme always defeated her. After bailing her out three more times, Anthony said charitably, "Take the second line this time."

"Oh, no!" Balkis protested. "You have had so little chance!"

"I've had small enough chance with the mid-lines, either," Anthony pointed out, "and I will be quite happy with the third line and the last. After all, I am the clean-up boy, am I not?"

"You are far more than that!" Balkis cried in anger.

Anthony looked deeply into her eyes, his gaze almost seeming to devour hers. She felt a fluttering inside and an impulse to turn away, but stood her ground, gazing back at him. "Never try to outstare a cat," she warned.

Anthony laughed with sheer delight, and the sound was balm to her heart. "I was staring, wasn't I?" he said. "Forgive, beautiful lady! But it is very good of you to think of me so—and if you say I am, I shall be so!"

After all, Balkis decided, the first lines were the prize he had been so long denied—and once the poem had been started, what was the difference between the middle lines of a verse and the first, save that the first could establish a new rhyme, and was therefore even easier to craft?

"Well enough, then, lad. You take the first line, and send Rustam off on the hunt."

"Then you take the second," Anthony said with a grin, "and lead him where he has never gone before."

Thus the evening passed, and when she lay down to sleep, warmed only by her cloak and the campfire, Balkis was surprised to realize that she was nonetheless quite content.

Stegoman thundered into the air and found a thermal to lift him higher. Matt scanned the sky but saw no sign of a slender red dragon. Then he looked ahead and saw beyond the mountains a vast expanse of beige.

"Southern desert ahead," he pointed out to Stegoman.

"I shall gain altitude while I can," the dragon said. "The air over that wasteland will not be rising until midday."

Matt took the hint—no landing until noon, unless it was an emergency.

Stegoman flew high indeed, enough so that the desert looked like corrugated iron—until Matt remembered that those corrugations were rows of sand dunes. After an hour or so, they crossed a long, pale line that snaked its way from the southern horizon to the northern mountains. "Follow that strand!" he called to Stegoman. "It's a road!"

"Who would have need of a road on so flat a land?" Stegoman asked, but banked to follow the track anyway. Matt bit back comments about quicksands, jagged rocks, and slippery footing and contented himself with, "Thanks."

As the sun rose higher and the land warmed, Stegoman settled lower, confident in the ability of the heated, rising air to take him aloft again. It was nearly noon when Matt spotted the cluster of dots on the roadway. "People!" he called to Stegoman.

"You wish to land and question them, I assume," the dragon sighed.

"You don't mind, do you?"

"Not at all—if they have a spare goat nearby." Stegoman wheeled back, then came in for a landing.

With his usual caution about public appearances, Stegoman slid to earth behind a sand dune a quarter mile from the road. It only took Matt ten minutes to hike in, but even so, the sun baked him so thoroughly that he arrived feeling dehydrated.

The travelers were riding camels and leading others laden with goods—all rather skittish, having seen a dragon overhead. The people stopped to stare at Matt. They wore loose coats and trousers of off-white, unbleached muslin, long enough to protect them from the sun, loose enough and light enough to be cool—or as cool as they could be in the desert.

"Hail!" Matt raised a hand and decided to start with the language of Maracanda.

"Hail," a graybeard answered, raising his own hand in return.

"I'm looking for a young woman."

"Most men your age are." The graybeard's eye twinkled.

Matt grinned in answer. "Not that way—I'm her teacher, and she's disappeared."

"She did not like your teaching?" a young man asked with a grin.

Just what Matt needed—a whole caravan full of comics. "Seems to have decided she knew enough to strike out on her own—and maybe she does, but I'm concerned anyway. You haven't seen a lone girl, have you?"

"We have not," the young man said, and another assured him, "We would have noticed."

"Noticed, but nothing more," said the young woman beside him, with a dagger-glance, "at least, if you wished to sleep easily."

"Let your heart be light." The young man caught her hand and gave it a squeeze. "I would have noticed her and called you to talk with her, nothing more."

The young woman's glance was somewhat mollified, but she was still suspicious.

So was Matt, suspicious enough to realize that Balkis would have been very foolish to try hiking in her human form. "She had a pet with her," he said. "I don't suppose you've seen a cat?"

"A cat?" The young men stared.

"Yeah." Matt was about to mention color, then realized he didn't know what robe Balkis had been wearing for her kidnapping. He hoped it wasn't blue or purple or green. "You know, small furry animal, long tail, whiskers, retractable claws?" Matt pantomimed as he talked.

The nomads stared at him as though he were mad.

"This is poor country for cats," the young woman told him.

An older woman nodded. "There is little to hunt, and less to drink."

Well, Matt wasn't entirely sure of that—he saw clumps of scrub brush here and there and knew it probably supported small colonies of mice who knew how to find the catch basins that watered it. Still, he wasn't about to contradict the locals. "If you do see one, could you take her in?"

"The cat, or the woman?" the second young man asked.

"Right," Matt answered. "I'll try to check back with you later."

"Be sure that I shall help her." The young woman gave her young man another whetted glance.

"We shall, us women together," the older woman confirmed.

"Thanks." Matt smiled. "I'd appreciate it. Have a good trip." He waved as he turned to start back to Stegoman.

"Beware, stranger," the graybeard called after him. "There was a dragon flying overhead not long ago."

"I'll keep an eye out for him," Matt said with a backward glance. "Thanks."

"It was not perchance your dragon, was it?"

"Mine? No, we're just friends. Take care, now." And Matt plodded back to Stegoman, oblivious to the stares at his back.

Each day's travel took Balkis and Anthony lower and lower; each noon's sun was warmer and warmer, though the nights stayed chill. By the end of the week they had come down into flat land, and Balkis found it was desert. The days were warmer than was comfortable, but not really hot; it was winter, after all. In her northern cloak, though, Balkis sweltered. She took it off, folded it flat, and slung it over her shoulder, retying her sash to hold it to her waist.

"Beware the sun's rays," Anthony warned her. "They can burn."

"I shall chance it," Balkis told him. "The sun is my summer friend." She doubted that the Central Asian winter could be that much worse than an Allustrian summer, which tanned her golden skin to bronze. She looked at Anthony with concern. "But your fair skin worries me."

"I have a hood." Anthony pulled it up to demonstrate. "Oh, my woolens are too warm for comfort, but I should be able to trade for a cotton robe as soon as we meet other travelers." He took a shiny stone from his pocket. "We find these in the streams now and then. It should do for trade."

Balkis glanced at the stone, then stared. It was gold. "Yes," she said, "that might even buy robes for both of us—and a dozen more."

"So small a stone as this?" A shadow crossed Anthony's face. "I wish we could find many of these, for then my father and brothers could cease this lifelong toil that makes them grow knobbed and bowed." Then he brightened. "Still, with this one, perhaps we can buy food—and water, too."

Balkis almost said that there was no sense in paying for water, but she looked at the desert stretching before them and said instead, "Could anyone spare water here, even for gold?"

"Some bring huge skins of it to trade, for it is dear in this waste," Anthony said. "Nonetheless, there is water for those who know where to look."

Balkis looked up at him in surprise, then remembered. "Yes, you have been here before, you said."

Anthony nodded. "During the hot months, we bring down livestock and grain to sell to the caravans. It is only a few miles, but it has taught us some knowledge of desert ways."

Balkis had dim memories of having traveled with a caravan

as a cat during her human infancy, but not enough to do much good. "How shall we travel, then?"

"By night." Anthony flashed her a grin. "Come, let me show you a cave where my family shelters when we travel."

He turned to go, but Balkis stayed him with a hand on his sleeve. "Will they not think to look for you there?"

"Do you truly think they will look for me?" Anthony asked, with a sad and weary smile that seemed to accept every dagger Fate threw at him.

He seemed so forlorn that Balkis spoke without thinking. "Of course they will! You are theirs, after all."

"A possession, you mean?" But Anthony's eye gained a gleam, even if it was only a sardonic one. "Perhaps they will at that—when several days have passed and they are convinced I will not come crawling back for food and shelter and they will have to do their own milking and mucking out. If they do follow, we will be gone long before they arrive. Let us find shelter."

The shelter turned out to be a hollow in the bank of a ravine which was plainly a dry watercourse.

"If it should rain, we will move to higher ground," Anthony explained, "and that quickly, for this gully will hold a raging torrent. There is a hidden pool; I know where to dig to find it."

"Has it rained so recently, then?" Balkis looked at the arid land around her.

"No," Anthony said, "but we came through melting snow, and some of it sinks down into a stream that pools out belowground here. Even when there is no rain, this watercourse stays damp."

Balkis had a vision of all that runoff filling the gully and shuddered.

The cave was a rough semicircle twelve feet deep. Anthony led the way to six pallets of straw at the back of the cave. "It is scarcely fresh, but is so dry that it will still do for beds—and will surely be more comfortable than the bare earth."

"It will that," Balkis said fervently, and spread her cloak over the pallet farthest to the side. Anthony spread his over the pallet at the back, with two between them, so they lay down as they always did, ten feet apart. Balkis wondered how she would feel if he tried sleeping closer, and was shocked to realize that she wished he would.

They rose in the sunset and sat awhile talking as the day cooled into night—talked of the Mazdans, who prayed to the sun as a symbol of Ahura Mazda, the god of light, then of the religions in which each had been raised. Anthony's ancestors had worshiped the old Greek gods, brought eastward by Alexander's armies, until Christianity had penetrated even the forgotten villages of their mountains. He learned quickly that she was a different kind of Christian than he, and listened to the Roman rubrics with knitted brow, clearly not understanding—but Balkis realized that he was trying for her sake, and the thought warmed her against the night's chill.

And it was chill; she was amazed to realize it as she shook out her cloak and wrapped herself in it. "Perhaps those cotton robes will not be needed, after all."

"Well, at least to sleep in," Anthony said. "Besides, will we not need them in your homeland? It should be cool enough to travel by daylight there."

The memory of Allustria in winter flashed through Balkis' mind; then she remembered that Maracanda was her home now. Even so, Prester John's city had certainly been cool enough when she had seen it last. "We will," she assured him. "Where shall we travel tonight?"

"To the oasis where we trade with the caravan drivers," Anthony answered. "There we can find water without having to dig."

That struck Balkis as a good beginning. She looked up at the wall of the ravine. "I think I can manage that in human form."

"But your beautiful garments will be ruined!" Anthony protested.

Balkis shrugged. "We were going to buy new robes anyway, and my sleeping chemise is scarcely priceless."

Anthony stared. "You wear so lovely a gown only for sleeping?"

Balkis found the comment oddly pleasing. She smiled and said, "I do not think my cloak will bear much damage from the climb—not if I wear it in this wise, at least." She belted the flat folds back into place over her shoulder again, then turned to climb the slope. Anthony followed her quickly.

The angle wasn't so steep that they needed to use their hands more than once or twice, but they were breathing hard by the time they came out onto the desert floor. Balkis stood a moment to catch her breath, then asked, "Now! Where is this oasis of yours?"

"We need only follow the ravine," Anthony said.

Balkis nodded and set off, preferring to travel beside him in her human form, though cat-guise would have been more convenient.

The sun was halfway up the sky before she saw palm trees appear, seemingly out of the sands. "I did not see these from the mountains," she said. "Have we come so far as that?"

"Oh, we could have seen them, surely," Anthony said, "but they would have seemed too small to notice."

It sounded right, but Balkis glanced back at the mountains to see if they looked much smaller—and gasped. "Anthony! What is that moving fire?"

"Moving fire?" Anthony turned back in alarm, and saw a flaming shape moving toward them. "I know not—but it follows us! Run!"

Balkis ran.

CHAPTER 10

Balkis outdistanced Anthony easily and had to slow down so he could catch up. When she did, she looked back and saw that they had left the fire behind. She halted and said, "It moves slowly."

Anthony stopped beside her and looked back, too, though his face was pale. He nodded. "We can outpace it easily."

"But why does it chase us?" Balkis asked. "And what is it?"

"I have heard of them, from the caravan drivers," Anthony said, his voice shaky. "They are called salamanders and can only live in fire, and are the caterpillars of some giant moth."

"Caterpillars?" Balkis shuddered at the thought of the butterfly such a creature would become—but the wizard in her was fascinated. She peered more closely. As the worm turned to follow a curve in the ravine, she saw it from the side; the flame was indeed much longer than it was wide, and its core was a long, crawling shape so bright that it was almost white.

"It is quite dangerous from the time it hatches out of its egg until it spins its cocoon," Anthony said, "since it is ravenous and its fire will fry anything it comes near."

Balkis wondered what kind of cloth the silk of that cocoon might make. "Could it be moving toward the oasis because it seeks water?"

Anthony shook his head. "It is made of fire. Water would kill it. No, it seeks food—at the moment, us. We are the ones who need water."

Balkis pursed her lips, musing. "If we can conjure up something for it to eat, we can fill our water bags before it chases us again."

Anthony considered the idea a moment, then nodded slowly. "A good thought."

"What does it most like to eat?" Balkis asked.

"Anything that lives or used to," Anthony said, "but the caravan men say it likes poppies most."

"Because they are the color of fire?" Balkis smiled. "There is sense to that, at least in magic." She stilled herself inside, let her eyes lose focus, and summoned a verse Matthew had taught her, written by one Edmund Spenser:

> "Fresh spring, the herald of love's mighty king,
> In whose coat of armor richly are display'd
> All sorts of flowers the which on earth do spring . . ."

She hesitated, unsure how the last line ran. Anthony, thinking it was his turn, cried,

> "With heaps of poppies gloriously array'd
> To our fireworm your vivid blossoms bring!"

"Um . . . thank you, Anthony," Balkis said somewhat uncertainly, for she was sure that was not how the original verse had been.

It worked nonetheless, and very well, too. Sparks flew up from the fireworm, hung dancing in the air, then grew into flame-red blooms and cascaded to the ground before the worm in a huge heap. It tore into the pile without a moment's hesitation—but it did stop to eat.

Balkis decided she might keep Anthony around for a while.

"Quickly, now!" Anthony caught her hand. "To the oasis!"

They ran hand in hand, holding each other up when one stumbled. The water bags weren't much of a hindrance—they were almost flat. Then they were running on soft grass beneath palm trees, and Anthony fell to his knees, gasping, by the pond. He pulled the straps of the waterskins over his head and pulled their stoppers. "Watch and tell me if it comes!" he said, and pushed the skins under the water.

Balkis looked back, "It has almost finished that whole mound of poppies!"

"Only a minute more." Anthony pulled one waterskin from the pond, stoppered it, and handed it up to her. "If worse comes to worse, flay it with a stream of that!"

Balkis took the skin and slung its weight over her shoulder. It seemed reassuring; she had no doubt a jet of water would indeed slow the salamander awhile. Then she saw the last of the poppies burst into flame as they disappeared into that searing maw, and the blind, questing head rose, weaving from side to side, then steadying on them. "It comes!" she cried.

"Then we go!" Anthony rose, the other waterskin over his shoulder, and caught her hand. "Come, around the pond and away! Perhaps it will fall into the water as it chases us!"

They ran, fragments of rhyme chasing one another through Balkis' head as she tried to forge a spell to stop a silkworm made of fire.

When they were sure they had gained enough distance to be safe, Balkis stopped and looked back; Anthony had to stop with her. They both stared, then Balkis said, "Well, we need no longer fear its chasing us."

"Indeed we do not," Anthony agreed. "That will be a blessing when we need to sleep."

The salamander was settling down for a snooze of its own. It had stopped to throw strands of silk between two trees that stood only a few feet apart. As they watched, it crawled out onto the net it had spun between the two and began to spin itself a nightshirt.

"It would seem your mountain of poppies finally filled it," Anthony said.

How like him to overlook his own part in conjuring up the flowers! "Perhaps it did not chase us, after all," Balkis said. "Perhaps it only sought a place to spin."

"Or perhaps the poppies sent it to sleep," Anthony said. "I have heard they have that virtue."

They watched as the creature swathed itself in silk. Balkis was surprised to see how small it was—on the desert floor there had been nothing to show its size, but she knew how tall the palms were, and realized that the salamander couldn't have been more than a foot and a half in length. Had she really been afraid of something no longer than her forearm?

Of course—if that something burned white-hot.

"We have only to wait until the creature is done spinning," Anthony said. "Then we can go back to the oasis for a proper rest. After all, if it is asleep in its cocoon, it will not be hungry or hunting."

Balkis nodded agreement, watching, fascinated. The net that held the salamander didn't burn, nor did the cocoon it crafted, but its own fire still enveloped it. Even after it had closed the hole at the top and settled down to sleep, the pupa was wrapped in flame—but the silk that held it suspended between the palms insulated the trunks from the blaze.

"I always wondered how the caravans harvested the cocoons they carried to market," Anthony said. "Now I know—they found them at oases all along their road!"

Balkis still gazed at the fiery cocoon. "Does each caravan bring a wizard to make the worms harmless?"

Anthony shook his head. "The drivers tell me that once the salamander has wrapped its cocoon around itself, it becomes harmless, and to kill it one need only drown the blaze. Then the merchants can take the silk to sell."

Balkis stared. "Now I know that form! I have seen palace servants buying giant silken eggs like this in the marketplace of Maracanda when the first caravan from the south comes!"

"The marketplace of Maracanda!" Anthony gazed off into space, his head filled with shining visions. He shook off the mood and asked, "What use have your people for cocoons?"

"They weave the silk," Balkis explained. "Spinsters carefully wind the thread onto spools and give it to weavers, who make it into cloth."

"Cloth? From salamander cocoons?" Anthony asked, wondering. "Why would anyone want them more than robes of true silk? The traders have shown me silken cloth, and it is beautiful!"

"This is even more so," Balkis told him, "and it lasts far longer, and is amazingly easy to clean! When they wish to wash the garments made of this cloth, the servants have only to put them into fire, and they come forth fresh and clean. They last so long that many people inherit them from their grandparents, and of course they never burn."

"How wonderful it must be in Maracanda," Anthony exclaimed, his eyes glowing, "if everybody there wears such silk."

"Not everyone, silly!" Balkis smiled, feeling quite the sophisticate. "Such cloth is very expensive, of course. Garments made of it are for royalty and nobility."

"So only the people who live in palaces can wear such cloth?" Anthony asked, disappointed. Then he shrugged, turning his face toward the north. "Even so, I wish to see Maracanda, for if it is your home, it must be wonderful indeed." He turned back to grin. "And if it is your home, I wish to take you there."

Heart warmed, Balkis smiled up into his eyes. "Thank you, my friend." She wondered why her voice had gone all throaty.

Anthony noticed; his grin widened and his eyes gleamed in a way that made her both excited and frightened at the same time—though whether she was frightened of the emotion she saw in him or of the feelings his look aroused in herself, she could not say.

Then Anthony turned back to the north. "It lies there, northward—but how far?"

Balkis shrugged. "I cannot say. I know only that its winter is much, much colder than this."

"Months away at least, then." Anthony shook his head regretfully. "Why did I not ask the caravan drivers how long it took to reach Maracanda? I only asked them how distant it was, and they always answered, 'Far, very far.' "

Balkis' stomach sank. "I cannot ask you to go so far from your homeland."

"But you did counsel me to leave that home behind and seek my fortune," Anthony reminded her.

Balkis felt a touch of pique; it might be true, but it was scarcely gentlemanly of him to remind her. "I do not recall saying anything about seeking your fortune."

Anthony looked up at the sharpness in her tone and saw he had erred. "You spoke of Maracanda, did you not? And surely my fortune lies there!"

Balkis gazed at him a second or two, then smiled. "I think it does, yes—not your fortune, perhaps, but your destiny."

"Then let us go!"

Balkis shook her head in amazement at his boundless optimism—or his foolish refusal to think of failure. Whichever it was, he would be pleasant company—for there was no question of her not doing all she could to return to Maracanda. "We shall, then—but let us rest while we may."

They sat down by the pond. As Anthony rummaged in his pack he voiced misgivings he'd been hiding. "I will be a stranger and a bumpkin in Maracanda. Dare I go there?"

"All are welcome unless they come in war," Balkis told him. "Every high holy day brings caravans of pilgrims who come to visit the shrine of St. Thomas."

"St. Thomas?" Anthony looked up, startled. "Doubting Thomas? The one who would not believe the Lord had risen from the dead unless he could put his finger into the nail holes in His palms and his hand into the rent the spear had made in His side?"

"Yes, and the one who, when the Lord appeared before him, dared do no more than kneel," Balkis said with a smile. "You did know it was St. Thomas who brought the Gospel to India, did you not?"

"To India, and thereby to all these lands of Asia," Anthony assured her, "but I did not know he had taken his preaching as far north as Maracanda."

"He died there," Balkis told him, "and his body sits in state in a golden chair in the cathedral that is part of Prester John's palace, preserved and uncorrupted, looking as though he only sleeps—but during the great holy days of the year, St. Thomas comes to life and preaches to the people."

"Truly?" Anthony's eyes were as round as saucers.

"I have not seen it myself," Balkis confessed. "I have a dislike of crowds." She knew why—she had a cat's fear of too many huge, booted feet stamping and shifting without regard for what lay beneath them. "People tell me the saint's body also gives communion, but closes its hand over the wafer if an unbeliever comes."

"Amazing!" Anthony exclaimed. "My family are Nestorian Christians. Will the saint count us as unbelievers?"

Balkis tried to hide her amusement. "Most of the Christians of Prester John's domain are Nestorians."

"Then let us find a caravan and go to Maracanda with it!" Anthony cried.

"Why, what a perfect notion!" Balkis clapped her hands. "It will surely be safer to journey with a caravan than by ourselves. But did you not say they do not travel in winter?"

Anthony nodded. "The trading season is over until spring, still a month away, but the first caravans should be leaving India even now—and did you not say we would be months on the road?"

"I did," Balkis admitted.

"Surely we will meet a train of camels long before we come to Maracanda!"

Balkis smiled; his enthusiasm was infectious. "Let us seek your caravan, then—but for now, let us eat, then rest awhile longer."

"We certainly shall not lack for a campfire," Anthony agreed, with a glance at the flaming cocoon.

"Is it safe, do you think?" Balkis asked, watching the flames.

Anthony nodded. "The fire will burn until the moth is grown—but it will not reach much beyond the chrysalis. If it did, it would devour the trees that hold it!"

Balkis could see the truth in that. "Not that it needs height for protection."

"The only creatures who would not be frightened away by its blaze are people." Anthony grinned. "Small wonder it did not chose to spin near the pond!"

"We should be safe enough," Balkis agreed.

They drank from their waterskins and ate dates from the palms with their journeybread and dried beef. As they finished the meal, the talk drifted to their pasts.

"Father taught us that we and all the people in our part of the hills are part Greek," Anthony told her. "Our ancestors were soldiers in the army of Alexander the Great. When he died and his generals settled down to rule the empire, his troopers followed Alexander's example and married women from the tribes around and about."

"So that is the source of your yellow hair and blue eyes!"

"Probably," Anthony said, "but the legends tell us that there were always redheads among these hill folk even before Alexander came, and my hair is as much red as yellow."

"Golden," Balkis agreed, trying to ignore the sensations that studying Anthony's looks aroused in her. "I expected all your folk to have black hair, though, as do so many of the peoples of these lands."

"Black hair and yellow skin, like the caravan drivers from the east? Yes. But our legends say the first mountaineers in these hills came from a wild people who crossed the mountains to conquer India," Anthony told her. "Their skins were bronze and their hair was red, brown, or black. But if so many in Asia have slanted eyes and yellow skin, how is it your eyes are round and your skin golden?"

"Maracanda has grown rich on trade," Balkis told him. "Caravans come from the west and south as well as the east, bringing not only goods but travelers. Some of the pilgrims choose to stay. My ancestors came from all lands."

"If all their descendants are like you, their mingling has produced a beautiful people!"

Balkis lowered her gaze, hoping he wouldn't see her blush. "You are kind to say so . . ."

"Not at all," Anthony breathed.

". . . but I think that all peoples are handsome, though others may not see it," Balkis went on, firmly ignoring his comment—but she kept her eyes, and her face, downcast. When her skin had cooled, she looked up and asked, "But what of this rhyming game of yours? Did Alexander bring that, too?"

"No one knows," Anthony said frankly, "though we think it was there before him. It is a contest for whiling away the long winter nights, after all."

Balkis gazed off into space, thinking, and nodded. "There is little point in sitting around the fire in summer, aye. But do you not sit out in the twilight, then?"

"We do," Anthony said, "but there is little time between evening chores and bed, for we work in the fields as long as the light holds. There is much work to be done if we wish to wrest a living from the rocky ground of the slopes."

"I suppose there must be." Balkis thought of the wide, flat fields around Maracanda and saw his point. "Do you never tire of retelling the old tales?"

"Never, for there are many of them, and some, like the Mahabhurata, are very long." Anthony seemed to see nothing odd in a Christian knowing a Hindu epic. "And, of course, you must never use a verse, or even a line, that you have used before."

"So you must always put the story into new words?"

Anthony nodded. "Always new rhyme and meter straight from your head, made up then and there. Some play it only as a game, but Father has always declared it to be a competition between his sons. At the end of the night, we discuss who has done best, and Father rules who won and who lost." His gaze slipped away and his face darkened. "Almost always, they agree I have lost, for I am clumsy in my rhyming and keep breaking the meter."

"Not the verses I have heard." Balkis felt a dark anger growing. "You seemed quite deft and your rhymes ingenious. Have you ever won?"

"Oh, of course not!"

"Of course," Balkis echoed with sarcasm. "You are the youngest, after all—how could they ever let you be first?"

Anthony frowned. "It is not their fault that I am slow."

"I am not certain of that," Balkis said, and before he could object again, added, "after all, they never let you begin the tale. You must always fit your thoughts to someone else's meter."

"Well, true." Anthony gazed out at the desert. "I have gained a great deal of practice at keeping the story going, though. Surely I will gain their respect someday, even though I may never win."

"Not theirs," Balkis said, "but mine, and that of any others who hear you."

"Yes, if someone else makes up the first verse!" Anthony said with a rueful grin. "I have little originality and less imagination."

"Or so your brothers would have you believe," Balkis said sharply. "I suspect your imagination is only lacking in regard to your own talents. For myself, I can memorize any verse at one hearing and coin a new verse easily, but I have a bitter time of it trying to finish a final couplet."

Still, Anthony had already proved that he was very good at improvising verses to add to her own spells. If she could start a spell, he could finish it, and make it much stronger in the process.

He did not say so, but looking into his eyes, Balkis saw that he realized it, too. She flushed and turned aside, not wanting to relegate him to being the clean-up man, even as his brothers had—but she had to admit his talent was useful. She resolved to give him a great deal of practice at beginning poems.

Anthony reached out for her hand but didn't quite touch it. "What are you thinking?"

"Only that it is a long way to Maracanda." Balkis took his hand. "A long way, and months in which to come to know one another. Let us sleep while we may, and when the sun is low, we can manage a few hours' more walking."

They walked northward until dark, with the setting sun on their left. They sheltered in the lee of a huge rock that stood alone and unexpected in the midst of the waste. Anthony kindled a small and smokeless fire with the dry brush that straggled about them while Balkis changed into a cat and crept downwind of some mice, watching them scurry about the brush finding dried berries to eat. Then a nighthawk found the mice, Balkis found the hawk, and they had fresh meat for dinner.

They traveled for two days, hiking northward from the first light of false dawn until noon, resting till the heat had slackened, then marching again until the twilight had faded into total darkness. On the third morning, though, they came to the rim of a valley and stared at an open river with groves of trees wherever it widened into a small pool.

"Do I see castles?" Anthony asked, eyes wide.

"You do, and I would guess them to be a day's march apart all along the river," Balkis said. "Upon my word, I do not know which is more amazing—the river in the middle of a desert or the castles!"

"We must be wary," Anthony cautioned. "Water is precious in this wasteland. The people who live here may raid one another to gain more acres of riverbank and may have built the castles to protect themselves from one another."

"If so, they will not take kindly to strangers," Balkis said, nodding. "But this valley runs northward for at least two days' travel, and the chance of having open water by us that whole way is too great a stroke of fortune to resist."

"If there is trouble, you can always turn into a cat," Anthony reminded her.

"Oh, can I!" Of course, Balkis had been thinking the same thing. "What shall you turn into?"

"A prisoner," Anthony said frankly, "but you shall free me with your magic."

Balkis stiffened in alarm. "Do not place too much faith in magic. You never know when your opponents will have a stronger wizard."

"Well then, we shall have to outsmart them." Anthony flashed her his dazzling grin again, then started down into the valley.

Balkis gazed after him, shaking her head—but his perpetual good humor did lift her spirits.

The going was easy on the valley sides, especially after they struck a winding path—apparently, the inhabitants climbed to the desert frequently, probably to meet the caravans. In fact, Balkis found herself wondering why so well-watered a place had not developed its own caravanserai and trade town.

They reached the valley floor before the sun had risen very high; in fact, they still walked in the shadow of the valley wall when they came to a huge heap of dirt beside a foot-wide hole.

Balkis stopped, staring. "What do you suppose made this? A fox?"

"A whole tribe of them, perhaps." Then Anthony's eyes

widened and, with a cry of delight, he bent down to the heap of dirt.

"What can be so wonderful about earth?" Balkis wondered if the sun had been too strong for her mountain-bred friend.

"This!" Anthony straightened up with something in his palm, holding it out for Balkis to see. She looked down and saw a golden nugget as big as a robin's egg. She stared, then felt fear reaching out from her stomach to weaken her limbs, though she did not know why. "This must be a miner's workings!"

"If so, he is a very small miner." Anthony gestured at the hole.

Balkis glanced about her, her apprehension growing. "I see other such heaps in the distance. These miners may be small, Anthony, but they are many."

"Let us see if they have brought up more of what you call gold." Anthony bent to dig in the pile of loose dirt. "Another! And another and another . . ." He gathered up a score of nuggets, then broke off with a yelp of alarm. Balkis leaped backward with a scream, for the miner came climbing out of the hole—a miner with six legs and long antennae above faceted compound eyes. It was an ant as big as a fox, an ant whose mandibles looked like the tusks of a forest boar.

"Run!" Balkis cried.

Anthony started running, but with reluctance. "Surely there is nothing to fear—it is so much smaller than we!"

"I assure you it is large enough to kill a man, or even an ox!" Balkis called back. "Have you never seen an ant pull a twig five times its size? Run as though the hounds of hell were at your heels!"

And well they might have been, for the ant gave a high chittering call as it charged after them, and dozens more came pouring out behind it.

Anthony ran.

CHAPTER 11

True to Balkis' word, the ant ran twice as fast as they, and so did its mates. The air filled with chittering as ants came pouring from other hills, darting across their path.

"There!" Anthony pointed toward a spire of rock off to their left, only ten feet ahead. "Surely they cannot climb stone!"

Balkis had seen ants climb vertical tree trunks, but these were so much larger that perhaps they could not stick as well—and they were almost at her heels. With a cry of loathing, she swerved after Anthony.

The ant swerved, too, and its mandibles caught in her robe. She screamed and yanked; the cloth tore, and she ran even faster.

Ahead, ants angled to cut her off. Others closed in from the sides.

Anthony shot up the spire, finding handholds with the ease of a mountaineer who has spent his life among sheer rocks. Eight feet up, he reached down. Mandibles clashed behind her, and Balkis leaped. The ant ran up the stone right behind her, but she caught Anthony's hand, he lifted as her feet scrambled, and the ant fell back, too heavy in truth for the acrobatics its smaller cousins managed without noticing. But more ants crowded around, more and more, pushing their front rank up by sheer mass of numbers.

"They will reach us yet!" Anthony unlimbered his sling.

"That will do little good against such a horde!" Balkis cried.

"We cannot sit and wait for them to come! You fight with your weapons, and I shall fight with mine!" Anthony set a stone in the cup and whirled it around his head.

It would buy them time, if nothing else—and Balkis needed time indeed, to craft a spell.

> "Loud and troublesome insects of the hour,
> Never shall we be within your power!
> Go back into the dirt from which you've come . . ."

Again she stalled. She floundered after a rhyme for 'come,' but while she floundered, Anthony called out,

> "And sleep within your deep and earthen bower!"

The tide of insects ebbed astonishingly as the ones at the back began to sink into the ground. They scrabbled for a foothold, but the soil gave way beneath them faster than they could dig. The ones that had been standing on them touched the ground and immediately sank, too. In minutes there were no ants visible, only churning earth; then it, too, was still.

"Quickly, down!" Balkis started climbing toward the ground. "Before they can dig their way out!"

"No, wait!" Anthony reached down to catch her wrist, pulling up to stop her. He pointed ahead, and Balkis, looking, saw a buck burst from a screen of bushes. A dozen ants shot after it, moving so fast their legs were blurs.

"No, look away," Anthony said grimly.

"I have seen beeves slaughtered, and deer butchered." Nonetheless, Balkis looked away as the ants surrounded the deer. She heard their furious chittering and its single bleat of terror.

"There is naught to see now but a mass of ants," Anthony reported.

Balkis turned back in time to see the throng of ants break apart, each with a slab of meat in its mandibles, gliding away toward their anthill, much more slowly now but still as fast as a human could run, leaving only a picked and gleaming skeleton behind them.

Balkis stared in horror and shivered with the chill that wrapped her back and shoulders.

"We dare not move at all in this valley!" Anthony said with a shudder. "How came we so far alive?"

"It was early morning," Balkis said. "Perhaps the ants do not come out until the sun does."

"Oh, for a cloud!" Anthony groaned.

The earth began to churn again, all about the spire, and antennae began to poke through.

Instead of increasing, what overcast there was lifted—and they saw a grim granite castle lowering at them atop another hill.

"This is why they have built their strongholds!" Anthony cried. "Not against one another but against the ants!"

"If we can reach that fortress, we shall be safe!"

Anthony swept his hand in a gesture including all the ants who were rising about them again. "How are we to wade through these?"

Inspiration struck, and Balkis cried, "The nuggets! It is not us alone whom they chase! Oh aye, they want meat, but they lust after gold far more! Throw the nuggets, Anthony! Throw them as far and as hard as you can!"

Anthony groaned. "You know not what you ask! Never have I seen such nuggets as these, only the golden pebbles in the stream! I have dreamed of having fortune enough so that my father and brothers need never toil again, and so we might journey as the traders do to visit fabulous lands such as Maracanda!"

"You shall gain your wish without gold!" Balkis cried. "Labor shall not harm your kin, and we are already on the road to Maracanda, with many fabulous sights on the way, I doubt not! Throw the gold, Anthony, please!"

With a groan wrenched up from the core of his soul, Anthony threw a lump of gold as high and as far as he could. The ants must have scented it somehow, for they turned and charged after it as it passed overhead. It fell to earth, and the ants piled into a churning, heaving heap, fighting over the ounce of metal.

"Quickly!" Balkis cried. "We must flee!" She scrambled down and ran toward the castle. Anthony dropped, leaped, dropped again, landed three yards behind her, and caught up quickly.

Behind them they could hear the frenzy of chittering slacken, settle, then boil up again, louder than before and still growing. Balkis risked a quick look over her shoulder and saw half the ants racing after them; the other half lay in bits and pieces, with a lone specimen limping toward his burrow to put the nugget back among the tailings.

"Throw another nugget, Anthony!" she cried. "Nothing else will slow them enough to save us!"

Anthony looked, saw the vanguard halfway to them already, and could have sworn the ant in the lead was the one who had first chased him. Ridiculous, of course, when they all looked alike. But they were coming fast, so with great reluctance, he took another nugget from his pouch, whirled it in his sling, and sent it spinning over the heads of their pursuers.

The result was electric—each ant turned as the lump of metal passed overhead, the ones in front scrambling over the ones behind, who were slower to scent the gold. Within moments they were all racing away from Balkis and Anthony. The winner pounced as the nugget fell to earth, and all the others pounced on him. Again they piled up, churning and tearing at one another, their chittering filling the air—but the heap was only half as high as the one before.

"Run!" Balkis cried, and Anthony shook himself out of his horrified trance to race beside her for the castle.

So it was that they ran and then stopped to throw another nugget whenever they heard the high, mindless chittering of pursuit. At last they were climbing the hill and voices were calling from the wall, calling and being answered, and the gates swung open as they neared. Anthony turned to throw one last nugget, then they dashed into the castle.

"Thank you, oh, thank you!" Balkis fought to keep the sob from her voice.

"Thank you from the bottoms of our hearts," Anthony said, holding out his hand.

The porter grinned and clasped it. "There would have been little left of you if we had not. Welcome to Castle Formigard, young travelers." His voice was oddly hushed. "I pray you, speak softly, for most of our folk have only now fallen asleep, and we would be loath to wake them. Time enough to tell them of your arrival when they waken this evening."

He was bronze-skinned, clean-shaven, and hook-nosed, wearing leather armor over desert robes and a turban with a leather neck-guard. Under his arm he cradled a crossbow, cocked and loaded. A quick look around showed Balkis that all the other guards were dressed and armed in the same fashion, though their robes were black, gray, or brown, and his was blue—presumably a symbol of rank.

His words surprised her—not only to find that the people were asleep in the coolness of the early morning, but also because he spoke in the language of Maracanda—a very deep dialect, one that took a great deal of effort to puzzle out, but the language of Prester John nonetheless.

Anthony, however, shifted into the same tongue with no effort at all, though his accent was just as barbarous. "You speak the language of the caravans!"

The porter grinned. "It is the language of Maracanda, young man, and all travelers and merchants learn it sooner or later, for every one of these lands that pay tribute to Prester John and accept his protection speak his language."

"You are of his empire, then?" Balkis asked.

"Our kings have boasted of their place at his table for two hundred years and more," the guard said. "His language may not be ours, but we all know it well enough to speak to strangers—as indeed we must in this valley, for each castle holds folk from a different kingdom, each sent here to help harvest the gold of the ants for Prester John. We must league with one another to survive, and admit one another to our castles without regard to nationality, or we would all be ants' meat."

"Praise Heaven for that!" Anthony said fervently.

The guard nodded, his smile touched with amusement. "Otherwise we might not have been so quick to admit you, eh? But the ants are the enemy here, and other rivalries seem to grow dim in this valley." He turned to call softly to a gray-robe. "Ahmed! Take these strangers to the kitchens, for they must hunger!"

Turning back to Balkis and Anthony, he touched forehead, lips, and breast with his fingers as he bowed. "Peace be with you, my friends."

"Peace be with you, and thank you for your hospitality." Anthony imitated the gesture, rather clumsily, but well enough so Balkis could tell it wasn't new to him.

She imitated it herself with considerably more grace, echoing, "Peace be to you," then turned away to follow the guide.

"He is a Muslim!" Anthony whispered to her.

"I would guess they all are," Balkis agreed.

"But Prester John is a Christian king!"

"All may worship as they please in his empire," Balkis told him. "There are Buddhists among his folk, too, and even folk whose religion is so primitive that they see spirits in every rock and tree. He has sent missionaries among them, of course, but he will not constrain any to believe as he does."

"A most prudent emperor," Anthony mused. "No doubt folk would fight against his rule if they thought he sought to banish their gods."

Balkis looked up at him with new appreciation. Anthony was showing considerably more intelligence than he had led her to believe, even more than she had seen in him herself.

The guide led them through a vast dining hall into a mammoth kitchen, where cooks and scullery workers were just finishing cleaning up after the morning meal and sitting down to dine themselves. They were quite willing to welcome two more to their table.

Anthony stared at his plate—meat, noodles, and vegetables all mixed together with a fragrant sauce. "What a hearty breakfast!"

The kitchen workers laughed—softly, of course. "This is our supper, young man," said a wrinkled woman across from him. "When your day begins, ours ends."

"How odd!" But Balkis picked up her chopsticks without much surprise.

Anthony asked, "Is the daytime sun as hot here as it is in the desert?"

That brought another laugh, and the old woman said, "No,

young man, it is the ants! They are our reason for being here, but also our reason for working by night, for that is when they stay belowground, deep in their burrows."

"I see," Anthony said thoughtfully. "So during the hours of darkness, they hide in the earth?"

"Not hide," said a plump man beside him. "That is when they work. From sunset until the third hour of the day, they dig for the purest gold and bring it up to pile in the dirt of their anthills—but when the sun is high enough to begin to heat the land, they come up to hunt and feed."

"Therefore you must stay in your fortress by day," Anthony said, understanding, "and if sunrise finds you too far from your own castle, you seek refuge in whichever is nearest."

The people nodded, and the plump man said, "That is why there can be no enmity between castles, no matter how long the blood-feuds between kings have been living in our homelands."

"And by night," Balkis asked, "you can leave your fortified places?"

The others nodded, and the old woman said, "That is when we work, and all take their turns outside the walls as well as in the kitchens or at repairs."

"None dare appear so long as the ants are aboveground," said another, "because of their strength and ferocity."

"So if we were to go to the battlements, we would see ants ranging the valley, but none besieging the castle?" Anthony asked.

"Oh, some," the old woman said. "There are always a few, like hopeful pups sitting by their master's table, hoping for a bone or a bit of meat to drop—but most know it is fruitless. Mind you, they tried to climb our walls when first our ancestors built these castles, but they fell off, and gave up quickly enough."

Balkis and Anthony went up to look. Sure enough, there were a few ants hovering hopefully by the gates—but only a few. Balkis looked up at Anthony's frown and asked, "What troubles you?"

"That one." Anthony pointed to the ant closest to the gate; it seemed to be exploring the wood with its antennae. "I know it is silly, but I cannot help feeling that it is the one who found me taking its gold, the one who was first to chase us."

Balkis brought up her sleeve to hide her smile.

"Yes, I know it is foolish." Anthony gave her a sheepish grin. "After all, we cannot tell one from another, and why should that one hold interest in me when none others do?"

"I suspect that the imagination you say you lack is too active." Balkis took his arm, letting her smile show. "But we must rest while we can, for I've no doubt we shall have to be on our way at sunset. Come, let us find our guest chambers and sleep."

The dunes rolled below them, Stegoman's shadow slipping over their contours like an iron over wrinkled cloth. Then Matt saw another shadow against the plane of the road.

"Traveler," he called to Stegoman. "Let's stop and talk."

But Stegoman peered down with eyes far sharper than Matt's and said, "I mislike the look of him. I pray thee, wizard, pass this one by."

Matt's interest sharpened. "Something odd about him? Let's have a closer look."

"You might frighten him into silence," Stegoman cautioned.

"That's what you want, isn't it?"

Stegoman thought that over for a moment, then said, "It is," and banked to sail back at a lower altitude. He passed the lone figure much closer, then banked into another U-turn and sailed over scarcely fifty feet above its head. Matt saw a solitary stranger in a cowled robe, staff in hand, pausing to look up—and showing not the slightest sign of fear. That bothered him, but he thought, *Hey, maybe the man is long on bravery and short on sense.* "Doesn't look all that unusual, Stegoman," he said. "What do you think is the matter?"

"It takes one to know one," the dragon said, "and this fellow seems distinctly cold-blooded."

"Oh, how can you tell that from this altitude?" Matt scoffed. "No point in hiding, since he doesn't seem scared of us. Just land ten yards away from him, would you?"

"I do this under protest," Stegoman grumbled, and spiraled down to land. It was no accident that he ended up with a short run directly at the traveler, but the man didn't even flinch, and the dragon did indeed come to a halt thirty feet from him. Matt dismounted and went up to the stranger, reflecting that his cowl was very deep—even on the ground Matt couldn't see his face. "Excuse me, have you seen—"

The stranger folded back his hood, revealing a snake's head.

Matt stood frozen in shock a moment, but came out of it when the snake grinned, unfolding two dripping fangs. Then it struck.

CHAPTER 12

Matt leaped aside and the reptile rammed its nose into the ground behind him. Matt danced away, fighting the atavistic fear of snakes, and drew his sword, chanting,

> "How strange this bitter chill doth thee embrace!
> The hawk, for all his feathers, groweth cold,
> The snake slows, blood thick'ning pace by pace,
> Lacking warmth of flock in woolly fold."

He hoped Keats wouldn't mind.

Frost appeared on the rock nearby, and a blast of cold air hit Matt, very welcome in the desert's heat. The reptile slowed in mid-strike, leaving Matt plenty of time to sidestep and jab it with his sword. The snakeman was made of sterner stuff than he'd thought, though—the sword's tip skidded on scales. The snake head turned—Matt could have sworn he heard it creak—and its body tensed, drawing in on itself, preparing for another lunge.

Stegoman, however, had his own internal heat source and wasn't slowed one bit. He came roaring up, blasting a ten-foot tongue of flame before him. The heat thawed the snakeman, whose strike caught Matt by surprise, bowling him over—but his feet came up by reflex, knees bending under the enemy's weight. As he did, the stranger's robe flew open, showing only a scaly-skinned humanoid body, very skinny, with no genitals or nipples, only scales—and around its neck a chain with a medallion showing a cobra's head. Matt didn't have time for close study, though—he grabbed a scaly arm and kicked with both legs, catapulting the reptiloid over his head and ten feet beyond. Matt rolled, came to his feet, and ran. Behind him, he heard the sound of a giant blowtorch. A second later the scent of roasting meat wafted his way. Matt wrinkled his nose—it smelled acrid—and turned back, afraid he knew what he was going to see.

He was right; Stegoman was just finishing a very long swallow, and the ashes of burned cloth lay at his feet with something bright winking among them. Matt came back, his feet dragging, and looked down—it was the cobra-head medallion, sure enough, and he suspected the ashes were what was left of the cowled robe.

He stirred them with his foot, seeking emotional refuge in business. "Could be a coincidence."

"What, that a snakeman wore an amulet with the sign of a cobra's head?" Stegoman's mouth lolled open in a saurian grin. "Scarcely a coincidence."

Matt waved away the smell of barbecue. "It has to be a coincidence, because the name of that Central Asian goddess the sorcerer told us about means 'black snake.' It sounds too paranoid to think it's anything but an accident that we should happen to meet a snakeman wearing a cobra medallion while we're trying to find the princess she attempted to kidnap."

"Perhaps." Nictating membranes slid over Stegoman's eyes, giving them a hooded look. "Show me how this 'paranoid' that you speak of thinks, Matthew. What, if this creature is not on this road by chance?"

"If it's not a coincidence," Matt said, "then it means somebody tied in with this snake-goddess cult knows where we're going and sent this creature to stop us."

"An interesting notion." Stegoman gazed off toward the horizon. "Who would its commander have been?"

"Possibly even Kala Nag herself," Matt said, "but more likely one of her generals—I don't believe in pagan gods much."

"Perhaps unwise, in this world," Stegoman commented.

"Perhaps," Matt agreed. "Primitive people could mistake a supernatural creature for a god, after all. Seems more likely, though, that it was a human mastermind who thought of reviving Kala Nag and of sending this monster after us."

Stegoman frowned. "There is more in your thoughts—I can tell by your tone."

Matt sighed and spilled the rest. "Well, if there really is a Kala Nag, and she didn't know where we were before, she sure does now."

"A sobering thought," Stegoman agreed, then turned away his head to belch, which involved a five-foot tongue of flame.

Matt looked up. "So how was our late enemy?"

"Like chicken," Stegoman answered, "a rather large chicken."

Late in the afternoon, the castle woke up. Delightful aromas wafted from the kitchens, and the people filed into the huge dining hall, taking bowls from a stack and filing past cooks who served them a porridge with a strange but enticing smell, and mugs of a thick, dark, aromatic liquid. Balkis and Anthony joined the line and found the food delicious, though they had difficulty eating, for their neighbors showered them with questions and kept them so busy talking that they had to sneak in quick bites.

As the sun neared the horizon, the castle began to buzz with activity. Looking down from the battlements, Balkis and Anthony saw dozens of camels and elephants being led toward the gate from huge stables built against the walls. People assembled with mattocks over their shoulders; more people lined up with baskets.

"They may sleep by day, but by night they look to be every bit as industrious as the ants," Balkis commented.

"But what amazing livestock!" Anthony said. "Could not oxen do the work they need?"

"Camels are for caravans," Balkis said thoughtfully. "Could oxen travel the desert?"

"Not very far," Anthony admitted. "But neither can elephants—unless some carry water for the rest."

"We shall discover soon." Balkis pointed toward the west. "The sun sinks even now."

The guard who had admitted them came up smiling and bowed, touching brow, lips, and breast. "I am Jabar, and I have been released from my vigil to be your guide tonight, esteemed guests."

"Oh, how kind!" Balkis said. "But surely we need not trouble you—we have but to follow the river."

"You could find your way," Jabar agreed, "but you will go more quickly if I am there to steer you to quieter places. The valley is a-bustle with activity at night."

"Then we shall be glad of your company." Anthony bowed, imitating Jabar's salute. "Thank you, esteemed one."

Trumpets blew from the gate towers, and Balkis looked up in alarm. "Are we beset?"

"Not at all," Jabar assured her. "That is only the signal that the ants have gone back underground and it is safe to come out of our strongholds—for see! The sun has set!"

Looking toward the west, Balkis and Anthony saw that the last sliver of scarlet had slipped below the horizon, though the sky was still lit with an afterglow of rose and lavender. Other horns took up the call from other castles until the whole valley resounded with their music. As the sound faded into echoes, the gate swung wide and the people streamed out to begin their night's work. After them came drovers with their line of camels, and last of all came the elephants, their mahouts astride their huge necks.

"Why do you need such giant beasts of burden?" Anthony asked.

"Because they will carry gold," Jabar answered. Then he laughed at their stares. "No, there are not so very many bushels of gold nuggets that we need vast baskets—but the metal is very heavy, and the pack that would hold a moderate load of corn would break a donkey's back were it loaded with gold."

Balkis stared at the line of elephants swaying away into the darkness. "That is still a great deal of gold! Where do your people find it?"

"Each takes his turn at each task," Jabar explained. "Some collect the gold the ants bring up, while others drive the elephants and camels out of the castles to bear it far away to our kings' treasuries. It is with this gold that they pay their tribute to Prester John."

Balkis had a notion that the kings kept more than they sent to Maracanda, but this certainly was neither the time nor the place to say so.

"Would you like to see the work?" Jabar asked. "You shall pass by it on the road along the valley."

"Very much," Balkis and Anthony said together, then glanced at one another with small embarrassed smiles.

Jabar said nothing, but his eye gleamed. "Come! Let us walk awhile in the coolness!"

He led them down a flight of stairs and out the gate. The night was soft, the breeze a caress of velvet, the air filled with the fragrance of wildflowers. Balkis glanced at Anthony again and found he was watching her. She smiled, suddenly feeling shy, then looked away, blushing.

"The moon comes," Anthony breathed, "and how huge it is!"

Balkis looked up and saw the golden bowl rising over the valley rim. It was three-quarters full and seemed gigantic indeed for a desert moon, no doubt magnified by the humidity of the valley. She sighed with happiness and started to reach out for his hand, then caught herself and stopped. He was only a traveling companion, after all.

At the bottom of the slope, they saw the cones of anthills as high as they were tall, breaking the flat floor of the valley at odd intervals, not even in a straggling row or wandering arc, but completely at random. Dots of light clustered around them, more dots moved across the plain, but others were distant, almost like stars come to earth. Balkis realized they were torches.

As they neared the first of the anthills, they saw the need for the clustered lights. They burned atop poles stuck in the earth, and by their light men and women sifted the dirt of the anthill with shovels and sieves. As they shook the wire grids, the soil fell through—and left nuggets of gold behind. These the workers poured into a padded basket.

Balkis stared. "I did not doubt when I heard it, but I never truly believed it until now!"

"Aye," Anthony agreed, then asked Jabar, "why do the ants bring up gold?"

Jabar shrugged. "Because it is in their way, most likely. Why do ants bring up any earth? To remove it from their galleries."

"Then why would they so earnestly pursue any who take it?" Anthony asked.

"Because it is theirs," Jabar answered. "They would as likely chase flecks of mica or pebbles of quartz that were taken from their hills."

"Why, then, do they not wage war against your castles?"

Jabar started to answer, but a voice out of the darkness called, " 'Ware! Make way!" and he caught their arms to hurry them aside. Balkis saw a huge shadow swaying toward them, looming higher and higher with every step. It came into the pool of torchlight and she saw it was an elephant with huge panniers strapped to its sides. The mahout rode its neck and steered it with prods of his ankus. Balkis noticed that the mahouts didn't use the hook of the goad, just the point. The huge beast shuffled past and halted by the anthill. The workers stopped their digging and sifting and stepped aside. The mahout gave the elephant a command, and it curled its trunk around the gold-filled basket, lifted it up, and dumped it into a pannier. Then the mahout tapped the side of its head and spoke again, and the huge creature swayed away into the night. The workers took their basket and went on to the next hill.

"Is the elephant taking the gold back to the castle so soon, or will he wait till both his panniers are filled?" Balkis asked.

"He will not go back to the castle." Jabar's teeth flashed in a smile. "When both his panniers are filled, his mahout will direct him to join the caravan, and they shall leave the valley well before sunrise."

"So soon as that?" Balkis asked in surprise. "So much gold in one night?"

"The panniers will only be half full," Jabar said, "for the metal is heavy, and there will be only half a dozen animals in the caravan—but yes, the ants do bring up that much of a night." He turned to lead them away into the darkness, explaining, "The caravan will journey a day's march to an oasis, where others will join it every evening. When there are twenty, they will depart for their homes."

Anthony asked, "So the ants do not attack your castles because there is never any gold there?"

"Never," Jabar confirmed. "The last camel leaves the valley at sunrise, and by the time the ants come up for the day, the scent of gold is too distant for them to follow."

"How clever!" Balkis said.

They had climbed high enough up the road toward the valley's rim that they left the anthills behind. The roadside torches now illuminated people hoeing rows of plants.

"So you grow your own produce?" Balkis asked.

Before their guide could answer, a voice from the darkness called, "Clear track!" Jabar pulled them back from the roadway. A string of camels came by with four elephants behind them. Each was piled high with bales of goods securely tied.

Balkis stared as they passed. "These do not carry gold, nor do they travel northward."

"Indeed not," Jabar agreed. "That is a caravan returning to the valley. Those bales hold salt meat and live poultry, vegetables and flour, cloth, and other goods that we need."

"Your kings send them?" Balkis asked.

"Why not? The caravan must come back for more gold anyway—why not let it bring supplies?"

"Do you never have fresh food?"

"Every castle has a garden within its walls," Jabar replied.

"But what of the fields these people cultivate?"

Jabar led them back onto the road as the last elephant swayed by. "By night, we all take turns in the fields, plowing and sowing—but the ants do the reaping."

"What a waste of labor!" Anthony cried with a farmer's indignation.

"Not at all, young man," Jabar told him. "There is little enough game in this valley, after all—as soon as an animal wanders in, the ants bring it down. No, they must have food to eat, or they will not live to dig us more gold—and they are quite content with grain and vegetables. We harvest some for ourselves, of course—but not by day."

Anthony shuddered. "I should think not!"

A mile farther on, Jabar led them out onto the plateau again. Balkis looked back over a long canyon sprinkled with warm yellow lights. "It looks like a garden of enchantment," she said, "but it holds so much danger!"

"It did for our ancestors, surely," Jabar said, "but with our castles and our knowledge of the ants' ways, it is safe enough now. Indeed, we scarcely ever lose a worker, and any large city has far more deaths due to footpads and accidents."

Balkis turned back to him with an uncertain smile. "You seem to like it well enough."

Jabar nodded vigorously. "There is a camaraderie, a closeness and sharing, that I have found nowhere else. It may be born of the constant awareness of the danger that lurks outside our walls, but it is all the stronger for that." He fairly beamed at her, still nodding. "It is a good life, maiden, and if you tire of the jealousies and backbiting of the wide world, remember us."

"I shall," Balkis promised, and Anthony nodded agreement.

The stars told them it was midnight when Balkis and Anthony came to another valley. He frowned, gazing at its rocky depths and single wavering strip of greenery, almost black in the moonlight. "The river must plunge underground," he said, "then rise again here."

Balkis nodded. "I would guess it has done so for thousands of years, and has carved out these valleys by its passage."

"If that is so," Anthony said, "it must have once been a mighty river indeed, for these valleys are a mile and more in width."

"Perhaps it still is, when the rains are heavy in the mountains." Balkis pointed downward at a line of broken branches and brush in the limbs of the trees nearest them. "How else would such wrack have been spread so high?"

"A good thought," Anthony acknowledged. "We are not likely to hear thunder so early in spring, but if we do, let us climb back up here as quickly as possible."

"If we hear thunder," Balkis agreed. "Since we do not, I would rather travel near water while we can."

Anthony agreed, and they started down into the valley as the moon swung lower in the sky. They found no road, only a deer-track, so it took them two hours to reach the valley floor.

"Strange that so few travelers have come here," Anthony said, but looked over his shoulder at the skeletal branches of oak and ash with the stars behind them and shivered.

"The night brings fear of spirits," Balkis agreed, "but only to us human folk. The animals who made this track have no dread of such things."

In the distance an owl hooted. A few minutes later they heard the death-scream of some small animal.

Anthony shuddered. "Perhaps we might do best to build a campfire against the gloom and walk this valley by day."

"Do you fear things you cannot see?" Balkis jibed.

"Quite right," Anthony affirmed. "I fear them far more than the things I can see."

His honesty disarmed Balkis, and she went onward feeling almost ashamed.

They followed the riverbank under bare branches. Balkis shivered in the chill of the desert night and drew her cloak more firmly around her. She had to admit that the leafless trees and silent flow of dark water were unnerving, and reminded herself that they would not be so by day. In the distance something howled, and something else screamed. She shivered—only from the chill, she told herself.

Then she began to hear a different sound.

It was soft at first, soft and distant, but she knew it at once—the drums of war. They rattled in time to men's steps, and they were coming closer, from in front of her, and coming quickly.

Anthony looked about desperately. "Where can we hide?"

A trumpet blared in the distance. Across the valley another answered it, but with a different rhythm.

"Why do they march at night?" Anthony cried.

"If they meant to catch their enemy unaware, they have failed," Balkis said.

The sounds ceased to approach; they stayed more or less distant, but shouting broke out, and with it the clash of steel, then the screams of the dying.

"Let us go out of this valley, and quickly!" Balkis turned toward the slope half a mile away. "I dislike the feel of this place."

"Flowing water seems less important now," Anthony agreed, and turned with her.

Across the meadow they fled by starlight, their eyes on the ground, watching for holes and rocks. The night wind sped no faster than they, nor the owl who sailed overhead, fleeing the shouting and the clamor.

"Only a hundred yards more," Anthony panted, and sure enough the ground was already rising toward the hillside before them. Then the ground dipped, and a soldier in leather armor rose up before them, circular shield barring their way, battle-axe already swinging down at them.

CHAPTER 13

Anthony shouted and threw himself against Balkis, knocking her out of the axe's path, but it struck at the base of Anthony's neck and cleaved straight through to his hip. Balkis screamed and threw herself at him, already catching up her gown to stanch the flow of blood before seeing it. Then she saw a spear-point emerge from her chest and stab on into Anthony, who was still intact, and through him and into the axe-wielder, who threw up his hands, mouth widening in a scream that sounded only faintly, echoing as though from a distance.

"Down!" Anthony cried as they both struck the meadow grass—and saw the metal sandals step before them, felt a chill that froze them clear through, and knew that the other foot had trod down through them, then risen. Their owner stepped on past the companions, showing greaved shins, then a kilt of leather straps stiffened with plates of brass, then a brazen back-plate beneath jointed epaulets and a brass helmet with a horsehair crest above all.

"It is a soldier of ancient Macedon," Anthony exclaimed in wonder.

"It is a ghost!" Balkis cried.

Sure enough, the soldier was smoky gray, and they could see stars through him, no matter how dimly, as he wrenched his spear out of his fallen enemy, who faded into nothingness even as they watched. The victor tucked his spear-butt under his arm and marched on toward the center of the valley, but his boots made no sound, left no print in the grass. The tread of marching men was distant, echoing down the canyons of time with the shouts and clashing and trumpets and drums of a battle long past.

"This is a haunted valley, and the ghosts can have it!" Anthony declared. "Come!"

His arm helped Balkis to her feet, and together they fled up the hillside. Twice more warriors rose to block their paths, but they ran on, shivering at the chill as the ghostly battle-axes slid through them but not pausing for a second, their fear of the ghosts only lending wings to their feet.

Finally they struggled up the last few feet of slope and collapsed on the level ground above, chilled to the bone, to the marrow, by the piercing of ghostly weapons. They gasped for breath and looked back the way they had come to make sure none of the phantoms had followed them. There were none near, but far away, in the center of the valley, ghost-lights swirled as a ragtag line of barbarians gave way foot by foot to the phalanx of Macedon. They hold their valley dearly, though—undisciplined or not, they were each of them valiant warriors, and two Macedonians died for each of them. But the phalanx clearly prevailed.

The breeze blew them the sound of battle again, and Balkis shivered. "What ghosts are these who fight a battle long past, again and again every night?"

"My ancestors," Anthony said, voice grim and face hard.

Balkis glanced at him and felt sympathy flow. To lessen the pain, she asked, "Which side?"

"Both." Anthony seemed shaken as he gazed down at the ghost-battle below. "I had thought the tale to be only someone's dream spoken aloud, nothing but some spinning of an after-dinner rhyme that held better than most—but I see now that it is more."

The tale clearly disturbed him as much as the ghosts he had just endured. "Tell me," she urged.

Anthony took a breath. "Long ago, hundreds of years, Alexander the Emperor sent a phalanx into the desert to take submission of each tribe who held a valley or oasis here. All surrendered without fight except the men of one valley—this, it would seem—and the phalanx marched into their land to conquer them. The defenders, though, were truly desert raiders to whom the valley was only one home of many; they had been hardened by the wasteland and by years and years of raiding caravans. They met the phalanx head-on, then sent outriders to the flanks, and though they lost, there were only a quarter of the Macedonians left alive."

"What of the raiders?" Balkis asked, her voice hushed.

"They retreated into the mountains, and the Macedonians followed. There they jockeyed for position, neither willing to strike first unless they held the higher ground—and finally settled in place, watching one another across a ravine and occasionally raiding one another . . ."

"And became neighbors?" Balkis asked, her eyes huge.

"Their grandchildren did," Anthony said. "The Macedonians would not budge, for they had their orders from Alexander and would not go back to him until the raiders submitted or every last soldier was dead. They married mountain women from their side of the chasm, while the raiders' wives came up to join them. Their children, though, married the children of the mountaineers on their side of the chasm."

"Who were kin to the soldiers' wives!" Balkis exclaimed.

"They were indeed, so the grandchildren saw no reason to fight their cousins. They made peace, and a few of the great-grandchildren married one another—so by the time my father was born, we were so much a mixture of raider, soldier, and mountaineer that we know not to whom we should swear allegiance."

"And therefore govern yourselves, and resist all who would conquer you?" Balkis asked with a smile.

"We do, though few care to try." Anthony still gazed at the echoing battle below. "My folk are a stubborn and stiff-necked breed, and yield to death rather than to kings—as the raiders did when they fought this battle."

"Whereas the Macedonians we see here are bound by loyalty to Alexander's commands," Balkis said softly, suddenly understanding, "and will therefore not willingly yield a single inch."

"Even so," Anthony agreed. "Therefore they stand here, obedient to the emperor's will, and every night their ghosts fight the battle again."

"You do not mean that each side is convinced that if they refight it often enough, they will finally win!"

"So it seems." Anthony's mouth pulled into a hard smile, gaze still on the ancient and current battle. "So the legend says. I had never thought it anything but an old wives' tale, a fable to make people realize they had to let go of the past and think of the future, but . . ."

His voice trailed off. Balkis watched him a moment, then finished the sentence for him. "It is no fable, but truth."

"It would seem so," Anthony said. "Alas! My poor ancestors! If their descendants marrying and becoming one people cannot end their fighting, what can?"

"Nothing," Balkis whispered, but she nonetheless wracked her brains as the two of them sat, spellbound and shivering, watching the ghosts slash and stab at one another until all had fallen. Even then she could think of no way to weave a spell to stop this ghostly carnage, and decided that this was a task for a priest, not a wizard.

It seemed an age before the battle sounds died away. Then Anthony spoke, face somber. "It is done. Let us leave this place."

But Balkis clasped his hand, looking back at the valley floor. "What noise is that?"

Anthony listened. It was soft at first, only a crunching here and there, but it grew in number and volume—ripping sounds, slurping and gulping, slobbering and grinding. He shuddered. "It is the carrion-eaters, come to clear away the ghost-flesh."

"But I see nothing!"

"They, too, are ghosts," Anthony said grimly, "and I never yet knew a vulture or jackal that did not hide from sight when it could."

Balkis buried her face in Anthony's tunic. "I dare not see their work being done!"

"Nor I." Anthony hid his face in her hair, and they sat shielding one another against the night, but the sounds of the gruesome banquet made them shiver until the horrid feast ended.

Finally the sky lightened with false dawn; finally the obscene noises dwindled. Still they sat huddled together, and neither could have said when sitting became lying, when shuddering stilled and warmth and solace grew, for at last they slept in one another's arms.

Balkis woke when the rays of the setting sun bathed her face. She sat up, blinking in confusion as she looked about, then remembered how she had come to this place of trees and grass in the middle of a desert, and shivered. She shook Anthony gently by the shoulder. "Wake up, sleepyhead! Wake up and tell me that last night's memories are only a nightmare."

"Hmmm? Wha . . . ? Nightmare?" Anthony sat up, blinking, and raised a hand to cover a yawn. "What nightmare is this? That I travel with you? I cry your pardon for the unpleasantness, but it is—"

"No, dunderhead!" Balkis gave him a poke in the ribs. "Fresh wakened, and you jest with your first yawn!" But she smiled. "The phantom army, and the ghastly banquet! Tell me that those were only a dream!"

"The battle!" Anthony came wide-awake. "No, I fear my ancestors were real."

"But their ghosts?"

Anthony shrugged. "Are any ghosts real? Still, we did see them—it was no dream."

"No, I fear not." Balkis gazed off toward the valley.

"Well, there is one way to tell," Anthony said. "We have only to wait and listen. If we hear shouting and the clash of steel, we will know."

Balkis glanced at the desert beyond and thought of the empty miles stretching northward. "Should we take the time?"

"An extra hour out of several months?" Anthony asked. "I think we can spare it." He unstoppered the waterskin and took a drink, then frowned and shook it. "We should take time to climb down to the stream in any event—we do not wish to march dry."

Balkis shuddered at the thought.

"Come, we need not stay longer than the first calling of trumpets," Anthony said.

"True," Balkis admitted, and together they climbed down to fill their waterskins, but climbed well back up the hillside while there was still some sunset left—at least high on the slope. There they turned to look down into the valley, already deep in gloaming—and froze, staring.

"What is that which moves so quickly?" Balkis asked.

"It is the size of a fox," Anthony offered.

"No fox I've ever seen had a jet-black coat!"

"No, nor was ever so shiny." Anthony stiffened. "Tell me I should not be so surprised—we are only one valley away, and the ants must forage here now and again."

"Surely they must," Balkis agreed, but neither of them believed it.

They could not deny, though, that the creature they saw scuttling abut the valley floor was definitely a giant ant. As they watched, it cast about, probing the air with its antennae, north to east, east to south, south to west—and stopped, facing them. It lifted its head . . .

"Be ready to run." Anthony's hand tightened on hers.

The ant shot forward—but a form rose from the ground before it, a form in leather armor, battle-axe swinging. The ant hesitated, then attacked the shape with fury—and went right on through. It halted in confusion, turning back—and saw a figure in brazen armor advancing on it with a spear. Instantly the ant charged, tearing through the apparition, then pausing in consternation, but only for a moment before another specter came running in its direction while a fourth came hurtling from the other direction. The ant whirled, tearing at the spectral warriors, about and about in a frantic dance of frustration, never able to come to grips with its foes.

Anthony and Balkis watched in amazement as the ant ran to and fro upon the ancient battlefield and the twilight faded. When the stars came out and full darkness descended in the valley, the ant froze for a moment, then dove at the ground beneath it, tearing and hurling, digging itself a deep, deep burrow, as it always did at night.

"It might bring up gold!" Anthony started down the hill.

"And it might not!" Balkis caught his arm. "You might stay there all night waiting, until your ancestors drove you mad! Come, say a prayer of thanks to them for distracting the little monster, and let us flee while we can!"

"Oh, very well!" Anthony grumbled. "But you will never be rich, Balkis, if this is how you treat your opportunities."

"You will quickly be dead, if this is how you treat yours," Balkis retorted, and tugged at his arm. "Let us be gone from this place!"

"Let us indeed." Anthony tore his gaze away from the new anthill and turned to follow her up the slope. At the top, he looked back and stood gazing at the glowing battle in the bottom of the valley.

Balkis observed the somber set of his face and said gently, "It was no mere nightmare after all."

"No, it was not." Anthony turned his face to the desert, and the future. "Let us go, sweet Balkis. It is not good to become mired in the past."

By degrees the arid land became more green; thorn and scrub gave way to grass and shrub. They began to find trees, first wide apart and stunted, but closer and closer together as they went farther north, until they found themselves roaming through a savannah with streams only a little more than a day's travel apart. A week after they had left the valley of ghosts, the nights were no longer so chill nor the days so unbearably hot, and they dared to begin traveling by day. So they were walking beneath a mid-morning sun when they met the urgent traveler.

They could tell he was in a hurry because he ran a hundred yards, then walked a hundred, and as he came toward them, alternately running and walking, Anthony took out his sling and fitted a stone to its cup. "What chases him, to make him run so?"

"Whatever it is, he must rest and take nourishment, or it will catch him." Balkis held up a hand as the man approached. "Stay, stranger, and break bread with us."

"You have bread?" The man skidded to a halt, and Balkis

saw that he wore only a tunic, cloak, and sandals, with no pack and not even a wallet tied at his waist.

"You have been long without food," Anthony guessed, and took off his pack to dig out biscuit and dried meat. "Is the land so empty of game as that?"

"I dare not tarry to hunt, let alone take time to roast my catch! Thank you, stranger, and bless you!" The traveler all but snatched the food from Anthony's fingers and began to tear at it with his teeth.

"What pursues you with such greed that you dare not stop to eat?" Balkis asked.

"Women, maiden." The traveler shuddered at the memory. "Warrior women."

Balkis and Anthony exchanged a startled glance, then turned back to the traveler. "Tell us of them," Balkis urged, "for we mean to go farther north. Dare we journey through their country?"

"*You* may," the traveler said, but jerked his head at Anthony. "You, however, dare only go there if you can run very quickly—or have far greater willpower than any man I've ever met!"

"Why should I need willpower to travel?" Anthony asked, bewildered.

"Because you will so lose yourself in pleasure that you will forget to count," the stranger said. "You will overstay your nine days, as I have, and will have to flee for your life."

Balkis felt a frisson of alarm, a thrill of danger, but Anthony was intrigued. "What nine days? And what pleasure could so ensnare a man that he forgets to guard his life?"

"Women," the man said again, simply, "warrior women," then added, "Without their armor, at play."

In Balkis, frisson turned to apprehension, but Anthony looked even more interested. "I would have thought that warriors' play was athletic contests."

"You could call it that," the traveler said with a sardonic smile, then took another mouthful and explained through his chewing, "You are about to enter the country of the Grand Feminie, young people. It extends for forty-two days' journey, and if you must go north, you must go through it, or take twice as long skirting it through the desert that lies to either side. It is a nation of warriors, female warriors, and no males are allowed to dwell within its boundaries, nor have been for hundreds of years."

"Hundreds of years?" Balkis frowned, puzzled. "Then where do new warriors come from?"

"From the brief stays that men are allowed." Again, the stranger managed a sardonic smile between mouthfuls. "No male may stay with them more than nine days, during which time he may carouse and amuse himself as much as he wishes and with as many different women as he can. Thus do they conceive."

Balkis's feeling of foreboding deepened. "What if he should overstay his time?"

"In such a case, the man will die—and therefore will I leave you." The stranger stood, wiping his mouth with the back of his hand. "Thank you for your food, good young people—but now I must flee." With no more ado, he took to his heels and ran.

Balkis turned to Anthony. "Let us go around this country, I pray you! No matter how many months it takes, it will be far safer!"

Anthony frowned. "I have never seen you fear anything before."

"True enough," Balkis admitted, "but I fear . . . I fear . . ."

"Not their women!"

"Not their fighting, no. Oh Anthony, please . . ."

High-pitched, ululating cries filled the air, and a dozen female warriors burst into sight around a curve in the road. They were armed like the Macedonian ghosts, with crested helmets, brazen breastplates, brass-braced kilts, greaves, and armored sandals. They caught sight of the fleeing traveler and doubled their pace.

"Aside, quickly!" Balkis pulled Anthony off the road.

It did no good—as the women warriors came even with them, their leader barked a command, and four of them stopped, looking darkly disappointed, and challenged the companions. Their accent was thick, but Balkis could understand it—the language of Maracanda had become the international tongue of these central lands. "I am Ramba, dozen-leader of Queen Harikot," the soldier said. "Why do you walk this road?"

A flippant answer came to Balkis's lips, but before she could defy the soldier, Anthony said, in tones of respect, "We travel to Maracanda, dozen-leader. May we pass through your country?"

"Aye, if you can come and go in nine days."

"But your land is forty-two days across!" Balkis protested.

There was a cry of despair down the road. Balkis and Anthony spun and saw the soldiers wrestling the stranger to the ground. Balkis whirled back to the dozen-leader. "Spare him, I pray you! He is not an evil man!"

"You must speak to the gross-leader about that," the dozen-leader said, her face granite.

As the warriors came back to them with the stranger struggling in their midst, Balkis cried to him, "I had not thought that giving you food would have slowed you to your death! Your pardon, I pray thee!"

"Given, bless you," the man groaned. "I had not known they were so close. Believe me, the ten minutes I spent with you would have made no difference."

Half the young women stared at him, then glanced uncertainly at one another.

"You gave this man aid?" asked a tall, older woman with cold gray eyes and a stern expression.

"I did, and I would do so again!" Balkis declared. "He is not evil, only weak to temptation! Spare him, I pray you!"

"He is lustful and licentious," the woman said grimly, "as greedy for our bodies as a miser for gold. Had he not lost his head in our embraces, he would have kept count of the days and departed in time to be safe. Indeed, if he had not indulged himself so freely with us, I have no doubt he would have had strength enough to run faster and make his escape."

"No man but a trained athlete at his peak could outrun your young cheetahs," the man groaned.

"Flattery may have served well you in the boudoir, but it will not aid you now! What of your wife, eh? What has she done these ten days while you dallied with us?"

"I am a bachelor," the stranger moaned, "and a poor man."

Balkis found herself wondering what sorts of men would avail themselves of the warrior women's invitation, and began to realize why they mistrusted males. "Many of your visitors may be cads and roués," she said, "but not this one."

"It is the law," the officer grated. "He thought us worth his life—and the bill has come due. Women! Take him to Queen Harikot and let her judge!"

The man gave a moan of despair as the women dragged him away.

"Take the woman to a guest house," the officer directed, and two women stepped up to either side of Balkis. "Go where they tell you," the officer said, "or they shall have to bind and carry you."

Balkis glared at her. "Poor treatment of a guest!"

"Few guests seek to argue the case of a reprobate," the officer returned, and told the remaining two soldiers, "Escort the young man to the pleasure dome!"

Balkis gave an involuntary cry and started toward Anthony, but hard hands clasped her arms, holding her back. He gave her an uncertain smile and raised his arms to guard.

"You have nothing to fear," the officer told him, "as long as you keep track of the days, and leave in time to be gone from this land before your nine days are up."

"But I would need forty-two days to cross your land! I would have to come back here!"

"Do you truly object?" the officer asked with a cynical smile.

"I do indeed! I have come to travel north, not to dally and lose days!"

"You shall abide by the law of the land," the officer said inexorably, "and even if you did naught but travel, you would still have to leave the Grand Feminie in nine days." She turned to Balkis. "Come, little sister. You, at least, shall be treated with honor."

"How can I, when I fear for my Anthony?"

Anthony's head whipped about, eyes staring at her.

"Is he yours, then?" The officer's gaze sharpened. "If he is true, you have nothing to fear—soldiers respect loyalty."

"I . . . I cannot truly claim him." Balkis' gaze faltered and dropped.

"Fear not, sweet one," Anthony told her, though his voice shook. "I understand loyalty, too."

"Think of St. Thomas, dear companion," Balkis said. "We shall see him together!"

"We shall." Anthony's tone was a promise; then he turned to follow his captors.

Still, as Balkis followed her escort, she wondered when Anthony had become "my Anthony" in her heart.

The guest house was clean and pleasant, fragrant with flowers and with curtained windows—but it was Spartan in its decoration. There were several chairs, two with arms, but none padded, a low table between them, and a low chest for linens and clothing. Against the wall stood a narrow bed which Balkis was sure was almost as hard as the chairs.

As they sat, a young girl came in with a tray containing a tea set. Balkis breathed in the aroma and began to think her spirits might revive—but she was desperately afraid for Anthony. She knew his goodness, but how could any man withstand temptation such as he was bound to confront?

The two soldiers with her sat down, taking off their helmets and shaking out long, lustrous hair with sighs of relief. Balkis was amazed—the one had a mane of rich chestnut, the other of red-gold, both long enough to cover their breastplates.

"It cushions the helmet," one said, "when we wind it about our heads."

Balkis realized she had been staring, and looked down at the tea set, but her heart shrank within her. Without the noseguards to hide their features, and framed by the glory of their hair, their faces were quite beautiful, and judging from the proportions of their cuirasses, she guessed they both had spectacular figures. How could Anthony hold out, indeed!

"Will you pour?" the redhead asked. "For the few days of your sojourn, this is your house."

Not that she had the option of choosing her guests, Balkis reflected sardonically. "I thank you, soldier, but it is more truly yours. Pour, if you will."

"Call me Alantha." The soldier bent forward and poured tea into three small cups without handles. "I trust you like the tea of China."

"I'm sure that I shall." Balkis had tasted Chinese tea before and preferred Indian, but she did not feel it would be diplomatic to say so. "I am called Balkis."

"And I am Illior," the brunette said. She accepted her cup and sipped. "Why do you travel toward the north?"

"Because I have been kidnapped from my home there and wish to return."

"Indeed!" Alantha's gaze fairly snapped, her tone hard. "Who stole you away?"

"A sorcerer," Balkis said.

The two soldiers stared, then frowned. "A man, of course," said Illior.

"He was, yes—but I think he may have been a woman's pawn."

"Why not?" Alantha gave her a hard smile. "They are so easy to manipulate, are they not? Or so we hear."

"I have not tried it myself." But Balkis thought of the way she had foisted herself onto the family of Queen Alisande and felt a trace of guilt.

"Why did he mark you for stealing?" Alantha asked.

Balkis shrugged. "I can only guess."

"Then do."

Balkis sighed. "Perhaps he, or the woman who sent him, feared that I might steal my cousin's inheritance."

"Your cousin is the woman?"

"No, but there are several who plan to marry him."

"Vanity!" Alantha snorted, and Illior said, "Would they not be better advised to make their own way to wealth?"

"That is a difficult undertaking, in our land," Balkis said.

"In any!"

"True enough." Balkis frowned at Alantha. "Is it so difficult, then, for a soldier to rise in rank?"

"There are many soldiers," Illior said simply, "and few officers."

Balkis nodded with sympathy. "Many soldiers, and all of

you brave and valiant. I have heard rumors of you in my homeland—though I confess I did not believe them."

"They are true enough, I suspect," Illior said, amused. "What do they say of us?"

"That you are furious in war—so courageous and so disciplined that none have ever beaten you."

Alantha's smile was complacent. "That is true indeed."

"None at all?" Balkis pressed. "Is not Prester John emperor over all these lands of Central Asia?"

"That he is," Alantha said, "but even his armies could not defeat our champions in the trial of arms to which he invited them. Nonetheless, all three of the queens of the Grand Feminie have allied with him and boast of that alliance, for they found him to be a paragon of morality and integrity, of justice and fair treatment to all. It is even rumored that he has recently found his niece who was lost, and has set her equal to his own son."

Balkis bit her lip, then said quickly, "Call it alliance though they may, the queens are still his tributaries, when all is said."

"They are, and the tribute they send him is a score of warrior women to swell his bodyguard."

So that was where the female bodyguards came from! Balkis knew from experience that they took orders from none but their own captain, scarcely spoke with any of the other soldiers, but were quick enough to talk with merchants and diplomats. She saw instantly that they might be helping to guard Prester John, but were also having an education in commerce, law, and statecraft. No wonder the three queens were willing to send a different score of women every year!

"Would that tribute not put your queens on a par with all of Prester John's other subordinate kings?" Balkis asked.

Illior nodded. "It does indeed, making them part of the most powerful empire in the Orient—and they have no fear of being enslaved, for we their soldiers are warriors by training and by inclination, who keep our skills honed by continually holding mock battles."

"And looking for excuses for going to war?" Balkis asked with sarcasm.

Alantha grinned. "I would not say we seek it—but perhaps

we bring it faster than it might otherwise come, by our pride and our loathing of compromise. When we must go to battle, we go eagerly, seeking the glory and honor that entitles us to become mothers, and we fight most bravely indeed."

Balkis could believe it, if that was what they had to do to win the privilege of having babies. Still, she was interested to learn that the mothering instinct was as strong in these women as in any others.

So they talked through that long afternoon, Balkis constantly on the watch for a chance to escape and go to Anthony's rescue—but her host-guards were too vigilant. Alantha happened to be sitting between her and the door, and Illior was quick to summon the servant girl to fetch food and drink from the other room at the slightest sign of Balkis' desire. Balkis began to feel as though she were bound with velvet ropes—comfortable, even pleasant against the skin, but binding her tightly nonetheless. She masked her growing desperation, and as the windows reddened with sunset, braced herself to work a spell into the conversation, hoping Alantha and Illior wouldn't realize what she was doing until it was too late to stop her with a blow.

Then Anthony lurched into the room, looking dazed. A soldier followed him, giving his shoulder another shove that explained his lurching. She wore no helmet or armor, only a linen tunic that clung to her figure and ended at mid-thigh, and her face flamed with anger—or was it embarrassment?

CHAPTER 14

"Take him, maiden!" the white-clad soldier snapped.

"Yes, take him, for we cannot!" said another soldier, coming right behind her.

"Aye!" said the first. "He is no use to us, that's certain!"

Balkis was on her feet and clinging to Anthony's arm, afraid he would fall, for he blinked around at the room, not seeming to understand where he was. "What have you done to him!"

"Everything we could short of rape. " Another soldier followed the first through the door with two more behind her, all clad like the first with their flowing hair unbound. "Stripped him naked and stripped ourselves, slowly and with every enticement we knew—and it did some good, as anyone could see, but not enough. Again and again he stammered that he had to refuse our kind invitation, saying he must be loyal to you."

"We accused him of being virgin, and therefore afraid of the power of the pleasures we would give him," another soldier said, "and he told us there might be truth to that, but still must he be loyal to his traveling companion."

"We assured him there was nothing to fear and every pleasure to gain, that we would ease him gently from his virgin state," the fourth soldier said, "and he thanked us, did you not, pale lad?"

That brought Anthony a little out of his daze. "Aye! How else could I respond to so kind an offer?"

"Aye, how could you?" the soldier said in disgust. "And you did not, to be sure!"

"As though we stood to gain nothing by our generosity," the first said with sarcasm.

"We danced for him, we offered him wine, we caressed and kissed him," the second said, fuming, "but still he stood rigid and protested he must refuse our kind offer."

"In the end, we dressed him and brought him back to you," said the first, lip curling in a sneer. She rounded on Balkis. "Why did you not tell us you are betrothed?"

"Why . . . because we are not!" Balkis gasped.

"In love, then—so deeply in love you might as well be engaged," the first soldier said. "Why, when we pressed him to take advantage of the opportunity he turned red-faced and stammered that he had to be faithful to his little cat." She wrinkled her nose. "He calls you endearments, and you do not know he loves you?"

"Well . . . perhaps I suspected . . ." Balkis didn't think it was time to explain that "little cat" was only a statement of fact, not an endearment—or was it?

"Take him and go." Alantha rose to her feet.

"Aye, take him, for he will surely be no use to us!" one of the soldiers said.

"We must respect such loyalty—it is a quality soldiers understand," Illior said, though she looked disappointed. "He has won you safe passage through our land, maiden, and so shall we tell the queens. It has been fifty years and more since a man so refused us through loyalty to his love."

Alantha stepped close. "If he is so much in love with you, you are a fool if you remain a maiden much longer."

"Per-Perhaps . . ." Balkis said, but her face flamed scarlet at the thought.

"If you do not realize the worth of what you have in him, you are truly a fool," Alantha said bluntly. "If you do not bind him to you with every tie you know of, you are a greater fool still."

"I . . . I shall ponder what you say." Balkis lowered her gaze, then looked up again at Anthony's face, anxious at his numbness, the trance in which he seemed to stand.

"You may stay the night." Alantha stepped aside from the inner doorway. "You will find the bed wide and soft, and if you have any sense about you, you will put it to good use."

"Thank—Thank you. But . . . we . . ." Balkis glanced again at Anthony, and saw that she would have to do the thinking for both of them. "You . . . are very kind, but I think . . . yes, I think that we had better go while we may. You have been very hospitable, but we have many miles yet to walk and must use every minute of daylight left."

"Go, then." Alantha nodded at the white-clad soldiers, who stepped aside from the outer doorway. "Go in peace, but go quickly, for though we respect his loyalty, there is something within us that must believe it is an insult."

Balkis took her Anthony, and went—and as she steered him down the road and out of the village, she marveled that he did indeed seem to have become her Anthony—for if the soldiers spoke truly, he most certainly was that.

The thought made her a little afraid. Afraid, but also excited—and that excitement made her even more afraid.

Matt and Stegoman came flying over the roadway, noticing how the desert had bloomed and turned from rock to scrub growth to verdant pasture and luxurious woodland. "We seem to be coming to a water source," Matt opined.

"Perhaps it is the drainage from that range of mountains we passed some days ago," Stegoman offered.

"That would make double sense—why this side is green and the northern side is desert," Matt said. "I have to say this for Prester John—at least he keeps communications open. The road just keeps going, straight through the mountains and the desert, even here hundreds of miles south of Maracanda."

"It is wise for merchants as well as soldiers," Stegoman pointed out.

Dimmed by distance, Matt heard something thudding. He looked up and stared. "Friend, that ain't no caravan!"

Stegoman lifted his neck, gaining a higher view of the sparkling mass that had come in sight over the horizon. "Indeed not. It fills the roadway and twinkles as it goes."

"I suspect that twinkling comes from the movement of marching—of the marching of armored soldiers," Matt said. "The only organism I know of that moves to the beat of a drum is an army! Let's get a little more altitude, Stegoman—say, out of crossbow range."

Stegoman felt for a thermal and tilted upward. "Ought we not avoid them completely?"

"An army marching northward, toward Prester John's territory? I think we owe it to him to take a quick survey, don't you?"

"We owe him nothing," Stegoman grumbled, but flew south toward the army anyway.

Before they could reach it, however, the soldiers turned west onto a side road—a very wide side road; if Matt hadn't known better, he would have suspected it had been made specifically for moving troops. Come to think of it, he didn't know better. "Follow those soldiers," he directed.

Stegoman glided over the marchers. Matt frowned down at them. "This isn't what I've been thinking of when I said I wanted to stop and ask anybody I saw, but hey, they could have seen Balkis as easily as the next man."

"I doubt it," Stegoman said dryly. "One sight of them and the lass would have hidden, if she had any sense."

"Don't worry—I'll just ask them if they've seen a cat."

"Pardon me if I think they may have ignored her," Stegoman told him. "Cats can scarcely be a rare occurrence in so fruitful a land."

"Well, it's worth a try, anyway," Matt sighed. "Just land on the other side of that grove up there ahead, will you? I'll walk back to the road."

"And if they decide to shoot you with their crossbows before you can come near them?"

Matt considered. "I'll sing the finale of *Iolanthe*. Meet me in midair."

"That would not be much of a change," the dragon grunted, but he landed as asked.

Matt clambered down. "Okay, back into the skies, soarian. If they get mean, I'll just start singing 'Up in the air, sky high, sky high . . .' "

"And I shall meet you on a zephyr. Aye, I know. How if they welcome you?"

"Well then, when I'm done talking, I'll hike back behind the grove again."

"I shall hope to land before I meet you again, then," Stegoman told him, "but I shall be watching you, never fear." He leaped into the air in a thunder of wing-beats.

"I'd say something about Big Brother, if he were only my species," Matt said to himself, then plunged into the grove, heading for the road.

He emerged while the soldiers were still five minutes away, so they had time to get used to the sight of him. It turned out to be a better plan than Matt had expected because he needed time to get used to them. Admittedly, for a man married to a queen who led her own troops into battle, the sight of female armor wasn't a surprise, but the sheer numbers were. He hadn't counted, but he was sure this army had to number more than a thousand—maybe more than three or four thousand.

He stood waiting. When they were close enough, he waved; after a pause, the leader raised her spear in salute. When she was ten paces from Matt, she called a halt, and the company stamped to a standstill. She bawled another command, and they all leaned on their spears—gratefully, Matt thought.

The officer paced up to him, junior officers flanking her. "Hail, wanderer!"

Matt understood her, of course—his translation spell seemed to have made a permanent change to his nervous system—but he hadn't expected to hear her speaking the language of Maracanda. Mind you, it was so heavily accented that he might not have recognized it without the spell, but it was Maracandese nonetheless.

"Hail," he said. "My name is Matthew Mantrell."

"I am ten-thousand-leader Liharl," the officer replied.

Ten-thousand-leader? Matt allowed for exaggeration and mentally converted her rank to colonel. He wouldn't ask about troop strength, though. There was such a thing as bad manners in the military.

"Why have you come to the Grand Feminie?" Colonel Liharl demanded.

Now, that was a surprise—but if Prester John was real in

this universe, there was no reason why the places he described in his letter to the Pope shouldn't be real, too. "I'm sorry to interrupt your progress, officer, but I'm looking for a young woman who's been kidnapped, and I was hoping you had seen her."

"A woman kidnapped to the Grand Feminie?" The officer frowned. "Scarcely likely. Women who have been badly used come to us of their own accord."

"Actually, this young woman might have escaped from her captors and be trying to walk home," Matt said. "She's young, about eighteen, dark-haired, golden-skinned—"

"You describe all the young women of Maracanda!"

"Yeah, that's her, Maracandese. Haven't seen any of them this far south, have you?"

"There are several in our army," the officer told him, "but none newly come, nor have we met any on the road."

"I was afraid of that," Matt sighed. "You do have cats here, don't you?"

"Thousands of them." The woman frowned. "Why do you ask?"

"She, ah, has an affinity for the beasts," Matt said, "and if they were rare here, and you'd seen only one . . ."

"That would have been a sign of her?" The officer smiled. "Clever—but in this country it would mean little."

"Oh, well, it was worth a try." Matt bowed. "Thank you for your time, officer. Sorry to hold you up." He started back to the grove.

The colonel snapped out a command, and her two subordinates caught Matt by the arms. He looked up, startled. "No reason to arrest me, officer. I realize you're on campaign, but I don't know your opponents." He hoped she didn't want him to prove that.

"How did you know we march to war?" the officer asked, frowning.

Matt glanced back at rank upon rank of soldiers. "Just an assumption I make when I see a few thousand soldiers on the march. Hey, I promise I won't tell."

"There is no harm in your knowing, since you will not be

going before us," Colonel Liharl said. "We march ten thousand strong to overawe the barbarians on our western border, and ten more armies like ours go to the battlefield by other routes."

Matt felt a chill down his back; the only time officers gave away military information was when they were sure the spies weren't going loose to take it anywhere. "Very interesting, but my business lies to the south, so if you'll excuse me . . ."

"We will not," the colonel told him. "Our rule is that no man may enter the Grand Feminie for longer than nine days, and no matter your questions, there is only one reason why men come here. Soldiers!" She rattled off a list of names; Matt managed to make out Adonitay as a single word, but the others ran together in unfamiliar syllables. Half a dozen young women stepped forward, striking their spears against their shields in what he assumed was a salute.

"Take him back to Asusu City," the colonel said, "and accord him every hospitality. See that all his wishes are granted."

The young women looked annoyed, but the one with extra horsehair in her crest stepped up to take Matt by the arm, and her companions surrounded him.

"About face," the extra-crest soldier—Matt assumed she was a corporal—told him.

Matt sighed and turned, deciding he would go along since they didn't seem to be planning any particular mayhem. He'd get a good night's sleep in a civilized bed, at least, have a good breakfast, bid them a good morning, and be on his way.

The corporal led her little troupe off to the side of the road and marched them back the way the army had come. Matt was surprised to see envy on the faces of the soldiers as they passed—he'd thought they were gung ho military, eager for battle, but it looked as though every one of them wished she were going back to Asusu with them.

There were a lot of them. He had assumed the officer was exaggerating when she said her force was ten thousand strong, but he began to think shc might not have been so far off at that. Each rank had five women, and he stopped counting ranks after five hundred. They went on and on, and after the soldiers themselves, there were teenage girls steering rank upon rank of carts, horses, and elephants loaded with equipment and provisions. The army seemed to go on forever.

Of course, he couldn't wait that long to go after a little information, so he asked, "Is this, uh, a regular custom of yours, to welcome male visitors?"

"Aye," the corporal said, "the few who have the courage to come."

Considering all the well-armed women he was passing, Matt could understand that the occasional male visitor might feel a little outnumbered. "Might as well get acquainted, if we're going to be road companions. My name is Matt."

"I am Adonitay." The corporal inclined her head in polite greeting. "Be welcome in the Grand Feminie—for nine days. Ladies, greet him."

"Welcome, stranger," the privates chorused. Matt glanced back, saw them nodding, and inclined his head in return. He noticed then a strange suppressed excitement about them; they fairly seemed to glow.

"You will have to pardon us if we seem short with you," Adonitay said.

"Oh, I understand," Matt assured her. "I'm making you miss out on the action. Sorry about that."

Adonizeb gave a mirthless bark of laughter. "We regret missing action, truly enough, but not in battle, and it is certainly not your fault, but that of the stranger who was here two nights ago and was too much the fool to take advantage of his good fortune."

"Oh. A bad guest, huh?"

"Very bad," Adonitay said, seething, "though we could scarcely condemn him for loyalty to the woman who traveled with him and her need to speed their journey."

Matt's mental ears pricked up. "Woman? His mother, maybe?"

The privates laughed, and Adonitay smiled, choking down glee. "Only if a mother could be a year or two younger than her son."

"Oh? A young couple, setting out in life?"

"On their way to Maracanda, so she said," Adonitay answered.

"So she could have rested for nine days, by your law?"

"As long as she wished, but of course she was as loyal to her traveling companion as he to her, and we do not allow men to stay longer than nine days." She glanced at Matt sidelong and hinted, "A day to Asusu and a day back to the border."

Matt took the hint; it left him an even week of hospitality, not that he was about to take advantage of it. He hated to eat and run, especially after they'd apparently just had a case of such rudeness—poor things must be hungry for news of the outside world. Well, he'd tell them what he could before he went to bed. "So you didn't even let them stay the full week?"

"We sent them on their way that very night," Adonitay said. "They could have stayed till morning, mind you, but they chose to leave directly—she was in a great hurry to reach Maracanda."

A very great hurry, no doubt, and Matt was sure that the young woman was Balkis. So she was traveling with a young man, was she? He could only think of one reason, and hoped he was right—Balkis in love with somebody her own age would certainly save him the embarrassment and difficulty of having to quietly discourage her interest in himself. And what could it be but love, when she could travel more safely as a cat than as a beautiful young woman, attaching herself to a caravan as resident mouser instead of road companion to a lone young man?

He must have been very trustworthy for her to take the chance—and from what Adonitay said, he was certainly faithful. Matt wished him all the best.

Matt resolutely put the young couple out of his mind. He'd stay the night, he told himself, then sneak out in the false dawn and call Stegoman—he was sure the dragon would be following him and would hide near Asusu and wait. There was the outside chance that Stegoman might attack Adonitay and her soldiers, thinking he was a prisoner—a reasonable assumption, after all—but Matt didn't think so. Stegoman was the soul of discretion. Total surprise made his attacks all the more terrifying.

No, no reason to worry about the dragon. Matt decided to concentrate on being a good guest, and wondered why Balkis' boyfriend hadn't taken advantage of his good fortune.

He found out in Asusu, when the fortune turned out to be a little too good.

Adonitay and her soldiers led him into a military compound right inside the main gate—but they went past the barracks to a smaller, circular house.

"This is the house for male guests," Adonitay told him. "Will you enter?"

"Why, thanks," Matt said, and stepped through the door into a sybarite's' dream.

The circular room had to take up most of the house, and the floor was one giant mattress, covered with soft rose-colored fabric, firm, but yielding enough under his step so that he stopped, afraid to damage it. Islands of cushions cropped up here and there, mostly around a low table that held a hookah, which Matt suspected did not hold tobacco. But the most outstanding feature of the room was the dozen young women kneeling on the floor, who stood up in a single sinuous movement and advanced upon him with low-voiced, throaty words of welcome.

CHAPTER 15

"Welcome, traveler!"

"Welcome to rest and refreshment!"

"Welcome to delight and pleasure!"

All twelve of them wore short-skirted tunics made by draping a length of clinging fabric around the neck, crosswise over each breast, then wrapped around the waist to form the skirt—simple but extremely attractive, especially considering how the fabric molded itself to their bodies. They advanced barefoot over the cushioned floor, smiling and eager. "May we aid you in taking off your boots, traveler?"

"Why, uh—yes, that would be very nice, thanks," Matt stammered, then wished he hadn't, for two of them pressed up against him on either side, ostensibly to brace his shoulders, while a third knelt to yank off first the one boot, then the other. Still kneeling and proving how low her neckline was cut, she looked up at him through long lashes. "May I perform any other service, O Guest?"

Matt had the first inkling of the true nature of his visit. He swallowed heavily and said, "Uh, no, thanks, I'm fine."

"I am sure that you are," the young woman said with a heavy-lidded glance. "A bath, then?"

Two other young women drew aside a curtain from an alcove, revealing a huge copper tub in a wooden frame, filled with steaming bubbles and emitting a fragrance of sandalwood.

"Yes!" Matt said. "That would be very nice. If you'll give me a few minutes privacy, a bath would be just the thing." He strode over to the tub before his hostesses could answer.

"May we not help you remove your clothes?" asked one of the women who had pulled open the curtain.

Alarm bells rang, but Matt knew the importance of abiding by local custom. "Yes, that would get me into the bubbles more quickly, thanks."

Slender hands unbuckled his belt as others plucked the jerkin, then the tunic, from his shoulders—but he stopped when they started pulling at his hose. "Uh, thanks, but I'll do that myself, if you'll just turn your backs for a minute."

"If you must," the oldest sighed with bad grace. "Turn your backs, girls." She set the example, muttering, "Foolish modesty!"

Matt stripped off his breeches and got into the tub quicker than he ever had. At the sound of splashing, the women turned back to look. He heard murmurs of approval at the contours of his chest; then a gentle hand drew a cool cloth over his forehead and murmured, "Lean back and enjoy the heat and moisture."

It sounded like a good idea. Matt leaned his head back—then felt the warm and yielding surface against which he leaned and decided it wasn't the wisest course of action after all. He glanced at the young women who gathered around the tub with avid eyes. It made him feel odd, like a side of beef on display at the butcher shop.

"A glass of wine, weary traveler?"

"Uh, yeah, thanks. Kind of you." Matt raised a soapy hand, but the young woman held the glass to his lips and tilted it just a little. Matt sipped, and his eyes widened. That wine was halfway to brandy! He could feel its warmth coursing through his limbs, and they hadn't needed any further warming.

"Drink deeply," the cup-bearer urged, and Matt did, again to be accommodating.

Then he leaned his head back and said, "Thanks, that's enough. Some more a little later, maybe."

"Whatever serves your pleasure," she murmured, and took the glass away—but her voice was husky and smoky, implying a greater pleasure than wine could provide, and Matt was alarmed to feel his body responding. What had been in that wine, anyway?

In fact, there was entirely too much emphasis on pleasure here. Surely these slender, smooth-limbed beauties couldn't be off-duty soldiers! But he took a closer look at the muscles beneath that smooth skin and decided that they probably were warriors—and that put a distinct limit to his relaxation.

One young woman reached in with a soft, soapy cloth to caress his chest. "Let us wash you, traveler."

"Uh, very nice, thanks." But the hand slipped below the water, and Matt protested, "Not really necessary, though."

"You wish to be clean throughout, do you not?" said the woman behind him. "Sit forward and I shall wash your back."

And she did, below the waterline and on down. When she passed his waist, Matt said, "Uh, thanks, but I think that's far enough." Then to the two young women who were working their way below his navel, one on each side of the tub, "You, too."

They giggled and withdrew their hands a little. "Do you not enjoy it?" asked one.

"Yes, but that's not the issue." The problem, Matt realized, was that he was enjoying it far too much, and didn't want them to realize it.

Light glared from the door, and he looked up, glad of the distraction. "Ah, mine host!" Then he stopped, staring, for Adonitay and her squadron were dressed like the others, and seemed far more feminine and appealing in short white tunics. No doubt about it—all his attendants were off-duty soldiers, Their exercises, however, were scarcely military.

"Have our sisters made you comfortable?" Adonitay asked.

"Uh, maybe a bit too comfortable," Matt said, but gave her a smile to soften it. Unfortunately, the smile felt mechanical.

Adonitay elbowed her way through to the tub and took the washcloth; the junior woman surrendered it reluctantly. Adonitay suggested, "Lift your legs, then, that we may wash them."

Warily, Matt lifted a leg, which drew another spate of murmured, excited discussion about his musculature, shape, and the aesthetic appeal of body hair. The washcloths worked over his toes, feet, ankles, shins, calves, knees, tickling, extremely enjoyable, and he could feet the submerged parts of his body reacting. When the cloths went underwater and worked their way up his thighs, though, he said, "Uh, that's far enough, thanks. I can wash the rest on my own."

"But we are quite willing to do it for you," Adonitay purred.

"Thanks, but I'm big on self-reliance." Matt took the washcloth and finished up. "If you'll turn your backs now, I'll hop out."

"Oh, but take another dram first," the cup-bearer urged, and pressed the glass to his lips—refilled, Matt noticed.

He drank half of it to be nice—against his better judgment—then said, "Just avert your gaze, okay?"

"As you wish," Adonitay sighed, and all the women turned their heads away, except one, who stood up, holding a huge towel high enough to hide her eyes.

Matt surged up from of the water, stepped out, and into the towel—but not quickly enough to keep a dozen women from peeking. They gave throaty chuckles and whispered to each other, and Matt's face flamed as he clutched the towel around him. He started to dry himself off, but soft towels touched his back and shoulders, and throaty voices murmured, "Let us attend you, brave traveler."

That part he could deal with—it was the towels rubbing softly around his ankles that worried him. "Uh, thanks, girls, but I think I'll just wrap myself in a sarong and air-dry."

He managed to swing the towel horizontal and wrap it without any more overexposure, but Adonitay, still kneeling, pouted and looked up at him through her lashes, saying, "Why do you spurn us, Matthew? It is the law of the Grand Feminie that any man bold enough to come among us may amuse himself in any way he wishes, as much and as often as he wishes. Indeed, if he does not, there will be no more warrior women born. Let us please you in any and every way."

"Uh, thank you very much," Matt said, "but I wasn't aware of your law, and it wasn't what I had in mind when I accepted your hospitality."

"But why not?" Adonitay looked up at him, genuinely puzzled, as were most of them—though a few appeared angry. "Do you find us plain and undesirable? Or is it perhaps because you feel at too much a disadvantage when you are naked and we are clothed? If so, let us be equal!" She pulled her tunic free of her shoulders.

Matt gasped at the sight. "Be-Believe me, it certainly isn't a matter of your being undesirable! You're all very attractive, very!"

"I had thought you found us thus." Adonitay reached out to caress high on his thigh. "Since it is obvious that you find us so, why do you hesitate?"

Matt looked down at her, and an irrelevant thought strayed thought his mind—that military training sure gave a woman excellent pectoral development. His own sweet warrior queen was similarly endowed; he had always suspected the same reason, and it was nice to have the thought confirmed.

Thinking of Alisande saved him. The arousal was still there, the stimulation still made him tremble, but it was now directed toward another woman, one who wasn't there. "I hesitate because I am married, fair hostess—very much married. But fidelity to a spouse isn't a matter of love and commitment magically making a man immune to the charms of all other women. There's a small matter of willpower involved, too. A husband can see beauty about him and respond to it, but still wish to be faithful to his wife."

Adonitay gazed at him unblinking for several seconds, while earnest discussion whispered around them, punctuated with muttered oaths of anger and groans of frustration.

Then Adonitay pulled her garment back onto her shoulders and rose, her face a mask. "I understand, and applaud your decision. We are warriors and prize fidelity in all its forms—fidelity, and honor. We have heard of marriage many times, though mostly through husbands who come to break their vows among us. It is very rare that we meet one who cleaves unto his wife in spite of all our charms."

Matt felt guilty, somehow. "I don't suppose you get very many men stumbling into your kingdom by accident."

"Very few indeed," Adonitay said with a sardonic grimace. "It is simply our very bad luck to encounter two in one week."

"Two?" Matt said, then remembered their earlier conversation. "Of course—the young man who didn't appreciate his good fortune."

"Nor do you," Adonitay said sourly.

"I'm afraid not," Matt said. "Sorry to be such a poor sport about the whole thing."

"I have a notion you would be excellent in sport, if you allowed yourself to be so treacherous," Adonitay said with a glint in her eye. "Nay, good traveler, go your ways back to your wife, and give her our congratulations, for she has a husband who is a jewel among men. Few indeed can withstand the blandishments of the Grand Feminie. Be sure that no woman among us who wishes a babe and has proved herself worthy to bear one has ever had to wait long." She glanced around at the thunderous-looking assemblage. "Though it seems that these shall have to wait awhile longer." She turned back to Matt. "Go your way, and if it takes you a month and more to cross our land, have no fear. You shall travel under a safe-conduct, for we must reward those few men who know how to keep faith."

Balkis walked beside Anthony in silence and confusion, deliberately fanning the coals of her anger, small though they might be. They were there at all only because Anthony, walking beside her in equal silence, had a faraway gaze and dazed expression that told her only too well how thoroughly he had been tempted, and how his body had longed to give in. However, it also told her how strong an act of will it had taken to refuse.

Of course, if he had never lain with a woman before, as the soldiers had said, there would have been some fear of the unknown to help him refuse. Surely it had been fear that made him shun the hungry warrior-women! Balkis thought. Surely his heart could not have become so deeply embroiled with her as to refuse such an opportunity!

Thus she fanned the flames of anger and tried hard to ignore the clear facts as the soldiers had told them—that Anthony was in love with her, so much so that he had refused to commit an action that would have hurt her deeply.

Or would have hurt her if she were in love with him, she qualified. But surely she had given him no reason to think so! Surely she was not! He was only a country bumpkin, after all, a rude and naive peasant who would be completely lost amid the alleys of Maracanda and the intricacies of Prester John's court!

She had to admit, however, that here in this distant land he was more knowledgeable than she, and just as capable. If she had the experience of traveling, he had some knowledge of desert travel and the places they would encounter, from his talk with the caravan drivers. And he was quite handsome. This thought slipped into her mind by itself. Indeed, she did not have to work at remembering the strange glow that the first sight of him had kindled in her, the rush of blood that had pounded through her veins. Rather, she had to work at forgetting it, for it was all too familiar, a mild version of the few times she had been in cat form when she had gone into heat. Unfortunately, the sight of him still aroused the same emotion; even remembering it made her pulse quicken and her breath shorten.

Again she used the energy to fuel her anger—how dare he so much as look at another woman with lust! How dare he gaze upon a naked female body—never mind that he had been given no choice. Worse, how dare he respond to the sight, even though he refused it! How dare he have longed to accept!

She had not, of course, given him any hope of such reward herself, nor would she—but that was beside the point. If he were in love with her, any other woman would have left him completely unaffected.

Wouldn't it?

She remembered seeing real cats in heat, though, and how they welcomed any and all males, and could not help the sneaking suspicion that there were human women who might wish to behave the same way, and only their willpower and love for their husbands prevented them from doing so.

But underneath all the effort of anger lurked the confusion arising from the conviction that the soldier women had seen Anthony more clearly than she had herself—had seen that he was in love with her, deeply in love with her, and she knew with a sneaking certainty that her own feelings were engaged with him far more than she liked. Anger was definitely the readiest answer to such confusion.

Balkis shook herself, putting the whole topic behind her, or trying to, as she looked up and saw a river before them. "Anthony, look! It is a boundary, surely! We can cross it and be out of this witches' country! We need not traverse the full length of the land!"

"Cross . . . ?" Anthony's eyes focused—a bit. "River?" He turned and looked at the broad gray-green stream before them. Finally the meaning of the words seemed to penetrate, and he shook himself. "Boundary . . ." Then he turned to look at Balkis, and she could see his eyes focus completely, could almost hear his brain click into gear, saw him shake off the trance. She tried to tell herself that it wasn't the sight of her that had done it, but the idea of leaving the Grand Feminie in a single day instead of forty-two.

"Yes! Leave the country! An excellent idea!" Anthony said, and strode toward the river.

Then, though, he roamed the riverbank in silence, gazing at the stream and frowning, deep in thought. Balkis felt the tension build, though Anthony seemed not to. Finally she burst out, "What are you thinking of?"

"The fate of that poor man we met on the road," he told her without hesitation, "and how unfortunate for him that he did not have a dream to protect him, as I have."

She almost asked what dream that might be, but bit back the words at the last moment, afraid that the answer might involve her, might be her. Instead she asked, "And that you might have shared his fate?"

"Oh, there was never any chance of that," he said with absolute certainty.

That nettled Balkis, and she spoke with some sharpness. "Why? Are you so sure you would have kept count of the days?"

"No," Anthony said, "I am sure that I would never have begun." He paused, considering. "Of course, I did not know what the punishment for refusing might be—but as it turned out, it was a reward, so it was all for the best."

Balkis stared at him, shocked by the ease with which he said it. Obviously he hadn't really considered at the time that there might be a punishment, or that the women's favors might constitute a reward. What had made him so determined to refuse that he hadn't even thought of the consequences?

She skipped over the answer to that with determination and demanded, "What are you seeking?"

"A bridge or a ford," Anthony answered. "There!"

She looked where he pointed and saw the bottom of the river undulating across its width. "It has shelved. How deep do you think it is?"

"Perhaps a foot or two, if we do not step too far to left or right," Anthony said. "See how the color of the water deepens so quickly to either side? But we can wade where it is shallow." He turned to give her a smile that was so open and ingenuous that he could not have had any ulterior motives as he offered, "Shall I carry you across?"

But wariness sprang up in Balkis, out of the emotions that had been warring in her breast. "I thank you, good companion, but I can walk by myself," she replied.

"As you will." Anthony sat to pull off his boots and pull up his bias-hosen to his knees, then stood and asked, "Will you go first? Then, if you should stumble, I shall be able to catch you."

The day before, Balkis wouldn't have felt at all reluctant to have Anthony walking behind her when she was holding her robes up to mid-thigh, might even have enjoyed the notion that he was watching her legs with admiration—but now she shrank from it. "Thank you, but I think not. I would rather you go before, so that if there is a sudden hole or soft place, I shall have warning."

"A good thought," Anthony said, abashed. "I should have thought of the danger." He turned and started wading.

Bemused, Balkis pulled off her slippers, gathered up her skirts and, holding them high, followed his steps as he crossed the river.

On the other side, Anthony sat down and leaned against a tree trunk, legs stretched out on the grass. "By your leave, I'll let my feet dry before I put my boots on again."

"That seems wise," Balkis said cautiously, and sat down beside him, but not too close—fortunately, the next tree was a good six feet from his. She did stretch out her bare legs, but kept her hemline below the knee. Casting about desperately for something to say, she came up with, "I should think such rivers would be new to you, that you have only streams in your mountains."

"There is one that is ten feet across," Anthony explained, "and wider in the spring, when the melt-waters swell it. We cannot avoid it, either, since it lies between our homestead and the upper pasture. We have to drive the cows across it twice a day, so I have become used to finding fords and bracing myself against the current."

"A stronger current than this, I would guess."

"It is indeed," Anthony said, "especially in spring."

That easily, they were back into their old friendship, chatting and exchanging experiences—but there was an undercurrent that hadn't been there before, an awareness of the other and the other's feelings, and Balkis realized that they could never again be simply friends, companions, and nothing more.

When their feet were dry, they pulled their shoes on again and set off down the road. Meadow quickly gave way to forest, and as it grew darker, Balkis muttered a spell, ready to recite the last line at sight of a wolf or bandit, but neither appeared. After an hour's time, Balkis paused and frowned. "Is there another river near?"

"It sounds as though there is," Anthony said. "I hear the sound of rushing waters . . . but is that shouting mingled with it?"

"People in peril of drowning!" Balkis hurried past him. "Quickly, we must see if we can aid!"

Anthony ran after her. As they went farther down the track, the water-sound became more distinct; they heard separate notes, and the shouting began to sound angry.

"Do the people fight the waters?" Balkis wondered.

Then they burst out of the woods into a field filled with grape arbors, posts linked by ropes upon which vines had climbed, bearing bunches of dark red fruit. But they scarcely had time to notice, for a horde of birds wheeled and hovered above the field, calling and warbling and making a sound like a waterfall as they dove, seeking to steal the fruit. They had little luck, though, for every aisle was filled with people scarcely higher than the posts, perhaps four feet tall, fighting with bows and arrows, spears and shields, to defend their crop.

"No doubt those people have watered and tended those vines," Balkis cried, "and now that the harvest is near, the birds have come to steal the fruits of their labors!"

"We cannot permit that to happen." Anthony drew his dagger and started forward.

"No, wait!" Balkis caught his arm, suddenly afraid she might lose him. "You can fight them far better by helping me craft a verse to send the birds away!"

Anthony frowned, turning back. "But it is you who are the wizard, you who knows the spells."

"For a hundred flocks of birds come a-stealing? I have never learned a spell for that, nor do I believe there is one! I shall have to make it up as I go, and you know what happens when I come to the end!"

She said it with a wrench of embarrassment, for she hated to admit her failing to Anthony—but with his great inborn tact, he only nodded and said, "You are right. I can do more good here with you."

She breathed a sigh of relief, then said, "Hold my hand! Perhaps we shall craft a verse better so!"

Anthony clasped her palm and turned to her expectantly.

"By vine and root and purple grape," Balkis began, and hesitated.

Anthony took that as his signal, and added, "By rain and earth that grew their state . . ."

"Close now those beaks that catch and gape!" Balkis commanded.

Somehow the birds sensed what they were doing; a squadron broke off and wheeled toward them.

Anthony said quickly, "Find flies and worms of interest great! Far from these fields go seek your bait!"

Balkis marveled at his facility, then clasped his hand more tightly in alarm. "Anthony! They are still coming for us!"

Anthony stared in alarm and awe. Sure enough, the whole avian army seemed to be banking to follow the squadron that was already bound toward the wizards, their beaks snapping shut as commanded—but all the sharper and stronger for that.

"These are not lovely songsters, but living arrows!" Balkis cried.

"Quick! Into cat-form!"

Balkis instantly felt panic at the thought of leaving Anthony to face the angry flock alone, but some perverse urge made her say instead, "When not a one of them but holds a grudge against cats? How shall I fare alone against them?"

"How shall we fare now?" Anthony returned. "What would you say to them if you *were* a cat?"

Without a thought, an angry yowl tore from Balkis' throat. She turned it into words:

> "To the King of Birds now flee!
> Your queen attend upon the wing!
> Flock around your royalty . . ."

She stammered to a halt, confounded by the need to rhyme. Anthony, thinking it his signal, called out,

> "Hither shall they fly, so sing
> Of their glory in loyalty!"

"That is where you wished me to improvise, is it not?" he asked anxiously.

"None better." Balkis clung to his arm with a sigh of relief.

Sure enough, two extravagantly plumed, flame-colored birds soared into sight, all trailing pinions, flowing crests, and undulating tails. They came flying from above the forest, calling out in musical tones that penetrated the sounds of battle.

The birds gave voice in a sound like a cataract and swirled in a huge half-circle to join the royal couple, surrounding them on all sides, some even flying on ahead, trilling a warning to all who encountered them.

The little people stared, letting their nets and weapons fall, eyes wide, drinking in a sight they had never seen, no doubt memorizing every detail to relate to their grandchildren.

The birds filled the sky now, and Balkis realized that others were streaking in from all points of the compass. Toward the east they flew, away from the sunset, darkening the earth below, but the sinking sun backlighted them in a golden glow. Then the sky began to clear as the huge flock soared away over the horizon. In its center, the king and queen of birds flew on, glorious song spilling from their throats, calling more and ever more of their kind to them.

Anthony stood transfixed, and Balkis was no better; the royal birds were so glorious that she had no thought for anything else in the world, all her mind devoted to drinking in the sight and engraving it upon her memory.

Then they were gone, the spell broken, and they were left two strangers in a foreign vineyard, surrounded by natives two-thirds their size but armed with spears and bows, slowly turning toward the two bigger people who had invaded their land.

CHAPTER 16

But the little folk dropped their weapons as they approached. They were all sweating and some were wounded, scored with the red trails left by birds' beaks, but grinning and bowing their thanks. They saluted the companions, and like the women warriors and the ant workers, they spoke the language of Maracanda with a heavy accent.

"Welcome, strangers!" said a gray-headed man. "I am Bunao, hetman of this village. Our great thanks for banishing the birds as you did!"

Anthony protested, "Surely we had little to do with—"

Balkis elbowed him in the ribs, and the hetman, grinning, said, "Be not so modest. Never before have the birds left us with so brief an attack—or so many grapes. We saw you pointing at them and chanting—but how did your call summon the yllerion?"

Anthony stared, and Balkis explained, "We only called for the king and queen of birds." She, at least, knew enough to accept her due credit in a strange land.

"You called well," Bunao said, "for the yllerion do indeed rule over all other fowl in the world. They are fiery of hue, their wings are as sharp as razors, and not even eagles can stand against them."

"How is it we have never seen them?" Anthony asked. "Is it because I am from the mountains, and they do not wish to roost there?"

"No, it is because there are but two of them in the entire world," Bunao explained. "They live for sixty years, after which span they fly off to plunge into the sea."

"It would seem we were fortunate to be summoning them at the end of that cycle!" Balkis said.

"So it would," Bunao agreed, "but it was definitely your magic that brought them here, for we have never seen them before, neither the oldest among us nor our ancestors, and doubly grateful are we for having seen the sight."

"If they fly to the sea to end their lives," Anthony asked, "how will there ever be more yllerion?"

"Oh, before they begin their flight, the queen lays two or three eggs, and they take turns sitting upon them for forty days. If the young ones have not already hatched, the royal couple will not have to begin their final journey. But it must have occurred, for what you have seen here is what we have been told happens—that all the birds who meet them fly as escort with them until they are drowned."

"The poor creatures!" Balkis cried.

Bunao shrugged. "I am sure their end is quick, for the water quenches their lives as it turns the fire of their wings to steam."

"But the nestlings!" Anthony protested. "How shall they survive with no mother or father?"

Bunao eyed him curiously. "You have a good heart. But fear not, for the nestlings are now the new king and queen, and the birds who served as final companions to their parents return to the fledglings, feeding and defending them until they have grown up and can fly and look after themselves."

"A most singular breed," Balkis murmured, turning to Anthony with wide eyes.

He nodded. "How fortunate we are to have seen them!"

"As though you had nothing to do with their approach," Bunao scoffed, and stretched out a hand. "Come! You must be our guests for the night, and let us honor you!"

"Oh, we could not intrude—" Anthony began, then grunted as Balkis' elbow dug into his ribs again.

"But it is very kind of you to offer," she finished.

"Not so kind as the lives you have saved by driving away the flocks! Indeed, we often lose a dozen or more of our people in this battle, and scores more die for lack of food in the winter. Everyone in this land of Piconye is in your debt. You must let us honor you for at least one night!"

"Well . . . perhaps only one night," Balkis said, with a meaningful glance at Anthony.

He looked down at her elbow and said, "One night will not slow our northward progress so terribly much. I must accept with thanks, good hetman!"

"Then come!" the hetman cried to his people, and the throng shouted with joy, then pressed in around the strangers as Bunao led them toward his village. They were surrounded by joyful singing, and if the warriors had picked up their spears and arrows again, at least none were pointed at their guests.

At the edge of the vineyard hundreds of horses were tethered—but what horses! They were as small as sheep, and the Piconyans swung aboard them bareback, taking the reins and turning them homeward.

"I regret that we have no mounts large enough for you, honored guests," Bunao said.

"We are accustomed to walking," Balkis assured him. "Your warriors appear quite proficient with their weapons. Must you march to war often?"

"Only against the birds," Bunao said. "We have no other enemies. We are content to spend our time laboring in the vineyards and going to worship the Christ on Sundays—though we also practice our archery and spear-play on the sabbath. It may not be rest, but for us it is recreation."

As they came to the village they saw another troop, even larger, approaching. At their head rode a man with an austere countenance, dressed in a loincloth like the rest of them, but wearing also a purple cloak and a crown of gold topped by ostrich plumes of purple and white. Like all his people, there was a shield over one shoulder and a quiver over the other, and he carried a bow and spear slung at his saddle. A man at his right called, "Bow to Tutai, King of Piconye!

"Hail Majesty!" Bunao cried, and fell to his knees.

All his people followed his example, leaving Balkis and Anthony standing in their midst, unsure what to do. Then Anthony shrugged, said, "Royalty is royalty," and bowed.

"Rise, good Bunao," the king said, "and introduce me to these strangers. Then explain how the birds have left."

"These are the wizards who called up the yllerion, Your Majesty, and bade the flock follow them away," Bunao said as he rose. "I fear I have not asked their names—one never knows, with wizards."

"We trust you well enough to tell you," Balkis said, smiling, "for the enemy of my enemy is my friend. I am Balkis, and this is Anthony."

Anthony held up a hand in greeting, somehow certain that Balkis wasn't being quite as trusting as she claimed. "Hail, O King!"

"Hail, O Wizards," the king returned, saluting them with an open palm. "How knew you of the yllerion, if you are strangers?"

"We called the king and queen of birds, Your Majesty, though we had never seen them," Balkis explained. "In truth, I was not sure there were such royalty among the feathered kind."

"A lucky guess, then." Tutai smiled, apparently relieved. "We thank you for kind rescue—this battle would have cost many lives without you!"

"It would seem that you shall not have as many birds to roast now, though," Anthony said regretfully.

"That is a small price to pay." But Tutai looked thoughtful. "In truth, most of those we slay go to waste—but now that you mention it, there should be some way to trap them when they come for the grapes next year. Perhaps we could ensnare them and gain as much food from their bodies as we lose to their beaks."

"A good thought," Balkis said with an admiring glance at Anthony. "Do you know anything about catching birds?" she asked him.

Anthony shrugged, seeming to swell visibly from her unspoken praise. "Only bird-lime and nets—but it would take many, many webs to cover all these vines."

"We have the whole winter to weave them," Bunao pointed out, "but what is bird-lime?"

Anthony started to answer, but Balkis laid a hand on his arm and said, "Let us discuss it as we dine."

"An excellent thought!" said Tutai. "Lead us to your village pavilion, Bunao. We shall feast with these wizards and fashion a plan for dealing with the birds!"

As the sun warmed the earth, though it was hidden behind gray pearly clouds that filled the sky, an ant the size of a fox dug its way out of the sand dune that had sheltered it during the night. The day before, it had had a narrow escape from a shouting horde of women who seemed not to know they should be afraid of it, instead chasing it with horrible clanging things that bit from twenty feet away and more. It could run much faster than they did, though, and had doubled back twice to bite some of them, deeply, too—it hadn't liked the flavor—but their insane comrades had chased it all the more angrily for that. Finally it ran out into the desert, and they had not followed. It then burrowed into a sand dune to spend the night.

Now, though, it followed the scent of its property—a tang no human could have detected but that the ant knew well: its own acidic scent mingled with the smell of gold. Strangely, the carrier seemed to have come this way, too, and the ant followed the trace far faster than any human could have run. To the ant, though, it seemed to be running slowly, and for good reason—its middle was hollow with hunger. It had to find food, and quickly.

Suddenly, there was a human foot in front of it.

The foot was at least twice the size of the ant. Looking up, though, the insect saw a human being not much larger than the ones in its valley. But where a normal human had hips that forked into two legs, this one had only one leg the width of its whole body, a massive column, slightly bent at the knee, which descended into the huge flat foot that lifted as the creature hopped into the air then plummeted down, its foot spread wide to crush the ant.

The ant stared, not understanding—never had it seen an ant being crushed. At the last second, though, it connected with a memory of a tree falling on another worker-ant and dashed to the side. The huge foot slapped down into the sand, and the uniped man bent his knee deeply, crying, "Vermin!" then hopped high and forward.

His foot caught the ant on its underside and hopped up again, sending the ant flying twenty yards. The impact hurt, but the ant had felt worse; it scrambled up and ran from the uniped man. Shouting, the man came hopping after it, but the ant was far faster than any human, especially one hopping. It ran until the uniped sank below the horizon behind it.

Then the ant slowed, its antennae probing for anything that might be edible. It quickly found a lizard, one almost gelled solid by the night's chill. Shortly after, it found a family of mice. As it was eating, though, it heard a distant thud. Looking up, it saw the uniped hopping toward it.

Ants don't have a wide range of emotions, but it did feel anger at the man's tenacity. It gobbled up the rest of the mice, turned and ran again.

Running is hungry work, and half an hour later, with the one-footed man out of sight, it slowed to hunt some more. It found some prickly vines and managed to eat the vines and leave the prickles. It was just finishing when it heard a thud again.

It looked up at the approaching hopper with fresh anger, then turned and ran north. Once more it slowed as hunger turned to famishment, and cast about, seeking something to eat. It found little except sand and another very small lizard before it heard another thud.

The ant looked up in a fury. Would the uniped never stop? Would it have to kill the uniped to get a little peace?

The thought struck it with pleasure—a way to satisfy both ends at the same time, safety and appetite. It streaked back toward the uniped, wary of that great slapping foot but also very much aware that the man was made of meat.

The uniped shouted with anger, hopping high and aiming for the ant. At the last second the ant dodged aside and, before the man could hop again, ran up his leg and over his hip and chest, its mandibles reaching for his throat. After all, when two anthills fought one another, biting off your enemy's head always stopped it, and if it worked with an ant, why not with a human?

But the uniped man shouted in anger and struck the ant with a huge fist. It fell, rolling, and struggled up to see that huge foot descending right toward it.

The ant dodged again, but when it tried to climb the leg a second time, the uniped was ready; the fist swung down out of nowhere and the ant went spinning. It sprang to its feet and ran in a half-circle, the great foot thudding behind it. Around and around the ant ran, watching out of its faceted eye as the uniped man spun about, stamping and shouting. Then, dizzy, he toppled.

The ant sprang in, mandibles wide, reaching for the uniped's neck—but the huge foot swung around, knocking it off its feet and through the air. This time the ant struck against a rock and landed dazed. It saw the huge foot approaching, hop by hop, but couldn't get its legs working again. The great sole lifted one last time to fill the sky, then descended . . .

The ant's legs started working and it shot out from under just as the great extremity slapped earth where it had been. All thoughts of food abandoned, the ant ran north, the direction the scent of the gold had been going. This time it knew better than to stop, and ran and ran northward, not even pausing to look back.

But as it ran, the clouds blew away, and the naked sun baked the desert with its rays. Between the heat and its hunger, the ant slowed, then finally stopped, trembling, and looked back—to see the uniped man hopping over the horizon. But he, too, had slowed, and now stopped, wiping his brow and lifting a waterskin for a long drink. Then, to the ant's astonishment, he lay down on his back and raised his foot. Its shadow fell across him, providing the uniped with shade in the heat of the day.

But he had also put himself low enough for the ant to reach.

Slowly now, shivering with hunger, fatigue, and heatstroke, the ant went back toward the man. This desert's heat was a far cry from the moist jungle of its home valley—but it was beginning now to suffer from thirst, treading as lightly as possible until it was ten feet from the uniped, angling around so it came upon him from beyond the crown of his head, where the stupid blind human could not see. Then it rushed.

The uniped never knew what bit it.

Matt pulled his cloak tighter about him; the wind of Stegoman's flying was chill, especially at this altitude. He drew a forearm across his face to shield it, and beyond the folds of his cloak he saw a sinuous shape flanking them and veering closer. "Female flying object at nine o'clock," he warned.

"I see her," Stegoman said in a carefully neutral tone.

Dimetrolas converged on their course in a matter of seconds, and Matt decided he had definitely been away from Alisande too long—he was actually thinking the female dragon's graceful S-curve was attractive. It was either pure aesthetics or having been with Stegoman long enough to perceive as he did.

"I have heard something of your woeful travels, wizard," Dimetrolas jeered. "What manner of man are you, who had the chance to fertilize dozens of females and refused?"

Matt felt a spurt of anger at the intention of the insult, if not its substance. "The only kind of man I respect, Dimetrolas—one who is faithful to his mate!"

"Oh, aye, even as dragons mate for life!" Dimetrolas jeered. "Have you been so long with this great scaly hulk that you have begun to think like our kind?"

Matt gave her a funny look, one he'd been practicing. "Humans mate for life, too, dragonette."

"Not those I have met, silly male! In truth, even those I have seen who claim to be married are quick to couple with any females who offer!"

"The more shame to them for offering," Matt called back. "I'm sorry you've only met such low examples of my kind."

"Every human male whom I call friend has been faithful to his mate, save one," Stegoman rumbled. "In truth, you have seen such sordid samples!"

But Dimetrolas picked up the mention quickly. "Save one? And who might that be?"

"A ragtag poet called Frisson, who rose to rule a kingdom as a wizard."

"And you call him friend even though he is unfaithful to his wife?"

"He is unmarried," said Stegoman, "and so far as I know, refuses to couple until he falls in love."

"He is a madman and a fool!" Dimetrolas snorted.

"He is a poet," Stegoman replied.

"As I said, a madman and a fool—and a paltry excuse for a male, as are you, O Most Celibate of Dragons!"

"Are you not celibate also?" Stegoman countered.

Red though she was, Dimetrolas's whole body turned redder. "Oh, then, let us praise the celebrated Stegoman! Would your fame be half what it was if folk knew you feared a female?"

"You have heard of me since last we met, I see," Stegoman replied, "but I fear no female, though some disgust me." He added pointedly, "And I have no fame."

"Do you not! I have heard human folk speaking of the great Stegoman, who carried the Lord Wizard of Merovence to victory!"

Stegoman flew on in silence for a few wingbeats, then said, "That is heartening to hear."

"Heartening! Do you think they would respect you if they knew that you are no more masculine than your rider, who fears women so much that he shrinks from coupling with dozens of willing and eager females?"

"Where I come from, that kind of self-control is regarded as a virtue," Matt told her.

"Then you come from nowhere upon this earth!"

"Right," Matt confirmed.

Dimetrolas stared at him, confounded just long enough for Stegoman to say, "He wooed a queen and won her heart. Would you not say that proves greater masculinity, not less?"

"Perhaps," Dimetrolas sneered, "if it were not she who had wooed him! Surely you must be so wooed, too, deficient drake, for you approach no female!"

"What, do you think the measure of masculinity is a male's drooling after every female in heat he encounters?" Stegoman asked with contempt. "A fine warrior he would be, a fine builder or protector, if any passing female could distract him from his work!"

Stung, Dimetrolas retorted, "Protector, are you? Then defend!" She dove toward him, tongue of flame licking out toward Matt.

"Hold fast!" Stegoman roared, and folded his wings to plummet from the sky.

Matt held tight, hearing the wind whistle past him as his stomach tried to make friends with his larynx.

"Leap!" Stegoman cried, swerving five feet above a mountaintop.

Matt sprang down into the center of a cluster of needle-sharp rocks and crouched as Stegoman swooped up and away. Dimetrolas bellowed in anger as she backed air sharply, jolting herself to hover just short of the rocks. Then she plunged down from the peak, caught the updraft that rushed along its side, and spiraled up after Stegoman.

But the male dragon turned, wings folding again, and stooped upon her. Dimetrolas squawked with anger—he was breaking the rules, after all—and shot away in an Immelman that Matt thought would have done credit to a World War I ace. Stegoman pulled out of his dive and went rocketing after her.

Dimetrolas caroled in delight and dove toward a mountaintop. Stegoman, reading her intention, soared after her but fifty feet higher, and as Dimetrolas pulled up to avoid the rocks, she found herself gliding straight toward him. She roared, sending a tongue of flame twenty feet ahead to scorch him, but Stegoman swung to the side. She barreled past him, and he veered to follow, bellowing a fifty-foot tongue of flame that did no more than warm her toes. She chortled victory and plunged down past the horizon.

Matt waited, knowing that Stegoman was too much of a gentleman to hurt a female who wasn't really trying to kill him, but also hoping he hadn't become such a stuffy old bachelor that he wouldn't remember how to have fun.

It seemed so; suddenly, Stegoman reappeared over another mountain peak, and even at a distance Matt could see the contemptuous set of his lip—of course, with that muzzle, Stegoman had a lot of lip. Dimetrolas came after him with all the finesse of a cargo jet, screeching with anger, spiraling high above him, then folding her wings to plunge downward, all talons out. Matt's heart quailed; she looked as though she were really out for blood, and he didn't know how Stegoman would react to actual injury.

He should have guessed, Matt thought as Stegoman swooped past his hiding place, calling, "Send her home, wizard, I pray you!"

Then he was gone, sailing away into an updraft. Furious, Dimetrolas came roaring in like a fighter jet, howling insults in dragonese, but Stegoman spiraled higher in his updraft, gaining so much altitude that she couldn't pounce on him. Screeching with anger, Dimetrolas soared over to a faster updraft and shot higher, then dove back to Stegoman's air column, wings folding to stoop—but Stegoman looped the loop to come out above her.

While they were playing "Can You Top This?" Matt sighed and went to work granting his friend's request, but with considerable disappointment. What else could he do, though? If Stegoman didn't want to play, someone might get hurt sooner or later. Still, some sixth sense warned him not to send Dimetrolas completely home; instead, he sang,

"Up aloft amid the jet stream,
Swiftly blows the favoring gale,
Soft as hatchling's scales in eggshells,
Filling out wings' leathery sails.
As it turns to catch and bear you
(For you are the wild wind's pride)
To the peaks you've left behind you,
Where we met and for truce cried."

A hot wind came howling in from the south and caught Dimetrolas. She squawked in outrage as it sent her tumbling through the sky, then managed to stabilize herself, leveling out, wings beating furiously as she tried to fly against the wind—but it bore her ever farther northward. Finally she tired and, just before it swept her past the horizon, turned to glide, nose pointing toward Maracanda and the mountains where she'd first met them.

Leather boomed as Stegoman cupped his wings to hover above Matt, then carefully lowered his legs. "Well done, wizard! That vexing female would have plagued me for hours if you had not sent her hence!"

"If you say so." Matt leaped, wrapped his arms around Stegoman's ankle, and let the dragon carry him past the spike-rocks to a more open peak, where Stegoman landed completely and Matt could climb back up between his shoulders. "You know, though, she might just have been trying to get your attention."

"That," Stegoman said grimly, "was quite obvious." He plunged off the peak, caught an updraft, and rose into the sky again.

Matt held his peace, waiting.

Finally Stegoman said, "I cannot comprehend why females find so great a need for attention that they must disrupt a male's peace to gain it."

Delicately, Matt suggested, "It could be that she finds you attractive."

"When she is at such pains to deny my masculinity? Hardly!"

"With most males, that's a sure way of getting their attention."

"Not mine," Stegoman snapped. "To what purpose, anyway?"

"It could be an overture to mating," Matt suggested.

CHAPTER 17

"Mating?" Stegoman squawked. "Me?"

"Hey, you are a big musclebound hunk, you know."

"But I have no notion how to deal with a female! All my adult years have been spent in exile from my own kind!"

"You *have* had more dealings with humans than with dragons," Matt conceded. "That's why you wouldn't realize that the females of your own kind might find you handsome."

Stegoman was silent for a quarter of a mile. Then he said, "There might be truth in what you say. Why else should she have followed us?"

"Why indeed?" Matt asked as casually as he could.

Stegoman was silent for half a mile this time. Finally he said, "She is a vibrantly beautiful dragon."

Matt nodded. "If Mother Nature is an artist, Dimetrolas is a masterpiece."

Stegoman was silent again.

Matt ventured, "You must admit, that little chase was stimulating."

"Must I?" Stegoman ground out.

Matt waited.

"Yes," Stegoman said, with great reluctance. "I must. Stimulating indeed."

"It makes a fellow think," Matt offered.

"I shall," Stegoman promised.

And he did, for the next dozen miles. Matt waited in silence and watched the road unwind below, knowing that when his friend wanted to talk, he would.

Finally Stegoman said, "We are not a promiscuous kind."

"You're not," Matt agreed. "Dragons are models of fidelity."

"We mate for life," Stegoman said.

"You do," Matt confirmed.

Stegoman was silent a little longer, then said, "Our lives are very long."

"Very," Matt agreed.

"A drake would be a fool to spend the rest of his days bound to a sharp-tongued female who insults and criticizes him."

"Even if she is beautiful," Matt mused, "and sensuous. Even voluptuous, maybe. In dragon terms."

"In dragon terms," Stegoman repeated, and flew on in silence a little longer. Then he said, "Perhaps I have been living among humans for too long, but I find I want a mate who is capable of gentleness, even sweetness, as human mates often are to one another."

The words evoked a vision of Alisande at her sweetest and most alluring, so powerful that it made Matt shiver. He forced himself to replace it with a picture of her at her most angry. It made him shiver again—unfortunately, he found his mate beautiful no matter what mood she was in—but gave him the impetus to remind Stegoman, "We can be pretty angry sometimes, too."

"I can bear the storms," Stegoman said thoughtfully, "as long as there is sunlight to follow, and far more fair weather than foul."

"Could be Dimetrolas has a gentler side to her nature," Matt suggested.

"Anything is possible," Stegoman huffed, "but I have not seen it in her."

"It's a little early in your acquaintance for her to let it show," Matt said, "at least, if I understand dragon culture at all."

"You understand the meaning of a dragon without a clan," Stegoman snapped.

That gave Matt pause. He had to think it over for a minute. "I see . . . I'd thought she was the lookout for a clan back there in the mountains."

"If she had been, why did they not come at her call?"

"Maybe because she didn't call?" Matt guessed. "Figured she could handle you herself?"

"No sentry would do such," Stegoman assured him. "At sight of a stranger, she would have called for a squadron."

"Since she didn't . . ."

"That means she had none to call," Stegoman said grimly, "and no clan to protect."

Matt was silent, absorbing the idea of Dimetrolas as an outcast.

"You know what it means for a dragon to fly alone," Stegoman challenged.

"Since I met you while you were in exile yourself," Matt said, "I can guess."

"Would her clan have banished her if she were truly gentle and sweet, with her brash abrasiveness but a facade?"

Matt tried for the delicate touch. "There could be reasons for exile other than a disagreeable personality."

"Such as drunken flying, for one who becomes intoxicated from the fumes of his own fire," Stegoman said with a sardonic tone.

"Or being half dragon and half griffon," Matt reminded.

"Like our friend Narlh? True." But Stegoman's tone was thunderous, and the unspoken statement was there: any dragon who had committed a crime great enough for banishment was a dragon to be avoided—the kind who would make your life miserable, or even very short.

Matt might have pointed out that Dimetrolas didn't have the look of a murderer or traitor about her, but he had sense enough to realize that conversation had awakened Stegoman's memory of his own tatter-winged banishment, and that returning sober and self-possessed, and being hailed as a hero among his own kind, had not completely erased the pain of that early trauma—indeed, that nothing ever could. Matt was shocked to realize that even now, ten years after his triumphant return to his clan, the humiliation of Stegoman's own exile made him doubt his worth as a dragon, as an individual, and most especially as a mate.

It was time to shut up and let the obvious conclusion work itself out inside the dragon's mind.

* * *

Balkis and Anthony were still feeling hung over as they waved good-bye to the Piconyans and set out again on their northward journey. They were rather quiet—it had been an excellent party, and each was somewhat dazed by the realization that neither had made a fool of himself or herself. Indeed, in spite of the amount of wine they consumed, they had each kept their heads and asked many more questions than they answered, and listened far more than they talked.

The Piconyans, it turned out, were an outgoing and garrulous people, and had been all too glad to talk about themselves. In the process, Balkis and Anthony had learned a great deal about Piconyan ways and history—and imbibed a great deal of wine. Each had only sipped now and then, but the wine was served in bowls instead of cups, and the party lasted into the wee hours. The Piconyans, after all, had a great deal to celebrate, as they pointed out to Balkis and Anthony with lurid accounts of the carnage they would have discovered had they come near the end of the day instead of at its beginning.

Thinking of that now, Balkis shuddered. "It is only our good fortune that we did not come when the mass of the birds would have distracted us so with their pecking and clawing that we would have been unable to think of a spell."

"Very true," Anthony agreed, blinking.

"We need a guide," Balkis said with the labored speech of one who had to work hard to drag a coherent thought from the wine-soaked wreckage of her brain. "We need to travel with someone who can warn us of such dangers before we come to them."

"Dangers such as this war with the birds?"

"No, dangers such as Piconyan banquets! Let us ask at the next village we find."

Anthony held up a small wineskin. "The king gave me this and told me to drink a mouthful if my head pounded too heavily. Will you drink?"

Balkis gave the skin a jaundiced eye. "What does it hold?"

"Wine that the Piconyans have boiled until it is three times as strong as that which we drank. That is why a mouthful will suffice, the hetman said. He also said to put a thimbleful in any cup of water that we think may be bad."

Balkis shuddered. "If that is so much stronger than the wine that made my head ache as it does, put it away, good Anthony! It may do to purify water, but not my blood!"

The land became dryer and less fertile as they walked; forest and field gave way to open meadow, a grassland that stretched as far ahead as they could see. Groups of dots moved against that green background, dots that grew, as they came closer, into antelope and wild oxen.

"Where there are grass-eaters, the flesh-eaters follow," Anthony said, becoming tense, "and they may not care whose flesh they eat."

"I shall keep a spell ready to seal their jaws," Balkis promised, and began to work one out.

Before she needed it, though, the savannah narrowed to a river gorge, a valley filled with trees and bushes and the clustered cottages of human villages. With relief, Anthony and Balkis sought out a footpath and followed it down.

As they came out onto the valley floor, Anthony looked about him with a frown. "We have seen at least half this valley from above, but I have seen no fields, neither crops nor meadows for grazing."

"Perhaps they are in the half of the valley that we have not seen," Balkis suggested. "After all, we did see villages, and the people who live there must have some form of sustenance."

"Let us hope they look kindly upon travelers," Anthony said nervously.

The road led them through a grove, and Balkis stopped to inhale the scent. "How lovely! I never knew apples could smell so sweet!"

"Perhaps you have never been in an orchard." Anthony looked about him. "I have, though these trees are far larger than those that grow in my mountains." He frowned. "How poorly they are tended, though! I do not see a single tree but needs pruning, and the apples are so small! It is clear the farmer has not thinned his crop to let the fruits grow larger!"

"How strange to see one tree blooming while another bears ripe fruit," Balkis said, looking about her, "and another has tiny green apples, while a fourth's fruit is half grown."

"I had never thought what could happen in a climate where there is never autumn nor winter," Anthony said, "but only ever-lasting summer. It seems almost magical."

"It does, does it not?" Balkis frowned, then stilled, letting her thoughts settle and rest, opening her mind to such tendrils of magic that might coil about this grove.

Dimly, as though at a distance, she heard Anthony ask, "Balkis? What ails you?" But when she did not answer, he desisted, only watching. It warmed her to realize that he was alert for the slightest sign of danger, but knowing that she was a wizard, he would not disturb her unless one emerged.

The constant exposure to magical creatures during her infancy had left Balkis not only with an unusual talent for magic, but also with a sensitivity to it. Now she listened, open to the touch of its tendrils, and felt them all about her. Slowly, she stepped over to an apple tree, pressed a hand against the bark, and thought a question to the dryad that lived within it. Instantly she felt the answer, guarded but intrigued, and was quick to think through her early days, to remember the nixies she had met in Maracanda, the same who had taken charge of her when her mother had set the infant Balkis adrift in a trunk because the barbarians were invading the city. Appeased, the dryad now gave her silent permission to walk her grove, gave her the freedom of the valley, and Balkis withdrew her hand, knowing that word would pass from spirit to spirit as soon as the human folk were asleep and the dryads felt free to come forth from their trees to play and celebrate life. Slowly, she let herself return to the world, feeling her pulse gradually speed up, felt the breeze on her cheek and the perfume of the apple trees become more vivid, until she was back in the world again.

She turned to Anthony with a smile. "There is magic here indeed, but it welcomes us and will protect us."

"Will protect you, rather," Anthony said with a smile, "but I suppose that as long as I am with you, I shall be safe, too."

"You shall be, surely." Balkis reached out to take his hand

with a smile. "Come, let us find a village. If the valley itself welcomes us, can its people do less?"

Fortunately, the answer turned out as she hoped—the people were friendly indeed, and just as welcoming as the Piconyans.

The apple grove opened out suddenly into a meadow filled with a score of round, straw-roofed cottages circling a central green. Some of the people practiced archery on the common while others carved statues or painted landscapes on the walls of their houses. Nearer to Balkis and Anthony, a circle of people sat with strange-looking but beautifully crafted musical instruments, setting up harmonies that were strange, almost weird, but hauntingly beautiful.

"What a handsome people they are!" Balkis exclaimed.

"They are indeed," Anthony agreed. "I see no one fat and no one skinny, and all have that lovely bronze-toned skin." He smiled. "How wonderful it must be to live in a land where you never need wear more than a loincloth! Though I must admit theirs are wrapped to cover the sides."

"The women's sarongs are beautiful in their jewel tones," Balkis said, "and how exquisitely they are patterned! Indeed, their weavers must love their craft."

"Love it, yes," Anthony marveled. "One more art among many. Does no one here actually work?"

One of the musicians heard; he looked up with curiosity, and all the others, seeing him, followed his gaze. Then they put down their instruments and rose as the first advanced, holding up an open palm in greeting and dazzling them with a broad smile. As he came close, Anthony and Balkis had to hide their expressions of surprise. Apparently they weren't successful, for the villager smiled and said, "Yes, you thought we were as tall as you, only farther away, did you not?"

"Of course," Balkis stammered, "for you are of the same proportions as we."

"Certainly! How could you know that we only came up to your waists?" the villager asked. "Welcome to Pytan, O Strangers. I am Rokin."

"I am Balkis, and he is Anthony," Balkis said, imitating the stranger's sign of greeting.

"We hope you have news of the great world outside our valley," Rokin said. "We will trade you songs for tales."

"We know something of what moves outside," Balkis said, smiling, "though we have traveled too fast for any news to catch up with us."

"At the least," Anthony put in, "we can tell you of the marvels that lie to the south, if you can tell us what you know of the obstacles ahead of us to the north."

"Do you travel to the north, then?" Rokin asked.

"We do, and my home is in the southern mountains."

"Then you are of the breed that Alexander's soldiers sired when they sought to conquer the hills!" Rokin shook his head in amazement. "It must be uncanny to live on land that slopes."

Anthony grinned. "It seems strange to me to see people dwell and farm on land that is level . . . well, it did seem strange when I started out."

"You have heard all we have to tell, then," Balkis said with disappointment.

"Surely not, for even in this little valley we hear the echoes of great battles and arrogant horsemen who sweep across broad plains, seeking to rule the world!"

Several of the Pytanians shuddered at the thought, but one said, "It must be amazing to be able to stand in one place and see completely to the horizon."

"I thought so, too," Anthony admitted, "the first time I came down to the desert to sell food to the caravans."

"Caravans!" cried several, their eyes lighting with wonder, and the young man said, "Strings of camels that sway on their way, eastward to China, westward to Samarkand and Persia, northward to Maracanda! Fabled cities and lands of wonder! We know only those that travel northward, and we must wander a day's march to meet them, so we see them rarely! Oh, tell us of them!"

"I can tell you little," Balkis said with a laugh, "though I can speak of Bordestang and the forests of Allustria, even some little about the Arabian galleys and the people of India."

"Tell us, tell us!" the Pytanians chorused, and led them to

the village green, where they sat around an empty firepit to listen eagerly.

Anthony looked around, disconcerted.

"You are looking for food and drink, are you not?" Rokin said, somewhat chagrined. "Panyat, I pray you bring a dozen of the finest apples."

The young man who had marveled at the thought of plains ducked into one of the straw-roofed stucco cottages.

"We do not eat or drink, as you do," one of the women said apologetically. "The scent of our apples is sustenance enough for us."

Indeed, every one of the villagers was bringing out an apple from a cleverly concealed pocket and waving it under his or her nose. Panyat reappeared with a bowl of beautiful rosy fruit in the crook of his arm, so perfect that Balkis noticed that the apples the villagers held had each the marks of insects or the lopsided shape that comes from growing too closely. In his other hand he carried a pottery beaker of clear water which he set down at their feet. "We always keep water near for washing," he explained, "for we love to be clean. I hope this will suffice as drink."

Balkis lifted her beaker and sipped. "Oh, how delicious! It is delightfully cool."

Anthony rolled a sip over his tongue as though he were tasting the Piconyans' wine and nodded. "Cool indeed, and with a wonderful tang to it."

"Has it really?" Panyat asked, intrigued. "To us it is merely water, for we do not taste of it."

"At least you will never be drunk," Balkis said with a laugh.

"Drunk?" Rokin asked, and the crowd murmured echoes of the word, puzzled.

"The dizziness that comes from drinking too much wine," Balkis explained, "such as your neighbors to the south make by pressing the juice from grapes and letting it ferment."

"What is 'ferment'?"

That took a bit more explaining and led to a discussion of the green grapes of Allustria and their wine-making, which led to the tale of Balkis' travels from Europe to Maracanda.

Anthony listened, as rapt as any of the Pytanians, and when they scoffed in disbelief at her tales of genies and evil sorcerers, Anthony staunchly assured them that if Balkis said it, it must be true. He did not say, though, that she had gone through half her travels as a cat, though she could see in his gaze that he suspected it. After all, he had never heard any of this, either.

When the Pytanians had left them alone in a guest cottage, Anthony asked her, "Did you really travel with the Lord Wizard of Merovence?"

"I did, and you need not look so impressed," Balkis said with a smile, "for I am sure you have scarcely heard of Merovence."

"Well, then, glad I am to have heard of it now! What is he like, this Lord Wizard?"

"A gentleman who is modest to a fault, completely faithful to his wife, devoted to her and to his children, and exceedingly patient with a skeptical, mocking maiden," Balkis told him.

Anthony frowned. "You make him sound like any good householder!"

"He is that."

"But does he not have a towering presence and a countenance of ivory? An imposing mien? An aura of mystery and magic?"

"He is on the tall side," Balkis admitted, "but as to the rest of it, he looks quite ordinary, even handsome for a man of his age. As to his aura of magic, though, he does his best to hide it and appear like any other man."

"Why?" Anthony said, flabbergasted. "Would he not want men to know his greatness?"

"I do not think he believes in it himself," Balkis confessed. "Besides, by appearing to be as ordinary as the people around him, he hears a great deal more than he would if they stared at him in awe."

That made sense to Anthony, she could see, but he was still puzzling over a mighty wizard trying to look ordinary as he fell asleep.

Balkis fell asleep thinking of Matt, too, and marveled that she thought of him only as another man. Her childish infatuation with him seemed to have disappeared. She wondered why, and decided that perhaps she was growing up.

The next morning, when they had breakfasted on more apples and thanked their hosts for a night's lodging, Balkis asked them, "Do you know where we might find a guide for hire?"

"A guide?" Rokin asked.

"Someone who knows the country between here and Maracanda," Balkis explained, "who can warn us of the pitfalls that lie ahead and lead us around the worst of them."

"Why, that I can do!" Panyat said, stepping forward, eyes shining. "At least as far as the border of Prester John's land." He turned to Rokin. "May I accompany them, hetman?"

"You have already had your year of wandering, Panyat," Rokin said with a frown.

"Yes, but not my fill of travel! Indeed, it is only because I have wandered toward the north that I could be of any use to these strangers."

Balkis' hopes rose. "We shall pay him a golden coin."

"Gold means little to us here," Rokin said, frowning.

"But it means much to the caravan traders who bring the luxuries we cannot make," Panyat pointed out, "and I shall return knowing where to find them. You were saying only yesterday that it would be good to have more northern ivory with which to fashion statues of the goddess."

"We have always traded apples, and our weavings," Rokin told him.

"But it would take so many tapestries to buy one small ivory tusk! I shall bring back the gold coin for the village, Rokin, not for myself."

An older woman stepped forth from the crowd, resting a hand on Panyat's shoulder. "There is no reason why he should not go, Rokin."

"The wide world is dangerous, Mishara," Rokin reminded her. "Your son might not come back to you."

"His chances are far better with these good people to ward him, especially since they are wizards, and therefore better able to protect themselves and him!"

"Aye, let him go," said an older man, stepping up to take Mishara's hand. "We must risk him in order to keep him, for if we do not, he will someday leave us."

"None of us can leave our apples for long, for we would die without their scent, Haramis." But Rokin was weakening.

"The traders assure us that there are apple trees in other lands," Haramis returned. "That is why they insist on so many for one little tusk."

"True enough, though I suspect ours have a far sweeter taste than any others they have eaten." Rokin sighed. "Very well, let him go—but see he is well supplied."

They left soon after, Panyat leading the way out of the valley of apples. He wore a wide sash around his waist, a sash that bulged all along the front.

Balkis counted the bulges and said, "Only three apples? Can that be enough to take you to the borders of Prester John's kingdom and back?"

"Easily, friend Balkis." Panyat looked back with a smile. "I need only their scent, after all."

The ant couldn't understand why it was taking so long to reach his stolen property. It knew those confounded humans were carrying the gold nugget, but why was it taking so long to catch up with them? Surely its encounters with all the things that tried to eat it hadn't delayed it all that long—had they? Though of course, once it had defeated them, eating had taken much longer than if it had been traveling with a score of its fellow workers. It didn't realize how much more slowly it had been traveling with an overfull stomach, but it couldn't resist eating as long as there was food.

Now, though, it was hungry again, and had come across a trail of honey that it followed avidly, licking the sweetness from the rocks on which it had been spread. It didn't fear the bees that had made the amber delicacy, for it knew they were small inconsequential things that would only try to strike it with their tails—as though that could do any good!

Then it rounded a rock, and saw the honey's source.

CHAPTER 18

The trail of honey came not from a hive, but from the mouth of a man lying on his belly, chin propped on his fists and mouth open with his tongue out—and that tongue was three feet long and fragrant with the sweet aroma!

Well, food was food. The ant started toward the man. Obviously he had set his mouth as a trap for ants. Well, he had caught one.

The man looked just as surprised as the ant felt, but he grinned with hunger and his tongue leaped into the air, swinging sideways at the ant. It glittered as it came.

The ant danced aside and the tongue smacked the ground, then rose again with a dozen pebbles sticking to it. The ant realized it would have stuck just as firmly to itself, possibly even with its legs in the air, helpless, waiting to be dashed against a rock. But it dodged the tongue again and, before it could swing a third time, dashed in to counterattack. Startled, the anteater man rolled up on his side, swinging a fist—but the insect leaped onto the arm and scuttled up to the shoulder, remembering how it had dealt with the uniped. All these humans were built alike, after all, and the neck was always on top of the shoulders.

Under the circumstances, perhaps it was justifiable that the ant ate the anteater.

As they walked northward the land grew daily more arid; grass gave way to rock, and trees to low thornbushes, though there was still the occasional small, tortured pine tree—usually dead and dry. Finally, when they had been traveling a week, they topped a rise and saw, stretching away before them, a rolling beige wasteland where nothing grew and nothing moved, except dust-devils and blowing tendrils of sand.

Balkis stared. "How beautiful—and how terrible! What is this place, Panyat?"

"It is called the Sea of Sand, Balkis—and it is a sea indeed, though one without water."

"A dry sea?" asked Anthony, who had never seen a body of water larger than a pond. "How can that be?"

"It seems still now," Panyat said, "but look at it again tomorrow from this same place and you will see a completely different picture. Each dune will have moved a dozen feet or so; some will have changed their shapes, and others will have disappeared completely. The sand is always moving, though far slower than water. It swells into waves like the sea and is never still, always slipping, remounding, and being blown about like salt spray—or as the traders tell me seawater is blown." He smiled sheepishly.

"It is beautiful." Anthony stared, dazed. "But it is terrible, too. So vast, and without moisture! How are we to cross it? Even our feet will sink in with every step!"

"That much we can cure with the aid of yonder tree." Panyat pointed to one of the dead pines. "We must cut wood, split it into planks, and tie them to our feet."

"Of course!" Anthony cried. "If it is like the water of a sea, it is even more like snow! We must make sand skis!"

"If that is your name for them, of course." But Panyat frowned. "What is 'snow'?"

Anthony and Balkis took turns explaining about the magical white powder that fell from the sky, mounded up into drifts, and pressed itself into ice by its own weight. Then they had to explain what ice was, and finished by telling Panyat that when spring came, the ice turned to water.

"Truly your mountains are lands of wonder!" the Pytanian responded.

Anthony laughed. "Your valley of apple trees seems just as magical to me, friend Panyat, as do your people. How wonderful would it be to survive on the aroma of our food alone in the dead of winter!"

When they had fashioned their skis, Anthony and Balkis

made a meal of hardtack and dried pork, with Pytanian apples for dessert—they had each packed a considerably greater number than Panyat brought. He managed quite well by sniffing one of his own.

"It is amazing how long our stores have lasted," Anthony said.

Balkis nodded. "We have been lucky to find game, and nuts and berries, so often."

"And the hospitality of those we have met," Anthony agreed. "Still, long though they have lasted, our supplies are very low."

Balkis shrugged. "Scarcely surprising, since we have been on the road two months now. They should last until we have crossed this desert, though."

They slept through the rest of the day in the shade of a boulder, then set out across the sand-sea at night. Very quickly, Anthony and Balkis lost their bearings. Balkis halted and asked, "How are we to know the way? Every dune looks like every other, when we are down here among them!"

Panyat pointed at the sky. "In the desert, you can always see the stars—and though they move through the night, they turn like a wheel, and its hub is one star that moves very little. It lies in the north; therefore, as long as we keep it before us, we march toward the land of Prester John."

"So that is what the caravan drivers mean when they say they follow the North Star!" Anthony exclaimed.

"You have seen it before?" Panyat asked.

Anthony nodded. "There is little else to see, in a mountain winter—but the cold makes the sky clear and the stars bright. We can tell the hour by their positions."

Panyat grinned. "Then there is little chance of your becoming lost, so long as you remember where to find the center of your clock."

They shuffled on through the night, and the sand-skiing was hard enough work that there was little breath to spare for conversation. They halted to rest at midnight, though, and Balkis asked, "Where shall we spend the day?"

"At an oasis I know," Panyat told them. "During my wander-year, I traveled with the traders all the way across this desert.

They knew how to follow a line of oases so that they never had to go more than three nights without fresh water."

"That," said Anthony, "has the sound of an underground river that comes to the surface now and again."

"Perhaps it is," Panyat replied, "but legend says the first caravan master told a djinni where to seek the most lovely djinniyah in the world, and in return the djinni dug him a string of wells from here to the northern edge of the desert. The oases sprang from those wells."

"As well the one explanation as the other." Balkis rose, dusting her hands and taking up her curving pine ski-poles. "But dawn will come and find us nowhere near your oasis, Panyat. Let us walk."

They shuffled rather than walking, but made surprisingly good time for so slow a mode of travel, reaching the first oasis when the east had begun to brighten with dawn. There, they washed their faces and hands, refilled their waterskins, and made a breakfast of hardtack and jerky. Panyat watched with amusement, sniffing his apple. They took turns telling stories as they ate, and Balkis was fascinated to discover how easily and naturally Anthony's speech fell into meter and rhyme. They fell asleep in the shadow of palm trees before the sun rose, and slept through the day.

They rose as the sun was setting, ate again, and set out on their night's journey. Thus they traveled from one oasis to another. Anthony and Balkis could see the fear in one another's faces when they had camped for two nights in a row and their water was growing low, but Panyat always led them to another oasis before that third dawn.

Still, he noticed their anxiety, and as they pitched camp at the fourth oasis he told them, "Sleep a little longer today, and when the sun has set I shall show you how to find food, even in this desert."

"Where?" Anthony looked about at the waste around them, totally confounded.

"You shall see," Panyat promised, "and there is no point in my telling you, for you would never believe me without seeing it."

He was right—they never would have believed him. They

had trouble enough taking him seriously when he showed them how to weave nets of palm fronds and bury them in the sand sideways, with one handle sticking up. When the handle trembled, Panyat said, "Now! Pull it up!"

Anthony yanked as hard as he could, Balkis caught the rim of the basket as it surfaced and threw her weight against it, and the basket sailed clear of the sand. In it was a flat, foot-long fleshy slab, about an inch deep and four wide, and pointed on each end. It thrashed and leaped.

"Hold it up by its tail!" Panyat directed.

"Which end is that?" Anthony cried in dismay.

"The end without the eyes!" Balkis answered, and caught it as Panyat meant. She had to use both hands to hold it up, head pointing downward, while Anthony hovered, ready to catch it if it slipped through her fingers, but the creature rapidly stilled. Then Anthony was able to make out two spots a bit darker than the tan of the rest of its body, but nothing he would have called eyes.

"Hanging like that freezes them, for some reason," Panyat said. "Now you may chop off its head, grill it, and feed upon it."

He turned away with a shudder.

Balkis stared at him in distress, but Anthony said, "Unlike him, we must eat," and took the creature, to prepare and cook it.

From her earliest days, when Balkis had been saved by nixies, she had not eaten fish, out of respect for the water-spirits. But these fish surely had little to do with water, and with her hunger now, she looked forward to eating.

"What are these called?" Anthony asked Panyat as the tantalizing aroma rose into the night.

"The traders call them sandfish," the Pytanian answered, still with his back turned. "After all, if this is a sea of sand, why should it not have fish? They come to the surface about an hour after sundown. Only then can you catch them, for they swim too deeply during the day."

It was surprisingly tasty, a savory flavor with a smoky overtone, though that could have been the result of the dried palm fronds that made their fire. Every night thereafter, Balkis and

Anthony caught three or four of the fish, and found there were many different kinds, from half a foot long to two feet, with many different flavors. Apparently, they weren't the only ones eating them, for several of the larger fish had smaller ones in their stomachs. Panyat always refused to look until they assured him that the meal was already cooked. The strips of crisp flesh bore so little resemblance to the whole fish that he could watch them eat without having to remember from where the food had come.

When they came to the fifth oasis, though, they found trouble. The pool teemed with water snakes, and Balkis drew back with a cry of distress. Anthony came at the run, saw, and blanched. "Quickly, away! They might squirm out onto land!"

They backed quickly, then watched warily, but the snakes seemed quite content in their watery home, darting and coiling and flashing about to feast on their smaller cousins.

"How can we dip up water?" Balkis asked, at a loss.

"We dare not," Anthony said, tight-lipped. "There are so many that we cannot hold a waterskin under long enough to fill before one of them bites us—and they might be poisonous! Indeed, their very presence may have contaminated the water."

Panyat stared at the pond, appalled. "These snakes were not here when I came by with the caravan last year!"

Balkis turned to him with narrowed eyes, thinking. "Someone may have brought in a mating couple," she said after a moment, "but surely so many could not have grown from one gravid female in a year! Someone has polluted this pool deliberately."

"Who, though?" Panyat asked.

Anthony gazed at Balkis and read her face. "Whoever did it could not have had us in mind, sweet lady. How could they have known we were coming?"

"A good question," said Balkis, "and I would dcarly love to know the answer." She turned to Panyat. "Perhaps we should not stay here today."

The Pytanian looked out over the desert to their north. "It

is only false dawn, and we could march another mile before the sun rises—but what if there is no shelter?"

"They we shall have to fashion a tent of our cloaks and our staves," Anthony told him, "but I think Balkis is right. I could not sleep with so many vipers nearby. Let us go."

They set out across the desert again, but Anthony was unusually silent. Finally Balkis asked, "What are your thoughts?"

"Hm?" Anthony looked up with a start. "Oh, only wondering how snakes would taste, and if there is any way to be sure their poison does not infect their meat."

Balkis smiled. "We lack time to experiment, sweet friend. Yonder is a dune with a face to the north; it should shade us for most of the day. Come, let us make a tent.

The day was a torment of thirst. Fortunately, they were able to fall asleep through the worst of it, but when they woke in the twilight, they were parched. Balkis and Anthony took only two swallows of water each, then asked Panyat, "How far to the next oasis?"

"I fear this is one that is three days distant," he said mournfully.

"Three days!" Balkis's mouth already felt like cracked leather. "How shall we last so long?"

"We shall have to ration the water very strictly," Anthony said grimly, "only one mouthful an hour."

But Balkis had to remind him to take even that. Several times in the next few nights, she caught him pretending to drink when he really did not. "I shall endure as well as you," she scolded. "Do not save your water for me! If we meet danger, we most both be able to fight!"

Anthony drank.

But three nights later, they still had not found the oasis.

"I am sure we have traveled in the correct direction!" Panyat said, on the verge of panic.

"Then we shall come to it." Balkis clasped his shoulder. "Fear not, friend. We go more slowly when we are thirsty, that is all."

They dared not eat salt beef when they had so little water, and the hardtack was almost gone. That evening, their traps caught no fish.

"I fear that even the sandfish do not like to go too far from water," Anthony sighed.

"It is not that," Panyat sighed. "It is only that they stay close to the rim of the desert, and we have traveled beyond their range."

"The oasis cannot be too far away now," Balkis said, and they marched hungry that night.

About midnight, they drank their last swallows of water. Anthony turned his waterskin upside down with a moan, catching the last few drops in his palm and licking them up.

When they stopped to rest an hour later, Panyat took out one of his apples, sniffed it, and held it out to them with a sigh. "Take and eat it, friends. There is moisture in it, and food enough to keep you another mile."

Anthony stared at the apple and swallowed convulsively but said, "Thank you, good Panyat, but I could not. You will need its aroma for many miles yet."

"Nor can I." But Balkis couldn't tear her gaze away from the lovely fruit. "Your health and vitality are far more important to us now than food, for without you we would be completely lost."

Panyat took the apple back, looking unhappy, but he tucked it back into his pouch with a sigh of relief. "We might have to go another night before we come to the next oasis," he warned. "I have lost my sense of time, for I can no longer judge our pace."

Small wonder that he couldn't—their feet dragged, and Balkis had begun to feel as though she were climbing a steep hill when she was walking on level ground. Anthony leaned heavily on his staff, his face drawn and pale under his suntan. On they went, forgetting why, only knowing that they had to raise each foot, swing it ahead, and set it down, following Panyat, who walked straight, sniffing now and again at an apple—but even he had begun to lean more heavily on his staff, weighted down by responsibility and the guilt they had told him he should not feel.

In spite of his warning of a fifth night, the sky's eastern glow showed them the silhouettes of palm trees.

Anthony ran toward them with a glad cry and an aching, waddling gait, but Balkis caught him and cried, "Not yet!"

They leaned together for a minute of sheer exhaustion. Panyat turned back and said, "She has the right of it. Those palms are a mile and more away." But his eyes glowed, and his face seemed to sag with relief.

On they slogged, mouths and throats dry, their steps wobbling now—but they managed to struggle to the palms before Anthony tripped on his own feet and fell. Balkis knelt to help him, but before she could pull him up, Panyat came to her with cupped hands holding an ounce or two of water. "Quickly, drink! Before it trickles away."

Balkis sipped the water gratefully, then held the last mouthful on her tongue and, with a supreme act of will, pressed her lips against Anthony's. They stayed obdurately closed, so she levered them a little apart with her tongue and let a little water trickle in against his teeth. His whole body stiffened; then his lips opened, and she let the water pour into his mouth. He licked her lips to draw the last drop, froze, then kissed her in earnest.

A minute later, she lifted her head with a gasp, then a shaky laugh. "What a pity that I am too weary and too thirsty to enjoy that as I should!"

"I am not." Anthony gazed up into her eyes with adoration. "Angel of mercy, who brings water in the desert!"

"In the oasis, rather, and it was Panyat who brought it." She turned away, feeling the need of a change of subject, and shrugged her flacid waterskin off her shoulder. "Please fill this, good Panyat, for I fear my companion will not go to the water yet."

"I shall crawl if I must," Anthony insisted.

"That would not be good for you," Balkis told him. "Your clothes are worn thin as it is." She managed to prop him up against a huge boulder that rose out of the sand like an exclamation of surprise.

It was only a minute or two before Panyat brought the waterskin back, bulging and wet. Balkis gave it to Anthony, but after a single swallow, he gave it back to her. "Strange—it had the taste of cherries."

"Strange indeed!" Balkis drank a single swallow too, then

handed it to him again with wide eyes. "Stranger still, my drink tasted like a pear!"

Anthony took another mouthful, swallowed, and said, "Pomegranate."

Balkis took back the skin, drank, and said, "Lemon."

"I pray you, do not drink too deeply!" Panyat said, alarmed. "A horse in the caravan did that, and he foundered!"

"I have no wish to become sick from too much water after too little," Balkis agreed. "Only one more." She drank, raised her eyebrows in surprise. "Mint!"

Anthony took the skin and rolled his last sip around his mouth as he handed the skin back. "Almond. What manner of pool is this, friend Panyat, that changes flavor with every sip?"

"Whatever kind it is, it is welcome," Balkis said, but she hid misgivings. She pressed the waterskin back into Panyat's hands. "You must keep this for us awhile, my friend."

Panyat took it reluctantly. "I cannot understand how this oasis came to be here. I do not remember one where the water was so various in flavor."

"Perhaps it was only that we took so much longer in coming to it," Balkis offered.

Panyat shook his head and pointed to the boulder behind Anthony. "That was not there on my last trip—not in the sixth oasis or in any other. I saw several like it as I rode with the caravan, but none were anywhere near an oasis."

Balkis felt a chill down her spine, but she forced a smile. "Perhaps some djinni took pity on us and made it for us."

"Perhaps," said Panyat, "but if so, he must have stolen away the oasis I thought to reach two nights ago." His expression became somber. "Either that, or I have lost my way and know not where we are, or where we are going."

"You have not lost your way," Anthony assured him. "I have watched the stars as closely as you have. The North Star is still before us, and at midnight, if I lift my left arm straight out from the shoulder, my fingers still point at the Archer."

"I thank you, Anthony." Panyat looked relieved, "It would seem this oasis is magical indeed."

"Magical or not, I feel as though I am made of sand myself, so encrusted is my skin," Balkis told them. "Avert your eyes, gentlemen—I mean to bathe."

"That will be mean to me indeed," Anthony sighed, but he turned to look out at the sunrise and said to Panyat, "Is it not amazing how the brightest stars may still be seen even in the sun's glow?"

"That is why we call that one the morning star." Panyat pointed. "We call it the Apple Maiden."

"My folk call it Aphrodite, for the goddess of love," Anthony replied, and they engaged in an earnest discussion of astrology while Balkis went down to the pool, took off her robes, scanned the water anxiously for snakes and, not finding any, waded in. The water was a blessing on her skin, and as she luxuiated in the bath, her thoughts drifted to the puzzle of its presence. She wondered who had really ordered her kidnapping, and if someone else had intervened to send her to Anthony. If so, the kidnapper might have filled the fifth oasis with snakes to stop her, and her invisible guardian might have directed their steps to this, an oasis Panyat hadn't known.

Her skin was parchment drinking up moisture, but she knew the sun would rise to bake her in minutes, so she stayed only long enough to wash away the dust of the trip, then came out, wrapped herself in her outer cloak, and told Anthony, "You may bathe now."

"Do I smell so strongly as that? But I know I must." Anthony made no request for privacy, but Balkis gave it to him anyway, feeling almost prim as she resisted the temptation to peek. Truth to tell, the thought also frightened her a little.

She ignored it and discussed their route with Panyat, guessing at landmarks that of course would have been buried by shifting sand during the last year. It was only minutes till Anthony rejoined them, again decently clad, though he grumbled, "Not much use to sluice the dust from my body, when I cannot purge it from my clothes!"

"Perhaps we shall find clean garments at the desert's edge," Balkis cajoled. "For myself, I feel remarkably refreshed."

"So do I, to tell the truth." Anthony stretched and sighed with pleasure, then froze, frowning. "How odd! I look within myself and find no hollow. I am no longer hungry, though I have not eaten!"

"Perhaps you have drunk too much, after all," Panyat said nervously.

"Perhaps," Balkis agreed, "or perhaps this water is more blessed than we think. My appetite, too, is sated. Come, let us fill our skins. If this water has such virtues as it seems, we must take as much as we can!"

They filled the skins, then lay down in the shade of the boulder and slept deeply and well, then woke in the twilight—and stared about them in disbelief. It was Anthony who spoke it first. "Where has our oasis gone?"

The sand stretched wide and empty for miles around.

CHAPTER 19

Balkis looked about her, wide-eyed, upon awakening. As she recalled, they had come to another oasis, bathed in it and drunk of its tasty water before going to sleep. "Has someone taken us from it while we slept?" she said now. "I see no palm trees, no pond, not even a puddle!"

"But I see the rock." Anthony looked up at the boulder in whose shade they had slept. "It is the same as it was last night."

Balkis looked, too, gave the stone a long and searching examination, then nodded. "You speak truly. It is the same."

"Could someone have moved both us and it?" Panyat asked.

"Not without waking us, unless they wielded mighty magic," Balkis answered.

"Less magic than it took to make the oasis disappear?" Anthony asked.

Balkis looked sharply at him, but he had not spoken in sarcasm—his face was open and confused. She considered the matter. "No, it would have required more magic," she said, "but not of a kind to wake us."

"How is that?" Anthony was befuddled.

"If someone created the oasis by magic," Balkis said, "all they would have to do, during the day, was let that magic fade, to cease supporting the illusion."

"If that was an illusion," Anthony said, "it was a most convincing one. I can still feel the water on my skin and taste its various flavors." He frowned. "Though an illusion would explain the changes in its taste. Still, I am no longer thirsty—

nor hungry." He held up his waterskin to demonstrate—then stared at it. The skin was as flat as slate.

"Strange," Panyat said nervously. "I did not know this oasis, and now it has disappeared. I think I would like to be gone from this place. Come, let us be off to the next oasis as quickly as we may."

"Quickly indeed," Anthony concurred, "and let us hope it is there, and real!"

They set off following the north star, shuffling their skis through the sand more quickly than usual. Illusion or not, the pond had renewed their strength. They traveled quickly.

Someone else traveled even more quickly.

About midnight, Anthony looked back to see if he could still spy the boulder where they had spent the day and yelped with dismay. "What is that which cuts the sand and comes toward us?"

Panyat and Balkis turned to look, too, and saw a great curve-sided triangle with a rounded tip moving toward them. Balkis gripped Anthony's hand. "I have seen such a thing on a lord's crest—but it was on the back of a dolphin."

"What is a dolphin?" Anthony asked.

"It is fantastical good luck!" Panyat cried. "The traders told me about them, but I never thought to see one! Step back from its path—but as it passes, leap and catch hold of that fin!"

They stood, waiting, as the huge fin rushed toward them. "What is it?" Balkis asked.

"A giant sandfish, and we can ride its back to our oasis!"

"Let us hope it does not mean to revenge its smaller cousins," Anthony said nervously.

"I think we need not worry about that," Balkis said. "It probably has a goodly number of them in its belly."

The sand hissed as the huge fin sped toward them.

"Now!" Panyat cried. They ran and leaped to catch the huge fin. Anthony's fingers closed on it first. Balkis clung to him, then swept an arm around Panyat. He clung to her while he set his feet down, then sat, gaining a secure hold. "We are well aboard now, I think," he said. "Anthony, have you a rope in your pack?"

"Of course," Anthony said, "but I am reluctant to loose my hold on this fin."

"Then, Balkis, would you dig out that rope and tie Anthony to the fin, so he can sit down on this creature's back? Then we can sit with him and hold onto his rope."

"A good plan," Balkis said, and did as he asked.

Pressing against Anthony while she cast the rope about the fin aroused the pleasant but frightening feelings that were quickly becoming familiar—and less alarming. Still, when they were all sitting on the creature's back, holding fast to the rope, there were only Anthony's eyes, shining in the moonlight as they gazed at her, and the admiring smile on his lips—and, of course, the moonlight itself . . .

Glad that Panyat was there, she tore her gaze away from Anthony's and asked, "How long should we ride this monster fish?"

"Until we come to the next oasis." Panyat smiled into the breeze of the fish's passage, his hair blowing behind him. "It will certainly be quicker than walking—and far less tiring."

Eventually they saw the oasis, far away on the eastern horizon. "Is that it?" Anthony pointed toward the palm trees, silhouetted against the reddening sky.

"It is indeed!" Panyat replied. "We would not have come to it for another day if we'd had to walk. Perhaps we should stay with this fish awhile longer."

"How far is the next oasis?" Balkis asked uneasily.

"Only a night's travel—or half that, at this fish's speed."

"If we had water," Anthony said, "I would not hesitate for a minute."

"Are you thirsty, then?" Balkis asked.

Anthony thought about it, then said, "No. It seems the water at that disappearing oasis has sustained me."

Panyat pointed east. "The palm trees have sunk below the horizon."

Balkis gazed at the flat sand stretching to the rose-colored sky and felt apprehension coil in the pit of her stomach. Still, the die was cast, so she said, "Let us drape our cloaks over our heads—and Panyat, do you sit in their shadow. If we are to stay with this fish, we must travel through the day."

But the heat wasn't a problem after all, for the fish actually traveled faster in the daylight, stirring up a breeze that kept them cool. They chatted idly, comparing more tales and exchanging songs, and never thirsted, thanks to the magical oasis.

"Amazing!" Matt said, looking down at the beige waste below them. "You'd swear it was an ocean, with those waves of sand dunes rolling across it!"

"If they roll, they roll very slowly," Stegoman said.

"Just a matter of rate," Matt said. "Watch it in time lapse and you'll see it move like an ocean."

Stegoman frowned. "What is 'time lapse'?"

"Watching it with time slowed down, so that its motion seems to be speeded up so much that a single day takes only a few minutes."

"Ah. Another one of your spells," Stegoman said, dismissing the matter.

His comment gave Matt pause. Could he craft a time lapse spell? Why not?

Better question: Why bother? But you never knew what spells might come in handy in this universe. Matt decided to try working this one out when they rested for the evening.

"There is a stripe of green ahead," Stegoman said.

Matt looked up, craning his neck and squinting. "I'll take your word for it, eagle eyes."

"Eagles," Stegoman said with disdainfully, "can see only a mile or so with any clarity."

"Nice to associate with a superior breed." For a dizzy moment Matt wondered what kind of country would select Stegoman for its national bird. He looked down and said, "But I can see a road, or some sort of track, anyway."

"A road indeed, and a traveler on it," Stegoman replied.

"Traveler?" Matt squinted and made out a dark speck. "Great! Let's drop down and ask him if he's seen anyone today."

"I suppose we must," Stegoman sighed, and banked into a downward spiral. "I assume I should land out of sight."

"It would help," Matt said, "though I don't think he's going to have too much doubt about where I came from."

Stegoman put a dune between himself and the traveler, then Matt hiked around the sandy hill. The traveler stopped as soon as he saw Matt, and waited, staff in hand but not leaning on it. Matt was automatically on his guard—the traveler had to connect him with the monster that had just flown overhead, but he looked neither frightened nor awed, only stood and waited. Also, he didn't seem to be fazed by the heat, but now that Matt was down and out of the wind of Stegoman's passage, he was already drenched with sweat and wilting.

Coming close enough to make out the traveler's features, Matt shuddered. The face was triangular, gaunt, snub-nosed and beardless, with a strange sheen to the pale skin and a hard glitter to the unwinking eyes. They stared, but without curiosity—or any other feeling Matt could detect. It made his skin crawl.

Still, politeness was an obligation, Matt told himself, then smiled and raised a hand in greeting. "Hail, traveler! May your journey be peaceful."

"And yours," the traveler answered with an oddly breathy voice. "What do you seek, stranger?"

"A young woman," Matt said, "a friend of mine, a former traveling companion." He waited for the suggestive comment, but when none came, he went on, even more uneasy. "She's about this high"—he held a palm up at shoulder height—"golden skin, black hair, last seen wearing white and gold robes."

"I have seen her." The traveler lifted his staff, turning to point toward the south. "She sojourned in a valley some distance yonder. There are two other valleys between, both of which hold little people. You must pass them and go to the third."

"Thanks!" Hope sprang, and Matt felt as though a weight had lifted off his shoulders; he'd been more worried than he'd let himself realize. "Was she . . . was she free? Happy?"

"Quite happy, so far as I could see, and quite friendly with the folk who dwelled there," the stranger said. "As to being free, she seemed to like the valley and had no desire to leave."

Suspicion stabbed at Matt, but he forced a smile and said, "Thanks. That's a huge relief. We'll go check it out."

"You should not arrive at night, or the people there will be wary," the stranger warned, "nor should you arrive in early morning, for they will be ill-tempered while they labor in the fields. But they stop to dine at noon and will then be more welcoming."

"Awfully nice of you to give us such great tips," Matt said slowly, though his brain was racing, seeking motives. He grinned, stepping forward quickly, hand out to shake. "Can't thank you enough."

The traveler gave his hand a hard-eyed stare, keeping his own palms deliberately on his staff, then lifted his hard glittering gaze to meet Matt's—and something flickered there. "You are welcome. Surely we of the road must aid one another."

"Surely we must." Matt lowered his hand, turned away—and lashed out a sweeping ankle-high kick.

It caught the traveler by surprise. He fell with a raging sound somewhere between a hiss and a roar—then froze, staring up the bright length of Matt's sword blade, feeling its tip poke his throat. "This is rude thanks for my courtesy."

"If it was courtesy. Stegoman! Help!"

Wings cupping thunder, the dragon was beside him, bellowing, "What moves?"

"Nothing, and I want to keep it that way. Hold him down, will you?"

At that the stranger writhed, trying to squirm away from the blade, but a huge claw descended, pressing into his chest. "Keep still," Stegoman rumbled, "for I have but to shift my weight, and you will be pinned to this road."

The traveler froze. Matt flicked his sword-point, untying the belt and opening the stranger's robe.

"Another of my kind!" Stegoman hissed, but the traveler hissed back and a forked tongue flicked out.

Matt saw a lean, sinuous body covered with iridescent scales. It had two arms and two legs, but nonetheless seemed more reptilian than mammalian, possibly because it had no genitalia. A bright circle winked on its chest, a medallion held around the creature's neck by a leather thong.

"You're as much snake as man," Matt said. "Who sent you here?"

"Monkeys chatter," the traveler hissed, "but they mean little."

Matt whipped his sword in a half-circle ending with the point at the creature's throat. "Snakes mean treachery. If you don't want an early molt, you'd better tell me your mission."

"Only warm-blooded fools would think molting a threat."

"Don't be too sure you can grow a new skin," Matt cautioned. "Who told you about this girl I mentioned?"

"You did, blind fool!"

"Enough of this game," Stegoman rumbled. "He will tell you nothing but more insults. Let me lean on him."

The stranger only hissed defiance.

"I think we might induce him to cooperate," Matt said, and chanted,

> "Once to every man and nation
> Comes the moment to decide.
> In the strife of Truth with Falsehood,
> For the good or evil side,
>
> New occasions teach new duties;
> Time makes ancient good uncouth;
> You must speak and fully answer
> From your knowledge of the Truth."

He didn't think Lowell would mind his patching verses from separate poems—after all, they dealt with the same topic.

"Now," he said, "who sent you?"

The traveler's lip writhed with scorn as it opened its lips—then its eyes went wide with shock as its tongue moved without its control and its voice said, "Kala Nag has sent me."

"What mission did she give you?"

This time the traveler clamped his jaws shut, his throat and face swelling with the effort of holding the answer in—but it burst out in hissing: "I am sent to stop the soul of destiny who could be her only serious impediment to conquering Prester John and his realm."

"An ambitious goal." Matt's eyes narrowed. "Why does she wish to conquer him?"

Again the struggle, again the bursting answer. "Because Prester John alone prevents her conquest of the rest of the world."

"She isn't modest in her expectations, our Kala Nag," Matt said. "Am I the soul of destiny? Is that why you tried to stop me?"

"Nay. You could aid the destined one, but you yourself are not."

Matt frowned, trying to puzzle out the cryptic comments, but sure they were true, and all the snakeman knew. "How will you know this soul of destiny?"

"There will be two traveling together," the snakeman answered, as though the words were torn from him. "For the aid you might give them, you must be stopped."

"Two?" Matt demanded. "Is one the woman of whom I told you?"

"Yes!" the snake screamed in torture.

"And the other?"

"The other is also young, is—" Then its hissing tore into a scream as its whole body burst into flames. An instant later it went limp, clearly dead, as inert as a log, though the blaze continued, consuming robe and skin.

Matt drew a shaky breath. "Well, that's one way to stop somebody from talking."

"A most gruesome way," Stegoman said, his voice hard, "though quick, at least."

"Yeah, the pain didn't last long at all. Still, if this is how Kala Nag rewards the followers who fail her, she must be as cold-blooded as her name."

"You know its meaning, then?" Stegoman asked.

"From a story I read when I was a kid," Matt said. "It means 'Black Snake.' "

"At least now we know what we seek," Stegoman said.

"Yeah." Matt turned away from the impromptu pyre and climbed back up to Stegoman's shoulders. "Somehow I doubt we'll find Balkis in that third valley to the south, Stegoman, and I'm very wary of landing there—but we'd better have a look, just to make sure."

"It should not take long," the dragon agreed, "and I am eager to be back in the clean air."

"Cool air, too." Matt wiped a hand across his brow. "How could that snakeman stand the heat?"

"He has cold blood, as do I," Stegoman reported, "though I think he would have sought the shade in an hour or so anyway."

"Yeah, this furnace sun would fry a stoker," Matt said. "Let's seek a bit of breeze, shall we?"

When night came, the giant sandfish did not slacken its speed, and Balkis asked, "How many more oases before the northern edge of the desert?"

"I have watched two pass us and fall astern," Panyat said, "so I calculate that only one remains."

Anthony gave a start, then looked about him at the empty sands. "The more fool I! I was so enwrapped in talk that I never noticed."

"Nor should you have," Panyat said, "for you did not know their distances. The last oasis was three days' journey from the edge of the desert, but this sandfish is going quickly now, very quickly. I think we might do well to stay as long as it travels northward."

"A good thought." But Balkis frowned. "I begin to thirst."

Before Panyat could answer, the fish began to turn. Balkis gave a yelp of surprise, thrown backward by the curve. Anthony tightened his hold on the dorsal fin and seized her wrist. Panyat went tumbling over her, though, and disappeared into the night with a cry of alarm.

"To him, quickly!" Balkis cried, and leaped off the sandfish. Anthony followed her, then ran to catch up as she sped back to the Pytanian.

"I am well, I am well!" Panyat protested, sitting up and brushing off sand. "My apologies, my friends—my clumsiness has lost us our steed."

"I think that it is well for us." Anthony pointed back along their trail.

Looking, Panyat and Balkis saw the great dorsal fin curving away, turning southwest, running back into the barren dunes.

"Why would it go back so suddenly?" Balkis asked, wide-eyed.

"It feeds upon the lesser sandfish." Panyat blanched at the thought. "That must be why it was coming north across the waste—because it had exhausted the shoals in the south, and fortunate we were to catch what we could before it came. Now, though, it has eaten all it can find here, for we have come too close to the northern edge of the desert for the small fish to swim. The giant must go west to find fresh prey."

"But if that is so," Balkis said, "our crossing is nearly done!"

Panyat faced north and inhaled deeply. He exhaled and said, "I think you may be right. Let us walk while we may."

They strapped their sand-skis on again and shuffled through the night. Balkis was feeling even thirstier now, but managed not to speak of it—one glance at Anthony's face showed that he was feeling it, too. She hoped they would soon find an oasis, if not the edge of the desert itself.

Through the darkest part of the night they traveled, speaking less and less as thirst sapped their energy. Finally, Anthony brought out a wineskin and offered it to Balkis. She stared. "From whence came that?"

"From Piconye," Anthony answered. "Do you not remember? Their king gave it to us as a parting gift."

"How welcome it is now!" Balkis said fervently as she took the skin. She squirted a few sips into her mouth, swallowed, then coughed and held it out, eyes bulging, hand at her throat. "Tay . . . take it, Anthony, but only a swallow!" she gasped, her voice hoarse. "It is terribly strong!"

"I had forgotten that." Anthony's face turned tragic. "Forgive me, sweet companion!"

"I shall thank you instead," she rasped, "for it is better than nothing—though not by much! Sip at it, Anthony. We shall surely make that last!"

Anthony drank, and they shuffled onward, following Panyat, who watched them with troubled eyes. Now and again they would stop and share a sip or two of brandywine, but the skin was still almost full when Balkis realized that she was hearing a distant roaring sound, had been hearing it for some time, but that it had grown louder so gradually that she had not remarked upon it.

"The river!" Panyat cried. "Hear you that sound? It is the river that flows into this sandy sea!"

Balkis stared. What manner of river made so much noise? Was it one huge waterfall?

"Then we have come to the end of the desert?" Anthony asked hopefully.

"To the end of the sandy sea, at least," Panyat said. "There is more desert between the seashore and the mountains, but it is far less harsh than this, and has more frequent water."

"That will be a blessing, certainly." The mere thought of water seemed to revive Anthony. "Come, Panyat, let us see this river of yours!" He set out at a quick pace.

Panyat looked up at the note of his voice and cautioned, "There is not much water there."

"Not much water?" Anthony stared. "How can there be a river without water?"

"Because it has many rocks," Panyat told him. "Come, you shall see for yourself."

They came to the river in the unreal half-light that comes as night is beginning to yield to day. First it was only a line of deeper darkness against lighter, but as they approached they saw it broaden even as its noise grew to thunderous proportions—not a roaring anymore, but a crunching and grinding. Coming closer, they stared in disbelief, for they saw a jumbled stream of rocks of all sizes, from boulders to pebbles, all turning against one another, over and over as they rolled on like a river swollen with springtime rain.

Anthony stared at it, aghast. "If there is any water in there, it would be death to dip for it!"

"Very true," Panyat said, "but there is moisture trapped beneath the stones, and if you dig a hole in the bank, it will fill with enough for a mouthful now and then. I saw the traders drink thus while they waited to cross."

"Waited to cross?" Balkis asked. "Did they not see a ford or a bridge?"

"There is none, for shallow or deep, the turning rocks would grind you to meal," Panyat said, "and none could build a bridge, for the pilings that hold it up would be swept away in minutes. For three days in the week it flows, casting up stones both great and small, and carries with it also wood to the sandy sea—but on the fourth day the river slows, then stills. Then we may cross it."

Balkis gazed out over the turning stones. "So we must wait three days?"

Panyat shrugged. "Perhaps three, perhaps one—perhaps even tomorrow the river will stop. Who knows on which of those three days we have come?"

As the day brightened, Balkis saw how the grinding rocks could carry wood—whole tree trunks slid along on its surface, the stones rolling beneath them. Following their course with her gaze, she saw the end of the river—the place where the huge stream of rocks and wood poured into the sandy sea, the stones and wood disappearing into the sand.

"Yonder is its ending!" Balkis pointed. "Can we not simply walk around it?"

"Nay, Balkis. You can see how the stones sink into the sand, how it swallows them up. It is a quicksand, and no one knows how far it extends."

"Do we have to cross the river at all?"

"Yes, for the land of Prester John is on the other side—far on the other side. This side leads only into more wasteland."

"A drink!" Anthony rose from kneeling beside a foot-wide hole, flourishing his waterskin triumphantly; it bulged very slightly at the bottom. He presented it to Balkis as though it were a treasure, which indeed it was.

"Many thanks, sweet fellow," she said, and upended the skin, letting a mouthful trickle past her lips. Then, with a supreme effort of will, she handed it back to Anthony.

He took and drank, too, afterward pushing the skin back into the hole he had dug. Looking out over the river, clear now in dawn's light, he said, "Can it be that all the sand of this sea has come from these rocks grinding themselves to powder as they flow?"

"Perhaps," Panyat said, "though I should think it would take a great many such rivers, and this is the only one of its kind in all the world—or so say the traders."

As the day brightened, Anthony's little well slaked their thirst a mouthful at a time; then he set himself to filling both waterskins. As he waited, Anthony scouted along the riverbank and gathered small branches and other bits of wood that had broken off the rolling trunks and been carried to the sides. As he stacked kindling and small sticks to build a fire, Balkis set out the baskets one last time. As Panyat had said, it was too shallow for good fishing, but they did catch several small sandfish and made one last meal of the savory creatures. Then Balkis and Anthony buried the butts of their branches in the sand and stretched their cloaks over the improvised frame to give them shelter from the sun.

They napped in the afternoon, sleeping peacefully in spite of the noise of the river—they had grown so used to it that it troubled them not at all.

The ant was faint with hunger; even for an ant, there was little to eat amidst the sand dunes. It had slowed to half its normal speed but kept plodding on as long as daylight lasted. Its thirst was raging; it had lost the humans' scent, but doggedly pushed ahead, sure it would find them. Poor insect, it could not know that it had strayed, that its path had curved amidst the shifting dunes, that it was far from their route of march.

Its antennae quivered; ahead, it detected moisture. Energy flowed, and it moved toward the source, if not with its old speed, at least faster than it had been going.

It came to an oasis and sped toward the water, ignoring the palm trees, the birds, the lizards that fled as the ant's acrid scent reached them, ignoring everything but the scent of water. It was a brackish pond, but it was wet, and the ant drank deeply. Finally, its thirst assuaged, it became aware of the pang of hunger again, and turned to seek the scent of living things.

They were all around it, six times as tall as it was, and all of them carried clubs.

Among the things the ant had ignored was the skin tents that circled the oasis, for it was home to a clan of humans—but rather strange humans, for their shoulders were level and uninterrupted by necks or heads. Instead, faces looked out of their chests, huge eyes just beneath the collarbones, mouths just beneath their rib cages. The women with babies in their arms stayed back by the tents, waiting curiously for the rest of the clan to deal with the little intruder. All the rest, men and women alike, gathered about the creature, raising clubs.

The ant ignored the clubs; all it knew was the scent of flesh. It charged the nearest of the men, then swerved at the last second to attack the woman beside him. Three clubs smashed into the earth behind it. The woman screamed in anger and swung; the ant shied in the nick of time, and the club pounded sand right in front of it. It leaped onto the wood and ran its length, then up the arm that held it, knowing how to deal with these soft creatures, for had it not killed the anteater-man and the uniped with a single clash of its huge mandibles? It scurried to the shoulder and reached out to bite . . .

But there was no neck.

Shouts rang in its ears as something struck its abdomen, knocking it from the woman's shoulders and sending it spinning through the air. It landed on its feet, though, and turned to charge back.

A dozen clubs pounded at it.

The ant danced, managing to avoid all the blows except the one that crushed the tip of one antenna. Even for a live eating machine like itself, the danger was obvious, and it turned and ran. The people ran after it, shouting and slamming clubs every time they came near. Having been revived by the water, however, the ant outstripped them and shot out into the desert.

Something struck it, and it fell to the side, then rolled and came to its feet again, not even stopping to look but running and running from these horrible creatures that did not die when they should. At last the clan's shouting diminished behind it.

The companions woke in late afternoon, drank, ate the last of the sandfish, and sat about trading tales again, then fell asleep for the night.

Balkis woke suddenly and looked about, wondering what had wakened her. She saw Anthony and Panyat likewise sitting up, blinking in puzzlement. The rosy hues of dawn made even the river of stones lovely, the rocks seeming to glow.

"What wakened us?" Anthony asked.

His voice seemed unnaturally loud, and Balkis suddenly knew the answer. "Silence woke us! The river has stopped!"

They turned to look, and sure enough, the stones had stopped turning. All three shouted with delight. They made a quick breakfast, tied their branches to their packs, left their sand-skis for anyone who might want to travel southward, and set out to cross the river of stones.

"Step carefully," Panyat warned. "One or two might turn beneath your feet, and even those that hold still may be uncertain footing."

Uncertain indeed, as Balkis discovered—she had thought it would be like crossing a brook on stepping-stones, but such stones had been flattened by long use, and these were all rounded from their grinding. They pressed painfully against the soles of her slippers, all the more because the long journey had worn those soles thin. She tried one large step, skipping a rock in between, and cried out with alarm, arms windmilling. Anthony instantly turned back and caught her wrist, steadying her enough so that she caught her balance—but he threw himself off and tumbled gracelessly to the stones. Balkis cried out and stooped to help him up.

He cast a rueful glance at her, then brushed himself off, avoiding her gaze. "It is not as easy as it seems."

"Not at all," Balkis agreed. "Pardon me for slowness, but I think I shall mince my way across."

So she did, stopping on only one stone at a time and making sure both feet were secure before she stepped to the next—or as secure as they could be on a rounded surface; she teetered each time, but caught her balance, then stepped on. Finally, though, one stone turned beneath her foot, and she cried out as she slipped and fell.

Again Anthony was beside her in an instant, lifting her to her feet—but pain stabbed through her ankle, and she caught her breath to stifle a scream.

"Carefully, then," Anthony said. "Lean on me, and hop with the good foot. Hold the other high."

"Be wary," she told him. "I do not wish you to be hurt, too."

But he wasn't, not until they were within ten feet of the northern bank. Then he stepped over a small pile of rocks, a sort of granite wave, and as he put both feet past it, one stone fell, crashing down at his heel. To escape it, Anthony stepped more quickly than he should have and fell with a cry of surprise. Balkis hauled back on his arm, almost upsetting herself, and cried with pain as her injured foot touched rock.

"Can you rise?" she asked.

"I think so." But Anthony spoke through stiff lips, his face white and strained. He shoved himself to his feet—then cried out and fell to his knees.

Panyat was there, though, shoving a shoulder under Anthony's and keeping his fall from having too rough a landing. "You must both lean on me now," he told them. "Come, it is only a few yards more."

That was how they finished the crossing, bracing themselves on Panyat's shoulders, which turned out to be just the right height. As they stepped onto the hard ground of the northern bank, they sank down with sighs of relief.

"I had not thought it would be so hard to cross a waterless river when it was still," Anthony admitted.

"Thank Heaven we did not have to try when it moved!" Balkis said.

They rested a little while, then pushed themselves to their feet and turned to look northward—and stared in dismay.

There were no dunes here, nor even very much sand—only hardpacked ground, bright here and there with salt-pans. There was actually plant life, but only outcrops of thorny brush, dry now but ready to bloom if rain came.

It had been a very long time since that happened.

The river of stones twisted across that wasteland, miles and miles to a distant range of mountains from which it flowed.

Anthony shuddered. "How could there ever have been life here?"

"There is water," Panyat told him, "but it flows deep under the ground."

"We cannot drink it when it is hidden," Balkis said in despair.

Anthony, scanning the landscape with narrowed eyes, remarked, "Perhaps there is a way to climb down to it—how else would people know it is there?"

Balkis searched, too, hope resurgent, before shaking her head sadly. "I see no cave, nor any other way to journey downward."

"Nonetheless, there is such," Panyat told them. "Let us each gather a few pieces of driftwood, for if we can find that stream, we may be able to ride it."

Balkis shuddered. "I have no wish to climb out among those stones again—nor will my ankle stand it!"

"Nor shall it have to," Panyat returned. "The smaller branches are torn off the trees and cast up on the banks." He proved his point by bringing each of them a driftwood staff. Leaning on them, they each managed to find a few good-sized branches about five feet long lying by the banks. They dragged them as Panyat led the way along a winding track, barely discernible in the hard-packed earth, to the lee of a huge boulder—and there, to their surprise, they saw a cave, a scooped-out declivity whose bottom lay below the ground.

Panyat took the sticks and tossed them in. They fell with a clatter that seemed to go on a long time, and Balkis paled. "How are we to descend so far?"

"Very carefully," Panyat answered, "especially with those turned ankles. But the way is easy enough, though rough."

They followed him into the cave, stepping down gingerly—and discovered a sort of staircase probing deep into the earth, made of slabs of rock and shelves of shale. The height of the steps was uneven, their depth varied from a few inches to several feet, and Balkis asked, as she sat down to descend a particularly high step, "Did people build this?"

"I think not," said Panyat. "Even the ancients would have made it more even. I would guess that the gods made this staircase and cared little about human convenience—but it will take us down to the stream. Be glad we will not have to climb back up laden with waterskins, as did the traders who showed me this."

Balkis shuddered at the thought, and was very glad indeed.

The stairs curved slowly in a great, uneven spiral, and the sunlight stayed with them almost to the bottom, though it became gray and dim. Finally Panyat encountered their driftwood and sent it clattering farther down—but before he did, he broke off a two-foot limb and asked Anthony, "Can you light this with your flint and steel?"

"Gladly." Anthony took some tow from his pack, struck sparks into it, nursed the flame to life, then held the tip of the branch in until fire caught firmly. Stamping out the tow, he gave the branch to Panyat, who held it high as he led the way down.

They followed into a darkness lit only by the torch. It gleamed on the stone walls about them—there wasn't much space to light, really. After a few minutes, they heard a gurgling sound, which grew louder as the daylight faded. Then, suddenly, the walls fell away and the torchlight glowed alone in the darkness—but at their feet, it showed them a shelf of rock and the winking turbulent mass of a flowing river.

CHAPTER 20

Panyat stepped forward and the torch lit the curve of a tunnel overhead—only ten feet high at the midpoint, no doubt gnawed out by the stream itself. Stone icicles hung from it here and there, glittering in the torchlight. They could see that it was more of a brook than a river, perhaps twelve feet wide but flowing quickly.

"So this is an underground stream." Anthony's voice was hushed, awed.

Balkis knew how he felt. There was something of the feel of a church in the solitude of the place, but something more of the awe of the underworld; she half expected to see Charon poling his boat toward them to take them into Hades. She shuddered at the thought and spoke briskly. "Well, we shall not lack for drink—but I thirst." She knelt by the bank—with difficulty, leaning on her staff—dipped up a handful of water and drank. The water was icy cold and tasted of the rocks through which it ran, but it was infinitely refreshing. "Shall we bother filling our waterskins?"

"Let us wait until we have come to the end of the river." Anthony turned to Panyat. "The ledge runs the whole course of the stream, does it not?"

"I know not," the Pytanian said, "for I have not yet followed it."

"Yet?" Balkis echoed him.

"It seems a more pleasant way to travel than slogging through the wasteland," Panyat offered, "at least, as long as our torches last."

"Well, we have brought enough wood to last us several

days," Anthony said judiciously. "I presume, though, that we are going to make a boat of most of it."

"That was my thought, yes," Panyat said.

"I mislike journeying into darkness when I know not what awaits me," Balkis said, her voice hollow.

"Oh, the river rises past the mountains," Panyat told her. "We know where it goes—but we also know it is the only water between the sandy sea and the foothills. If we had camels to carry bags and bags of water, why, we might manage—but since we have only our own legs . . ."

"And two of them are injured," Anthony finished for him. "I see your wisdom, Panyat. Well, let us set about lashing these sticks together." He took the coil of rope out of his pack.

Anthony was clever with his knots, and had clearly done this often. Bound together, the driftwood made a raft that was just big enough to carry them all safely. Anthony crouched, holding onto the raft, and said, "Climb aboard now, and we will be on our way."

Balkis bridled. "Why should you be the one to hold it?"

"Because the last one aboard may fall in," Anthony said, "and cats do not like wetting."

Balkis smothered a laugh and took a playful swipe at his head as she stepped aboard. The raft teetered under her alarmingly, and she quickly sat down. She loved a bath in her human form, but not when the water was icy cold.

Panyat came after her, puzzled. "Why should you care if a cat does not like to be dampened?"

"I have a deep affection for them," Balkis explained, and wondered if she should tell Panyat about her other life. He might run in fright, though, so she decided not.

Sure enough, when Anthony made to climb aboard, the raft, no longer anchored to the shelf, moved faster than he did, and in he went with a splash.

"Anthony!" Balkis cried, but he clambered aboard, grinning, while the echoes repeated his name as they faded. "Only wet to the knees," he assured her. "The water is shallow here."

"Thank Heaven for that!" Balkis pulled his feet into her lap. "Come, off with those wet boots!"

"I can fend for myself," Anthony protested.

"But would not!" She peeled his boots off and wrapped his lower legs in her cloak. "I prefer a traveling companion who has not lost his feet to frostbite, thank you!"

Panyat gasped, and the two of them turned to look ahead—then caught their breaths in wonder.

The torchlight waked a thousand points of light in the roof and walls of the tunnel, the glitter of mica flakes, the glint of sapphire and emerald, the glow of ruby. They sailed through a multihued world surrounded by garnets, opals, carbuncles, topazes, chrysolites, onyxes, beryls, sardonyxes, and even, here and there, the pure white gleam of diamonds.

Anthony groaned. "So much wealth, and I cannot reach it!"

"It is well I have hold of your feet, then," Balkis said tartly. "I would not put it past you to dive in and drown yourself trying to wrest a stone from its matrix!"

"I am not so great a fool as that," Anthony protested, "but I am a hill farmer born and bred who has watched his father struggle and sweat to wrest a meager living from a barren hillside. I have heard him say again and again that we must never let anything of value pass us by, for we will need it when the hard times come—and I am the one passing by all this wealth with no way to stop the raft!"

"Indeed there is not." Panyat's voice was sympathetic. "The current is too strong."

"It whirls us along through this tunnel," Anthony agreed, "and here I ride surrounded by ransoms for ten kings! Fortunes pass me every second, enough to keep my father and brothers in luxury the rest of their lives, and I cannot even touch the wealth I see!"

Just as well, Balkis thought—his father and brothers certainly deserved no such reward for their abuse.

Suddenly, a huge dark lump rose from the middle of the river. Glowing eyes the size of platters opened, and a huge hand with writhing, snakelike fingers slapped down to grip the edge of the raft as a glutinous voice asked, "Did you wish to stop your ride, mortal?"

"Not that badly!" Balkis slapped a hand over Anthony's mouth, for his eyes lit even as he shrank away. "What creature are you who rises from lightless depths?" At the back of her mind, she readied a banishing spell.

"I am Negation, the emptiness that hungers for everything that exists." The monster smiled, opening a lipless, toothless maw that stretched across the whole of its head as it drew the raft in.

"You are Greed," Balkis snapped, "and you mean to drag us down with you!"

"Feed, then!" Anthony cried, and threw something into the monster's mouth.

It swallowed automatically; then its eyes filmed over and its fingers slipped from the raft. "What exshellent flavor!" it said, speech slurred. "More!"

"I have no more, and be glad—it is very potent, and more would kill you."

"I cannot die. I feed on ev . . . everyshing, I shupershede Deaph, I . . ." The monster's eyes rolled up as it fell back into the river.

"What did you feed it?" Balkis asked, staring.

"The brandywine the king of Piconye gave us," Anthony said. "He spoke truly—it purified this water." Then he sighed with regret. "Still, if I had let him hold the raft, I could have swum to the wall and gathered a fortune in jewels!"

"Then you would have come back to an empty raft," Balkis told him, "for Panyat and I would have been in his belly, and you would have followed us—then the raft for dessert, like as not!"

Anthony shuddered and admitted, "Free jewels come at too high a price—this time, at least."

Balkis wished he hadn't said "This time."

Suddenly the raft sped faster.

"Seize hold of the ropes!" Anthony cried, and followed his own advice. "Has the monster wakened already and come to pull us to him?"

"No," Panyat said, his voice faltering. "Can you not hear?"

They listened and heard a roaring, faint but swelling quickly.

"I know that sound!" Anthony cried. "I have heard it many times in my mountains! There are rapids ahead!"

"I did not know," Panyat wailed. "The traders told me that people had sailed this river before, but they said nothing about rapids—or monsters!"

"Balkis, your staff, quickly!" Anthony jammed his feet back into his boots. "Use it to push us free from rocks on your side! I shall fend us off on this! Panyat, hold that torch high!"

Then the current turned and tossed the raft. Balkis saw a boulder looming out of the darkness and aimed the pole at it. A second later the pole lurched in her hands. It was all she could do to hold onto it, but the rock slid past them safely. Water dashed off its sides, splashing her from toe to collarbone, and she prayed Panyat's torch wouldn't be drowned. The raft jolted under her, and she knew Anthony had fended off a boulder on his side. Another huge stone came tearing at her, and again she pointed her staff like a knight tilting. Her aim was accurate, and the pole met the rock with a shock that seemed to vibrate through her, but she held fast to the pole, and the raft swung around the stone. A second later it shuddered from a blow to her left, and she cast an anxious glance at Anthony, but he was still whole, though his face was taut and pale with strain, and over the roar of the water she heard his wail: "That boulder was alabaster!"

On through the maze they sped, bouncing from side to side, never quite striking a rock. Now and again Panyat's torch hissed and Balkis' heart nearly stopped, but always the light blazed up again, and Balkis' pulse with it.

Then, abruptly, with a last torrential roar, the stream tilted at a sharp angle. Balkis screamed, afraid she would slide off, that the raft would topple and spill her, and Anthony's arm closed around her waist—but the raft struck water with a huge splash, spray drenched them, and the raft leveled. It spun twice, and the brave, constant torch showed them a view of precious stones flowing above them, limestone pillars polished mirror-smooth by the passage of the waters—but no banks. As the raft stopped its spin, they were able to make out the sides of the channel by the winking of gems, but they seemed tiny with distance.

"That was only a stream," Panyat said, voice shaking with

wonder. "It has carried us into a proper river—an underground river!"

In spite of herself, Balkis looked about for Charon, the pale ferryman, then breathed a sigh of relief when she did not see him.

"We are safe, sweet one, safe and still together." Anthony pressed her against him. "Do not tremble. After that ride, what could affright you?"

"Only my own silly imaginings," Balkis told him, "only old wives' tales." Of course, the wives in question were Greek, and very old indeed. "And I do not tremble, Anthony, I shiver." Perhaps because of that, she did not try to pull away.

"We are soaked to the skin," he agreed, and shivered in a sudden breeze. But it did not pass, it kept blowing, chilling them to the bone.

"What could make a wind in an underground tunnel?" Balkis moaned.

"A door to the outer world!" Anthony sat straight up. "Our journey ends already!"

"It has seemed quite long enough to me," Balkis said, exhausted as well as chilled.

"The torch is nearly consumed!" Panyat wailed.

"Toss it into the river," Anthony directed. "Do not take a chance on burning yourself."

"But the light . . . !"

"Unless I am very wrong," Anthony told him, "we will not be in darkness long."

"You have been wrong before," Balkis reminded him. Then honesty impelled her, and she admitted, "So have I."

"We have no choice, unless we wish our friend to be burned. Cast the torch away with a blessing, Panyat—it has served us well."

The Pytanian tossed the butt of the torch into the river. It sizzled and went out. For a while the darkness seemed total, and Balkis said, "Panyat, take my hand and press against me! Only all our bodies together will survive the cold!"

She felt the Pytanian press against her, his fingers clasping her arm, and she wished she had some light to see Anthony's face—would it show jealousy?

Almost it seemed that her wish had come true, for the darkness became less opaque. Wondering, she said, "I see the glint of gems above us!"

"I think there is light ahead," Anthony said.

The breeze strengthened and the current bore them shivering onward. The light grew stronger, and they heard another roaring.

Panyat groaned. "Not more rapids!"

"No, this is a stronger sound." Anthony tensed. "I think we come to a waterfall, my friends."

"A waterfall!" Balkis cried. "How are we to survive?"

"Pole to the sides, if we can!" Anthony took his staff, probed, and cried, "I feel rock beneath! Pole, Balkis!"

She went to his side of the raft and pushed as he did, straining with every fiber—and the raft moved to the side, slowly, by inches, as the roaring grew louder and the current strengthened. Suddenly, that current spun them about, then cast them aside into much calmer water.

"Keep poling!" Anthony cried.

The light was strong enough now for them to see the side of the tunnel. Balkis poled with her last ounce of strength, and the raft floated across what looked to be a still pool to bump the rock at the side of the tunnel.

"It is a ledge!" Panyat cried, and threw the top half of his body onto the stone to hold the raft. "Quickly, my friends! Take your packs and step off!"

They did as he bade, Anthony handing Balkis across the gap, then she steadying him as he stepped across to her, then both leaning down to take Panyat's arms and pull him up as he stepped off the raft. It shot away from his foot as he did, though, floating out toward the middle of the channel.

"Go toward the roar," Anthony called above the sound of the stream. "Go toward the light." He turned to suit the action to the word, probing ahead with his staff—but Balkis noticed that he held to the wall and saw that hand go to his wallet. She realized he was taking any pebbles he could break loose. For his sake, she hoped they were gems and not limestone lumps.

The light brightened, the wind freshened, and a bright oblong appeared in front of them. Anthony led them toward it; it grew until they saw it was thirty feet across. There, Anthony stopped, calling, "Let our eyes adjust!"

"Spy out our route!" Balkis shouted over the roar of the water.

Anthony squinted, then nodded and beckoned as he set off. Balkis followed, heart in her mouth, hoping he had indeed seen clearly whether or not the ledge continued.

It did, and they came out into sunlight. She looked, and gasped, flattening herself back against the rock wall, for beneath her a cataract fell fifty feet into a churning, frothy pool. Panyat came up behind her, blinking, then stared with her as they watched their raft tilt over the edge and plunge down to lose itself in spray. Balkis shuddered, realizing that they could have been on it when it fell.

Anthony must have thought the same, for his eyes were wide and round as he called, "There is no danger, really. The ledge is six feet wide, and I feel no wind." He turned and walked away.

Feeling foolish, Balkis sidled after him, keeping her back to the rock; she somehow felt as though, if she kept her eyes on the sheer drop before her, it could not claim her. It crossed her mind that this trip would be much safer as a cat, but she did not want to startle Panyat.

Anthony had spied his route well, though, and led them from one ledge to another, switching back and forth across the face of the cliff but always going farther and farther downward until at last they stepped onto level ground beside the pool into which the water thundered. Balkis stared upward for a long while, awed by the sight. Finally she looked down to ask Anthony if it was not indeed wonderful—and found him sitting on his heels by the bank, picking pebbles out of the gravel at the edge. Balkis sighed, not needing to ask—she knew the "pebbles" were uncut gems. She felt a touch of exasperation—did he not know that life and beauty were more important than wealth? Then she realized that she had lived in luxury for months, and tried to remember how she had felt as a peasant in the Dark Forest, newly orphaned and alone, and acknowledged that she would have been every bit as hungry for jewelry as he.

When Anthony rose, his belt-pouch bulged with gems. He turned to her with a grin and gestured toward the bank away from the cliffside. Balkis smiled and nodded—there was no point in trying to talk amidst this thundering. She walked with him away from the waterfall. Panyat fell in beside her.

Looking about her, Balkis saw high hills to either side, trees lining the edges of the valley floor, but broad meadows before them. The banks of the river were bright with glinting pebbles, many uncut gems and semiprecious stones. Anthony gazed at them with huge and hungry eyes, his face gaunt, but did not stop to gather any more. Balkis took his hand and pressed it for comfort, and as soon as the noise of the waterfall had faded enough to be heard, she said, "You are strong to resist the temptation to load yourself down with jewels."

"That would be foolish indeed," Anthony sighed. "If I could scarcely walk for their weight, I would never manage to bring them to market, and what worth would they be then?"

Balkis nodded, eyes bright with sympathy and pride. "They would be only gravel to harden a path against the rain."

Anthony gave a bark of humorless laughter. "Imagine walking on a path strewn with jewels!" Then he frowned. "But that is what we did as we walked away from the waterfall, did we not?"

"We did," Panyat told him, "so your gems could not be worth much here. This river is called the Physon, friends, and it is the broadest river that flows through Prester John's lands."

Balkis looked at him in astonishment; she had heard people mention the Physon at court, had seen it from her window, for it was indeed the most important river in the land, carrying passengers and cargo from the borderland all the way to Maracanda—and rumored to have its origin in the fabled Garden of Eden. If it did, most of its course had to be underground, for as far as the waking world knew, it began in this valley.

Panyat stumbled, bumping into Balkis' thigh. She reached out to catch him instinctively, then noticed his paleness and the unsteadiness of his gait. "What ails you, Panyat?"

"Merely hunger," the Pytanian said, his face gaunt. "I regret that I must leave you and go home, for I have only one apple left, and am feeling faint."

"One?" Anthony's gaze went immediately to the Pytanian's loincloth. "Balkis! His pouch is flat!"

"Nothing to trouble you," Panyat insisted. "One apple will suffice . . ."

"One apple? You have lost all your apples in the rapids!" Balkis cried.

"Even so, that was only today." Anthony knelt before his little friend with a frown. "You have been hiding this weakness for some time, have you not, Panyat?"

The Pytanian looked away.

"When did you lose the apple?" Balkis cried.

"In the rapids, as Anthony guessed," Panyat protested.

"How long since you smelled of its aroma?" Anthony demanded.

"Since the desert," Panyat admitted. "I feared we would not find food for you, and . . ." his voice trailed off.

"And you saved the apples, thinking to feed us if we found nothing!" Balkis cried, and hugged him. "Oh, bless you, best of friends! But we did find food, and now it is you who are like to die of hunger! Anthony, how can we feed him?"

"Leave me." Panyat sank down to sit by the bank, his face gray. "There is no hope, for there are no apples. I do not wish you to see me die."

"We cannot let a friend die alone," Anthony said, tight-lipped.

"We cannot let a friend die at all!" Balkis cried. "Anthony, carry him! This river is still too turbulent to drink, but if we can take him to a spring, mayhap its moisture will revive him at least a little."

"I . . . do not drink," Panyat protested as Anthony picked him up.

The farmer glanced at Balkis and told Panyat, "Nevertheless, we shall do as Balkis recommends. If any can find you nourishment, it is she." He gave her a severe look that as much as told her to work magic.

What spell could she do? Balkis wondered. Could she conjure up an apple tree? Well, she might at that—but surely Panyat would die before it could bud, flower, then bear fruit, even with magical speed.

"It can do no good," Panyat protested, and his voice grew more and more feeble. "Save your strength . . . it is useless . . ."

"We have strength to spare, now that you have brought us to water, and a fruitful land where we may find food," Anthony told him. "Be still and save your own vitality, Panyat. Trust our Balkis."

Theirs? When had she become theirs? But Balkis silently acknowledged the truth of his words—she might not have belonged to them, but certainly belonged with them. She strode ahead, searching for some sign, some hint of a way to feed Panyat, trying to ignore the despair growing within her.

CHAPTER 21

To make it worse, the sunlight was fading. They were at the bottom of a valley, after all, and the sun had fallen behind the ridge to the west. If Balkis was going to find an apple tree, she would have to do it quickly.

Did apples even grow in this country?

Apples grow everywhere, she told herself, and shrugged off tendrils of despair. She cast about her, found a forked stick and picked it up by the branching twigs. It was four feet long, and she held the stem of the Y straight out before her.

"We seek apples, not water," Anthony said with a frown.

"So you have heard of divining rods in your mountains," Balkis said with absent interest, her mind on Panyat. "Know, then, that a wizard can make a rod seek whatever he asks, not water alone." She stroked the branch with her right hand, crooning,

> "Wooden fork with barky suit,
> Sprung from seed and grown by earth,
> Seek your own kind, trunk and root.
> Show me trees of apples' birth.
> Take us . . . Find—"

She broke off in frustration and cried, "Anthony, finish it!"

"Take us to the rosy fruit!" Anthony called.

Thc rod jerked sharply to the right.

"Well done, my lad!" Balkis cried. "Follow fast!"

Speed was needed, and fortunately speed they found. The forked stick guided Balkis by pressure first against one palm, then against the other—and in the last rays of sunset, brought them to an old, gnarled, withered tree with a few last wrinkled fruits still hanging on its boughs.

"Succor!" Balkis cried, and reached up to pluck—but the apple fell into her hand. She dropped the divining rod and plucked another—it fell even as she touched it—and carried both to Panyat. "I regret they are such poor and withered things, my friend, but perhaps—"

"They will do! Oh, bless you, my friends!" Panyat's eyes opened wide; he moved a hand, but it trembled and fell. "I cannot . . . cannot . . ."

"Here." Balkis thrust the apple under his nose. The Pytanian inhaled deeply, then closed his eyes, trembling with the sensation as new life coursed through his veins. He inhaled again and again; color came back into his skin, and he seemed to swell with vitality even there in Anthony's arm. Then a hand, no longer palsied, reached up to take the apple. He held it under his nose, inhaling its fragrance with every breath, though it seemed to shrink and wrinkle even as they watched.

"The tree!" Anthony cried out, aghast.

Balkis turned to look and saw that amid a shower of its own yellowed leaves, the apple tree had shriveled. As they watched, limbs broke off and fell, the trunk caved in on itself, and the bark shredded into motes, until they found themselves staring at a pile of sawdust.

Finally Anthony spoke, his voice trembling. "What manner of tree was that?"

"A blessed one," Panyat said, his voice no longer faint, but still not as rich as it had been. "By your leave, my friends, let us spend the night here, for I am not yet strong enough to walk."

"Surely," Balkis agreed. "After all, where there is one apple tree, there may be others." She sat down, reaching up for the Pytanian, and Anthony set him down with his head and shoulders in her lap. Then he turned to gathering wood and building a fire.

They woke in the predawn chill. Anthony fanned the fire to life, fed it a few sticks, and brewed a porridge of crumbled journeybread. They ate, watching the east and talking in low tones, savoring the freshness of morning and the scents of life around them, so welcome after the dearth of the desert. Then the first rays of sunlight broke over the eastern ridge and Balkis threw back her head, closing her eyes and letting the warmth bathe her face.

Panyat cried out with joy.

Turning wide-eyed, Balkis saw a green spike stretching up from the heap of sawdust. As they watched, the shoot grew taller and the dustpile smaller, giving its substance to the life of the plant. They stared, entranced, as the shoot grew into a foot-high sapling and put out thread-thin branches.

"What manner of tree is this?" Anthony asked, his voice shaking.

"It is a thing of Faerie, my friends," said an old quavering voice.

They turned in alarm, Anthony leaping to his feet, but the old man who approached only raised one palm, saying, "Peace, peace. I am the guardian of this grove and mean no harm to you, unless you mean harm to my trees." He was bald, with a white beard falling almost to his waist. He wore a robe the color and texture of bark, and carried a staff in his hand that still bore twigs and leaves. Balkis thought it must have been her imagination that made the leaves seem to freshen when he stopped, resting the butt of the staff on the ground.

Panyat folded his hands over his midriff and the slight bulge of the dried-up apple within it.

"Peace, my friend—you may keep the apple," said the old man. "Indeed, you may take as many as you wish."

"A safe offer," Balkis said with a cynical smile, "since there are no others that have not rotted to dust."

"Ah, but there will be," the old man said.

"We cannot wait four months."

Panyat cried out in joy.

Turning back, Balkis saw that the shoot had grown into a sapling and put forth buds. Even as they watched, those buds opened into lovely, pale pink blossoms. Buzzing began and grew, and bees appeared as if by magic to crawl into the flowers and collect pollen.

"This tree thrives remarkably," Anthony said, wide-eyed. "If I could take only a dozen of its seeds home to my father and brothers, they would grow such an orchard as the neighbors would never believe!"

They watched spellbound as the tree grew and grew. The old man carried buckets of water from the stream to moisten its roots, pruned it carefully, and pinched off flowers that were too close together. The blossoms withered and fell to reveal small hard fruit that swelled as the tree waxed. The old man still carried bucket after bucket of water, then shovelfuls of the mud of the riverbank, rich with decaying weeds to pack around the roots. By midday the fruit was full and ripe and the whole grove filled with the sweet aroma.

"How marvelous!" Anthony reached up to pluck an apple.

"You must not eat!" the old man warned.

Anthony's hand froze an inch from the apple. "Why must I not?" he asked, eyes still on the fruit.

"Because it is a thing of Faerie," the old man answered, "and if you take within you anything of that mystical land, it will shackle your heart forever to illusions. I have seen people thus bound, forever seeking, never satisfied. Everything they see they feel they must own, for that will make them happy, but an hour or a day after they have gained it, their delight in it fades and dies, and they grow restless, once again looking for their hearts' desire. Poor fools, they do not realize that what they truly seek, no one can attain in this world."

"Is not this the common state of men?" Balkis asked, eyes wide.

The old man turned to her, a gleam of approval in his eye. "Perhaps, and of women, too. All of us are fools, but the wiser know that what they truly seek cannot be held or weighed. But if you eat the food of Faerie, you will never gain that insight."

"I, however, need not fear it," Panyat said, "for I shall take only the perfume, as all of you do, and that much has not harmed you." He reached up a hand. "May I?"

"You may indeed," the old man said, smiling with approval, "for your folk at least have realized the value of the insubstantial. Nay, take of the fruit as many as you can carry, and may they serve you well."

Anthony lifted Panyat; he plucked three apples and stowed two of them in the fold of his loincloth. As Anthony set him down, he held the third to his nose and inhaled. Immediately the flush of health returned to his cheeks; his eyes sparkled with vigor, and he smiled. "Oh, thank you, my friends! I am well-provided now."

"But how is this?" Balkis cried. "It ages!"

They looked, and sure enough, the apple tree had begun to look old; dry leaves fluttered from dying branches, and as they watched in shock and grief, the bark thickened, dead branches broke off, bark closed over the knots, and the limbs became gnarled and twisted. The dust of dry rot poured from the trunk, leaving a portion of it hollow. The apples fell, soft and wrinkled, and as the rays of the setting sun touched the leaves, they turned yellow and fluttered to the ground. As twilight descended, the tree itself began to crumble away to powder until, as gloaming thickened into the darkness of night, it was again only a heap of sawdust.

"How could such vitality and beauty fade so quickly?" Balkis protested, tears in her eyes.

"You shall ask that of yourselves in thirty years, my friends," the old man sighed. "Set your hearts and minds on things that endure."

"What things are those?" Anthony asked. "Ho! Do not leave us in ignorance!"

The old man had turned to go, but now he looked back, a smile glimmering. "What endures? Why, the beauty of music and poetry, which is gone in an instant but awakens again at a singer's thought—but you and your lady have something far more lasting about to spring into life between you, though like this tree, it requires tending and care to grow to its fullest. See you prove as good in gardening as I." Then he turned away into the shadows and was gone.

"Who was he?" Balkis asked, staring after him as though by doing so she could ignore his advice.

"Who tended the garden from which the Physon flows?" Panyat asked with a smile, but would not answer his own question.

The next morning Panyat told them regretfully, "I fear I must leave you now, my friends. These three apples will see me safely home, but if I go much farther with you, I shall not be able to carry enough fruit to last me, even though I take only its aroma."

Tears in her eyes, Balkis embraced him. "Thank you so for guiding us safely to this borderland!"

"It was my pleasure," Panyat assured her. "When I come home, I think that I shall have had my fill of adventuring."

"If you do not, perhaps I shall see you again when I return," Anthony said, clasping his hand, "and we may travel southward together."

Balkis felt a stirring of alarm within her breast at the thought of Anthony leaving her and returning to the harshness of his father's farm—but she had no claim on him, no right to bid him stay, so she bit her lip and said to Panyat, "Fare you well, then, my friend. We shall miss you sorely."

"And I you," Panyat assured them. For a moment he held both their hands, his eyes shining as he looked from one to the other; then he turned and walked away, back along the shores of the river Physon.

They watched him until he had disappeared among the trees. Then Balkis turned away with a sigh, wiping a tear, and Anthony said, "I hope he will not go hungry."

"If his provender fails," Balkis said, "he has only to travel by night, for he can plant an appleseed every morning, sleep until the tree is grown and its fruit ripe, then pluck an apple and walk south under the moon again."

"I wish we could accompany him and guard him," Anthony sighed, "but would we not then be the merry company, forever going back and forth over the wasteland and the Sea of Sand?"

Balkis smiled at the thought, but assured him, "I had some concern for his safety, too, and I plan to recite a spell every morning to shield him. For now, though, perhaps we should continue our own journey—or have you no longer any wish to see Maracanda?"

"Maracanda!" Anthony's eyes lit. "Yes, of course we must march northward, for I must see you to your homeland and discover the city for myself!"

Balkis set off with him on the northward path, somewhat nettled that his reason for traveling onward seemed to be Maracanda, and not more time spent with her.

The ant heard the rumble from far off but, knowing only the drives of hunger and the need to regain what was its own, had no idea what the sound meant, nor even thought of it. When it came to the river of stones, it was half dead of thirst and hunger, but its antennae quivered at the scent of water. It leaped upon the rocks, never thinking of danger—never thinking at all, seeking only water. The stones rolled under its feet; it leaped and danced, but a rock came rolling over the others and struck it a glancing blow. It scrabbled, trying vainly to keep its feet, then fell, rolling, and felt itself being pulled toward two rotating rocks. In desperation, it flailed with its fore-legs, mandibles opening and closing, striving to catch hold of something, anything—and its jaws closed on driftwood, a broken branch five feet long and half a foot thick. Its fore-legs found footing, pulled its middle and back legs up, and it perched precariously on its makeshift surfboard, dancing as the branch turned under it. Then the bank was coming closer, closer, and at last it leaped and caught firm soil. Its back legs tangled in the branch's twigs, though, and it hobbled away from the river of stones hauling a large piece of wood after it. The poor insect was too tired to try to wriggle free—but it smelled water again! Much safer than the water beneath the rolling rocks, which it had not found. It hurried forward as best as it could with the branch dragging behind it, and found the hollow in the huge boulder. The scent of water was stronger still, and it plunged downward into the darkness, the log bump-ing along behind. Down and down it went, impelled by the swelling scent, then by the sound of water rushing. Faster and faster the ant ran—and plunged straight into the water.

Its legs flailed and water shot into its spiracles as it tried to breathe, wracking it with pain. Then, suddenly, it burst through to air, flailing about with its forelegs, for its spiracles were still submerged. A leg caught; it pulled itself up—onto the very log it had hauled from the river of stones.

Water drained from its spiracles; the blessed air flooded in. It clung, then danced as the log turned under it, clung again until the log spun, when it danced again—and so, bedraggled, chilled, but no longer thirsty, it rode its former burden, clinging and dancing by turns, plunging and rolling through the darkness with absolutely no idea where it was going.

Above its head, far above, Panyat walked south under the moon, now and again sniffing the apple in his hand.

Matt studied the valley below and said, "Funny how from this height all the people look like ants."

Stegoman glanced down and informed him, "Those *are* ants."

"Impossible!" Matt scoffed. "If those are ants, that castle down there must be a mile high!"

Stegoman looked more closely and said, "Perhaps we should fly lower." He banked, dove, and passed over the castle again at a much lower altitude.

Matt stared. "There are people on the walls!"

"So I see," said Stegoman.

"They can look over the crenels! That castle can't be more than five stories high!"

"I would estimate fifty feet from the moat to the tops of the towers," Stegoman said.

"But that can't be! Those ants would have to be the size of foxes!"

"Perhaps there are no such predators, and they have . . . how did you explain it? 'Evolved to fill an ecological niche'?"

"Ants that size would certainly be all the predators you'd need." Matt shuddered. "In fact, one would wonder why there would be anything else left alive in that valley."

"In truth," Stegoman said, "I see no other animals—only the humans."

"Yeah, and they're penned up in the castles. No wonder,

with wildlife like that running around." Matt frowned. "Wonder why they stay there?"

"You have told me of people who dwell in frozen wastes, and we have seen desert nomads," Stegoman reminded him. "Why do *they* stay?"

"Because it's home." Matt nodded. "I see your point. But I also see cultivated fields. Either the people find some way to come out now and then, or those are mighty smart ants."

"I would not wish to test them," Stegoman said.

"Neither would I." Matt frowned. "Wait a minute! I wondered why the snakeman was so open about telling us where to go!"

"Of course," Stegoman said slowly. "He knew what we would find here—or what would find us."

Matt shuddered. "He was very insistent that we show up in the middle of the day. Wonder why?"

A wailing cry made him look up—just in time to see Dimetrolas plunging toward him, all claws out. Matt shouted with anger, but Stegoman only sideslipped in the air, and Dimetrolas plunged past them. She cupped her wings; air boomed as she slowed, then circled back up to them. "Someday, overgrown newt, I shall see the same shock and anger on your face that I have seen on your friend's!"

"I am somewhat larger than he," Stegoman said, unperturbed. "How came you here, maiden?"

"How came I? Forsooth! I flew, overbearing worm!"

"To see rare sights?"

"I will own I have never seen ants so large," Dimetrolas admitted, "though it could be that the people are very small. Shall we land among them and learn?"

"Uh, thanks, but I think I'll pass on that," Matt said quickly. "Somehow I suspect those people are a little taller than one inch."

"No sense of adventure," Dimetrolas scoffed. "Well, if you are so sure of the people, perhaps you will take pity on them and find ways for them to sally forth." She turned to Stegoman. "What say you, snake? Would it not be tempting to dive and torch a few of those anthills so that the people could go free during the daytime for once?"

"I had considered it." Stegoman sounded surprised.

So was Matt. Dimetrolas was being a lot nicer than she had been—nicer, but still tart enough for the transformation to not be suspicious; which meant Matt automatically was.

"Then let us go!" Dimetrolas cried.

"Be not so hasty, slender beauty."

Dimetrolas stared in surprise at the compliment.

Stegoman, however, ignored it completely, plowing ahead. "I have, as I said, considered the proposition, and bethought me that if the people have not fled this valley, they must have need of these ants in some way—or at least benefit from their deeds."

It was an interesting idea, Matt thought. He wondered if his friend were quick on the uptake, or quicker at improvising to keep the pretty one—at least in dragon terms—talking.

"A point worth considering." Dimetrolas sounded surprised at finding a brain inside that hunk of a dragon. "I have flown over this valley before in my wanderings and have seen that when the ants go back into their hills at sunset, the people come out to harvest some sort of crop from the sands of those very hills. They load it on elephants and camels to haul it away."

That also explained when they did their farming, Matt thought, and wondered what kind of crop the ants provided that was worth hauling away by the elephant-load. "The ants come out again at sunrise?" he asked.

"No—mid-morning," Dimetrolas replied.

Stegoman turned his head to fix Matt with a glance. "That explains why the traveler who told us of this valley bade us come at noon."

"At noon!" Dimetrolas cried. "Those ants would have minced you in minutes!"

"I believe that is what the stranger intended," Stegoman agreed.

"Strange indeed! Show me him, and I will torch *him* for you!"

"I thank you for the thought, lass." Stegoman sounded surprised, but he inclined his head gravely. "However, his employer already did that."

"Employer?" Dimetrolas stared.

"How I know not, but he burst into flame before our eyes. It would seem that, when Matthew cast a spell that made him tell what he knew, his employer had to silence him before he told all."

Dimetrolas shuddered. "How could such a one command any loyalty?"

"Surely not mine," Stegoman said.

"Nor that of these people below us." Dimetrolas looked down. "They are well-guarded, after all, for no invader could besiege their castles for long."

"True," Stegoman said agreeably. "It seems the ants may be the jailers, but they are also protectors."

"Still, there is no one seeking to invade at the moment." Dimetrolas' mouth spread wide in a dragon's grin; she lashed her tail. "Let us torch just the one anthill nearest that castle below, so that its people may be free for one single afternoon."

"A charitable thought," Stegoman said, "but I fear I must not join you. I do not know enough of the way of life here. By doing what I think is a kindness, I might truly upset some sort of delicate balance, inviting disaster."

"Disaster!" Dimetrolas scoffed. "What disaster could you bring by fusing the sands of this one hill to glass? You would not even kill many of its ants, for they are doubtless deep underground."

"But other ants might come to defend them," Stegoman pointed out, "besieging the castle by thousands instead of hundreds, and keeping its inhabitants closed in even by night. I must not act where I do not know."

"Stodgy old prig!" Dimetrolas' lip curled in disdain. "Must you withdraw from any act that might prove frolicsome?"

"I am indeed boring," Stegoman acknowledged. "I see little to amuse me in this life. Far better for you to seek the company of someone more gamesome."

"Oh, you are impossible!" Dimetrolas snapped and peeled off to dive-bomb an anthill, her fire roaring out fifteen feet ahead of her.

Stegoman looked down with regret.

CHAPTER 22

"She expects you to go down there and try to stop her, you know," Matt told him.

"We do not always do as one expects," Stegoman returned, unruffled. "Who knows? Perhaps she is right, perhaps she will do those people a favor. Certainly there are enough ants to repopulate that hill quickly enough."

"I don't think ant welfare is the issue she's really concerned with," Matt demurred.

"And I am? Well, we must not let her know how foolish she is, then," Stegoman answered.

Below, Dimetrolas leveled off, blasting the top of the hill into glass, then veered upward, rising away.

"It does kind of look like fun," Matt said, "especially since she's probably right about the ants being far enough underground to be safe."

"They will have a longer way to dig in the morning," Stegoman acknowledged, "but I am sure that they will. In the meantime, they will have difficulty disappearing back into their tunnels."

A wail of distress rose, clear even so far above the castle. Looking down, Matt saw Dimetrolas making a second torching run on the anthill. The castle's people gathered on the battlements, and it sounded as if they were lamenting.

"It would seem that burning the anthill has upset the people in some way," Stegoman noted.

"Yes, it surely does," Matt said. "You're really in for it now, old saur—you were right."

Sure enough, Dimetrolas came rocketing back, eyes ablaze

with anger. "Did you not see? Or can you not even deign to watch others have fun?"

"It did seem enjoyable," Stegoman allowed, "the feel of the wind screaming past, the satisfaction of seeing your fire strike the target squarely, the air bearing you up again—all a warrior's delights."

"Oh, how surely you must mean what you say," Dimetrolas sneered, "for you are so quick to join in the game!"

"I can at least delight in watching those who can enjoy such frolics," Stegoman replied with benevolent calm.

It was just the thing to send Dimetrolas into the stratosphere, of course. "Watch? Am I your clown, then, your mummer's play, to sport and juggle for your amusement? Am I nothing more?"

"Am I anything less?" Stegoman countered.

"Less? Aye! You are a wooden sobersides who has absolutely no sense of fun!"

"That is quite true," Stegoman agreed gravely, "and I would be a fool to deny it. I have attempted such antics in the past but have never understood why it gives others such pleasure. Nonetheless, I wish them joy of it."

"Joy? What of the joy of battle, of the thrill of conquest? Are you a sobersides or a coward? Surely you seem to lack even the courage to engage in a duel of wits! Nay, surely you would turn tail and run from a real battle!"

"I do not see much to fear in an ant," Stegoman replied, "but I do fear to upset a balance between Nature and humanity, for Nature has its ways of revenging itself upon those who injure it. In that, yes, I must be a coward."

"Then you shall live and die a lonely old bore," Dimetrolas spat, "for cowards deserve nothing more, and those who will not play must live without playmates!" She banked and shot away, arrowing toward the sun.

"Am I supposed to chase after her again?" Stegoman asked wearily.

"Well, now that you mention it," Matt said, "yes. You're also supposed to explode in wrath at being called a coward."

"I might, if I were not so sure of my courage," Stegoman replied, "but you know as well as I, Matthew, that I have fought in several battles and never shrunk from the fray. I know my courage well and feel no need to prove it again, especially not upon so frail a female."

Dimetrolas looked about as frail as a bulldozer to Matt, but he did have to admit that next to Stegoman, she looked fragile. "Even so, she meant to hurt enough to anger you, and stings like that are more painful coming from a female. I'm amazed you were able to stay calm."

"She surely will not anger me by questioning the one virtue of which I am certain. If she insulted me for being cruel or petty, I might indeed respond with anger, for I know myself to be a selfish bully."

"You could fool me," Matt said. "In fact, you have—I would have said you always put your friends' welfare before your own, and I don't think you've ever attacked anyone who wasn't a real danger, not even an ant. As to being cruel, the term 'soft-hearted' comes to mind."

"I thank you." Stegoman inclined his head. "She did not accuse me of cruelty, though, but of being prudent and careful, which is only true, and anyone who thinks it an insult is obviously someone with whom I desire no further acquaintance."

But Matt heard pain beneath those words and the fire of anger rumbling deep below, and knew that the last thought, at least, had held nothing of truth.

Anthony and Balkis came to a halt, even though it was only mid-morning. They stared at the gloom of the forest before them for several minutes. Then Anthony said, "I have never seen so many trees together. Is it not threatening somehow?"

"Not a bit." Balkis' eyes shone. "It is much like the great forest in which I grew up. I am sorry if it bothers you, Anthony, but it will be like coming home to me."

"Well . . . if you see no threat, I shall hold myself foolish," Anthony said. He went ahead again.

As they came under the first boughs, Balkis breathed a sigh of pleasure. "It is so cool after that sizzling sun of the desert! So moist, so fragrant!"

"So dark, and the air so oppressive." Anthony glanced around him warily. "Is the air always so thick in these lowlands?"

"Yes, my poor friend." Balkis turned and caught his hands. "I fear this journey will be a sore trial to you, who are used to the brisk, dry air of your mountains."

"Well, I wanted adventure," Anthony sighed, "and I shall not complain if it becomes somewhat . . . inconvenient. Still, I think I begin to understand the trader who told me that, after years of travel, the most important thing he had learned was that the best place in the world was the village of his childhood."

Balkis tried to smother feelings of alarm, telling herself once again that Anthony was a friend and not a possession. She turned away, saying, "Come, then! Before you fare back to your mountains, see a little of my forests!"

After a quarter of an hour, though, even Balkis began to feel that there was a presence about them that did not like them. She looked at Anthony anxiously and saw his lips pressed tight with the determination to ignore his own fears. "I shall recite a spell to protect us," she told him.

Anthony nodded, obviously relieved that she seemed to feel the danger, too. "Wise."

Balkis thought a moment, then recited,

> " 'Gainst forest sprites who'd mean us harm
> We shall raise a warding arm
> Of unseen shields that all make good
> This dark impenetrable wood,
> Deflecting as a buckler should . . ."

As usual, she ground to a halt, and Anthony said, "I have the final line in mind."

"I should have known." Balkis flashed him a smile. "Hold it there until we've need."

"I shall." Anthony smiled in answer.

They went on together, feeling the menace grow. Then they saw grass at the bough-arch ahead and a minute later stepped into a sunlit meadow.

Balkis caught her breath and squeezed Anthony's arm, pointing with her other hand. Looking, he froze, staring in wonder.

A unicorn stepped into the meadow from the other end of the path, stepping daintily over a fallen log and lowering its head to graze. Its coat was white, its mane and tail golden, but its horn was black.

Balkis and Anthony gazed, spellbound by the creature's beauty and rarity.

The unicorn looked up toward the side, then bleated.

Balkis and Anthony looked and saw another unicorn entering the meadow. This one's coat was also white, but its mane and tail were silver and its horn green. It came trotting over to the first unicorn and nuzzled it briefly, bleating in greeting; then both turned to graze side by side.

Balkis squeezed Anthony's arm again, wanting to exclaim, to marvel aloud, but not daring to make the slightest noise.

Another bleat sounded. Both unicorns looked toward the west; so did Anthony and Balkis. There came a third unicorn, its coat golden, its mane and tail silver, and its horn white. The first two lowed in greeting; the third joined them, rubbing noses with them. Finally they turned to cropping grass, all three side by side.

Balkis let her breath out in a whispering sigh and glanced up at Anthony, to find him smiling at her with bright eyes. She smiled back; they might not exclaim, but both proclaimed their wonder silently.

A guttural roar broke the stillness, and a lion paced out of the wood, mane a tawny glory, tail lashing.

All three unicorns whirled to face the beast, heads down and horns leveled, neighing warnings—and two lionesses sprang from the trees to either side, bounding in silence toward the backs of the unicorns.

Balkis couldn't help herself; she cried out, and the white-horned unicorn whirled, saw the danger, and bleated warning.

The male lion roared in anger at the spoiling of his ambush and paced toward the trio, but the black-horn charged and the lion swung aside. The unicorn turned its horn, though, and raked a trail in the lion's side as it passed. The beast roared in pain, but the other two whirled to surround it, thrusting with their horns, one skewering the lion in a foreleg, one catching it in a ham. Baffled and outraged, the lion leaped back in among the trees. One of the unicorns stayed on guard against him while the other two turned to meet the lionesses' charge.

Faced with two long, sharp horns, the lionesses aborted their attack, leaping aside and roaring in frustration. Then followed a few minutes of standoff with lioness and unicorn circling one another, watching for an opening. A unicorn saw one and charged, horn lancing the lioness' flank. She tried to leap aside, and certainly saved her heart, but the tip of the horn came away reddened as the unicorn sprang back out of reach.

The other lioness roared with anger and charged the unicorn who dared stab her sister—but the unicorn whirled to attack from the side and the other unicorn stabbed. The wounded lioness leaped in to join the fray, but the third unicorn left sentry duty long enough to stab at her eyes, and she leaped away, coughing in confusion. The other lioness leaped away, too, both limping back in among the trees.

The unicorns shied away from the woods, too wise to venture in where a lion could spring from a branch, and came together again in a ring, hindquarters in, horns out, watching and waiting.

"They are wondrous!" Balkis breathed. "Who would have thought a unicorn could best a lion?"

"I would not want to go up against one of those horns," Anthony whispered back.

Quiet though they were, they still made enough sound for the unicorns to notice; the beasts looked up, horns half lowered, but when the humans made no threatening moves—no movement at all, really—the unicorns slowly lowered their heads to graze again. The companions watched, spellbound, until the grass-eaters had filled their stomachs. Two of them sauntered off into the woods, side by side, wary and watchful. The third lay down about ten feet from the trunk of a huge spreading oak, under the shade of its broad canopy, curled its head into its forelegs and fell asleep.

Then Balkis sank her fingers into Anthony's forearm, pointing with her other hand.

"I see," he whispered, wincing.

The male lion came silently out of the underbrush, creeping between the unicorn and the tree. As Balkis and Anthony watched, horrified, it roared. The unicorn sprang up, still half asleep and confused. It saw an enemy and charged.

The lion sprang aside at the last second. The unicorn was going too fast to stop. Its horn struck deeply into the trunk of the oak with a meaty sound. It set its heels and yanked back, yanked again and again, but the horn wouldn't come out. Unable to free itself, the unicorn thrashed about in panic, bleating for help.

The lion closed in for the kill.

"This must not happen!" Balkis cried and thought of the grass higher than her head, of how the meadow must smell with the mingled scents of lion and unicorn—and the world went out of focus as the grass and trees seemed to shoot upward, swelling to giants.

The lion, alarmed by her shout, turned to defend itself, but saw only a puny human who was rooted to the spot. It didn't see the little brown cat at his feet, saw only prey that would wait, and turned back to finish the unicorn.

Balkis sprang up from the grass at its feet and tried to speak in the limited language she had learned from other cats, something to the effect of felines needing to stand together, tales of better food only a day or so away. The lion gave her a cough of contempt and a swat of its huge paw. Pain exploded all through Balkis' side; the grass and trees reeled about her as she shot through the air, spinning.

"Beast!" Anthony shouted, and ran to pick up his cat.

The lion growled in anger and swatted. Anthony shot into the air and landed on the ground, hard. The lion advanced on him, roaring. He struggled to sit up, hand on his dagger, but the lion swung a roundhouse blow and knocked him down, then put a huge paw on his chest and opened its cavernous jaws to bite.

Balkis had wanted to save the unicorn, but not this badly! She started to recite the protective spell with a feeling of despair, knowing it would be too late, that Anthony would no longer be able to speak by the time she finished her part of the verse . . .

Something small and bronze-colored shot out of the trees, moving so fast it was a blur. It leaped upon Anthony.

"Anthony, roll!" Balkis screamed in her cat-voice. He heard and rolled without asking why as the lion's head plunged and its jaws closed—on the metal-hard body of the giant ant.

The ant turned its head and sank its mandibles into the lion's neck. The lion dropped it with a roar of pain, then swatted at it with a huge paw—but the ant danced aside and shot in to tear flesh from the lion's leg. Then it danced back to bolt down the delicacy, for though the hunting had been better recently, it was still famished.

With a bellow of pain, the lion collapsed on one side.

Balkis dashed over to Anthony and started changing back into a woman.

The ant charged in. The lion swatted at it with its good paw, but the ant danced aside from the blows and fastened its jaws in the lion's throat. The beast reared back, bellowing in pain and swatting at the small creature that plagued it, but the ant was still hungry and chewed as it held on. Finally a blow from a huge paw connected, sending the ant spinning, but it rolled, came up to its feet, and charged back in for more dinner.

Balkis caught Anthony under the arms and started dragging him toward the cover of the forest.

The lion reared to swat at the ant but lost his balance when the creature struck and fell onto his back. The ant sank its mandibles into whatever flesh was nearest, which happened to be the lion's deep chest. It raged with pain, drawing its huge hind legs up to rake and claw. A piece of the ant's carapace went flying, then the whole ant itself—but with a piece of lion-flesh in its jaws. Bellowing with pain, the lion tried to roll up to meet its next charge, but the ant dodged between its swatting blows and followed the scent of blood to sink its mandibles in where it had begun. They grated as they broke through ribs, then sank deeply under into the heart of the lion itself. The beast gave one last rattling cough, its body spasming, legs pulling in and kicking in one last blow—and tore the ant's body from its head. The jaws went on chewing for a few seconds more, as though the insect were not aware that its body was missing, that it was itself dead. Then the jaws tightened in the realization of death, its body ten feet away stopped kicking even as the lion did, and the two lay silent in the stillness of mutual murder.

But Balkis didn't notice; it was another murder that concerned her. "Help!" she cried, forgetting all caution. "Whoever can hear, come and aid! My love is dying!"

She knelt over Anthony's unconscious, bleeding body, weeping and pressing her hand over his heart, feeling the erratic beat, beside herself with terror as she realized too late that she really did love him.

CHAPTER 23

"What a deal of nonsense!" said a grating voice.

Balkis broke off her lament and looked up, staring.

"I have seen dead fish, dead rats, and dead lizards, damsel," the voice said, "and I assure you that the man you bewail is none of them—neither fish, rat, nor lizard, nor, for that matter, dead."

Balkis could not stop staring, for the one who spoke to her was a bird.

"As to him being your love," the bird said, "why, that is only an excuse for insane behavior. It is something of which we birds are blessedly bereft, but I have seen something of its effects on you silly wingless folk and know that it makes you all fools."

It was a very striking bird, though, very brilliantly colored, for it was green with a large curving red beak, red feet, and a red band around its neck. Balkis gave herself a shake—after all, if she could talk as a cat, why should not a bird talk as well? "What could you know of love, avian?"

"Enough to know that if you love him, you should mate with him and be done with it!" the bird answered. "Really, such a deal of fuss over something so simple!"

Balkis blushed and looked down at Anthony—but sure enough, his heartbeat had steadied, and he was blinking. There were four long slashes in his chest, though, all oozing blood, and the side of his face was darkening with a huge bruise—all for love of her! Frantic with fear for his life, she reached under his shirt to press and see if any ribs were broken.

"Ah, she paid attention!" the bird croaked. "Even now she begins to caress him."

Balkis blushed even more deeply and snapped, "Mind your own affairs, birdbrain, and leave humans to theirs!"

"Is it only an affair you shall have with him, then?" The bird cocked its head to the side. "Really, maiden, you should hold out for marriage!"

"Be still!" Balkis' face felt so hot she was sure she must be crimson. "You speak nonsense, gaudy crow! Be silent unless you have some notion how to save my love!"

"I thought you would never ask," the bird said, amused. "Of course, I have only a bird's brain, so I cannot really know much—but if you were to help the unicorn wrest its horn free, I doubt not it would be willing to carry your friend where help awaits."

"The unicorn?" Balkis looked up, distressed. "The poor thing! But how can I leave my Anthony to tend it?"

"Oh, he will live," the bird said carelessly. "Your concern is in restoring him to health, maiden, not to life. I would be far more anxious for your heart than for his health."

Balkis bit back another retort—rude though it was, the bird seemed to have some sense and might even know where she could find help. Anthony showed bleeding enough on the outside, but she was even more worried what the lion's blows had done to his organs. Still, with the worst of her concern for him abated, she had time to learn what she might need, if the bird proved to be more interested in mocking than in helping. "What manner of bird are you?"

"I might as well ask what manner of woman are *you*, who can appear and disappear in the midst of a fight!" the bird said with an acid tone.

"One who is adept at hiding," Balkis answered, wondering how much of the fight the bird had seen. "I am a woman who is as much a cat as a lass."

"Alas indeed!" the bird lamented. "Well, I have known many women who made better cats than lassies."

"Knowledge for knowledge," Balkis reminded. "A name for a name."

"I would not say that you had really given me your name," the bird retorted.

"Know, then, that I am Balkis, and tell me a word for what you are!"

"There is indeed a word for what I am, one that your kind have called me many times, but I would hesitate to speak it into such young and tender ears. Naetheless, the one that fits best is 'sidicus.' Think not to use it for power over me, though, for it is not my name, but a term for my kind; I am a sidicus bird."

"A ridiculous bird would be more apt," Balkis said tartly. "Well, I shall do as you suggest and hope I shall not regret it."

"Be it on his head, then," the sidicus told her, "and on your heart."

"It shall be on your neck, if harm comes to him." Balkis wondered from where this bad temper had come, then remembered how cats felt about birds. Certainly she would be irritated by a lunch that talked back! "Guard him well, sidicus bird, for if he dies before I return, I shall dine upon roast fowl!"

"Then your dining should be foul indeed." But the bird sounded nervous.

They were past the valley and crossing a barren plain when Matt saw the three men walking northward below them. "More local lore available," he told Stegoman.

The dragon sighed, circled down, and landed behind an outcrop of rock. Matt hiked around it to the road and arrived just as the three men came up.

They were hulking young hill men, dressed in dun-colored tunics and bias-hosen, looking sullen and arguing as they came closer.

"Hail, friends!" Matt held up a palm.

They looked up, startled, and Matt realized they had been so busy arguing that they hadn't seen Stegoman come in for a landing. "Hail, stranger," one of them said, but he didn't raise his hand and looked about as friendly as a bulldog on guard. The other two rested their hands on the clubs in their belts.

Matt turned so his sword was showing and rested his hand on its hilt. "I'm a traveler from the north, seeking a friend who has gone before me. Can you tell me if you've seen any strangers here?"

"Not a soul on this road," the dark-haired one said. "We're on a search like that ourselves. Have you seen our little brother?"

"Littlest," said another. "Moti stayed at home."

"Be still, Philip," the dark-haired one snapped. "He's almost as tall as I am, stranger, and has yellow hair and a stupid look about him. Have you seen him?"

With a description like that from his own brother, Matt understood why the youngest had hit the road. He shook his head. "Haven't seen anyone like that. Some traders, some very odd travelers, but none young and strapping."

"He left a perfectly good home, left us short of hands for the spring plowing," the middle brother growled, "and all over a silly cat! We waited two weeks for him to come crawling home, but devil a sight of him we've had!"

"All over a cat?" Matt's pulse picked up, but he frowned as though puzzled. "He argued that much about a cat?"

"Aye, a plain little yellow cat! Had found it and kept it a secret, if you can imagine that, smuggling it table scraps and letting it drink of the cows' milk! All we wanted to do was play with it, but he turned into a demon and fought us tooth and claw!"

"Never did a thing like that before," Philip grumbled.

Matt could understand that—one look at these three surly louts and he had no doubt what sort of games they had wanted to play with the cat. "How long have you been on the road?"

"More than two months now," said the dark-haired one in disgust. "We went as far as a valley where all the people had to live in castles for fear of giant ants that roamed their land, looking for people to eat. I don't doubt for a minute that Anthony blundered in there and turned into ant-bait in minutes."

"At least it was quick," said Kemal.

None of them seemed to be terribly upset by it. Either they were calloused to the point of being incredible, or they didn't really believe their brother had met a mishap.

"So we're on our way back to our clean, cool mountains," Philip said, "to tell our dad that Anthony must be dead. He'll mourn, I suppose, but he'll get over it."

Matt began to wonder just how unloved Balkis' escort had been. He suspected Papa would be far more upset than the boys thought, but they clearly wouldn't mind at all if the youngest never came back. "Well, good luck in your search," he said. "Myself, I'm looking for a young girl, about shoulder high, very pretty, dark brown hair, large dark eyes, golden skin. Haven't seen her?"

All three developed hot eyes before he was halfway done with the description. The dark-haired one said, "No we haven't, but be easy in your heart, stranger—if we find her, we'll take very good care of her."

Somehow Matt found room for doubt.

As he came back to Stegoman, the dragon said, "You seem to have found some news of her at last."

"I think I have," Matt said, "though these three farmers never saw her as a human being, that's for sure."

"She was only in cat form? But how would they know her from their barn's mouser?"

"They wouldn't, of course, but she seems to have persuaded an abused younger brother into going along with her—escaping, I should say."

"Unpleasant men, eh?"

"Very," Matt confirmed. He climbed up onto Stegoman's back, squinted south, and said, "We saw mountains on the southern horizon, didn't we?"

"We did indeed," said the reptile who found eagles shortsighted.

"Well, those boys are going home to mountains—and they turned back at the valley of the giant ants—and if we assume their brother and his little yellow cat traveled that road before them and kept going—" He traced an imaginary line from south to north. "—they should be well on the road to Maracanda."

"Then we have flown over them at some point in our quest."

"They wouldn't have been hard to miss, if they were traveling by night," Matt said, "and if Balkis is doing the smart thing and traveling as a cat." He frowned. "If, that is, they survived the ant valley."

"I take it, then, that we must now turn northward to search again."

"Yeah, if at first you don't find what you're looking for," Matt sighed, "you keep on seeking."

"Is that a rule of life, Matthew?"

Matt shrugged. "What can I tell you? It worked for me. Let's fly."

Balkis went over to the unicorn, who was still huffing and puffing, its feet set, trying with all its might to pull its horn from the tree. Balkis wrapped both hands around it and tugged with all her might. She was still marveling over the fact that she was actually touching a unicorn's horn when the tip came free, the unicorn jolted back onto its haunches, and Balkis went rolling head over heels. She picked herself up and turned, wary of the trapped beast she had just helped—but the unicorn rose with dignity and grace and came to nuzzle her hand.

Balkis smiled, thrilling at the touch of its soft, velvety nose. "Do you thank me, then? But I rejoice that I could aid, for beauty such as yours should not be hidden—especially in a lion's stomach."

The unicorn stepped a little closer and nuzzled her cheek.

Balkis recoiled a step, laughing, hands coming up to fend off the muzzle, but somehow they wound up stroking its soft, warm hide. "Would you thank me, then?"

The unicorn nodded.

After encountering a talking bird, Balkis certainly wasn't disconcerted by a unicorn that could understand human language. "A gift for a gift, if you will. My companion has been wounded in your defense. Will you carry him to one who can heal him?"

The unicorn looked wary but gave an uncertain nod.

The provisional nature of that nod made Balkis nervous. She led the unicorn back to Anthony, pouring on the flattery. "Never have I seen so wondrous a beast as yourself! You are so graceful, so noble, so glorious in your strength!"

The unicorn lifted its head, seeming to preen; by the time they neared Anthony, it was prancing.

"So gallant a creature, so courageous, so—"

"So saccharine and nauseating!" the sidicus snapped. "If

you had an ounce of modesty, horsehead, your hair would turn pink with blushing!"

The unicorn gave the sidicus a narrow glare and lined up its horn on the red band around its throat.

"Here is my Anthony," Balkis said quickly. "Will you carry him?"

The unicorn lowered its gaze, took one look at Anthony, and nodded. It lay beside him. Balkis realized it was waiting to be loaded, and she pulled on Anthony's arm, turning him over and hauling his torso across the animal's back, amazed how heavy he was. Then she grasped a foot and tugged on it until his legs flipped over to more or less straddle the unicorn.

"Rise carefully, now," she begged her hooved friend, "and I will hold him on your back."

The unicorn rose with fluid grace, but it was all Balkis could do to stabilize Anthony and keep him from falling. Then she arranged his face to lie on the unicorn's mane and took his hand to steady him as the unicorn walked.

"See? Nothing to it!" the sidicus crowed. "I knew the beast would carry your lover."

Balkis blushed at the term, but insisted, "It was not so foregone a conclusion as that. A unicorn will only come near a maiden!"

"Not a maiden, foolish lass! A virgin! And men may be virgins as easily as women! Indeed, most of them are born that way." It cocked its head on the side and fixed her with a beady eye. "How long have you been traveling with this man?"

"Traveling? Why . . . why, for weeks!"

"Four weeks? And you call him your love and your lover, but he is still a virgin? Are you so ugly as that, or merely a shrew and a termigant? Or could it be that you are afraid of your own passions?"

Balkis blushed furiously. "Hold your tongue, impertinent bird! He has never told me he loves me, nor I him!"

"Not only your passions do you fear, but even your emotions! Do you not know your own heart?"

"No," Balkis grated, "but if you keep on in this vein, I will empty yours, and know *your* heart—by taste!"

"*Rawk!* A fine way to treat one who has aided you!" the

sidicus said in mock indignation. It turned its back, flirted its tail at her in insult, and flew away.

Balkis watched it go, not knowing whether to be glad or sad—the bird had been amusing, after all.

She plodded onward beside the unicorn, saying to it, "You, at least, are a true companion, neither insulting nor belittling!" and other such protestations of friendship—but she began to worry. Where would they find help?

The sidicus came arrowing back and lighted on a twig nearby. "Are you blind and ignorant? Help is this way! Come!" And it flew off, but only a hundred feet or so, where it perched and waited. As Balkis and the unicorn came up, it cried, "So slow! You should trade your feet for a pair of wings!" then flew away again before Balkis could manage a retort. It perched a hundred feet farther on, though, and Balkis followed it, reassured—it might be a caustic friend, but it was a friend nonetheless.

Stegoman carefully bypassed the Valley of the Ants before settling down for the night, even though it meant flying in the dark. Out in the wasteland he found a cave in the lee of a hill which Matt declared to be adequate housing for the night—he'd slept in worse hotels. He kindled a fire and started his stew boiling while Stegoman went looking for something fresh. They must have finished dinner about the same time, he thought, for Stegoman came circling down to the top of the hill as he was scrubbing his plate clean. Matt gathered brush for bedding and heaped it in the cave, campfire for a door, secure in the knowledge that if anything dangerous came along, Stegoman would see it far away from his perch above. The moon rose three-quarters full, but its light didn't penetrate far enough into the cave to be a problem.

Then a shadow swept over him. He looked up to see a long, sinuous dragon folding her wings to settle up above. The gal had tenacity, he had to give her that. Whether or not Stegoman would remained to be seen.

Stegoman was, at least, polite. "Good evening, maiden. You must be weary, for you have traveled far."

"What else am I to do with my time?" Dimetrolas demanded.

"There are no eggs to hatch, no hatchlings to ward, no companions to join me in games."

"That seems odd," Stegoman said.

Matt could hear the frown in his voice, and told himself he shouldn't be listening. Himself acknowledged that it was being naughty and stretched its ears with relish.

"Odd?" Dimetrolas asked. "Why would you think it odd? All other female dragons taunt me because the males find me ugly, even as you do."

"I do not," Stegoman said evenly. "I find you beautiful."

"Then why do you reject me so!"

"Because beauty is not enough for even a mild friendship, female. It makes the difference between liking and desire, yes, but I have found that if the liking is deep enough, I begin to see a female as beautiful, and the desire comes."

"But you do not desire me?"

"Not yet, no."

"Yet!" Dimetrolas snapped. "How much future will there be, far traveler? How long before you have fled from my range? Better to take what you can while it is offered!"

"Nothing has been offered yet," Stegoman returned.

"With no sign that it would be accepted? Of course not!"

"What good is the offer and the acceptance if you regret it on the morrow?" Stegoman challenged. "I have been too long among humans, female, and have spent far too little time among my own kind. I am alien among dragons now, and those of our kind who admire me at first become distant when they discover that I do not think like a true dragon."

Dimetrolas was quiet awhile, then asked, "In what ways do you not think like our scaly breed?"

"Comradeship has become too important to me," Stegoman replied. "Oh, there is camaraderie enough among our own kind, but it is only for convenience. No dragon in his right mind would fight to defend any but the Free Folk, and would seek closeness only with those of his own blood."

Dimetrolas thought that over, then said, "Such a yearning for kinship is not entirely bad."

"Indeed? And what experiences have you had that would make you think so?"

"Experiences!" Dimetrolas snapped. "What need for experiences? Kin is kin! Were you hatched without a clan?"

"Not hatched, no," Stegoman said judiciously.

Matt thought his friend did an admirable job of hiding the pain the words had to awaken in him.

"Surely you were not born alive, like a cow!" Dimetrolas said scornfully. "Though mayhap if you were a bullock or steer, you would better understand the need for sibs and kin."

"I understand the need for friends," Stegoman said, musing. "My kinfolk would be loyal to me in great need, but they mistrust me."

"What have you done to them, then? Are you as caustic and aggravating to them as you are to me? You are arrogant and condescending, patronizing and impatient! Do you think yourself a sorcerer?"

Now, "sorcerer" was the second worst insult a dragon could give, since sorcerers wanted dragons' blood, and the only way to get it was from hatchlings. The only insult worse was "hatchling hunter," the men who actually tracked and killed the hatchlings for their blood, to sell to sorcerers—and Stegoman, in his own infancy, had had a very bad experience with one such. Matt held his breath, waiting for the explosion.

But someone had blown out the fuse. Stegoman said only, "I think I am a dragon who keeps company with a wizard, and I own to have given him a drop or two of my blood when there was great need."

"Oh, you are impossible!" Dimetrolas cried. "Have you no pride, no sense of honor?" She was working herself into a royal rage now. "To give your blood to a wizard—not to have it wrested from you by sorcery, not to fight to the death to defend it, but to actually give it meekly, like a lamb to the slaughter! You are no dragon, but a human's pet!"

"I have told you that I am alien among my own kind," Stegoman said with deadly calm.

"Small wonder, if you league with wizards! You are right in this much at least—that no dragon in her right mind would seek your company! Go your way, and may it not cross mine again!" She leaped into the air, wings beating hard and fast, and flew away into the night.

Stegoman crouched immobile on his hilltop.

Matt waited for the explosion. After a verbal drubbing of that sort, his friend had to let off steam somehow, and it did him great credit that he hadn't tried to vent it on Dimetrolas. But right now Matt had a notion he should stay out of Stegoman's way.

Wrong again. The dragon's voice came floating down out of the dark, calm, even sad and, strangely, tender. "Matthew?"

"Uh . . . yeah, Stegoman?" Matt called up.

"You heard?"

"Well, there was a downdraft, and—"

"You could not easily have done aught but listen. Aye."

Matt took a breath. "I thought you did a masterful job of being patient."

"But was patience what she needed of me?" Stegoman asked. "Did she not wish some sign of passion from me, even if it were anger?"

Matt chose his words carefully. "She might have wanted that, but she would have been frightened and hurt if you had given it to her."

"Then there was no way to do what was right for her," Stegoman sighed. "Patience frustrated her, but anger would have frightened her."

"Well, you could have given her a compliment or two when you realized she was trying to get a rise out of you."

Stegoman was silent awhile, then said, "Perhaps. But would that not have seemed odd?"

"Oh, I don't think she would have minded."

"Perhaps not." Stegoman was silent awhile longer, then asked, "Was she angered only because I was not, or did I reveal myself to be something too strange, too frightening?"

"Maybe you did cut a bit close to the bone there. Certainly you were a bit guarded about your own background."

"Guarded!" Stegoman snorted. "Has she given even that much indication of her own?"

"Well, no, but the frightening parts of your biography aren't exactly going to inspire her with a desire to trust you with the secrets of her own hurts."

"Even though I have entrusted her with my own," Stegoman said with a sardonic tone.

"Well, yeah, but you were using them to explain why she should stay away from you. Can't blame her if she decided to take you at your word, can you?"

"I do not blame her at all," Stegoman returned, "neither for her coming nor for her going."

Which was to say, of course, that he blamed her for both, for if all she were going to do was to cause him grief by firing off a few insults and flying out of his life, why should she have come into it in the first place?

Still, he thought the two dragons were making progress—if Dimetrolas came back for more.

He had to admit that having Stegoman at his beck and call was very handy, and knew that a female and a full nest would end all that. Nonetheless, he wished that his friend would indeed find a mate—he'd be much happier for it. But if this courtship were anything to go by, he couldn't understand how the species had survived this long—though maybe it wasn't as hopeless as it seemed to human eyes. Dragons, after all, were a naturally prickly breed.

The sidicus finally flew out of the forest into a broad plain that stretched as far as Balkis could see. She looked about but saw only tall grass as high as her knee—and one huge boulder, gilded by the setting sun with a grove of trees behind it.

The sidicus hovered near her, beating its wings furiously and demanding, "Why are you so slow when aid is in sight? Come, bring your swain and hurry!"

An angry denial came to her lips, but the sidicus was already darting away over the plain to perch on the rock.

She quickened her pace, mad with worry about Anthony; the unicorn matched it without effort. She touched Anthony's throat, felt the pulse, and felt somewhat reassured. She also felt a little uneasy, knowing that her leading a unicorn marked both herself and Anthony as virgins, and scolded herself—virginity did not of itself make one more vulnerable.

They came up to the rock, which proved to be about the

size of a dining table, though oval in shape. Looking down, she saw that its surface was hollowed in the shape of a mussel shell—like a clam's, only longer. There was clear water in it, about four inches deep.

"Now, pay attention!" the sidicus rapped out. "This boulder is of incredible medical virtue, for it cures Christians or would-be Christians of whatever ailments afflict them—even wounds made by lion's claws."

Balkis stared at the depression in the boulder's surface, then tried not to let her skepticism show. "Why should it cure only Christians and folk who wish to become Christians?"

"*Rawk!* Have you no brains, girl? We are in the land of Prester John, the foremost Christian king of Asia! Who else should it cure—the pagan shamans whose people threaten him?" The bird tilted its head back and burst into song.

The music amazed Balkis, for its voice had thus far been only a grating and raucous noise. With even greater surprise, she recognized the notes for a hymn!

The sidicus finished its song and fixed her with a beady eye. "Surprised, are you? Well, witty lady, know that if I can imitate human speech, I can mimic any other sound as well, even the songs of the nightingale and the skylark! If I can manage that, why should I not be able to copy something so simple as one of your hymns?"

The song had acted as a summons, for two old men came from the grove—and with that much of a clue, Balkis was able to discern a cottage in the center of the trees, its walls faced with bark, its roof thatched with leaves, so thoroughly a part of its environment as to escape notice. A suspicion formed in her mind that perhaps the trees that made the little house were still alive and had grown as they did out of kindness to the hermits.

Certainly they seemed to be religious men, for the crowns of their heads were either shaven or bald with age and fringed with white hair, and their brown robes were belted with hempen cords. Each carried a staff, the top carved into a cross. As they came near, they inclined their heads in bows, smiling through their long white beards. The one who looked marginally older said, "Good evening, maiden. Is your companion ill?"

"Not ill, good sir, but wounded." Balkis noticed that the unicorn seemed completely at ease with the two old men, and she drew her own conclusions. Oddly, it made her more comfortable with them, too.

"We can heal him, if you will," said the other old man.

Balkis' heart leaped, and relief almost made her weak. "Oh, thank you, sirs! He was mauled by a lion, and I have been so terribly fearful for his life!"

"He will live, be sure," the first said. "Is he a Christian?"

"He . . . he is, sir—a Christian of the Nestorian sect."

"As are we," said the first hermit.

"Most are, here in Prester John's land," said the second. "I am Brother Athanius, and this is Brother Rianus. Does your friend wish the healing of the entire body?"

Balkis didn't stop to think and wasn't about to count Anthony's wounds. "Oh, yes, sirs, if you can! Heal him entirely, heal him all!"

"Why, we shall, then." Brother Athanius went to the unicorn and took hold of Anthony under the arms. "Aid us in laying him within the mussel shell, maiden, for we are old men and no longer as strong as we once were."

"Of course, holy brother!" Balkis hurried to the other side of the unicorn with Brother Rianus and took hold of Anthony's left leg while the monk grappled with the right. Together the three of them managed to wrestle Anthony off the unicorn's back and onto the surface of the huge boulder but not yet in the depression.

The unicorn snorted.

Balkis turned back to throw her arms around its neck. "Oh, thank you, beautiful one, for bearing my Anthony hither! I shall ever be grateful to you!"

The unicorn nuzzled her cheek, whickering low as though to reassure her, then turned away and trotted off into the trees.

"Go apart from us now, maiden," Brother Rianus bade her. "We must take the clothes from his body, for he must go into the shell as bare as he was born."

"I—I shall, sir, yes." Balkis turned away as they began unbuttoning Anthony's jerkin—but with a strange sense of foreboding that made her pulse beat like twin drums in her ears.

CHAPTER 24

"Why leave it to them?" the sidicus demanded. "After all, you should have done that months ago!"

"Be silent, bird!" Brother Athanius commanded. "This work will be hard enough for her without your carping."

"Hard forsooth! It would be the greatest ease for her and, when he is mended, the greatest pleasure!"

"Be not obscene, feathered one!"

Balkis walked away toward the grove, but her anxiety churned so high that she couldn't keep from turning back to watch, frantically concerned that Anthony could not be healed.

Brother Athanius managed to pull the jerkin off one massive shoulder, then the other, as Brother Rianus was pulling off Anthony's boots, then skinning off his breeches. Balkis resolutely turned her eyes away, determined to trust the two monks.

"Aye, avert your gaze, maiden," the sidicus jibed. "You will long to gaze back there again soon enough, and with good reason, too."

Balkis blushed a light mauve. "Do not be absurd, sidicus." But she couldn't help an anxious glance. Brother Athanius was pulling Anthony's shirt up over his chest. As he did, her hands tingled with the imagined feeling of pushing against Anthony's skin, and she felt a wave of dizziness—she hadn't realized he had such a powerful belly and chest, all muscle from the look, and a great deal of it, too. But the wounds across it wrung her heart.

"So, then, I am a bird absurd?" the sidicus mocked. "Or do you mean to say that a bird should be obscene and not absurd?"

"He should not be either, if he wishes not to be roasted

with herb dressing!" But from the heat in her face, Balkis knew she was blushing furiously.

Anthony's shoulders were too broad and seemed to be entirely of muscle. Brother Athanius managed to pull the tunic off first one arm, then off the other, and Balkis gasped, amazed at the size of Anthony's biceps. Finally he was naked from the waist up. A glance at Brother Rianus showed that Anthony was naked from the waist down, too, and she looked away, feeling her face grow hot again.

"Aye, avert your gaze!" the sidicus chided. "Wait until he is healed, then gaze your fill!"

"Be still, bird!" Brother Athanius pointed an admonishing finger. "I have endured your carping while it did little harm, but I will not have you mock this maiden's virtue!"

"Will not her virtue be its own reward, Brother? And it had better be, for it will be her only rawka squawk rawka craw!" The sidicus broke off, eyes wide with surprise at its sudden incomprehensibility.

"You may have your speech back when the lad is healed and dressed," Brother Rianus informed it. "For now, it were best you perched elsewhere."

"Or you may be dressed for dinner," Balkis told it with a warning glare.

The sidicus fluffed its feathers in indignation, gave a last raucous cry of protest, and flew off to perch on the monks' rooftop.

"Do not let the sidicus upset you, maiden," Brother Athanius told her. "It has a brazen tongue, true, but it has also a heart of gold."

"It has indeed aided me thus far," Balkis admitted, "but nonetheless, for this brief time I am relieved to be shut of that dirty bird."

Brother Rianus gave Balkis a slight understanding smile. "You need not watch, maiden. If his faith is strong, the stone shall cure him."

Then he took Anthony's legs while Brother Athanius managed his shoulders.

Again Balkis could almost feel the long, thick muscles of Anthony's thighs; the sight aroused warmth within her again.

She fought a feeling of faintness and tried to look away, but anxiety for her companion kept her gaze on the monks and their patient.

"Lift, now," Brother Athanius directed.

Together they heaved and dragged, lowering Anthony into the mussel-shaped depression and the water at its bottom. Balkis' heart began to hammer in her bosom again—from anxiety, she told herself. What would happen if this stone did not cure Anthony?

"Peace be within your breast," Brother Rianus called in comforting tones. "If his faith is sincere, the water will increase and rise."

Balkis fought to keep her face immobile, to keep the twist of skepticism from her mouth and the panic contained within her breast. How could the faith of an unconscious man affect the level of water? And how could more water rise in a bowl that had contained only four inches? All they were likely to do was to give Anthony a chill from lying naked on cold stone!

"Ah, there—it rises!" Brother Athanius said with satisfaction.

Balkis stared. Sure enough, the water level was rising, slowly put perceptibly. It was as high as Anthony's ribs, then as high as his chest, over his chest—she looked away, blushing and ashamed of her own anxiety.

If the monks noticed, they kept silent on the subject, but Brother Athanius reached down to pinch Anthony's nostrils shut with one hand while the other pressed down over Anthony's mouth a moment before the water rose to cover it, to cover his face, then his hair, and Balkis' heart clamored with a new fear.

"Be calm, maiden," Brother Rianus called in reassurance. "He will not drown."

It was hard to believe that, with Anthony's hair floating about his head like a halo and making him look like an angel, especially since he was so pale, but surely no angel had ever inspired such feelings in a woman.

Then his hair was floating no longer, the water was sinking below his head, and Brother Athanius released Anthony's nostrils. She heard his breath rasp in, saw the color return to his cheeks, and felt the knot in her chest loosen, a knot that she hadn't realized was there until it was gone.

The water receded until it was halfway down Anthony's sides, then started to rise again. The mussel shell filled nearly to the brim, and Brother Athanius had to prevent Anthony's breathing again; then the water ebbed away. A third time it rose, then sank down to its original level. Balkis gasped in amazement, for the ugly wounds left by the lion's claws were gone, and not even the bruise from the blow of that huge paw remained on Anthony's face.

"Why are you surprised, my daughter?" Brother Athanius asked. "Thus everyone who enters the shell leaves it cured of whatsoever infirmity he had."

"Now we must take him out and dry him," Brother Rianus said, "for it would be a shame to heal him only to have him catch cold."

Brother Athanius took hold of Anthony's shoulders while Brother Rianus took his legs. Balkis turned resolutely away, but couldn't help another anxious glance back, aching to see if Anthony was truly healed. The monks heaved, dragged, and managed to lower Anthony to the ground. Each of the hermits produced a length of soft cloth from his sleeve.

Anthony's body was smooth and unmarked by any scar. Balkis' heart swelled with gratitude to the hermits. For a few minutes she drank in the sight of Anthony's body, whole and glowing with health again as the hermits rubbed his bulging muscles. Then the warmth inside her increased to the point where she looked away blushing again—but the feeling would not stop, only intensified into a fluttery feeling in her stomach, one that spread both upward and downward until she could no longer deny that she was in heat, or the human equivalent—and rather intensely, too, though not so badly as she would have been in cat form. This was quite different from her few early experiences with the feline version of the sensation, though, for beneath it, above it, and throughout it was an intoxicating soaring of the heart that cats never felt. She trembled within as she acknowledged to herself that the sidicus had been right—she was in love.

The bird saw the difference in her as the three humans carried the reclothed fourth to the grove and the shelter of the cottage. "How now, maiden?" it teased. "Have you fallen so forcefully that you can no longer deny it?"

Balkis blushed furiously. "Be still, foolish bird! Remember the roasting pan!"

"How could I forget, when you are yourself so clearly roasting in your own broth?" the bird carped.

"Holy man, what day is it?" Balkis asked.

"Why, the sixth day of the week, good maiden."

"Not so good as she thought herself," the sidicus said, "though I'll wager her young man thinks her even better."

"Rejoice that it is Friday, foul fowl, for I cannot eat meat!"

"No matter how it tempts you? And I see a hunk of meat that tempts you indeed; 'tis well you dressed it."

"People are not the only creatures who may be adorned with dressing!"

"Come, foolish lass! If love is a virtue, sure 'tis a vice to deny it."

"Deny it I will, to you and to everyone who may hear!" But with a sinking heart Balkis noticed the two hermits exchanging a glance of gentle amusement and admitted that she could no longer deny it to herself. She was not only in love, but had been for weeks, though it had taken a lion and a healing bath to make her realize it.

What was she to do now? What was a girl to do with a love that was so great it made her tremble, especially if she did not know whether or not the boy loved her in return? She was sorely tempted to return to cat shape, in which form the anti-heat spell cast by her teacher Idris would have protected her. It would have had the additional benefit of making the sidicus a bit more respectful and, hopefully, less talkative—but she didn't think the old men would approve.

Brother Athanius noticed her embarrassment and said gently, "Let the sidicus not twit you."

"He is all a-twitter anyway," Balkis said darkly.

"Twitter yourself!" the sidicus returned. "You must deal honestly someday, maiden!"

"Speak sense, bird," Athanius said, still smiling.

"Why should I?" the sidicus returned. "Where has it gotten *you*?"

"Why," said the hermit, "it allows me to see things in their true forms."

Nervously, Balkis wondered if Athanius could suspect her ability to change shape—then wondered which was her true form, woman or cat.

Ridiculous! She had been born a woman and would always be one in truth! Besides, a cat could not know the sort of love she was now feeling.

That brought her up short. Was that what he had meant by recognizing true forms? If so, it would do no good to transform herself into a cat—it would not protect her from love, only allow her to avoid it. Besides, she couldn't stay in cat form forever without explaining to Anthony, and she might as well do that right away and get it over with—though she did wonder if he would react like a tomcat. Worse, she wasn't entirely sure she didn't want him to—though with a bit more gentleness.

The hermits laid Anthony in a spare bed as the sun set. Brother Athanius sad, "We have a hut for female guests, maiden, only a few yards from the cottage."

"Thank you," Balkis said, "but by your leave, I will sit by his bed until I can fend off sleep no longer."

"As you wish—but when you find yourself beginning to nod, do go to the guest house; you will find a bed with clean linen, though it may not be of the softest."

"I have slept on hard ground more nights than not in these last few months, holy one," Balkis said. "Your guest house will be a delight to me."

"Good night to you, then." Brother Athanius set a stool by the bed. "You need not trouble yourself, though. He will sleep blissfully, and wake in the morning feeling a new man."

Balkis wanted the old man, not a new, but she understood what the hermit meant. "It is myself I wish to reassure, holy sir. I know it is foolish, but I feared so for his life that I have need to gaze upon him well."

"There is sense in that, though it is sense of the heart and not the head," the hermit said. "Good night to you, then, maiden." He went out of the room and closed the door.

Balkis sat by the bed for an hour or so—not really to be sure Anthony was well, but to feast her eyes on the sight of him while she could, without worry that he might wake and see the glow in her eyes. The old man had spoken truly, though—in less than an hour her eyelids grew heavy, then her head fell forward with a jolt that woke her from a doze. With a smile of self-mockery, she rose, then bent to kiss Anthony on the lips, long and lingeringly, and whispered, "I might not do that while you were awake, my lad, so I shall do it now while I can." Then she straightened, went out of the room, and found the guest house.

It had been long since Balkis slept in a bed, and the previous day had been exhausting, so she slept a sleep that was dreamless—blessedly so, considering her state of mind. The sunlight woke her, however, and she stretched like a cat, delighting in the feeling of well-being. She lay still a moment, gazing out the window at the sun-flooded grassland and the boulder in its midst while the events of the previous day came once again to the surface of her mind, and with them a decision that she hadn't known she had made:

Today she would tell Anthony that she was in love with him.

If he wasn't in love with her, of course, telling might frighten him or disgust him, in which case she would have to travel on alone, though she would find it difficult to do so and still keep an eye on him to make sure he didn't fall prey to any of the dangers of these strange exotic lands—but she felt she had to take the chance and tell him. She had denied it too long, and now that she had acknowledged it, thanks to the sidicus and the healing bath, she couldn't keep it hidden any longer. No, she would tell Anthony and take whatever consequences came.

The decision made and acknowledged, Balkis rose, feeling lightened, freed, and went out to greet the day with a song on her lips. She made her ablutions, then went to the little side door of the cottage to look in on the invalid.

She was overcome with a strange timidity then, and knocked very lightly—but a few seconds later the door swung open, and Anthony stood before her, bare-chested as she had left him, hair still tousled, face still flushed with sleep. He smiled at her with such delight that it raised the strange fluttering warmth within her again, and overcome with a sudden shyness, she lowered her gaze. "Good morning, sir," she said.

"Good morning, lady," he replied with equal gravity. Alarmed at his formality, she looked up, saw the twinkle in his eye and the smile on his lips, and reassured, managed a smile of her own.

"Your pardon," Anthony said. "I should not greet a lady when I am half undressed." He went back into the room and pulled his tunic on, then came out and offered Balkis his arm. "Let us walk while the morning is cool and fragrant."

"Yes, let us." She linked her hand through his elbow and strolled in the sunlight with him. Both of them were silent for a few minutes, and she realized that the moment was ideal to tell him her feelings—but that odd shyness swept over her again, and she lowered her gaze, overcome with modesty. "Do you remember anything of yesterday?"

"I remember walking through a woodland with you." Anthony frowned, trying to bring the events to mind. "We came to a clearing—why, we saw a unicorn! No, three of them!" He turned to her, eyes alight with wonder and delight. "How strange and wonderful a world it is, to hold such enchanting and beautiful creatures!"

His eyes said that the unicorn was not the only enchanting and beautiful creature, which roused the strange fluttering in Balkis again, and she dropped her gaze once more. "Do you . . . remember anything else?"

Anthony gazed off into the distance, frowning, trying to concentrate. "I remember . . . lions! Yes, and the unicorns drove them away! Two went off into the woodland and the third lay down to sleep beneath a big tree!"

"Better and better." She glanced up at him. "What more?"

Anthony frowned, wracking his brain, then gave it up and shook his head. "Birdsong, sunrise through the window of a strange room, then a knock at the door, and yourself, brighter than any dawn."

Balkis caught her breath at the compliment, especially since it was given as a matter of fact, as plain and undeniable as the sunrise or the birds' music—but shyness overcame her again and the words of love froze on her lips.

"What happened in between?" Anthony asked.

"You . . . the lions came back—one of them, at least—and tricked the unicorn into burying its horn so deeply in the trunk of the tree that it was defenseless. I changed into a cat to try to reason with the lion in its own tongue, but it struck me aside, and you came running to pick me up with courage that shocked me, for the beast struck you down."

"Did it really?" Anthony stared at her. "That does not sound like me, the least brave of my family!"

Anger at the brothers who had mistreated Anthony rose to give Balkis more boldness. "Whoever told you that was clearly wrong. I saw it myself. You are a very brave man, Anthony, so brave as to be foolhardy."

Anthony turned away in confusion. "But I rarely fought for my own pride, and that only when they pushed me past bearing!"

"For yourself, perhaps," Balkis said, feeling the warmth kindle at her core again, "but for others you are quick to defend. Be sure—you did indeed fight to save the unicorn, though it did you little good."

"Then why am I still alive?" Anthony asked, confounded.

Balkis tried not to make it an accusation, but it came out so anyway. "You still have a few nuggets of gold from the valley of the ants, have you not?"

Anthony flushed and said, "You have caught me. I fear I cannot wholly contain my greed." Then he remembered the topic at hand and turned to her, puzzled. "What has ants' gold to do with a man-eating lion?"

"It seems one ant followed you—or should I say, followed its gold," Balkis explained. "It caught up just as the lion was about to devour you—" She broke off and turned away, tears flooding her eyes. "I tried to craft a spell to save you, but it happened too quickly, and I could not think of a final rhyme!"

His arm came around her shoulders, his muscular chest pressed against her cheek, his voice soothing. "I am sure that you did, and would have triumphed to save me even if it meant forcing the beast to disgorge me. Did the ant save you the trouble somehow?"

"It was a match for the lion." Balkis shuddered, remembering. "I am amazed that anything so small could be so strong—and deadly. It slew the lion even as the lion slew it."

"Heaven cares for fools and madmen," Anthony said softly, "and I thank Heaven, for I was both. How is it that I live, though?"

Balkis started to answer, then caught herself, overcome with shyness—and with misgivings, for she did not want Anthony to love her simply out of gratitude, and certainly not from a sense of duty.

Brother Rianus saved her. He came up to them, smiling and cherubic. "Good morning, young folk!"

"Good morning, good sir," Anthony said, puzzled that the old man seemed to know them, but unfailingly polite.

"Good morning, Brother Rianus." Balkis gave him a smile of thanks and relief. "Anthony, this is one of the two saintly men who healed you."

"Healed me?" Anthony stared at Brother Rianus. "You are? A thousand thanks, good sir!"

"You are welcome thrice over," said Brother Rianus.

"But how could you cure me of a lion's wounds in one single night?" Anthony asked, bewildered.

"In less time than that, young man—indeed, less than an hour." Brother Rianus turned and pointed outside the grove to the huge boulder. "Do you see that rock?"

Anthony looked where he indicated. "I do, reverend sir."

"It is a thing of incredible medical virtue," Brother Rianus said. "There is in that stone a cavity in the shape of a mussel, in which the water is always four inches deep. If any Christians desire the healing of the entire body, they lay aside their clothes and get into the shell; then if their faith is sincere, the water begins to increase and rise over their heads; when this has taken place three times, the water returns to its usual height. Thus everyone who enters leaves it cured of whatsoever infirmity he had, and thus your wounds were healed."

"It is a miracle!" Anthony gasped. "I can only offer you my thanks, good sir."

"Offer them to God, young man, for it is God who healed you." Brother Rianus glanced at Balkis and smiled. "Though you might spare some thanks also for the maiden who brought you to us, and the bird who led her."

Anthony stared at Balkis in amazement. She said defensively, "Well, I could not leave you to die."

"Surely she could not!" Wings battered air and the sidicus lit on Brother Rianus' shoulder; he winced as its claws dug in but said nothing. "Of course," the bird went on, "she was too frantic to know what to do if she had not had expert advice."

Balkis shot it a glance of annoyance. "Anthony, this wordy bird is called a sidicus, and it is he who bade me free the unicorn and ask it to carry you—which the unicorn did."

"Once I made her angry enough to start thinking again," the sidicus crowed. "Then I led her to these kind old men and their magical boulder, though I had to keep insulting her to catch her attention—her mind kept wandering to worrying about you."

"It could not, of course, be merely that you enjoy insulting people," Balkis said darkly.

"Why not combine charity with pleasure? *Rawk!*"

Balkis finally realized that its raucous noise was laughter.

Anthony managed to overcome his stupefaction at hearing a bird talk and bowed gravely. "I thank you, kind creature, for fair rescue and aid."

"Well, doesn't he speak prettily, though!" The sidicus, still sitting on Brother Rianus' shoulder, fixed Balkis with a beady eye. "As you should know!"

Anthony turned to Balkis, puzzled again. "What does it mean?"

Balkis lowered her gaze, blushing furiously.

Before she could speak, the sidicus said, "*Should* know, I said! If she told you how she really felt, you would speak just as prettily to her, and she *would* know!"

"How you really feel?" Anthony turned to Balkis, suddenly intent. "Of which feelings does this bird speak?"

CHAPTER 25

Balkis bit her lip, blushing furiously, confounded to find herself so completely tongue-tied and cursing the sidicus in her heart.

"Of course! You need not say, for I know!" Anthony said warmly. "Your feelings are care and concern for a companion and, I hope, for a friend." Suddenly his arms were around her, her cheek was against the rough cloth of his tunic and the hard muscles beneath it, and his voice filled her ears as the fluttering began inside her again. "How fortunate I am to have so loyal and caring a companion! Thank you again and again, Balkis, for kind rescue!"

She was about to protest that it was more than friendship that had made her act so, but the words jammed up in her throat and would not come out.

"She doesn't want you to thank her, young idiot," the sidicus said, "she wants you to kiss her!"

"Kiss her?" Anthony pulled back from Balkis, blushing but staring down at her doggedly. "Don't speak foolishness, bird! Why would so exquisite a creature wish for so lumpen a fellow as myself to kiss her?"

Balkis gazed up at him with longing, speechless but dying to tell him that he was anything but lumpen.

"Why, because she's in love with you, dolt!" the sidicus said. "Can't you see it? Really, you humans are so stupid! Any cock sidicus can tell when a hen takes a fancy to him! Do you really have to hear her say it?"

"Yes, and even then I probably shall not believe it." Anthony's gaze held hers, and his eyes seemed to swell, to fill her whole world. She felt herself on the brink of falling into them, and his voice seemed to surround her. "Do you love me, Balkis?"

Her mouth opened, her lips parted, but the words would not come.

"Pray Heaven you do," Anthony said softly, "for I am most overwhelmingly in love with you, and have been since first I saw you in human form."

Her lips parted farther, her eyes widened in surprise; she was filled with a sweet aching, but still she could not speak even as his lips came closer and closer to hers.

Then they shaped the soft words, "Do you love me indeed?"

"Heaven forgive me," she whispered, "but I do."

Then his lips touched hers, gently, lightly, moving enough to raise a sensation that sank more and more deeply into her, and she closed her eyes to savor it the more, to caress his lips with her own, until nothing existed except his kiss.

A raucous laugh broke the spell, and the sidicus crowed, "Well enough, well enough! We don't mean to have to put you both into the mussel shell to revive you from smothering each other!"

Anthony broke away from her, red-faced and fighting down an angry retort. "You are a most unseemly savior!"

"Oh, but I have to save humans," the sidicus explained. "Your follies are endlessly amusing, and life would be so boring without you!"

Brother Athanius came up to stand next to Rianus in time to hear this. Smiling, he said, "I own I find your jests amusing, sidicus, though they are frequently annoying, too." He favored Anthony with a conspiratorial smile. "Indeed, I would rather have one like him, who carps and mocks but does good, than one who speaks me fair and does me ill."

"Well, there is some truth in that," Anthony allowed, and bowed. "I am Anthony, reverend one."

Balkis remembered that they hadn't met. "Anthony, this is Brother Athanius, the other gentle hermit who healed you."

"I am pleased to have aided, young man." The hermit returned the bow, then glanced from one to the other, his eyes bright. "Of course, your fair young friend aided us in bearing you the mussel shell, where the curing waters healed your wounds."

Anthony turned to stare at Balkis. "You have cared for me in every way!"

"Cared very much," the sidicus agreed. "Of course, that might have had something to do with the fact that you had to go naked into the water."

Anthony's stare widened. Balkis lowered her gaze, blushing. "Bird, do you know the meaning of the word 'discretion'?"

"Of course," said the sidicus. "It is what people call for when they want to keep secrets."

"Annoying he may be, but I have never known him to speak falsely," Brother Athanius said.

"Of course," Brother Rianus demurred, "that's not to say he won't mislead people if he thinks he will have more pleasure watching their confusion."

"Of course," the sidicus agreed. "What are humans for, after all? And you two have been great fun this morning!"

"I must not criticize one who has helped me," Anthony sighed.

"Quite so," Brother Rianus agreed, speaking up now. "Still, young people, I would say you have endured enough of his taunts. You are healed in both body and spirit now, and must go your ways to make enduring this treasure that you have hidden from one another, but that the sidicus has discovered within you."

"I suppose we must thank him for that," Balkis said grudgingly.

"Of course." The sidicus' tongue lolled out in an avian smile. "You never would have told it by yourselves. Birds are much more practical."

"Go hatch an egg," Balkis muttered, then aloud she said, "Thank you I shall, then, for you have been a great help."

"Yes, thank you, good bird," Anthony said, "and I thank you, reverend sirs."

"Go with our blessings," Brother Ranius said, smiling, "and may love lead you."

* * *

With Anthony's arm about Balkis, they walked in silence, stopping to gaze into one another's eyes now and then, smiling but still shy. After half an hour they overcame their shyness enough to stop and kiss again, then went on, talking in low tones of things they had never discussed in all the months they had journeyed together. All that day they drifted in a sweet dreamland, and though Balkis occasionally felt the touch of apprehension, wondering what would happen when evening came—though it sped her pulse, too—she was able to put it aside well enough to enjoy these first few blissful moments to the fullest.

When the sun went down, they walked awhile in the moonlight, Anthony talking of his love for her and of her beauty, stopping frequently for kisses that inflamed her thoroughly. Finally, though, Balkis' head began to droop with weariness, and Anthony stopped. "We have come far enough for one day, my love. It is time to sleep," he said.

Apprehension clamored in her breast, surging up into her throat, but Balkis managed to only gaze up at him shyly and say, "Let us lie down, then."

The ritual of pitching camp had become so routine that they were able to go through it without thinking—which was good, for Anthony began to grow silly, making foolish remarks that soon had Balkis giggling and breathless—but when they had supped and she knelt by her bed of bracken, again overcome with shyness, Anthony said, "Sleep, now, and I shall watch, for that bath in the magical shell has made me so completely well that I feel no weariness, and doubt I could sleep."

Relief flooded her, though she could have wished for a better reason to keep him from sleep. "How long shall you watch?"

Anthony shrugged. "I shall waken you when I tire. It shall be half the night at least, and perhaps all of it, since I shall have the sweetness of your sleeping face to gaze upon and fill me with strength."

She blushed, looking down. "May the night be calm for you, then." She lay down, careful to arrange her cloak with all modesty—if he would gain strength by gazing, it should be only her face that he watched.

"Sleep lie sweetly on your brow." Anthony leaned over and kissed her forehead. "And on your eyes." He kissed each closed lid. "And on your lips." The last kiss was substantially longer than the others and guaranteed to keep him awake. When he lifted his head, Balkis smiled shyly up into his eyes, then deliberately closed her own and breathed out a long sigh of happiness. Anthony echoed it with a sigh of his own that perhaps held as much longing as contentment, then turned away to sit by the fire where he could watch both the night and her.

Sleep would not come to Balkis, though, and all that lying still with her eyes closed merely made her acutely aware of the strange warmth and trembling within her. As the hours passed she began to wonder whether to feel relieved or disappointed at Anthony's self-control.

Then she remembered that the unicorn hadn't hesitated to carry him, that he must be virgin, too, and wondered if he were as apprehensive as she. She even wondered if he knew what lovers did together, then remembered that he was a farm boy, after all, so had certainly seen animals couple, as had she herself in growing. Then she remembered the crudeness of the household in which he'd been reared, and a strange thought struck her, the possibility that he might not connect mating with love.

If that were so, she would definitely have to do something about it. She was still wondering what when she finally fell asleep.

Anthony woke her after the moon was down, woke her with a kiss on the forehead. Heavy-lidded and flushed with sleep, she smiled and said, "Is that all you can offer me, sir?"

Smiling, he kissed her on the lips, a long and lingering caress that quickened the blood in her veins well enough. Then, though, he released her and sat back on his heels to say, "I have grown wearied at last, so I shall let you watch for the last hour or two of the night, if you wish."

Balkis realized that he was waiting for her to rise from the bed, even though she had made only the one this night. She rose with a sigh, went to sit by the fire, and gave him a smile that spoke more than her lips as she said, "Dream sweetly, love."

He pulled his cloak over his shoulders, smiling back and saying, "If my dreams have been as sweet as my musing, I may not wish to wake."

"Oh," Balkis said, "I think I can see to that." She gave him what she hoped was a look filled with promise. His eyes glowed in answer, but he forced his lids shut with firm resolution.

She turned back to the fire with a sigh and fed it twigs. Really, she was going to have to do something about his excess of gallantry.

She woke Anthony with a kiss, and the magical mood wove itself around them again as they ate breakfast. Then they drowned their fire and took to the road again, or rather, the path. The early sun cast a rosy glow over the landscape, the dew twinkled like stars all about them, and they both felt that they were walking on air as they strolled along, chatting of inconsequentialities—and stopping now and again for a kiss.

Early in the afternoon the mountains that had been before them in the distance for so long were suddenly near, and they saw that the path led into a gorge a hundred yards wide at the bottom. As they came into it, they saw that the walls were high rugged cliffs. They looked about them, marveling at the wild beauty of the place—then heard shouts in a language that Balkis recognized again as akin to that of Maracanda, but so heavily accented that she couldn't really understand it. She did, however, comprehend one word. "Anthony! Someone is telling us to stop!"

"There may be danger ahead, then." Anthony looked all about him. "Where are these people who send kind warning, though?"

"I see them not, either," Balkis said.

The voices shouted again, then began to chant with a heavy beat.

"That has the sound of a war song," Balkis said nervously. "Where are the singers?"

"There!" Anthony pointed upward, staring in amazement.

Balkis looked where he pointed and saw a dozen dragons—small ones, only twelve feet long—saddled and bridled and with people riding them as they flew. As they spiraled down toward the intruders, their war-songs grew more harsh. Anthony and Balkis stared, thunderstruck, as they came. Then three riders dropped spinning packages that spread open into nets, and Balkis jolted out of her reverie. "Run!"

They ran hand in hand, stumbling and staggering over rough ground. Balkis followed the pressure of Anthony's grip, first left, then right, with a total lack of pattern; they were running toward the western wall, but so unpredictably that first one net, then three, fell to either side, but none caught them.

A voice above called out a command, and two dragoneers dove between the fugitives and the cliffs, then arrowed toward them.

Balkis cried.

"Fires scorch and waters drown!
Fear that earth might drag you down!
Air betray you, tumult-fed!"

Anthony didn't even give her a chance to run dry; he called out,

"Hurl you high above our heads!"

The dragons cawed in fright as a wind rose out of the earth itself to hurl them high, tumbling; their riders shouted in terror. They didn't fall from their saddles, though, and Balkis suspected they were tied in. She ran on, letting Anthony direct their course, but glanced back over her shoulder and saw that the two dragons had dropped as suddenly as though they had been tossed, but managed to halt their fall by cupping their wings. Steadying, they didn't try to chase Anthony and Balkis, but flew ahead toward the eastern cliff, then swooped upward and spiraled higher, regaining altitude.

"Down!" Anthony cried and dove, pulling her with him. She fell, and scaly bodies shot by overhead. A rider shouted and a net fell but didn't have time to open; it struck Anthony between the shoulders as a solid lump.

"My love! Are you hurt?" Balkis cried.

Anthony flashed her a grin as he struggled to his feet, then managed to catch his breath and say, "I've taken worse knocks than that."

Balkis caught his hand again with a sob of relief, then saw the lumps of lead in the packed-up net. "It is weighted around the edges!"

"Therefore it spreads when the warrior gives it a spin and lets it go," Anthony said grimly. "Very clever—but so are we. Run! If we can find a cave in that stone wall, they cannot come at us!"

Balkis ran, glancing back at the riders who had just attacked them—but saw that they were sailing onward toward the eastern cliff, just as the last two had. She thought they were going to strike directly into it, but at the last second they swooped upward, then spiraled aloft. She remembered Matthew Mantrell saying something about updrafts. "Anthony! We do not need a cave! If we can even come near to the wall, the riders cannot reach us. Their dragons are far better at gliding than at real flying, and need the air that blows upward along the cliffs to take them back into the sky!"

"To the wall let us flee then!" Anthony said grimly, and kept up his broken-field running. Nets fell to the left and the right of them, they even had to bat aside the edges of one, but none caught them. They came closer and closer to the wall, and the riders must have known it meant safety for the couple, for they set up a hue and cry as they dove at their quarry.

Then one flew directly overhead, only twenty feet up, his net already spinning. It fell open, fell far more quickly than most, fell on them and all around them, and they floundered in the midst of it with cries of despair. Anthony reached for his dagger to cut their way free, but the rider pulled sharply on a drawstring rope and the net closed about them, yanking them off their feet, swinging them high into the air. They cried out in fright and clung to one another, staring down at the ground that receded so quickly below them, spinning and swaying.

"What spell can take us far from here?" Anthony cried.

Balkis tried to remember—yes! There was a verse that she'd heard the Lord Wizard recite.

"I know a bank where the wild thyme blows—"

She broke off in fright as the net began to swing down. They had come to the top of the cliff, but there was only a hundred-foot shelf before it began to climb again, honeycombed with shelves on which the men had built a whole village complete with dragon-cotes. and they were sinking directly toward that village's square. She sang out louder and in a rush,

"Where oxlips and the nodding violet grows—"

Then the net struck rock with an impact that knocked the breath out of her. With wild hope she looked at Anthony, but saw that he was gasping for air, too, and despair and fear gripped her.

Thunder shook the ledge. Looking up, Balkis saw a huge reptilian shape that blocked out the sun, stooping upon the twelve-foot dragons with a twenty-foot tongue of flame. The smaller dragons sheered away in terror, their riders screaming, and as the leviathan passed, Anthony saw a rider with no saddle or reins, only the dragon's great triangular plates to hold him on its shoulders.

"What horror is this come upon us?" Anthony cried.

"It is not horror, but a friend!" Balkis told him, almost weeping with relief. "I know that dragon! He is Stegoman, and the man who rides him is the Lord Wizard of Merovence, my teacher!"

Stegoman completed his first pass and turned to rake the air again, but the dragoneers rallied, calling to one another and forming small groups to either side, surrounding the behemoth. One daring rider sailed overhead, dropping his net, but Matt's sword flashed, cutting half its ropes and batting the rest aside. It plummeted downward and tangled a rider below it.

But the dragoneers were singing again, chanting their warsong as they swooped and darted at the huge dragon who had come to wreak havoc upon them. Balkis had heard their accent long enough so that the words began to make sense, and she realized they weren't boasting or trying to buck up their own spirits—they were giving directions to their mounts and compelling them to obey! The tyrants had not made friends with the dragons—they coerced them by magic! She understood what they were ordering and cricd a warning—but too late, for the separate knots of riders suddenly swooped all together and attacked in a pack.

Matt laid about him frantically, and Stegoman scythed his flame from back and forth, but a few dragoneers managed to duck in from his blind side and swords raked his ribs. Balkis bit her knuckles to keep from screaming as one dragoneer's sword caught Matt's blade and knocked it back against him, making him reel in his seat. She could see that Matt and Stegoman could hold the dragoneers off a goodly while, but in the end they would be borne down by sheer numbers.

Anthony saw that, too. He worked frantically with his own dagger, sawing through ropes. "If you know a spell to help your friend, sing it! We must be free of this net and away where we can aid in our own defense!"

Balkis tried to think of some verse that might disperse the horde of fliers that beset her friends, finally remembered something she had heard Idris sing, and began,

"Blow, winds out of the north!
Chill them to their bones!"

Another roar split the air.

Anthony froze, staring up. "What lyric brought you *that*?"

Another full-sized dragon came tearing down from the sky, a reddish dragon a little shorter and considerably more slender than Stegoman, but with a lance of flame just as long.

The dragons scattered with scandalized screams of rage, and for the first time Balkis heard them utter words.

"It is Dimetrolas, bigger yet than when we cast her out!"

"It is Dimetrolas, turned against her own kind!"

"Even as we knew she one day would! Gather all! Slay the renegade!"

CHAPTER 26

"I am not a renegade but an outcast!" Dimetrolas roared. "If I turn against you now, it is because you cast me out of your tribe; I can fight without turning against my own, for you have made me no longer one of you!" Then her roaring turned inarticulate and her flame swept the air to guard Stegoman's back. Dragoneers howled as their mounts rolled aside from the flame.

But the dragons were shouting the alarm, and more of their kind came bolting from the round doorways of every cote. Some circled down to the shelf to gather their riders, but most came with bare backs, flaring their rage against the rogue who sided with a stranger against her own clan. Soon the whole village was aloft and attacking from every side, only oldsters, children, and hatchlings still on the ground to watch the battle. Gradually the cloud of fliers separated into two wedges, one on each side, like the jaws of a forceps.

"We must aid them!" Anthony cried.

"We must indeed." Though why the Lord Wizard was not himself using magic to fight off the fliers Balkis couldn't understand. Perhaps he feared killing them, for if you knocked a dragon unconscious at that height, both mount and rider would die in the fall. She had watched closely enough to identify the leader of the dragoneers, though—the one who rode the largest dragon and wore an emerald jerkin, where all others wore brown or grayish-green, and if they had tamed the flying dragons not by friendship or skill but by incantations, they offered a very serious weakness for her to exploit. She began to chant, adapting a verse Matt had taught her, and so worried not at all about rhyme.

"How happy is the dragon taught
To cease to serve another's will;
What armor is his honest thought . . ."

"Take it, Anthony!" She was chagrined not to remember the last line of the verse.

"And simple flight his utmost skill!"

Anthony replied.

Balkis' voice rang with delight:

"Dragons, be freed from servile bands,
Of goad to rise, or fear to fall;—
Lords of yourselves, though not of lands . . ."

She floundered again, and Anthony came in on the instant:

"And having nothing, yet have all!"

A cry came echoing down, Matt's voice: "Wotton!"

"What in Heaven have we wrought, indeed?" Anthony exclaimed, looking up.

Every dragon who carried a rider roared with delight as he or she dove toward the village ledge, roars that resolved into, "Off my back, midge, ere I swat you!"

The riders shrieked frantic verses, but nothing would regain them control. The dragons swooped within five feet of the ledge; a few riders were smart enough to leap off. The others howled with fright as the dragons looped the loop to make a second pass—fright that their spells did no good, that the dragons were completely out of their control, that their conquered mounts did exactly as they pleased. On the second pass most of them jumped, and the dragons flew away to attack Dimetrolas. The few diehards nearly did—die, that is, because their dragons simply turned their heads and blasted flame. None actually struck the riders, they missed by a foot or more, but the men and women took the hint, untied their saddle-ropes, and as the dragons dove toward the ledge, leaped to save their lives.

They ran to gather weapons, but they were safe for the moment, for all the little dragons were concentrating their attack on the renegade—Dimetrolas.

"Do you act in concert still?"

Balkis cried, spreading her hands up toward the flock.

"Remember each your mind and will!
Render up your own opinion . . .

"Anthony, a rhyme!" she shouted. Obligingly, he answered,

"Of none other be a minion!"

"Well sung!" Balkis said with a sigh of relief. "Give me now a second verse."

"Second . . . ?" Anthony spread his hands, at a loss how to begin.

"A last verse! Give me a last verse!"

"Ah!" Anthony cried, and chanted,

"Let discord foment in your clan!"

Then he spread his hands again, brow furrowed.

Balkis leaped into the breach.

"Guard with zeal your independence!
Each dragon form a different sense . . ."

"Of wisest course and soundest plan," Anthony cried triumphantly.

Balkis almost collapsed, limp from tension.

"Attack from the left!" one dragon cried.

"Fool! Attack from the right!" another shouted.

"Idiot! They have heard you and will expect us now!"

"Attack from all directions at once!" another commanded. "Some may die in the glory of flames, but others will come behind, no matter which way they face!"

"Lead, then, and die yourself!" cried a fourth. "All attack from the back! Now!"

In minutes they were quarreling among themselves so viciously that the real quarry was forgotten. A few dragons remembered and dove toward Dimetrolas and Stegoman, but a single blast of flame was enough to make them sheer off. Finally there was a space of a few minutes, during which Stegoman and Dimetrolas put their heads together; then Dimetrolas flew east and Stegoman west, both turning to descend with flame on half a dozen dragons on the fringe of the tribal argument. The half dozen shrieked at the first touch of flame and went zigzagging across the sky, but Stegoman rose above them and in front, flying faster than they, then turning to roar fire. The smaller dragons turned, shrieking, and dove to escape Dimetrolas' flame. The two larger dragons drove them down to the ledge, where they shot into their stone cotes for safety. Then the two behemoths soared back to chip another half dozen off the mass and drive them similarly down to their cotes. Again and again they soared and stooped, working in perfect unison to harry the outliers down. Finally, the dozen remaining realized the mass had shrunk tremendously and turned to fight, but at one blast fled shrieking for cover.

Then Stegoman strafed the ledge, roaring flame at the dragoneers. The few who had not already fled for safety did so now, running back into their granite-block houses. The great dragon dipped low over the ledge as he passed Anthony and Balkis, and his rider sprang off, running a few steps to shed momentum, then stopped, grinning and spreading his arms.

Balkis gave a joyful cry and ran into his embrace. "Oh, my teacher, I have so longed to see a face from home!"

"Your real home, yes, I know," Matt said, then stepped back to look at her companion. "And who is this strapping young man to whom I'm sure I owe your safety?"

Balkis turned with delight that faded as she saw the look of resentment on Anthony's face.

Matt muttered, "Don't worry, he's just jealous!"

Joy sprang in Balkis' heart, and she ran to her love. "Oh, Anthony, it is Matthew Mantrell, my teacher, of whom I've told you! Come, you must meet him, for he and his family have been such good friends to me!"

Anthony's face cleared at the word "family." He came forward and bowed to Matthew. "An honor to meet you, my lord."

Matt bent an accusing glance at Balkis. "You weren't supposed to tell him I'm a lord."

Balkis laughed, a sound of sheer delight. "Lord Matthew, this is my love Anthony, my own true love to me!" She demonstrated by stepping into the circle of his arm and pressing her head against his shoulder.

Matt smiled, trying to ignore a feeling of indignation that the girl who'd had such a huge crush on him a year before should now be so thoroughly besotted with a callow youth—but he didn't try to quell the feeling of relief that overrode all. He bowed to Anthony in his turn. "Well met, Master Anthony."

"Oh, no master!" Anthony protested. "I am only a farmer's son, and quite innocent of any knowledge save tilling the soil and tending livestock!"

"Oh, aye, and now with knowledge of every land between here and your southern mountains," Balkis chided, "and a skill at verse that leaves me far behind!"

"No, it is I who am the one behind," Anthony said, grinning down at her, "for I have only the skill of ending a verse, whereas you can begin them with ease that astounds me."

"Sounds like a good match." Matt tried to hide a smile of amusement. But he saw how the two gazed into one another's eyes and realized how truly Balkis had spoken when she called him her own true love.

Then Balkis broke away to give Matt as stern a look as she could manage. "Why did you not send those dragons fleeing with your magic, my lord?"

"Oh, I did my share," Matt told them. "When Dimetrolas and Stegoman started herding the beasts home, I chanted a spell about discretion being the better part of valor, and none of them even thought of fighting back."

Balkis laughed with delight, still clinging to Anthony's hand. "I should have known! But had you realized that these dragon-riders had tamed their beasts with magic, not friendship?"

Matt stiffened. "No, I hadn't. How'd you find out?"

"I have heard enough of their barbaric accent to understand their words," Balkis explained.

"So you cast a spell that gave the dragons their freedom." Matt nodded. "Very smart—but how do we keep the dragons from killing off their erstwhile captors?"

"Should we?" Balkis' eyes glittered.

"Balkis!" Anthony protested, shocked. "I own what they have done is horrible, but I would not wish to see a bloodbath!"

Matt nodded approval. "I think we can take our time working out a solution—neither the people nor the dragons seem terribly eager to come out while Stegoman and Dimetrolas are on patrol."

"Dimetrolas, yes, that was the name the dragons called out." Balkis turned a curious gaze on the female dragon crouched next to Stegoman in the center of the village, the two resembling hawks waiting to pounce on the first rabbit careless enough to poke its head out of its burrow. In fact, whenever a dragon dared to poke its head out of one of the circular doorways of a cote, Stegoman sent it ducking for cover with a blast of flame. If a human face peered out a window, Dimetrolas sent it back with a torch. Neither of them was within fifty feet of the buildings, but the point was taken.

Balkis smiled at their cooperation. "Is Stegoman courting, then?"

"I'm impressed," Matt said. "How'd you know it was a she?"

"By her slenderness and grace," Balkis answered, "but chiefly by the dragons calling her a she. Where is her origin?"

"Here, it would seem," Matt said, "though she didn't tell us—we met her guarding a mountain pass alone, no doubt waiting for fat sheep to wander by. How she got there is no doubt a long story."

"But one she has not confided to you?"

"Right. One look at Stegoman, though, and she wouldn't leave him alone—and now we know why."

"That she found him handsome?"

Matt nodded. "Handsome, and the first male of her species she'd ever seen who was anywhere near her own size. Speaking of long stories, though, how did you get here?"

"Tell me first," Balkis said, "how you came to happen by when we had such need of you."

"Mostly luck," Matt said, "but your uncle called us in as soon as you were kidnapped. We've been searching for you ever since and just managed to pick up your trail a couple of days ago—in the nick of time, it would seem. Okay, your turn. I can guess how you came to be in the foothills of the Himalayas." At the blank look both young folk gave him, he explained, "Anthony's southern mountains. But how did you travel from there to here?"

"Why, we walked," Anthony said.

Balkis flashed him a smile and said, "We have simply come north, Lord Wizard—no need to be sure of the road to Maracanda until we were near enough for it to matter."

"I'll accept that," Matt said, "but how did you survive the valley of the giant ants? And that griddle of a desert? And . . . but maybe you'd better tell it to me from the beginning."

They did, Balkis and Anthony taking turns as the three humans sat down and Matt took a wineskin from his pack. They drank only to wet their lips when they went dry, but the tale took an hour anyway. Matt listened as closely as he could, but his attention was split, trying to keep track of the conversation between the two dragons.

Stegoman said to Dimetrolas, "So you are of this flock, but grew too big for their liking."

"Were you not cast out, too?" she asked angrily.

"I was, and for a far better reason—I could not help but breathe fire whenever I flew, and when I breathed fire, I became drunk from my own fumes and attacked any whom I imagined had offended me. My clan ripped my wings and cast me out to crawl about the land."

"Ripped your wings?" Dimetrolas shuddered. "What a horrible punishment!" Then she stared at his half-spread, unmarked leather vanes. "But they are whole, and so handsome! I mean . . ."

"I thank you for the compliment," Stegoman said gravely. "My friend Matthew healed my wings with his magic and cured me of my drunkenness. Therefore do I carry him and fight his battles."

"I can see that such courtesy is merited." Dimetrolas' eyes turned dreamy. "If someone were to transform me into a wee, winsome thing, only eleven feet long—"

"You would lose half your beauty," Stegoman said instantly, "and all your fascination."

Dimetrolas turned to him in surprise. "Do you truly find me fascinating?"

"Do you not truly find me alien?" Stegoman returned.

"No, only strange enough to intrigue me," Dimetrolas replied with equal candor. "Your mind does not work as those of other dragons do."

"I have been among humans too long," Stegoman acknowledged, "and one of them has a most odd sense of humor. But now I see the reason for your own solitary anger that has struck a chord of kinship within me."

"Kinship?" Dimetrolas stared. "Then why would you not chase when I jibed?"

"I am, as you said, too serious by nature," Stegoman told her. "Perhaps it is this removal from my own kind that has done it—or perhaps I am simply too grim and forbidding a beast."

"I think it is lack of practice," Dimetrolas said with a saurian smile. "I shall have to teach you to play again." Then she raised her head high, staring down at him with the loftiest manner she could manage. "Have you anything to teach me in return, ancient lizard?"

Stegoman's lips lifted in a faint echo of her smile. "I might remember a very old game or two, chick."

Matt smiled and focused all his attention on the young couple before him; he had a notion that any further eavesdropping would constitute an invasion of privacy.

"Thus we left the gentle old men," Balkis finished, "and came here."

Matt suspected that there was a lot she was leaving out, but the tale of how she and Anthony had fallen in love was none of his business. "You don't know how glad I am to see you safe." He inclined his head toward Anthony. "Thank you for guarding her sleep."

"I must thank her for guarding mine," Anthony returned, "and for my look at the wide world."

Balkis turned to him anxiously. "You do not regret leaving your hills?"

"Not a bit, strangely," Anthony said, "and if I ever grow homesick, I can always return."

Balkis' eyes clouded.

Anthony smiled into her eyes. "Of course, the company here is far more agreeable."

Balkis grinned and leaned forward, head back. Anthony took the hint, and met her lips with his own.

Matt whistled the Liebestod as he gazed off toward the village, then turned back to the young lovers as they broke apart but still gazed at each other with shining eyes. He felt a pang as he remembered his first days with Alisande, and longing for her welled up in him. To get his mind off it, he said, "So you weren't deliberately walking into danger when you came into this gorge."

"If we had known what we would find, we would surely have gone around it," Anthony said grimly.

"We certainly did not expect to have to evade capture," Balkis said.

"It is odd that these dragoneers do not even challenge a traveler before they attack," Anthony mused.

"Yes, very odd." Matt stood up, gazing at the largest building in the village. "Maybe we ought to find out why." He set off toward the structure.

Balkis and Anthony exchanged a look of curiosity, then hurried after him, Balkis muttering under her breath.

Anthony caught the cadence of her words and asked, "What spell do you prepare?"

"One to call down lightning," Balkis said grimly.

Matt stopped fifty feet from the building, close enough to be heard easily, far enough to avoid any surprise attacks by giving him a chance to dodge an arrow. He set his hands on his hips and called, "Parley! I'd really rather not stay here for the rest of your lives making you behave, but I can set spirit sentries if I have to!"

"You would not!" wailed a voice from within. "How should we live?"

"How do you live now?" Matt returned. "By robbing travelers and selling them into slavery?"

"We are not such cravens as that!" A lean, gray-bearded man appeared in the doorway, ramrod straight, fists clenched. "Who are you who comes to insult us so?"

"One who came to make you mend your evil ways," Matt retorted. "Come out and talk—if you have the courage."

The man eyed Stegoman and Dimetrolas. "Come out, to be burned by your pets?"

Stegoman rumbled warning, and Dimetrolas hissed with anger.

"I think you know Dimetrolas well enough to realize she could never be anyone's pet," Matt said, "though she could choose to be a strong ally—and might want a spot of revenge. Nonetheless, I don't think either of them would want to fry me, so if you're standing near me, you'll be safe."

"What of the distance between this hall and yourself?"

"Let's make a deal," Matt said. "You don't shoot any arrows, and the dragons won't crisp you until after the parley's over and you've gone back inside."

The man glanced at Stegoman and Dimetrolas again. "I will accept those terms, if they will."

"I shall hold my fire," Stegoman rumbled, "though I shall bid you mind your speech, human!" He turned to the female. "Dimetrolas?"

"I shall withhold also," she replied, though warily. "You and I have an old score, Lugerin!"

Stegoman stiffened. "Was it he bade the dragons exile you?"

"He it was who began the talk," Dimetrolas replied, "though he left it to the lizards to do his shabby deeds." She showed all her teeth and spoke toward the building. "He feared my size, but would have had no cause if I had stayed. Now, though, he is right to fear! Still, Lugerin, I will wait for my revenge—but bring Ginelur, for no bargain will be binding without both of your assents!"

"She shall come," Lugerin grumbled, and so darkly that Matt was sure he had planned on an escape clause.

Lugerin leaned back into the hall for a few muttered words, then came out side by side with an older woman, tall and striking, with a mane of raven hair streaked by a central band of silver. They came forward, both clad in leather embossed with brass—not quite armor, certainly more than casual wear.

They halted five feet from Matt. Ginelur demanded, "Why have you come here?"

"Looking for my young friends," Matt answered, "who are traveling to Maracanda and certainly did not deserve attack. Why did you try to kidnap them?"

"We do not sell slaves!" Lugerin snapped.

Matt caught the implication. "But you do enslave travelers. Do they farm for you in hidden fields?"

Both dragoneers flushed, and Matt knew he had scored. "If they offend us, and if the gales are too strong," Ginelur said stiffly, "we sacrifice them to the wind-spirits at the changing of the year."

The equinoxes, Matt guessed, those being the windy times. "What on earth makes you think you have the right to capture anybody you please?"

"The right of revenge!" Lugerin snapped. "Our ancestors farmed this valley in peace, but again and again barbarians swept in to raid. At last our ancestors built these cliff-houses for retreats when the reavers came, and thus saved their lives, saved their wives and children from capture and slavery—but lost their crops and became prey to starvation."

"So you're taking revenge on people who didn't commit the crime." Matt shook his head, remembering a girl or two who had treated him with suspicion and jealousy because old boyfriends had loved them and left them, and a man he knew who had loved and left a young woman in revenge for others' abandonment. "Well, it's a human failing. Still, you should have outgrown it by now."

"That revenge was taken against the barbarians at first, you may be sure!" Ginelur told him. "Olien, our ancestors' shaman, learned how to tame the dragons with his magic. We then had mounts more fearsome than the barbarians' horses, and have repelled every raid since."

"Repelled, and taken slaves and warriors to sacrifice in our own turn, as they did to us!" Lugerin spat.

"How many centuries ago was this? Not much for holding a grudge, are you?"

"Our safety lies in our savagery!" Ginelur retorted. "The barbarians have not ridden against us in three generations, you may be sure!"

"So when you ran out of barbarians, you started in on random travelers."

"Would they not loot and pillage if they had the chance?" Ginelur said defiantly.

"Not these two." Matt nodded toward Anthony and Balkis. "And not quite a few others over the centuries, I'll wager. They would now, of course, after suffering your enslavement. Even gentle people tend to do to others what you've done to them. But if dragons are your strength, why were you afraid of Dimetrolas?"

"Because she grew far more than was acceptable," Ginelur said. "Now and again one of the huge wild dragons would turn rogue and burn houses, even people—so our ancestors bred them to become smaller and more manageable."

Stegoman spat an oath. "You robbed them not only of their freedom, but also of the size that was their birthright?"

"They were dangerous to us," Lugerin said, flint-faced. "Therefore do we cast out the throwbacks who grow toward ancestral size."

"Stand away, Matthew," Stegoman growled. "He deserves burning. They all do."

CHAPTER 27

"There!" Lugerin pointed at Stegoman. "Do you see? If they can hurt us, they will!"

"Just like people?" Matt asked softly. "Any stranger might be a powerful wizard, is that it? So you trap them and enslave them to make sure they can't hurt you. Who do you choose for sacrifice—the ones who are big enough and strong enough to be threats?"

Lugerin flushed, but Ginelur said evenly, "They, and those who come riding, for any on horseback will surely attack us if they can."

"Why? Because the barbarians who originally attacked your ancestors came mounted?" Matt shook his head. "Your whole culture is built on fear."

"Indeed," Stegoman rumbled. "I have seldom seen a band of fainthearts so devout in their cowardice."

Lugerin reddened. "You would not say that if this sorcerer had not robbed us of our dragons!"

"If you had treated them well," Dimetrolas retorted, "they would have become your friends, and no wizard could have robbed you of them by simply giving them their freedom."

"Friends may turn against you, too." But Ginelur was looking doubtful.

"Oh, friendship takes work, no doubt about it," Matt said. "You have to treat each other well, you always have to be polite, you have to be there when they need you and vice versa. Sometimes you can even drift apart for a while just from having spent too much time together. But you can find ways to keep your alliance going, if it really means anything to you."

"You shall have to now, in any case," Dimetrolas called, "for your spells will no longer coerce your dragons!"

Lugerin brought the words up with great reluctance. "I shall apologize to your sorceress, if shc will restore the power of our spells."

"After you tried to capture her and enslave her?" Matt asked. "Who knows, maybe you meant even worse."

Ginelur cast a dark glance at Lugerin.

"No, I don't see any reason why she should remove her freedom spell," Matt said.

"But she must!" The words ripped out of Lugerin. "If she does not, the dragons are sure to destroy us!"

"They have old grudges to settle, too, huh?" Matt glanced at the dragon-cotes.

"Then we should let them come out and be about their business," Stegoman rumbled. "That would be justice for any who sought to compel so wondrous a creature as Dimetrolas—and more than just recompense for her outcasting!"

Dimetrolas looked up at Stegoman with pleased surprise; then her eyes began to glow.

Matt was wary of glowing dragons. "I don't know, Old Smoky," he called to Stegoman. "There is another side to the issue. Okay, the dragoneers enslaved your breed and cut them down to their own size—but the winged ones always had plenty to eat, and they certainly have multiplied. The humans even made them very secure roosts. If they just had the courage to trust the beasts, they might have a very profitable alliance here."

Stegoman was silent. Dimetrolas burst out, "Such an alliance would require great changes in their ways! Can they bear it?"

"Well?" Matt looked from Ginelur to Lugerin and back. "Consider the alternative—a giant barbecue fueled by some very vengeful dragons. Even if we talk them into leaving you alone, you're going to find you have a lot of people with scores to settle—starting with your slaves. And if word gets out, the barbarians may come riding in to settle *their* old grudge."

Lugerin paled. Ginelur looked up at him with anxiety, then asked, "What would the dragons want of us?"

"No slavery, that's for sure," Matt said promptly. "Your dragons are already free, but you'd have to let your human slaves go, too."

"Who, then, would till our fields!" Lugerin cried.

"Why," said Matt, "you will. Have to do your own farming, I guess."

Lugerin glared daggers at him but said nothing.

"And this matter of casting out must cease!" Dimetrolas snapped. "The dragons will not think of it if the humans do not urge it!"

"How should we deal with fifty-foot mounts?" Ginelur cried.

"The same way I do," Matt said.

The dragoneers stared at Stegoman, then back at Matt, frankly disbelieving—but doubt of their ancestral ways stirred in their eyes.

Matt nourished it. "If you can make friends with twelve-foot dragons, you can make friends with fifty-footers. All it takes is honesty, sincerity, and the ability to keep a bargain."

Lugerin still stood stiffly, but the doubt was growing. Ginelur glanced at him, then at Dimetrolas, and nodded slowly. "It might fare." She called to Dimetrolas, "Do you wish this alliance?"

"It matters not to me," Dimetrolas said with lofty carelessness, "for I shall not be here. But I shall warrant your safety while you parley." She turned her head and called to the nearest dragon-cote. "Ho within! It is Dimetrolas who speaks! Let Brongaffer come forth to confer with the humans!"

The cote was silent.

"Come *now*," Stegoman thundered, "or you shall wither away in shame!"

Several heads poked out of doorways. "How now, drake?" said one. "Why should we wither, and what should be our shame?"

"Why," said Stegoman, "if the humans you guard were to die at the hands of barbarians, you would be shamed through all the world of dragondom—and the news would travel, be sure! As to why you would wither, you soft creatures who have let humans feed you and build your nests for hundreds of years—is there a one among you who can be sure of bringing home game to feed mate and hatchlings every night? Even if you could, where would you travel when you have eaten all the game in these hills? How will you live, if not in truce with these who have bred you?"

There was silence; then a tumult of conversation broke out in the dragon-cote—and in the other cotes all along the ledge.

Ginelur and Lugerin looked at one another in astonishment.

The ruckus died down, and one dragon came out of his cote. "I come, Dimetrolas."

"I am your bond, Brongaffer," she warned him. "Do not think to attack these humans who stand for parley."

"I have not so little honor as that!" Brongaffer said indignantly.

"So, then," Stegoman said softly, "these have learned human ways, too."

"Is honor so human, then?" Dimetrolas asked in surprise.

"Honor is of humans, yes. Pride is of dragons."

"Then I, too, have something of human ways."

Stegoman's head whipped about to stare at her, then his mouth lolled open in a dragon's smile. "You do indeed."

Brongaffer spread his wings, sprang into the air, and landed ten feet from Lugerin and Ginelur. "What speech would you have with me, mayor and broodmaster?"

"I would suggest," Ginelur said, "that we make a pact between dragons and dragoneers, Brongaffer—your backs and wings in exchange for the works of our hands."

"The two folk together arc far stronger than either one alone," Matt pointed out. "In fact, if you can work out a functional agreement, I suspect Prester John would be delighted to have you join his army as an aerial corps."

"Work for hire?" Lugerin cried indignantly.

"No—swear fealty as vassals." Matt turned to Brongaffer. "You might even be able to gain wealth of your own by setting up an express delivery service for the emperor—you'd certainly be the fastest way for him to communicate with his kings and governors. You might even be able to open a transportation service, carrying diplomats to and from Maracanda."

"Why should we wish to serve in so menial a fashion?" Brongaffer said disdainfully.

"To get rich. You could charge exorbitant rates, after all—say, ten head of cattle for each message delivered. Of course, after a while you'd have to build a lot of barns to hold them all and spend hours and hours tending them—so maybe you'd prefer to take a few pieces of gold instead of the cattle. That way, you could always buy dinner."

Brongaffer looked thoughtful.

"Well, I'll leave you to sort it out for yourselves. No cheating, now—and no attacking while my back is turned."

He sauntered over to Stegoman and Dimetrolas but glanced back after a few paces. The humans were already deep in discussion with the dragons' emissary.

He came up to his old friend and his new one and said, "Score one more for the benefits of commerce."

"They shall hammer out a bargain," Stegoman agreed.

"I hate to admit the truth of it," Dimetrolas said, "but these humans have provided well for their dragons."

"The dragons have a lot to lose if they burn the hands that build for them," Matt agreed.

"If they ally, though," said Stegoman, "will they not be a danger to any other travelers who happen by?"

"If they get that far," Matt said, "I'll start bargaining again. I'll extract a promise to parley before attacking strangers, unless those strangers are clearly a war party. If the dragoneers want to charge tolls, all well and good, but no raiding and no more enslaving."

"Why should they obey you?" Dimetrolas demanded.

"Because I'm the Lord Wizard of Merovence. They don't know that yet, but they'll pay attention once they do. I can make some pretty dire threats, especially if I claim I have Balkis to back me up."

Dimetrolas considered this.

"No, I won't deliver the dragon equivalent of itching powder," Matt said quickly. "You've punished them enough already."

"Punished them?" Dimetrolas stared at him. "How?"

"Pride is very important to dragons," Matt reminded. "The adolescent they cast out just came back with a bigger, meaner drake than any of them and made them all behave. You handed them a thorough humiliation, lady. Worse, you turned right around and did them a favor—you helped enforce the truce, and one of the people you were defending freed them from the dragoneers' spells, so they can't even hate you for attacking. How's that for humiliation?"

Dimetrolas' eyes gleamed as she raised her head proudly. "I have had my revenge, haven't I?"

"You have indeed," said Stegoman. "The one they scorned become their champion? I would say you have!"

"With some help, of course." But Dimetrolas seemed suddenly both coy and arrogant. "The other females mocked me and told me a great lump like myself could never find a mate—and I have come back with one grander and stronger and wiser than any of them!"

Stegoman visibly swelled under her regard. Nonetheless, he reminded her, "We are not yet mated."

"Shall we not amend that soon?" Dimetrolas said, her voice low and pulsing.

Matt decided it was time to see how Anthony and Balkis were doing. He strolled back to them and said, "Looks like the dragons and the riders will work things out. We'll just wait until they make a bargain and see that they sign a formal treaty, then fly on home. Can we offer you two a ride?"

Balkis cast a quick glance at Anthony, then gave Matt a look that was almost furtive. "I thank you, Lord Wizard, but—" Her eyes seemed to plead. "—I may not have set out to come to know my mother's homeland, but I have found it most instructive and . . . rewarding." She took Anthony's hand by reflex. "I am sure there are more wonders in store, more kinds of people to meet between this place and Maracanda, and I would like to come to know them all. By your leave, we will continue on our way as we were."

"But to fly . . ." Anthony gazed at Stegoman with mingled fear and excitement.

"We'll give you a chance when you reach Maracanda,"

Matt promised. He had his own ideas about whom Balkis wanted to come to know better before she made it back to her uncle's capital. "Sure, you two walk and we'll fly along. I'll go tell Stegoman what's going on."

He walked a bit more slowly as he passed Brongaffer and the humans, listening a moment to their spirited exchange:

"If we are to continue to sacrifice the freedom of the air, we will want strong covenants from you!"

"And we from you," Ginelur said. "Who among you has learned to read? For this covenant must be carved in stone for all to learn!"

They'd made faster progress than Matt had expected. Seemed he wouldn't have to nudge them too hard after all.

He came up to the two dragons and said, "Balkis and Anthony have decided to go on home on foot."

"Have they indeed!" Dimetrolas exclaimed with a knowing look. "She wants him to herself for a while longer, does she?"

"I think that's most of it," Matt admitted. "Certainly she's not ready to tell him she's a princess."

"She is?" Dimetrolas looked at Stegoman with astonishment.

He nodded. "The niece of Prester John."

"Truly!" Dimetrolas looked at the young lovers. "No wonder you deemed it worth your while to search her out!"

"No, her worth is that of a friend," Stegoman said, nettled. "What are emperors and kings to me?"

"Or to her, from the look of it," Dimetrolas pointed out. "She is as besotted with that farm boy as she would be with a belted knight!"

"Well, she may be a princess, but she didn't find that out until a year ago," Matt explained. "Before that, she grew up in a cottage as a woodcutter's daughter."

Dimetrolas stared at him in surprise. "How strange are the ways of you human folk!"

"Don't expect me to argue," Matt said grimly. "Still, I'm glad I only said 'your uncle' to her when Anthony was around—and not his name. I think she wants to make sure he's as besotted as she is before she breaks the news. Why else would she want to spend their quality time on the road, instead of in a chamber full of luxuries?"

"There is sense in that," Stegoman said, musing. "Still, are they certain they wish to chance the journey? Have they any idea what manner of dangers stand between them and the capital?"

"None all that bad, as I remember from the trip down here," Matt said. "Certainly they've already survived worse. After all, Balkis is a pretty accomplished wizard already, and it turns out her young man has some talent along that line, too."

"Does he indeed! Ought you not stay and teach him the use of it?"

"Somehow I don't think the two of them want company just now."

"I am not sure that we do, either," Dimetrolas said, with a glance at Stegoman.

"We must know each other better ere we spend too much time unchaperoned, sweet chick," Stegoman said, his eyes glowing. "After all, it is only this day that we have begun to talk as friends—more than friends, but not yet close enough for a sweet and fragile creature such as you to entrust herself to a gnarled old beast such as myself."

"Gnarled and old, forsooth! You are no more aged than I am fragile!"

Matt noticed that she didn't deny the "sweet" part, though, and thought that was promising. "Just give me a lift back to Maracanda, okay? Then you two can go off and find a nice isolated mountaintop where you can get to know each other in detail."

"How many days to this Maracanda?" Dimetrolas asked.

"One at the most," Stegoman answered. "With a tailwind, less."

"Oh, well, I can spare you for that long," Dimetrolas grumbled.

Stegoman gave her another saurian smile. "Mayhap I shall not wish to be spared." Before she could answer, he turned to Matt. "How soon shall we sail, then?"

"Well, I'd better help them put their treaty into words."

Matt glanced at the dragon/human conference. "They might need a neutral party at that point. By then it'll be night. How about taking off at first light?"

"Done," Stegoman agreed. He turned to Dimetrolas. "Thus can we ensure at least one night of peace between your tribe and the humans."

"They are not mine!"

"They are even if they have disowned you." Stegoman gazed deeply into her eyes. "Deny your origins, and you deny yourself, weakening the core of your being—this I know from bitter experience. Then, too, you are their savior now, and an example to them of what dragons were once and can be again, once they are freed from the tyranny of sorcery."

Dimetrolas stared at him, speechless.

"I think that they shall acclaim you as one of their own again," Stegoman finished.

"Shall I want it?" Dimetrolas erupted. "After the shame they have heaped upon me, should I not scorn them?"

"You would have every right," Stegoman said grimly, "and I doubt that you would feel welcome if you tried to stay—but you must make your peace with them for your own sake."

"And theirs?" Dimetrolas challenged.

"And theirs," Stegoman acknowledged, "but it is far more obvious that they would gain by your presence, than that you would gain by theirs."

"It was not so years ago, when they cast me out!"

"It was not," Stegoman agreed, "but they weakened themselves by letting the humans manipulate them into rejecting you, and they have learned that today. Nay, sweet chick, show mercy, and humiliate them further by your kindness—acknowledge them as your own, even though you do not choose to stay."

Dimetrolas raised her head slowly, neck forming an S-curve, looking toward the dragon-cotes with pride, even arrogance. "Perhaps I shall . . ."

Stegoman had certainly learned human diplomacy over the years, Matt reflected, and far more about the soul's need than he had realized. "I'll just tell Balkis the plan, okay?" he said.

"Do," Stegoman agreed, "and see if you can sound out that young man, to learn how much he has of the gift of magic."

Matt glanced at the peace conference in time to see Ginelur, then Lugerin, hold up a palm, and Brongaffer press his taloned paw against it. Then all three started back to their respective halls.

Matt caught up with the humans in a hurry. "Made progress?"

"We have hammered out the bones of an agreement," Lugerin said, his hostility barely veiled.

"Now we must put flesh on those bones." Ginelur hid her resentment a bit better; it only showed in flashes. "We must ask our people for their approval, and for their suggestions and additions."

"Then meet with Brongaffer again and negotiate the details." Matt nodded. "You are going to stipulate that you'll ask strangers their business before you attack them, aren't you?"

"Unless they are clearly a war party, yes." Lugerin's gaze was pure hatred. "If they come in peace. we shall let them pass unmolested—if they pay us tribute."

"Call it a toll instead of a tribute and I don't think you'll have much argument," Matt said. "I predict that within a year word will get around among the travelers, and you'll start having caravans coming through. Give them a discount for having a lot of people in one party and they'll make it a regular stop."

Ginelur looked at him in surprise, then gazed off into the distance, her expression calculating. Lugerin didn't get past surprise. "You offer us advice to make us prosper when you have only now defeated us?"

"Hey, if I'm going to insist you let your slaves go, I've got to show you some way to come out ahead, don't I?"

"Why do you think you can insist on anything from us?" Lugerin demanded, his rage an inch below the surface. "Without your dragons you are nothing!"

"No, without my dragon friends, I'm the Lord Wizard of Merovence."

Both leaders stared at him in shock.

"You haven't heard of Merovence, I expect," Matt said. "It's a kingdom far to the west, but between its warrior queen and myself, we've held it secure against half a dozen invasion attempts."

Lugerin was having second thoughts. Nonetheless, he blustered, "You could be lying!"

"I could," Matt agreed. He looked around the village and saw a huge boulder filling the space between two houses. "You ever think about getting rid of that rock?" He pointed.

Lugerin turned to look. "Aye." His smile turned vindictive. "None can move it, of course. We must build around it."

"Well, you never know," Matt said. "Erosion can wear down a mountain." He drew his wand, pointed at the boulder, and started chanting.

CHAPTER 28

"Break, break, break
Your cold gray stone—oh, see!
Demolition my tongue shall utter,
Become a heap of stone blocks for me.

"Break, break, break
To the foot of this crag that I see.
Shiver into a thousand shards
With no pebbles or gravel or scree.

Break, break, break
Into a heap of gray cubes and stone blocks
A new dragon-cote for to make,
All formed of this obdurate rock."

He hoped Tennyson's ghost wouldn't object. After all, it was in a good cause—clearing living space in a congested area.

The boulder started to vibrate. With sounds like gunshots, cracks appeared at its top, then ran down its sides until the whole mass was segmented like an orange. All at once it fell in on itself with an avalanche's rumble. Where there had been a huge boulder, there was only a heap of tumbled blocks.

The humans poured out of their houses to gaze in amazement.

Lugerin and Ginelur could only stare, thunderstruck.

"Those blocks will need finishing, of course," Matt said, "but they're basically squared off. Should make fine building stone."

The two leaders turned to him with awe and fear. Beyond

them, their people glanced at the stranger in terror, then looked quickly away.

"So you see, I really am a wizard," Matt explained. "The young lady who cast the spell that freed your dragons was my apprentice, but she learned everything I could teach her in a year. I'm sure she'd be glad to come back here for a visit if I asked her. So would Stegoman and Dimetrolas, for that matter."

"How would you know what passes here?" Ginelur asked through stiff lips.

Time to bluff. "I have a dozen ways, of course. I'm sure you've heard of crystal balls and ink pools. Then there are animal sentries, supernatural spies, and . . . well, I won't bore you with the list."

They weren't bored. Lugerin glared defiantly, but Matt could see in his eyes the certainty that he was boxed in. Ginelur, on the other hand, was clearly aware that Matt might be bluffing—but it was even more obvious that she didn't dare call him on it.

"Not that my insisting would be necessary, of course," Matt said. "I'm sure your people will realize the good sense of these ideas. You may have to explain it a bit, but they'll see the wisdom of it."

"No doubt they shall," Lugerin said in a monotone. He looked down at Ginelur. "Let us tell them the plan to which our colleague Brongaffer has agreed."

They went on toward the biggest building, which Matt was more sure than ever was a meeting hall. He smiled to himself as he turned to go back to the young couple.

"You told me a wizard should never make an exhibition of his powers," Balkis accused as he came up.

"An *unnecessary* exhibition," Matt reminded her. "In fact, as I remember it, I said not to be a show-off—don't go working magic without a good reason."

"And your reason was to make clear to these dragoneers how little choice they had in agreeing to your terms?" Anthony asked.

Matt nodded. "Some people never get beyond thinking that a law only exists if it's enforced. I just showed them that Prester John has a long arm when it comes to his laws."

Balkis' eyes widened in surprise. "Why, my—" She bit back the word "uncle" and went on. "—emperor has outlawed slavery and banditry, has he not?"

"For a century or more, I'm sure," Matt said, "and this valley is well within his jurisdiction. They just thought they could do as they pleased because they were so far out of the way from him."

Anthony's gaze turned distant. "I had not thought of wizards as enforcing laws."

"Magic can be used for good or for ill," Matt explained, "and the temptation to use it selfishly is always there, as these bandits demonstrated by enslaving dragons and people with the spells their ancestors' shaman worked out."

Anthony frowned. "It is well I'm not a wizard, then. I might not prove equal to the temptation."

"You would use your powers for naught but good." Balkis clasped his upper arm with both hands. "I can think of few men I would trust with such power as readily as I would you, my love."

He looked down into her face, drank deeply of the glory of her eyes, and smiled. "With you to strengthen my will, I could."

"Well, let's find out if you have any power to speak of." Matt sat down on a big rock, as Balkis moved away, to afford them privacy. "Now, here's a little spell that comes in handy on rainy camping trips; it's for starting a fire . . ."

Half an hour later Anthony had learned a dozen verses, each on the first try, and was cheerfully making rocks move into fire rings, lighting small blazes, and conjuring up three-foot-wide storm clouds to put them out. Worse, he had managed to come up with improvements on three or four lines in each spell.

"Where did you develop such a quick memory?" Matt asked.

"Whiling away long winter evenings making up new verses for old stories, with my brothers," Anthony told him. "The first line I crafted was: 'Thus Alexander's sword swung high to slice the ropes clean through.' "

"Your very first line?" Matt stared. "How old were you at the time?"

"Six, before they let me join the game," Anthony said, "but I really did very little crafting; I made the line by remembering pieces as my brothers had told them."

"At six," Matt echoed, "remembering half a dozen different versions and putting them together."

"Aye. There was nothing original about it. A year later I improved it to become: 'His sword swung high to slash the ropes.' I revised it over the next few years until I made it thus: 'Then with one blow he cleaved the knot.' I like that best, but I've had to finish that verse many times since, and had to make the line anew each time. Still, that was the best I phrased it."

"If you say so," Matt said. "Do you remember every line you ever made up?"

"I'm sure I have forgotten a few," Anthony said, "and I only remembered the three or four best versions my brothers crafted of each legend."

"Oh, is that all."

"Aye. I fear I have little prominence in memory," Anthony sighed. "I will remember these verses you have taught me, though."

"Just use them well," Matt said. "Tell me, was there a reason why you always made up a variation of the same line?"

"Oh, aye. I am the youngest, so the last line in each verse always fell to me."

"Seems to me your brothers might have wanted a bit of variety," Matt said, "though there is something to be said for predictability. Listen, what if somebody shot an arrow at you and you had to make it break before it hit you?"

Anthony frowned in thought. "It would have to be a couplet, for an arrow's flight leaves little time—and iambic or trochaic trimeter, for the same reason."

"Good thinking," Matt said. "Give it a try."

"Why . . . 'Arrow, cease your . . .' No, that would be to stop it, not to break it. 'Snap in flight, arrow of . . .' No, the meter's wrong. 'Turn and crack, speeding . . .' No . . ."

Balkis came back as he was fumbling, growing more red-faced with each failure. Before he started stuttering, she said, "Speeding arrow, break in flight."

"Pieces, fall! Begone from sight!" Anthony cried. "You have made the line again, genius of music!"

"I would rather be your genius of love." Balkis sat down beside him and smiled into his eyes. He gazed back, blissful and speechless, and his hand stole out to cover hers.

Matt coughed delicately. Both of them gave a start and turned to him, abashed.

"I see how it works," Matt said. "If Anthony can memorize a verse, he can work a spell—but if he has to make one up, he just can't get started."

"Like to me," Balkis said, "save that I can begin a verse, but make weak endings, slowly and with difficulty."

"So he can't make magic on his own," Matt said, "but he can make yours ten times more effective." He nodded. "Good basis for a partnership. Better teach him all the magic you know. If he's really going to Maracanda, Prester John will be delighted to meet him."

"Meet the emperor himself!" Anthony cried, sitting bolt upright.

"Sure," Matt said. "He needs all the wizards he can find."

"As to that . . ." Balkis looked suddenly nervous. She turned to Anthony. "I have given you time alone with my mentor, Anthony. Will you grant me the same privilege?"

"Why . . . of course, my sweet." Anthony hid his jealousy with an effort, smiled, then rose and went over toward Stegoman and Dimetrolas, moving warily and timidly.

Dimetrolas noticed and said something to Stegoman, who boomed out, "Welcome, son of the mountains! Have you never seen dragon folk before?"

"Never." Anthony came forward, though shyly. "Might I speak with you awhile? I am bursting with a thousand questions!"

"I will answer only a hundred," Stegoman said with a twinkle in his eye. "Ask, mountaineer."

They settled down to conversation. Balkis glanced at them,

then leaned closer to Matt and asked in a low voice, "How is it you searched for me?"

"Prester John—"

"Shh! Do not say his name!" Balkis gave a frantic glance over her shoulder at Anthony. "Say rather, 'my uncle,' as you did before—and a thousand thanks for that tact."

"Just good luck," Matt said. "Okay, 'my uncle' sent word that his niece was missing . . ."

"Oh, be not so silly!"

"Okay, *your* uncle sent word—and asked me to come find out what had happened to you. We tracked down the sorcerer who had kidnapped you, but he wasn't much help—seems you foiled his transportation spell at the last minute, so he didn't know where you'd gone."

Balkis smiled with grim satisfaction. "Not where he intended, at least."

"Yes, and I'm very glad of that." Matt beamed at her. "Very proud of my pupil. But your uncle did a bit of divination, found out which direction you'd gone, and I started searching. Stegoman insisted on coming along for the ride—or so that I could ride, rather—and we headed south, stopping to ask about you whenever we could." He spread his hands. "When we found chaos happening, we thought it was worth a look."

"Praise Heaven that you did! But Pres—my uncle is still seeking me?"

"Not officially," Matt hedged. "If I can't find you, he'll send his son with a small army to search."

"Oh, such noise and furor will certainly not affright a kidnapper!"

"Careful, my dear—with your coloring, sarcasm doesn't become you, and I sure hope the converse isn't true. I also hope you're reassured to know your uncle's willing to shake heaven and earth to find you, though."

"It is a warming thought." Balkis smiled. "The problem, though, Lord Wizard, is that I would prefer not to be found for a while."

"Need to cement a new relationship before you jeopardize it by revealing you're a princess?" Matt eyed Anthony, who was in earnest conversation with the two dragons. "You could tell him you're a woodcutter's daughter, you know."

"I could," Balkis said, "but would he believe that I could be that and a princess, too?"

"Should be enough old legends around to give him a basis for accepting it," Matt said, "and as I understand it, he's steeped in them so thoroughly that they've dyed his soul—but why take chances, right?"

"Exactly," Balkis said. "I wish to journey with him through Prester John's tributaries and his own domain, all the way to Maracanda itself. We should be so firmly bound by then that he will not be affrighted—not if he truly loves me."

"Assuming he doesn't feel you deceived him, of course."

"Ridiculous!" Balkis said. "I am myself! Why should it matter whether I am a princess or a beggar?"

"Good point," Matt said, "but it does matter. Still, it's your play, and I won't try to rewrite it for you."

"Please do not." Balkis' face was taut with anxiety. "I am not ready to be a princess again! We have survived dangers and privations on this journey, it is true, but we have also seen wonders, and come to know amazing people. I wish to see the country all the way into the capital itself as ordinary people do, so that I may come to know them better."

Matt looked into her eyes and drew his own conclusions about which ordinary person she wanted to know better. He smiled, remembering his first few days of rapture, and reached out to pat her hand. "Don't worry, I'll keep quiet about it. Just don't wear out the honeymoon before the wedding, okay?"

Matt took dictation, refereed the disagreements on wording, and kept them from breaking up the newborn alliance, then carved it all into a cliff at the side of the village—magically, of course. The villagers were suitably impressed by the stunt and swore to uphold the treaty, possibly more out of fear of the power that had engraved it than of the threat of civil war that could have resulted from breaking it.

Matt, the two huge dragons, and the young couple stayed on through the celebrations that evening, then slept the sleep of the sober amid a thousand drunks—with one always awake as sentry, of course. The next morning, Anthony got the exhilarating and terrifying experience of a dragon ride, because Matt insisted on seeing his young charges well beyond reach of the dragoneers before he let them go north on their own.

Thirty miles north, Stegoman and Dimetrolas came in for a landing, and Balkis and Anthony slid down, Balkis running to hold Anthony upright while he got his land legs again. He gave her a foolish grin and a sloppy kiss and said, "I wish another such ride someday."

"I shall give you one," Stegoman promised, "though you shall have to come to Maracanda to have it."

"One more reason for traveling north! Many thanks, noble beast! I shall see you in Maracanda!"

"In Maracanda, then," Stegoman acknowledged, and took off with Matt on his back and Dimetrolas flying convoy.

"You have most amazing friends," Anthony informed Balkis.

"I know." She pressed herself against him and wrapped her arms around his chest. "Though I had hoped you were more than a friend."

"Far more." Anthony grinned and kissed her.

They traveled northward for three more days, though they did not exactly hurry. Balkis chafed at Anthony's gallantry in asking nothing of her but kisses, especially since those inflamed her so that her entire body burned to give and demand more—but she remembered what the Lord Wizard had said about not wearing out the honeymoon before the wedding and fancied there might be some truth in it, so she wandered northward arm in arm with her swain and waited for them to happen upon a priest.

Her hopes soared when they came to a crossroads and saw a little chapel glittering in the light of later afternoon. "We can at least give thanks for a safe journey, Anthony."

"We can indeed," he said, and together they went to the chapel.

As they came closer, Balkis gasped in wonder. "How marvelous!"

The chapel stood surrounded by trees; its roof reflected the green of their leaves, but with spots of blinding light here and there where the sun's rays came through. It was ornamented with a delicate tracery of leading, and the sides were every color of the rainbow, depicting scenes from he Bible.

"There is Noah," Balkis breathed, "and there Abraham and Moses!"

"There David fights Goliath," Anthony said, "and there Esther stands before the king!"

"There Mary and Joseph kneel at the creche," Balkis said. "The whole church is made of glass!"

"How can it ever stand against a storm?" Anthony wondered.

"There is either magic in it or a genius of an architect," Balkis answered. "Shall we see more of the Savior's life on the other side, do you think?"

"Let us enter and discover," Anthony urged.

They went in, and the room was quite full, the congregation standing, but they were so spellbound by the beauty around them, they barely noticed. The glass of the roof was indeed green, dimming the sun so that it did not hurt their eyes—but that same sunshine poured through the western wall, throwing jeweled light upon all the people within. Even on the eastern wall, the windows glowed with the light from outside—and sure enough, it showed scenes from the Savior's life. Wherever they looked, they were surrounded by pictures that almost seemed to breathe with the light that infused them.

But Balkis' gaze went to the man who stood in the pulpit. She was disappointed to see that he wore no chasuble, nor any stole around his neck, only a simple white robe, though it glowed with half a dozen colors from the light that struck through the leaded walls.

"We shall not hear a true Mass," Anthony said, disappointed, "for if he wears no stole, he is no priest, but only a deacon at best."

Balkis felt a surge of chagrin and fought to keep it from showing—there was no chance of a wedding here. She tried to be philosophical, telling herself that Anthony had not asked her to marry him in any event.

There were no pews, which was why the people stood to hear the service. Anthony and Balkis edged their way in and stood with their backs against a wall.

It certainly was like no Mass that Balkis had ever attended, but Anthony nodded, smiling, obviously familiar with the words, even speaking them himself when the congregation gave the deacon their ritual response.

Then Balkis stiffened and clutched Anthony's forearm. He turned to her in concern, and she stretched to whisper in his ear, "The wall no longer presses against my back!"

"Surely we have stepped forward." Anthony turned to look at the people in front of him, then stared. "No, we have not."

Balkis turned to look, almost afraid of what she might see, and noticed that the wall was a good three feet behind her. She turned back quickly, as though to keep the chapel from hiding its dimensions from her. "Anthony—the roof is a little higher, and all the walls a few feet farther apart than they were when we entered!"

"This cannot be," Anthony said nervously. He would have explained, but just then some people came in through the doorway behind them. They wore pilgrims' gowns, dusty with travel, and looked wearied, but the beauty of the little chapel seemed to refresh them instantly. The new arrivals filed along the wall behind Anthony and Balkis, then along the wall to the other side of the door—and kept coming. Thirty or forty of them filed in, standing on line behind another—three rows, where there had been only three feet! Moreover, the wall was a foot or two behind the backs of the rearmost line!

Balkis and Anthony looked at one another in amazement. then looked back at the walls, feeling a strange prickling along their backs. Anthony leaned close and whispered, "The deacon will explain it when we are done."

They listened to the rest of the service in silence, but Balkis had a deal of trouble in keeping her mind on it. Her gaze kept drifting to the walls.

Finally the deacon bade the congregation go, and they filed out of the chapel—or church, for it had grown amazingly in the short time they had been there.

Anthony touched Balkis' arm. "Let us stay behind, so we may talk to the deacon at leisure."

"Well thought," Balkis agreed. They drew aside.

A woman in pilgrim's garb stepped up near them. "Is not this a wondrous church?"

"Wondrous indeed," Balkis agreed and smiled, drawn to thc woman even though they were total strangers. She was middle-aged, with a full, kind, smiling face. Her skin was the dark tan of the Afghans, wrinkled with laughter and smiling. Iron-gray curls peeped from under her hood, and although she wore the same dusty cream-colored robe as everyone else, the embroidered cross on her breast was a work of art in five colors. "Have you come far?" Balkis asked.

"From Kashmir, young woman—a land far to the south, glorious with mountains." She pressed Balkis' hand in greeting. "I live in a little town there; my name is Sikta, and my husband and I grew prosperous from the caravan trade. Now all our children are grown and married, though, so he sold his business, and we have time and money to go to see St. Thomas and the wonders of Maracanda. What of yourselves?"

Balkis was a little taken aback by the woman's openness and friendliness, but Anthony responded to it like a flower turning its face to the sun. "I hail from a farm in the mountains far to the south, good woman, but only a day or two from the caravan route. Belike my father and brothers sold you foodstuffs as you passed."

"I do seem to remember a man of my own years, with four stalwart sons." Sikta peered into his face. "Yes, one of them looked much like you—but that was three months ago, and only a few weeks from Kashmir!"

"I had heard of your land," Anthony said. "You grow sheep whose wool is wondrously soft, do you not?"

"Goats, young man, and yes, the quality of their hair is known far and wide." Sikta beamed at his knowing of her land. "Are you newlyweds?"

She had her answer in Balkis' lowering of her gaze and her covert blushing glance at Anthony. He pretended not to notice, saying brightly, "No, good Sikta, we have only been traveling companions. I am Anthony, and this is Balkis, stolen from her home by a foul villain. I set out only to escort her, to bring her safely to her homeland and see something of the world along the way—but I have fallen in love with her, and have cause to think that she is not indifferent to my suit."

"Suit forsooth!" said Balkis. "You have asked me for nothing but a kiss! Well, several . . . all right, many."

"And shall ask for many more." Anthony devoured her eyes with his gaze. "I would ask for your hand, too, and your life with mine, were I certain we could find a priest."

"Do not let that stop you," Sikta told him. "Long engagements have their virtues—if you can be virtuously engaged."

"I could try," Anthony sighed, "but I fear my own urges."

Balkis blushed furiously and noticed that the pathway to the church had fascinating brickwork.

"You shall be quite safe if you have an abundance of chaperones," Sikta said somewhat primly. "Travel with us, young people, and you may be sure you will be so closely watched that you shall be hard put to sneak a kiss now and again."

Balkis wasn't sure she liked the sound of that, either, but Anthony leaped at the chance. "Why, how good of you!"

"We are bound to Maracanda," Balkis admitted. "I have dwelt there with my uncle this last year."

"Of Maracanda yourself!" Sikta cried. "Why, then, you must journey with us, for you can show us the town!"

Balkis was saved from having to answer immediately, for Anthony said, "The deacon is done with his churchgoers. Let us speak to him before he goes to his home."

They stepped up and the deacon turned to offer his hand. "Welcome, pilgrims! I regret that we could not offer you the Eucharist, but there is only the one priest for these five parishes. He shall come two Sundays hence. We must fare without him as well as we may, and I can, at least, say vespers."

"You said them very well, too," Anthony said. "Tell me, deacon—was it my imagination, or did the chapel truly swell as more and more pilgrims came in?"

"It did indeed, good people! We are singularly blessed, for no matter how many come for our services, there is always room for more. We are overwhelmingly grateful to the good Lord for the favor, for none should be turned away from a church for lack of room."

"That is fortunate for a chapel on the caravan routes," Anthony said.

"Even as you say—three of the routes converge here to become one broad road leading northward to Maracanda. We frequently have more travelers than parishoners—so we have cultivated the modesty to believe we were given our chapel for pilgrims as well as ourselves. We strive to maintain it as a sacred trust—and the caravans are generous in aiding us."

Balkis recognized a plea for contributions when she heard one. She elbowed Anthony in the ribs.

He turned to her with a sad smile. "What a pity we have no coins—but when we have sold our wares in Maracanda, we can send money for this church."

"That would be good of you, young folk, but we do not ask money of those who have little." The deacon smiled and raised a hand in blessing. "May St. Christopher guard your passage!"

They traveled north with the caravan, enjoying the lighthearted company of the pilgrims and taking their turns telling stories—their own adventures, which everyone agreed were too fabulous to be believed. There was a holiday mood about them, and Balkis studied them, remembering Sikta's tale of being free to go on pilgrimage after a lifetime of earning, and realized that most of them were of her kind—hardworking, devout people who were finally free to travel after a lifetime of toil and responsibility. They were able at last to shed that burden for a while and were enjoying life with the delight of release. They were quite sincere in their religious zeal for witnessing the miracle of St. Thomas, but they were also eager to see something of the world, even as Anthony was, and the wonders of Maracanda. They were on holiday indeed, and meant to enjoy the experience to the fullest. Balkis found them to be wonderful company and listened to their gossip of child-rearing and grandchildren with yearning. She was beginning to realize that she, too, wanted to be a mother some day. She hoped their stories would arouse some stirrings of the same feeling in Anthony. There did seem to be a new quality of longing in his gaze now, but that might simply be due to the plethora of chaperones. As Sikta had promised, it was indeed difficult for them to be alone long enough for a satisfactory kiss.

Thus they wandered northward on a road a good twenty feet wide, passing small towns and prosperous farms, gossiping and singing and resting frequently. Their progress was slow, but Balkis was in no hurry to reach Maracanda and take up again the mantle of princess—and with it, to risk losing Anthony.

Then, after they had been on the road a week, they heard the distant noise of trumpets. Balkis' heart sank, for she recognized the pitch and timbre of the instruments. They blew again and again, coming closer and closer, until two soldiers on horseback shouldered through the crowd with two heralds between them and two trumpeters behind. The heralds cried out, "Make way, make way for the emperor! Clear the road, for Prester John passes!"

CHAPTER 29

Then the trumpets blew again. When they were done, the heralds took up their cry once more.

The pilgrims broke into excited talk, hurrying their mules and horses to the sides of the road.

"Why is the emperor riding?" asked one.

"He returns from a tour of the provinces!" answered another.

The rumor must have come from southbound Maracandese who knew some accurate news, for Balkis suspected exactly why Prester John had been visiting his outer districts. She did the best she could to lose herself among the crowd, keeping her face down.

"Balkis? Balkis!" Anthony followed her, catching at her hand. "Think—the emperor! Do you not wish to see Prester John himself?"

"Surely, surely!" Balkis assured him. She just didn't want Prester John to see her.

Then the procession was upon them. Balkis stood riveted to the ground, peeking up under the edge of her hood—and was astounded to realize that, when you were watching the parade instead of riding in it, the sight was very impressive indeed!

First came a rider carrying a six-foot-high wooden cross fastened to his saddle.

"Wooden?" Anthony stared. "Why would an emperor not have a cross made of silver or gold and filled with priceless gems?"

"He wishes to be reminded of the passion of Our Lord, young man," Sikta told him. "We have heard of his humility even in Kashmir. If wood was good enough for the Savior, it is good enough for Prester John!"

"His name does mean 'John the Priest,' " Balkis reminded.

"True—but I did not expect him to be as humble as a monk."

"I would not call such a train as this humble," Balkis answered.

Then came courtiers bearing a single golden vase.

"At least this metal is precious!" Anthony said. "But why has it no flowers or shrubs within?"

"It is full of earth," Balkis answered, "to remind the king that his flesh, too, must one day return to its original substance, the earth."

Sikta looked up. "That must be so—for if you have lived a year in Maracanda, you must have seen processions such as this more than once. Tell us the meaning of the symbols."

The last thing Balkis wanted to do was to watch the parade closely—but she sighed and braced herself.

After the vase came another courtier carrying a silver bowl full of pieces of gold.

"Well, this is more like an emperor!" Anthony said, satisfied. "Surely Prester John wishes to impress the people with his wealth!"

"A good guess," Balkis said, "but not quite on the mark—the king wants all to know that he is lord of lords in these lands, and that his magnificence surpasses all the wealth in the world."

"Do you truly know this simply from dwelling in Maracanda?" he asked.

What was Balkis to say? She couldn't exactly tell him that she had heard the explanations from the emperor himself. "Prester John goes about frequently within the city," she said. "People discuss his processions."

"With such pomp as this?"

"Oh, this is only his ordinary coming and going. When he travels in state, or marches to war, it is much more magnificent."

Anthony looked frankly skeptical, but Sikta said, "I can believe that easily! Why, he has only a dozen soldiers going before him!"

They watched the troopers ride by, backs as straight as the poles of the pennons they bore, eyes firmly toward the front.

"Who are those gaily dressed fellows who follow the soldiers?" Sikta asked.

"They are courtiers," Balkis explained, "dukes and counts of the land. Do you see those last seven coming, and the crowns they wear?"

"Why, yes!" Sikta gasped. "Surely they are not truly kings!"

"They are indeed. Seven of his tributary kings are always in attendance upon him—more, when they march to war with all their soldiers."

"But who is that young man riding behind them, who also wears a crown?" Anthony asked. "He cannot be a king—he is scarcely older than I am!"

"He is the crown prince." Balkis lowered her gaze. "He shall become emperor upon Prester John's death."

"So much power to fall upon such slender shoulders!" Anthony murmured.

Balkis could only agree. She thought Prince Tashih a good man, but Anthony a better—and he had far broader shoulders to bear such a burden.

"Look, Balkis!" Anthony gripped her arm, pointing. "It is the emperor! It is Prester John himself!"

Resigned to her fate, Balkis looked up and hoped her uncle wouldn't see her. Then she stared, for as he rode in state, he seemed far more impressive than he did at home.

He even looked taller—broader, too, bigger in every way. Perhaps it was the huge horse he rode, a western charger, gift of Queen Alisande—or perhaps his robe was deliberately padded and stiffened. He rode with regal bearing, straight as a rod and seeming on the verge of casting thunderbolts. He raised his hand in blessing as he rode, but his face was stern, and there was nothing of the tender, doting uncle she knew.

Suddenly his head snapped around and his eyes met hers. Too late Balkis realized that, being a wizard, Prester John had been alerted by her magical aura. For a few seconds he looked directly at her, and she straightened, lifting her head proudly, gaze defiant, virtually daring him to acknowledge her before all these people.

But the emperor glanced to her right at Anthony, tall and golden beside her, then back at her, and a slight smile touched his lips. Somehow, Balkis felt the vast wave of relief coming from him.

Then the emperor turned his head to the fore and rode on. Balkis stared after him, numb—overwhelmingly grateful that he had not declared her station in front of Anthony, but even more overwhelmed by realizing how deeply he loved her.

The Lord Wizard must have reported to him, she realized, and her uncle must have ridden down this road specifically so he could ride back when she had passed his sentry—probably the deacon at the chapel—and see for himself that she was well.

The Lord Wizard had no doubt reported Anthony's presence and place in her life, too. So much for her fears that Prester John meant to marry her to his son! She lowered her gaze again, tears of joy coming to her eyes. The man and woman she had thought of as mother and father might be dead, but she had true family here, in her uncle.

"A dozen more courtiers behind him," Sikta exclaimed. "Such state! Ah, so that is the source of the martial music—a whole wagon filled with musicians that comes after the emperor! And oh! Here come the soldiers! There must be a hundred of them! Are they the palace guard, Balkis? . . . Balkis?"

"Why do you weep, my love?" Anthony's voice was tender with concern.

"Because I have realized that I am almost home," Balkis told him. In fact, for the first time since she had left her parents' cottage, she knew that she really did have a home.

Anthony squeezed her hand and she clung to it, watching with him as the spellbound crowd gazed after the procession until the last of the soldiers was out of sight. Then they broke into a babble of excitement.

Anthony turned to Balkis, eyes shining. "Isn't it amazing, darling? Never in my life did I think I would ever see Prester John himself! Have you ever seen anything so glorious? But of course—in Maracanda, you said you witnessed such processions many times!"

He babbled on, now to Balkis, now to his neighbors, tremendously excited by what he had seen. Watching him, Balkis thought it ironic that a man who had witnessed so many marvels was overawed most by something so human—but she watched him with a gaze that became more and more tender, and found herself exulting even as he exulted, for his joy was hers. She made polite replies to all his exulting, trying to match his enthusiasm but not succeeding.

Finally, the storm of his excitement having passed, Anthony discerned her mood and frowned with concern. "Why has such a marvelous sight only saddened you, my love?"

Balkis burst into tears and buried her face in his tunic, sobbing out her tension. Sikta looked surprised, then concerned, but as the storm passed, she began to smile with understanding. "You are troubled to realize that your journey together with your Anthony is almost ended, are you not, my dear?"

It was a better explanation than anything Balkis could have devised herself, and she was astonished to realize there was truth in it. "Even so, good Sikta. These months have been so wonderful that I do not want them to end."

"But why should they?" Anthony asked softly. "Why should our journeying together have an end, ever?" Then he kissed her in front of all their chaperones, a kiss that became far longer than he had intended.

The pilgrims marveled at the sight of the gates of Maracanda and marveled all over again at the wonders of the city. They were exhausted from their travels, though, and saw only as much as stood between the gates and the hostel to which their guide led them to spend the night. There were basins of water for them to wash, facilities for them to bathe separately—and when the women came back to join the men, Balkis was amazed to discover Matt there, chatting with several of the middle-aged pilgrims.

He turned as she came up to him, giving her a smile. "Didn't think you could make it through the gates without my finding out, did you?"

She couldn't help but smile in return. "Of course not." She glanced at the men. "Let us go aside to talk."

"Well, that's what I came for." Matt lifted a hand in salute. "If you'll excuse us, gentlemen?"

The pilgrims did, but Balkis could feel their curious eyes on her as she led Matt to a chair at the side of the room. They didn't trust this stranger. She was grateful for their concern, but was very glad the talk was so loud that there was little chance of anyone hearing their conversation.

"So has he asked you to marry him yet?" Matt teased as they sat down.

Balkis blushed. "Not quite, but he has come very close."

"I hoped you looked receptive," Matt said. "You'd be surprised how many of us weak-willed men don't want to ask such an intimate question if we think we're going to be rejected."

"I gave him as tender a look as I could." Balkis didn't explain the circumstances. She leaned closer to say, "But I am worried, Lord Wizard. I fear I may not wait for him to propose."

"Bad idea," Matt said promptly. "Very bad, in a medieval culture. Wait. Make it a quick wedding if you have to, but wait for it."

"I . . . I may not be able to stand against the tide of my own desire." Balkis gave him a pleading look. "You know how such feelings may overwhelm a cat."

"Then stay in human form."

"But there is enough of the cat in me now that . . . well . . . to be blunt, Lord Wizard, I fear I am in heat, and more and more deeply with every passing day!" She lowered her gaze. "Sometimes I think that I cannot bear it, that I . . . should perhaps . . . should . . . give in."

"No you shouldn't," Matt said firmly. "Besides, even if you wanted to, you'd have to seduce Anthony—he has you on a bit of a pedestal."

Balkis grimaced, looking away. "Then pedestals are quite uncomfortable."

"Yeah, and kinda windy," Matt sympathized. "Still, it's not quite the animal lust you seem to think it. Odds are the only reason you're feeling this way is because you're in love."

"Yes . . . I think so . . ." Balkis looked up at Matt beseechingly. "What if he should not propose, though? What if we should not marry?"

Matt studied her for a few seconds, then said gently, "I think the real problem is that, way down deep, you don't want to miss the chance of learning physical intimacy when you're in love."

Balkis lowered her gaze, blushing, but only repeated, "What if he should not wish to marry? What if he should leave? Do I still wish to be a virgin when he does?"

"From all the women I've seen in your predicament who gave in," Matt said, "the answer is definitely that if you're still a virgin when he goes, it hurts less." He laid a hand over hers. "Don't worry, lady—if he's as deeply in love as I think he is, there's no way he'll leave."

She blushed and looked up at him with gratitude. "You are right, of course. I only fear what may happen when he learns I am a princess."

"Just tell him you'll give it all up to live in a cottage with him," Matt advised.

Balkis stared at him in shock, then realized his meaning and laughed with pure joy. "Of course! It matters not what I am now, does it? It is how I grew up that affects him!" She reached up to give Matt a kiss on the cheek. "Thank you, Lord Wizard! Oh, thank you, thank you!" She leaped up. "I must go to find him now! I shall tell him all straightaway!"

Matt almost stopped her, almost told her it might not be the wisest course, then realized she had to do it while her courage was up. "Right. Go find him."

Balkis ran off among the crowd, twisting and turning and seeking.

Matt relaxed with a sigh and thought gratefully of his wife. He'd forgotten how wearing the angst of the search for love could be.

Then Balkis was back, was running up to him with tears in her eyes. "Lord Wizard! He is gone, he is fled!" She collapsed beside him, her face on his knees, sobbing. "He has gone out into the streets of Maracanda, alone and without a guide!

Sikta saw him go, and what will happen to him alone among those sharks and thugs who are ready to prey on any they find?"

Matt just held onto her and wondered if it was really as bad as she thought, then admitted to himself that it probably was—a country boy in the big city was always at something of a disadvantage. "Let's go," he said. "You can change into a tabby right outside the door. You take the back alleys and I'll take the bazaar." He tilted her chin up and smiled as reassuringly as he could. "Don't worry—it's too late for him to get out. They closed the gates half an hour ago."

"It was not the predators outside the gates that worried me," she told him.

Matt didn't have to search very long. Anthony was right there in the bazaar, haggling at a goldsmith's booth.

"You know this nugget isn't gold, don't you?" the goldsmith was asking.

"I know very well that it is true gold." Anthony gave the man a hard smile. "Still, I did not ask you what it was—I only asked you to make it into a ring, and to cut and polish this stone to mount on it."

The goldsmith looked at the dull white pebble in his palm. "I suppose you think that scrap of quartz is a diamond."

"No matter what it is, it is what I want in the ring. How much will you charge to make it?"

"Two silvers."

"I have no coins." Anthony held up a small blue stone. "Will this do?"

The goldsmith glanced at the stone, then looked again, his eyes hot with avarice, but he said only, "It is very small."

Matt decided it was time to step in. "Very small, and completely unnecessary," he said, stepping up beside Anthony. "The gold that's left over from the nugget and the chips of the diamond will be more than enough payment."

Anthony looked up in surprise. "Lord Wizard! How come you to be here?"

The goldsmith stared at Matt, then looked away, tidying up his counter with nervous glances at the new customer.

"A wizard always has to keep an eye on the bazaar to see if any exotic substances show up," Matt said. "For example, I'm running low on cinnabar at the moment."

The goldsmith looked up with chagrin. "I do not deal in that ore, I fear, Lord Wizard."

"No, but one of your neighbors does." Matt picked up the nugget and gave it a close inspection. "The young man's right—that's gold, sure enough. I'm sure you just don't recognize it because it's in such a raw state. Don't you think so, goldsmith?"

"Belike, belike," the man muttered.

"Then the leftovers will surely be enough payment." Matt looked up at Anthony. "You want it nice and wide, don't you?"

"Not terribly." Anthony gave him a bashful smile. "It is for a lady, after all—if she will have it."

"And you with it, of course." Matt gave him a grin. "A ring that size wouldn't take more than half the gold. I think the rest is more than enough payment."

The goldsmith gathered courage to bargain a little more. "Once I have smelted it—"

"You'll still have twice as much as you need for such a little ring," Matt said. "And no more than one-tenth copper in it, mind you!"

The goldsmith frowned. "That will make it very soft, my lord."

"Hard enough," Matt told him, "and so am I." He turned back to Anthony. "Any more shopping to do, or shall we have a sherbet together and go back to the hostel?"

"I would delight in your hospitality." Anthony said. "I did want to see what other baubles this street has to offer, though."

"Well, you go explore a few of the other booths while I have a word with this goldsmith, okay? He might have one or two items I'm needing."

"A good thought," Anthony said brightly and drifted off to another booth.

The goldsmith, reassured by Matt's pleasant demeanor, asked, "What do you wish, Lord Wizard?"

"A little honesty." Matt fixed him with a very stern eye. "When that ring is ready, the stone had better be real diamond, and the gold had better be true—or do you think I can't tell brass and quartz when I see them?"

"I—I am sure you can, my lord!" the goldsmith stammered. "I have heard the tale of your magicks that saved this city, have seen you riding beside the emperor! I would never doubt you!" He frowned. "But I had heard you had gone back to your own country."

"I did, but I came back for a visit," Matt told him. "I'm likely to do that, from time to time. I can find ingredients for magic potions here that I never find in the West—but I only deal with honest merchants. You are honest, aren't you?"

"The very soul of honesty, my lord," the goldsmith said fervently.

Balkis was already back at the hostel, pacing and wringing her hands, when Matt came in the door with Anthony.

"Anthony!" Balkis rushed into his arms. "Oh, I so feared for you, my love!"

"Feared for me? Why?" Anthony asked, his arms tight about her. "Surely you know I can take care of myself!"

"Hey, did you worry about her safety in your home mountains?" Matt asked.

"Well, of course, but there are fearsome beasts there."

"We have some pretty merciless predators here, too," Matt told him. "The big thing, though, is that you're always at a disadvantage in strange territory. Just reassure the lady and take her in to dinner, will you?"

After the meal, though, the pilgrims started swapping stories again, and Anthony became interested. Matt was able to take Balkis aside.

"Lord Wizard, where was he?" Balkis demanded.

"In the bazaar, trying to trade a gemstone." It wasn't really a lie, and it did preserve the secret of the ring. Gravely, he asked, "Balkis, how did Anthony come to have a gold nugget and a jewel in his pockets?"

Her eyes flashed with anger. "The gold he took from a

valley where giant ants mine the stuff, and people who live in fortresses by day collect the nuggets at night. Greed is his one fault, and because he kept some of the gold, one ant followed us for months. It might have slain us, but as good luck was with us, it slew instead a lion who was trying to kill Anthony."

Matt gave a low whistle. "And the lion squashed the ant, huh? But where did he get the gems?"

"From the banks of the river Physon, which we navigated underground with only torchlight to guide us. Our friend Panyat showed us the way. I bade Anthony not to burden himself, but he could not bear to leave without at least a handful of stones."

"I can understand that, at least." Matt nodded. "Gold that was apt to draw retribution, no, that was stupid—but a handful of gems wasn't going to slow him down any, and could last him the rest of his life." He fairly beamed at her. "I'm very glad to find out he came by them honestly."

"Did you think my Anthony a thief?" Balkis asked, her anger returning. "Never! He is the soul of honesty and loyalty! Never would I question him! Save, of course, in the matter of that one flaw: greed."

"I'm glad to learn it hasn't undermined his honesty," Matt said. "It has broken the integrity of many good men before now, Balkis." He gave her a sly smile. "The boy just might be worthy of you, after all."

"I should think he is!" Balkis said indignantly, then turned shy. "But Lord Wizard—do you think I am worthy of him?"

"Definitely!" Matt said. "You don't know what a gem you are, cottage girl!"

She frowned at him. "I am a princess now, sir."

"Yes, and doing a very good job of it, too," Matt agreed, "and if you can, so can Anthony."

The next morning, they woke to find the pilgrims all astir, milling about in the yard of the hostel. They went out to join their friends, Anthony asking, "What is the cause of your excitement, good Sikta?"

"Today we go to the palace!" the matron exclaimed. "Will

it not be wondrous, Anthony—to see the grand home of Prester John himself?"

"It will indeed!" Anthony's eyes were shining. "Will it not be a delight, Balkis?"

"It will indeed, Anthony," she said faintly.

CHAPTER 30

They came out of a boulevard into a great open plaza and saw the palace rising above a high wall. Directly before them was a huge portal closed by two massive, pale gates with the sheen of polished stone, inlaid with geometric patterns in a translucent yellowish material. The pilgrims milled about, discussing the sight with one another in tones of excitement. Then a trumpet blew and they fell silent, all eyes turning toward the gateway.

Drums began to beat and soldiers filed out of the palace. They formed into four ranks and marched toward the pilgrims, shifting their weapons from side to side at the calls of a sergeant. The pilgrims murmured in awe, for such drill was unknown anywhere else in the world. It made a brave spectacle indeed.

The soldiers marched up to them, stamped to a halt, then opened an aisle in their center, down which came a man who strutted with self-importance. He wore a brocaded gown and hat embroidered in gold. As he came, the sergeant bawled orders again, and the soldiers wheeled to the sides, files lining end-to-end until they formed a broad avenue down which the pilgrims could march.

Balkis hid a smile. She had never seen this display before but could tell it was calculated to awe and entertain the pilgrims—and, without their realizing it, to contain them in case any wished to make trouble. She thought she detected Matthew's hand in this.

The courtier came to a halt in front of the band and gave them a condescending smile. "Good morning, good pilgrims! I am Hajik, and I shall guide you through such of the palace as the public may see! If you have questions, I shall answer as many as I may."

The pilgrims murmured to one another, but none asked any questions, though each had a dozen clogging his throat.

"The square in which you stand," said Hajik, "is where our glorious emperor witnesses the judicial contests of trial by combat: It is paved with onyx in order that the courage of the fighters may be increased by the virtue of the stone."

Balkis shuddered. "Horrid custom!"

"It is indeed," Anthony agreed, low-voiced. "We must find a better way to decide which is the worthier case."

Balkis looked up at him in surprise; he spoke with the sound of a man who had pondered the issue. She had not expected Anthony to have given any thought to such matters.

"These great gates before you are made of sardonyx inlaid with the horn of the serpent called 'cerastes,' so that no one may enter with poison."

The pilgrims murmured, suitably impressed.

"So if any of you come with poison about you," the courtier said, with a twinkle in his eye, "you were best to leave it on the ground!"

The pilgrims gazed at him in shock. Then one or two realized that he spoke in jest and managed a weak laugh. Hearing them, the rest of the company joined in, halfheartedly but relieved.

"Come in, then, come in!" Hajik stepped to the side, spreading an arm toward the sardonyx gates. "The emperor invites you!"

He stepped aside and the pilgrims surged forward with cries of delight and awe, scarcely noticing that the soldiers closed in to their sides and their rear, shepherding them and making sure none went running off to investigate on his or her own.

Exclaiming to one another, the pilgrims came through the twelve-foot-high portal and saw vast lawns stretching away to the distant castle.

"How awe-inspiring, how huge!" one of the pilgrims exclaimed.

"It is indeed," said another, "but why should the emperor need veritable fields within his walls? Why, you could drill an army in here!"

"He probably does, neighbor," a third man said. "He probably does."

Anthony looked the question at Balkis. Eyes twinkling, she nodded.

"If the city were invaded," said another thoughtful pilgrim, "he could house half his people here, in tents and such."

"All his people, actually," Balkis confided to Anthony.

He grinned down at her, then turned away to regard the palace itself. Soldiers herded straying pilgrims onto the flags of the broad paved apron before the palace. Gradually all of them came there to stare at the graceful building.

"The emperor's palace is patterned after the heavenly mansion St. Thomas constructed for the Hindu King Gundafor," Hajik explained. "The king appointed the apostle to build him an earthly palace, but St. Thomas gave the money to the poor instead. When the king indicted him for it, St. Thomas replied that he had used the gold to build the king a palace in Heaven. Soon after, King Gundafor fell into a deathlike sleep and was transported to Heaven, where he gazed upon a palace much like this, only grander and even more magnificent. An angel told him it was the castle St. Thomas had built for him by his charity to the poor, then sent the king back to the world of the living, to be baptized as an example to all his people."

The people murmured, marveling at the tale and the palace both. The building was three hundred feet long and a hundred deep, with a huge central dome and four smaller domes at the corners, all bulbous and pointed—but the central doorway was a Roman arch flanked by Corinthian columns. The window opening onto the central balcony, right above the main door, was a smaller version of its arch, with railings of ivory. The windows were Moorish arches with balconies enclosed by elaborately carved railings. The roof, however, was completely black.

"Good sir, why is there so dark a roof on a palace so light and colorful?" Sikta asked, frowning.

Hajik puffed himself up with the pride of knowledge. "It is made of a precious wood called ebony, good woman, and it has the virtue of taking and holding a spell that will make it immune to fire."

"You mean it cannot burn?" a pilgrim asked, wide-eyed.

"Not once Prester John enchanted it, no," Hajik said. "The gates of the palace itself are likewise of ebony so that no enemy may burn them down to enter." He turned and pointed at the eastern end of the roof. "Notice the gables at either end! Above each are two golden apples—see how they shine! But set in each of them are two carbuncles; as the gold shines by day, so the carbuncles shine by night."

"That must have been the glow I saw in the sky last night!" one pilgrim exclaimed.

"It was indeed." Hajik turned sideways with a flamboyant gesture toward the castle. "The windows are of crystal. At night you shall see them glowing with light from a thousand lamps . . . ah, I see by the wonder in your faces that you gazed upon the sight last night! Know that in this palace all the lamps are fed by balsam, and the sweet aroma permeates all the chambers."

"Even in the emperor's personal rooms?" a pilgrim asked.

Hajik gave the speaker a forbidding frown. "I cannot speak of Prester John's private chambers, for none but the emperor, his family, and his privy ministers know what lies therein."

Balkis smiled secretly, barely managing to keep from showing off by telling Anthony that the emperor's withdrawing room was marvelously bedecked with gold and all manner of precious stones. But hold it back she did—she was trying to keep him from knowing that she was part of the emperor's family, not display it.

"Whenever an onyx is used for ornament," Hajik orated, "four carnelians are set about it so that the assertive effects of the onyx may be tempered. When it is used for its magic, of course, the onyx is inlaid by itself."

From the top of the palace's dome a gong sounded. Its tone faded, but before it was quite gone, another boomed, then ten more. The crowd gasped, staring in awe, trying to see the man who struck the great tam-tam—for that matter, trying to see the instrument itself.

Hajik smiled. "Yes, good people, the emperor has a wondrous machine crafted for him by a smith of magical powers, and that machine reminds us of the hours of the day, even as you have but now heard. The stroke of noon tells us that hours for viewing the palace are ended. Go back to your hostel in peace; your guide shall bring you here again tomorrow, for it is a holy day, and you may hear the apostle Thomas preach from the balcony above the main gate."

The crowd stirred, exclaiming to one another in delight and surprise.

"Go your ways now," Hajik said, "and come back on the morrow." He saluted them with a slight bow, then turned to walk back toward the palace. The soldiers closed in, ushering the people out the main gate. The pilgrims dispersed with happy chattering, but Balkis, so close to the palace, realized that if there was a proper time to tell Anthony her true rank, it had better be now—and she dared not risk his learning by another source, for every minute in Maracanda increased the chances of some acquaintance greeting her by her title. She nerved to the deed and caught Anthony's arm as he was about to exit the black portal. "No, Anthony! I wish to see inside the palace."

"Mere country folk like us?" Anthony exclaimed, horrified. "They will think us assassins and execute us on the spot!"

"They will not." Balkis said, gazing at him with an intensity he found unnerving.

Anthony's eyes went to a man approaching over her shoulder. "Lord Wizard!" he cried gratefully. He waved.

Matt waved back, smiling as he came up. "I thought that might have been your band of pilgrims. What do you think of the emperor's palace?"

"It is beautiful and wondrous—but Balkis thinks to look inside."

"Does she really?" Matt stared at Balkis.

"She does, and I fear we will be struck down on the spot! Lord Wizard, I pray you—for her safety, persuade her of her folly!"

Balkis gave Matt stare for stare and moved her head up and down a fraction of an inch.

"No," Matt said to Anthony, "you're my friends, and therefore privileged people. Besides, Prester John likes wizards—as long as they're on his side. Let's go have a look at the throne room."

"The chamber of state?" Anthony goggled.

"Well, we couldn't expect him to show us the private apartments, could we? Come on, let's go." Matt turned to talk to the captain of the guard, who nodded and led the way. Soldiers formed up about them.

Anthony eyed them nervously; then apprehension was drowned in a rush of enthusiasm. "To think, we shall actually see the wonders inside the palace! Balkis, what great fortune that your teacher was someone of such influence!"

"Yes, great fortune indeed." But why did her heart feel like lead?

They walked between the Corinthian columns, under the Roman arch, and Balkis was struck once again at how Prester John's palace was a thorough mixture of the styles of East and West, for his empire comprised people of all cultures. Somehow, the architect had made them work—not surprising, if it really was copied after the work of an Israelite prophet for a Hindu king.

They walked down a broad hallway paved with semiprecious stones, between pillars of sandalwood and cedar. Tapestries hung on the walls, depicting scenes of strange slant-eyed, yellow-skinned people with elaborate coiffures and silken robes, playing at games that seemed quite ordinary and plucking musical instruments that seemed quite exotic. Anthony exclaimed with wonder at every step, but beside him Balkis was silent, growing more and more nervous.

"How polite these people are!" Anthony marveled. "They bow to us at every step! But why do they stare?"

"No doubt they are unused to seeing people in humble clothing amid such grandeur," Balkis replied. She bit her lip; it hadn't been a complete lie, after all. The servants knew her face, but they certainly had never seen her in rough travel garb.

At the end of the corridor were two huge portals with guards holding crossed pikes before them—but Matt turned down a side passage. The ceiling was only ten feet high and there were no pillars here, but the walls were marble.

"Even the servants walk amid splendor!" Anthony marveled.

Matt led them to a smaller set of doors, only seven feet tall, but still with two guards holding crossed spears.

"We are expected," Matt said, and Balkis' heart beat so heavily and rapidly that she was sure Anthony could hear it.

He didn't, though, only beamed down at her. "Be not apprehensive, my love. If the Lord Wizard conducts us, surely there is nothing to fear."

"Surely not," Balkis said faintly, and clutched his hand, hoping it would not be the last time.

The soldiers bowed—apparently to the Lord Wizard, though their gazes were fixed on Balkis. They opened the doors and the little company went in.

They entered a circular chamber that seemed a veritable cavern, but one floored with marble, walled with lapis lazuli and jasper, and framed by gilded columns upholding a ceiling that stretched away into the dimness of the great central dome. Some window must have been opened there, for it let a shaft of sunlight spear down to bathe the throne in a golden glow.

That throne stood atop a dais ten feet high, and in it sat a man with golden skin, black hair, and black beard. There was an elaborate jewel-studded golden crown on his head and robes of cloth-of-gold on his body. He held in his left hand a golden scepter while he gestured with his right as he spoke to the richly dressed men on the floor before him, their leader honored to stand on the lowest step of the dais. The emperor looked larger than human, glorious as a pagan god, awe-inspiring and intimidating, and if she had been in cat form, Balkis thought, she would have hissed.

"We'll have to wait until he finishes with the delegation from Kazakhstan," Matt murmured to them.

Balkis was quite willing to wait till Doomsday. Anthony scarcely seemed to hear; he stood with head tilted up, gazing with shining eyes at the magnificence around him.

Then Balkis had the uncanny feeling that someone was watching her. She looked up, glancing from side to side, first at the guards before the dais, who stood with spears braced and eyes firmly forward, then up to its top—and saw Prince Tashih standing behind the throne and to the side. He should have been taking mental notes on the formalities he would have to conduct himself one day but was instead looking down at Balkis with a smile of joy. He caught her look and started to raise his hand.

Balkis shook her head ever so slightly.

Prince Tashih's smile faded; his eyebrows rose.

Balkis nodded toward the bemused Anthony.

Tashih glanced at the young man, gave Balkis a long, speculative look and a grin, then studied Anthony again with curiosity, then with favor.

Balkis sighed with relief. She had been aware of Tashih's resentment, but it seemed to have vanished. She wondered if that had anything to do with Anthony's presence.

Finally the delegation was done. They backed away from the throne, bowing as they went. Guards threw the doors open, and the delegation retreated out of the throne room. The portals closed behind them.

Then Prester John himself was rising from his throne and descending the steps of the dais, the emperor of Central Asia approaching Anthony and Balkis, the Lord of Maracanda holding his arms open wide.

Balkis could contain herself no longer. With a cry of delight and relief, she threw herself into the embrace of the uncle who had been so kind to her, the mother's brother who, with his beaming son, was all the family she had left in the world.

Prester John lowered his crowned head, laid his cheek against Balkis' hair and murmured soothing words as her body heaved and she began to cry.

Anthony stared, uncomprehending, and his hands closed on Matt's arm like talons. "Lord Wizard—what—how—what can this mean?"

"It means that she is his niece." Prince Tashih inclined his head toward Anthony a few millimeters. "I am Prince Tashih, and I am her cousin."

Anthony's mouth dropped open. He stared, thunderstruck.

"He saved me!" Balkis cried, deep within the folds of her uncle's robe. "He gave me food when I was lost and weak, he gave me friendship and left his home to bring me safely to you!"

"Then I cannot thank you deeply enough." This time, Tashih

bowed fully, head and shoulders. "If you have given my cousin safe passage, I can only offer you whatever is mine to give."

"But— But—it was she who saved me! Who rescued me from a life in which I was despised, who has given me my life again and again!"

"Yes, even as you gave me mine." Balkis stepped back from Prester John's embrace, wiping away a few last tears. "My uncle, this is Anthony of the southern mountains, without whom I would have died a dozen times before I could come safely home to you."

"A prince's thanks be upon you." Prester John stretched forth a beringed hand in blessing. "Ask what you will, and you shall have it."

Anthony's eyes automatically went to Balkis. She blushed and lowered her gaze—quickly enough so that she did not see Anthony look away again, appalled at his own temerity, or the reddening of his face as he remembered all the kisses he had given—to a princess!

But Prester John noticed. "I see there is more to this tale than the Lord Wizard has told me—though he did bring me word of her safety, and of her escort. Come, let us repair to my private chambers, where I may divest myself of this heavy regalia and sit in comfort to hear your tale."

"Your private chambers!" Anthony gasped, remembering Hajik saying that only the family and privy ministers had ever gone there.

"You would not expect the emperor of half the East to sit in a public dining room to take tea and hear your tale, would you?" Prince Tashih smiled and reached out in welcome as he turned to follow his father and Balkis. "Come, let us follow them."

Prester John was tactful enough not to insist that Balkis put on a royal gown. He persuaded Anthony to sit in spite of the fact that he was a mere commoner, "For surely the man who has saved my niece merits the courtesy of reclining at table beside her."

Tongue-tied and goggle-eyed, Anthony sat and listened to Balkis telling of her kidnapping, her aborting of the shaman's spell, her rescue by the Wee Folk, and her convalescence in Anthony's barn. His eyes began to focus then, astonished at hearing how the events had appeared through her eyes. She explained the number of times that her spells would have worked too slowly to save her had Anthony not improvised a final line. There he broke in to protest, and to enumerate the times she had saved him by beginning a verse for him to finish.

"You are certainly comrades in arms," Prester John said, amused, "and both mighty wizards in the bargain."

"But I have only begun to learn, Majesty," Anthony protested, "to learn at her hands."

"You are nonetheless to be numbered among the natural resources of the realm," Tashih informed him, also amused.

Anthony noted his smile and turned away, blushing angrily. "Am I so humorous a bumpkin, then?"

"If you do not know your own worth?" Tashih asked. "It is amusing that you are the only one here who does not."

"I am only a peasant and the son of a peasant," Anthony protested.

"It would seem you are more," Prester John said quietly. "It would certainly seem that my niece would not have come home to me without your aid."

"She has the protection of a most powerful wizard," Anthony objected, not meeting the emperor's eyes, "one who saved us from the dragon riders."

"Yes, with the help of two full-sized dragons and your own spell that set the small ones free," Matt countered. He turned to Prester John. "Might I point out, Majesty, that I only caught up with them a few weeks ago, and Balkis had found plenty of opportunities to get herself killed before then."

Anthony looked up at that, opening his mouth to object, but Prester John said, "Would you argue with the Lord Wizard of Merovence, the most powerful kingdom of the West? Accept our thanks and believe your own credit, young man, for if the Lord Wizard says you saved my niece, be sure that you did."

"But she—"

"Yes, I know that she saved you as often as you her, and I

can think of no better example of comradeship than that. But my niece is wearied at last—I see that all this excitement makes her eyelids droop. She is in need of rest and refreshment now that she is come home to me."

He clapped his hands and half a dozen women entered. Seeing Balkis, their mouths dropped open and their eyes widened; they started to rush forward, then caught themselves and knelt instead. "Mistress and princess! You are returned to us!"

"Faithful companions!" Tears came again to Balkis' eyes.

"Go with them," Prester John directed. "Bathe, take tea, rest awhile, then come to speak with us again."

Balkis glanced anxiously at Anthony, who resolutely refused to meet her gaze, face still red.

Matt winked at her and made a shooing motion with his hand.

With misgivings and many backward glances, Balkis went off with her ladies in waiting. She cast one last wide-eyed imploring look back at Anthony as she went out the door, but he still refused to meet her eyes.

The emperor clapped again and four servants came in, liveried alike. They bowed.

"Here are men of your own rank and station," Prester John said to Anthony, "or at least what you deem to be yours, in spite of our telling you that you are indeed what you have proved yourself to be—a wizard worthy to escort a princess. Go now with these men, whose opinions I think you are more willing to trust than mine. They shall bathe you and attire you as befits a gentleman of the court. When you have rested, we shall meet again, that we may discuss the ways in which an emperor may thank a subject who has served him well."

"I . . . I thank Your Majesty." Anthony rose and backed away. The servants bowed and backed out with him.

Then Prester John turned to Matt, his demeanor suddenly grave. "Now, Lord Wizard, we must speak of justice for the villain who tried to steal and slay my niece."

"And who tried to tear the realm apart by creating a rift between son and father." Tashih's eyes glittered with anger. "How shall we serve this upstart, Lord Wizard?"

CHAPTER 31

"Instead of justice," Matt said, "we might do better talking about the security of the realm. From the sources I encountered, it seems this villain—Kala Nag, as she calls herself—has plans to conquer your empire and do away with both of you."

"Therefore she began with my cousin?" Tashih asked, an edge to his voice.

"She seems to be operating according to some sort of prophecy that Balkis is one of a pair who can stop her conquests—but only if the two are joined."

"That would be, of course, my niece and her mentor, yourself," Prester John said grimly.

"If that's the case," Matt said, "I can always be with you quickly, if you need me—and the threat this Kala Nag poses is scarcely immediate."

Prester John shook his head. "It is wisest to deal with enemies before they feel ready to attack. Let us call up our army and march southeastward into barbarian lands, that we may besiege this quondam goddess in her lair."

Matt sighed and set himself to planning.

Dinner that night was the usual ceremonious affair, with Prester John listening closely to a religious debate between a Nestorian prelate and a Greek Orthodox patriarch.

Anthony, seated beside Balkis, said little or nothing, watching wide-eyed and eating token mouthfuls, completely overawed. Balkis tried to draw him into conversation, of course, but he answered her questions with short sentences, not looking at her eyes. In desperation, she asked Prince Tashih if he had succeeded in translating any more of the poetry of Tu Fu and Li T'ai Po, and the prince responded by reciting several verses. That caught Anthony; he listened in rapt attention, but when the prince had finished, he said only, "They were masters. May I read more of this poetry, Your Highness?"

"I shall delight in having copies made for you," Tashih assured him.

"I shall thank you deeply," Anthony said.

"You already have," Tashih replied.

Then the conversation lagged again. Finally Balkis was struck with inspiration. "I wish we could discover who polluted the fifth oasis, Anthony."

"Do you?" he asked, startled. "Surely that is of no moment now!"

"A polluted oasis is of great moment to us," Prince Tashih said, frowning. "We seek to guard the pilgrims who journey to us as best as we may."

"We do indeed," said Prester John. "Where was this oasis, young man?"

"In the midst of the Sea of Sand," Anthony replied. "Our guide Panyat led us from oasis to oasis—he had traveled with a caravan the year before—but when we came to the fifth, we dared not drink the water."

"Why not?" Matt asked. "What was wrong with it?"

"It was full of snakes."

Suddenly he had their full atention.

"Snakes?" Matt asked. "What color?"

"They . . . they were black," Anthony stammered.

"What matters their color?" Balkis asked.

"The has-been goddess who ordered our kidnapping calls herself 'Kala Nag,' " Matt explained. "It means 'Black Snake.' "

Balkis gasped and exchanged a horrified glance with Anthony.

"We shall have to ask of the pilgrims who came after you if it was still polluted," Prester John said, scowling, "and if it is, we shall have to send a force to clear it. How did you endure without its water?"

"We came to an oasis Panyat did not know," Anthony answered. "It was most strange, for whenever we sipped water, its flavor had changed." He exchanged a warm glance of reminiscence with Balkis. She returned the smile, her heart leaping—but Anthony suddenly remembered at whom he gazed and looked away, seeming almost frightened. Balkis' heart twisted; she fought back tears.

"I have heard of such a pool." Prester John tensed. "Though rumor has it that its flavor changes with every hour, not with every sip. Did you bathe in it?"

"Bathe?" Again Anthony glanced at Balkis in surprise, but quickly looked away. "Why—yes. Of course," he said quickly, "we turned our backs and watched the desert while the other bathed."

"Of course." Prester John's eyes burned. "Know, young folk, that you have bathed in the Fountain of Youth."

Anthony stared at him open-mouthed, then exchanged a brief, shocked glance with Balkis.

Prince Tashih's face lit up. "Majesty, we must go there without delay! You must bathe in it so that you may rule over us forever!"

"It would avail us nothing, my son," Prester John said with a rueful smile. "We would not find it—no, not though we searched for the rest of our lives. The fountain reveals itself to very few and is rarely seen in the same place twice." He turned to his niece and her escort. "Did you look back at the fountain after you had left it?"

"We could not," Anthony said helplessly. "It was gone when we awoke."

Prester John nodded with sad satisfaction. "And will not appear in that place for a hundred years and more, I suspect—if ever."

"But—But why should it have revealed itself to us?" Anthony stuttered.

"Maybe somebody doesn't want Kala Nag to win," Matt suggested, "and therefore wants Balkis to stay alive."

"I think it just as likely that young Anthony is also destined for great deeds, Lord Wizard," the emperor said, "perhaps even for the protection of my realm." His look told Matt exactly from whom Anthony would protect the land.

"How can you think it is the fabled fountain?" Anthony protested.

"Anyone who drinks of its water three times without having eaten will feel as if he had dined on the finest meat and spices," Prester John said. "After your bath, did you feel hunger or thirst?"

Balkis remembered their first night in the wilderness, and how they had felt no weariness nor thirst. She almost said so, then caught herself in time—her goal was to draw Anthony out, not to speak for him.

"Not for days," Anthony admitted.

"It strengthened you amazingly." Prester John nodded. "More importantly, you will discover that you will never be sick again, and any wounds taken in battle will heal very quickly."

"But—But it did not make us younger!" Balkis protested in confusion.

"That is because you are already young," Prester John explained. "Those who drink of this fountain grow older as any will—until they attain the age of thirty years. Then they remain thus as long as they live. Moreover, a person who bathes in that fountain, whether he be a hundred years old or a thousand, will regain the age of thirty-two."

Balkis turned to Anthony and found him staring at her—finally. She kept her gaze locked with his as she asked, "Then we will age for some years yet, but grow no older than thirty-two?"

"Save in experience and, I hope, in wisdom—no," Prester John said. He grew thoughtful and glanced at Matt. Matt returned the look with a glance loaded with meaning.

A protopapas said, "I have heard that the fountain appeared only to the worthy—"

"That is certainly not me!" Anthony burst out. "I am only a lowly peasant!"

"It would seem you are more," the protopapas told him severely, "and to deny your destiny will lead to ruin, not only for yourself, but also for those whom you would have saved—for look you!" He raised a palm to forestall Anthony's objections. "When I say 'worthy,' I mean that the fountain appears to those who devote their lives to others, and whose destinies are so important to humankind that they must have longer lives and stay in good health for the full term of those lives, in order to benefit their fellows to the fullest. You have been given this miraculous bath not for yourselves alone, young folk, but for the good of us all."

Balkis and Anthony stared at one another in astonishment. Then Anthony broke off, blushing, to stare at his plate again.

Balkis' heart turned to lead. She turned to her own plate sadly, knowing that his taciturnity could mean only one thing—that he did not wish to spend so vastly lengthened a life with her. No doubt he had gone suddenly from thinking himself beneath her to thinking himself above her, for she saw clearly now that it was Anthony whose life was vital to the land and therefore to all the world.

Matt, though, watched Anthony's face and knew otherwise.

He had a chance to explain it to Balkis after dinner in her apartments, when she was done weeping bitterly on his shoulder. Then Matt dried her eyes and told her, "He's denying the truth about himself. That's why he's gloomy."

"No, it is because he despises me as a deceitful woman and will never trust me again!" Balkis wailed. "Rightfully, too—I should have trusted him, should have taken the chance and been honest with him about my rank and station!"

"Yes, you should have," Matt agreed, "but if you knew he'd react this way when he found out, you shouldn't be surprised at his gloom."

Balkis stepped back, glaring at him from a tear-streaked face. "You speak as though there is hope!"

"I think he'll be able to understand that you were afraid to lose him," Matt said, "but only after he's gotten over feeling like the lowest worm who ever crawled."

"But he is not! He is a brave, loyal man of amazing talent and—" She caught her breath. "—amazing beauty!" Her eyes began to fill again. "I should have taken the chance to learn what I wish from him, and wish to learn from no other man! I should have tempted him into bedding me!"

"Yeah, then he could have hated himself for the rest of his

life for seducing you, and that *would* have made him leave you for good," Matt said. "Let him get over his self-esteem problem. If he's in love with you now, he'll be in love with you forever."

"Not when he knows me for a deceiver, who did not tell him my true rank!"

"No, I think he simply doesn't believe he's good enough for you," Matt protested. "I watched his face while we were talking about the fountain, and Anthony flatly did not believe he was worthy of it. Instead, he convinced himself that it was you who are the important one."

Balkis stared at him, then demanded in a hushed voice, "How could he?"

Matt shrugged. "It confirms the tragedy that hit him this afternoon."

"What tragedy is that?" Balkis asked in a quandary.

"Discovering that you're too good for him, of course," Matt said, "that you're above and beyond him. Why else would he lapse back into gloom so quickly?"

Balkis' eyes glimmered with hope as well as tears. "Then—Then he may forgive me?"

"In an instant, if we can convince him that he's good enough for you."

"But how can we do that?" Balkis wailed.

"Let me have a chat with him," Matt said. "I can't guarantee results, mind you—but I can point out a few things that might change his mind."

"Oh, Lord Wizard, would you?"

"Be glad to—and I have a notion that it's in my best interest anyway." Matt thought of the Mongol conquests of his own universe, which had not happened here yet, and of the potential for mayhem posed by an animist spirit who was a Central Asian shaman's nightmare. "I think he'll believe me if he thinks it's for somebody else's benefit."

"Anyone's but mine!" And Balkis was off into another storm of tears.

Matt sighed, pulled her close, and set himself to comforting, while he wished wildly for Alisande to take charge of the poor kid. By the time he had calmed Balkis enough for her to sleep, it was past midnight, and he thought he'd better leave Anthony alone until morning.

The next morning, though, when they'd finished breakfast and he was about to invite Anthony to go for a walk, the Lord Privy Minister brought the bad news—that there was a hooded stranger at the gates who refused to show his face but who claimed to be an emissary from Kala Nag, and who insisted on speaking with the emperor immediately.

"Bring him to the throne room, but hold him at the door until we arrive." Prester John rose with a frown. "Send gentlemen to attire me in my court robes." He nodded to Matt. "Let them attire you also, Lord Wizard—I shall have need of you by my left side, with Tashih by my right." He turned to Balkis and Anthony. "Do you watch from the hidden chamber, that you may add the weight of your magic to the Lord Wizard's if there should be need."

Anthony looked up, startled, then rose hastily and bowed. "Of course, Your Majesty."

Balkis went with him to the small chamber high in the wall of the throne room, where they peered through spyholes. Her heart sang; when it was a matter of someone else's good, her Anthony never hesitated. His own good, though, he would ignore in a second. How could she make him understand that he *was* her good?

Looking down, she saw Prester John arrange himself on his throne, then call to the guards, "Admit him."

The stranger came in, a tall and ominous figure in a gray hooded robe, the cowl pulled so far forward as to hide his face. He stepped up to the bottom step without a bow—an insult in itself—and said in a rasping voice, "We do not appreciate being kept waiting, foolish prince!"

Tashih uttered an exclamation of anger and started forward, but Prester John restrained him with a hand. "I see that you are as lacking in courtesy as you are ignorant of protocol. Are you also a coward, that you dare not show your face?"

"Nay. It is you who shall prove coward when you see it." The emissary threw back his hood. Balkis gasped, and Anthony spat a whispered oath, for the stranger's head was that of a snake.

Below them, Tashih's hand went to his sword but froze there. "Be glad that your status as an emissary precludes attack!"

"Yes, you should be glad of it," the snakeman hissed, "for thereby are you safe from me." Then he focused his unwinking stare on Matt and said, "You have met two of my broodmates already, wizard. We shall remember that."

"Good idea," Matt answered, "and you might want to remember their fates, too."

The snakeman's eyes flashed with anger. "You shall not always have your tame lizard with you!"

"Takes one to know one," Matt said, "and you will always have your mistress with you, ready to burn you to a crisp if you fail her."

The snake head hissed in anger, forked tongue darting out and back. "Do you treat your own failed warriors better?"

"Much," said Prester John. "We may chastise, but we are more likely to console and heal, for we are too wise to waste warriors."

"That is because you have no warriors to waste! Because there are too few of you! But a snake-mother can make dozens in a single hatching, and there can be dozens of snake-mothers—no, hundreds, thousands!"

"So you're planning to bury us in vipers?"

"If you have the courage to meet us in open combat, yes," the ambassador said. "If you do not, we shall lay siege to your city and our young shall come up your drains and tunnel under your walls, then grow in a matter of months into warriors within your city."

"They will not have the opportunity," Prester John said evenly. "Name the time and place of your battle. We shall march to meet you."

"Let it be on the Plain of Redest, then," the snakeman said, "and the time an hour after sunrise tomorrow."

"At Redest, then," Prester John said in a voice that should have frosted the air. "Go now in safety, while we can still rein in our temper."

"As though you would dare strike at the emissary of Kala

Nag!" the snakeman sneered, then deliberately turned his back on the emperor and strolled out the door.

As the guards closed it, Prester John said, "See that hc is well and closely guarded until he is beyond the city's walls, but do not let your soldiers march too near. Give every man a forked stick to use should any little vipers fall from his robe."

The guard bowed and departed.

"Good thought," Matt said approvingly. "They probably grow fast, and a corps of snakemen inside the city could be very handy for Kala Nag."

"They may be here already," Prester John said grimly. "Send dogs out to hunt for snakes."

"And mongooses," Matt reminded him. "I know I've seen them for sale in the marketplace. Set people to breeding them. I'll give them a spell that will increase the speed of the process enormously."

"A good thought," Prester John agreed. "How else shall we guard against snakes?"

"I have a spell involving pigs and an Irish saint that should make the very earth anathema to them," Matt said. "Just pass the word that it's a citizen's patriotic duty to keep a mongoose on the premises. That should take care of the fifth column."

"Well thought again," Prester John said. "Why do you think they have set the time as an hour after sunrise?"

"Because snakes are cold-blooded, and it takes some time in the heat of the sun before they can begin to move at full speed. If we want to fight dirty, we can just start attacking at first light."

"Lord Wizard!" Prince Tashih gasped in shock.

"We would not fight in so dishonorable a fashion," Prester John reproved.

"Okay." Matt shrugged. "Kala Nag will, but don't let that stop you. Where's this Plain of Redest?"

"Ten hours' ride southeast of the city."

"So your army will be facing east and have the sun in their eyes."

"A good thought; I shall bid the generals circle and come from the north," Prester John said. "What do you make of this ultimatum, Lord Wizard? Surely if Kala Nag felt able to conquer Maracanda, she would merely have marched, not issued a challenge!"

"Right—she knows she's not ready," Matt agreed. "Besides, it's clearly a ploy to get the army away from the city, so make sure you leave a strong home guard to man the walls and a police force to deal with any hidden snakepeople already in the city. Beyond that?" He shrugged. "It's a last-ditch attempt to knock you out before you become too strong; apparently, the configuration of which Balkis is the key hasn't formed yet, but will soon. Kala Nag has to try to knock you out, do or die, before it's too late."

"But how can she hope to triumph?" Tashih demanded.

"She obviously has some sort of secret weapon that gives her a fighting chance—probably magical." Matt frowned. "I'd recommend leaving Balkis and Anthony for the home guard, Your Majesty, and taking the rest of your wizards with you."

Balkis' heart soared, but she kept her tone level. "Do you think we are proof against a siege, Anthony? . . . Anthony?" She looked up, looked around the little room, but Anthony was gone.

"Gone?" Matt said. "What do you mean, gone? Where could he go?"

"I fear he may have gone after the snakeman to prove his worth—and the viper may slay him!" Balkis clasped her hands, tears running down her cheeks. "Lord Wizard, save him!"

"I'll run an aerial reconnaissance," Matt promised, "but I don't think he could get near Snake-eyes, not with the kind of guard your uncle put around him. Come on, up to the ramparts—Stegoman can't land indoors."

They went up to the rooftop, where Matt recited the spell to call up his dragon friend, hoping he wasn't interrupting a honeymoon. Then he and Balkis looked down at the army assembling before the walls of the city.

It was truly spectacular. When Prester John rode forth to war, he marched in real state, preceded not by banners but by thirteen huge and lofty crosses made of gold and ornamented with precious stones. Soldiers formed up behind each of the crosses—a thousand cavalry and ten thousand infantry, not counting those who had charge of the baggage and provisions.

One of those infantrymen had blond hair, a uniform a little too small for him, and a marked southern accent. He stood out like a sore thumb among the black-haired, golden-skinned Maracandese, but he wasn't the only outlander; there were hundreds of soldiers from Prester John's tributary states.

"What manner of stones are those in the golden crosses?" he asked the soldier next to him. "They look quite ordinary to me."

The man looked up at him in surprise, then laughed outright. "You are an outlander, and newly come! Know, then, that each of the first ten crosses holds embedded in its gold a marvelous gem that can work magic of the sort soldiers love."

"Martial magic?" Anthony frowned—for of course it was he, determined to defend Maracanda, and the woman he loved but knew he could not have; if he died protecting her, so much the better, for without her there was no reason to live.

"The first stone can freeze the very air, and certainly enemy soldiers," the trooper told him. "The second can heat their weapons till they are too hot to hold—or broil the soldiers themselves in an instant. If the enemy uses ice or fire as a weapon, the third stone can reduce either to an even temperature. The fourth can flood with light everything within a span of five miles; the fifth can cast darkness as far."

"Amazing virtues," Anthony said, eyes wide. "What can the others do?"

"The sixth and seventh are unconsecrated; the one turns water to milk and the seventh to wine, which is greatly to be valued by any soldier. The eighth, ninth, and tenth are consecrated; the eighth will cause fish to congregate, and the ninth will compel wild beasts to follow one. The tenth, when it is sprinkled with hot lion's blood, will produce a fire that can be quenched only by sprinkling it with hot dragon's blood." He grinned. "That standard is ours."

Anthony peered up at the huge cross, frowning. "But I see no stone there, only a gaping hole."

CHAPTER 32

"What!" The soldier stared, horrified. "It is so! How can this be? Who can have stolen it? Why has no one seen this before?"

Good questions, Anthony thought, especially the last. More to the point, how was it he had seen it gone when no one else had? He could only think that his bath in the Fountain of Youth had given him the ability to see through glamours—either that, or Balkis' magic was rubbing off on him. He shied away from that notion; thoughts of Balkis hurt, and deeply.

"Captain!" the soldier cried. "The stone! The stone that starts and quenches fire is gone!"

The alarm went up and Matt was there to investigate within minutes. They lowered the cross. He glared at the hole a minute, then said, "Yep. It's gone, all right."

"But who could have stolen it?"

"One of those crawlie enemies we were worried about." Matt looked around the ranks reflectively. Anthony ducked behind another soldier and pressed his helmet down farther over his telltale hair.

Matt turned to the captain again. "While their ambassador distracted us, a fellow snake got into the treasury somehow."

"Ridiculous!" the captain snorted. "What manner of thief would penetrate a royal treasury and steal only this one stone?"

"A snake with a mission," Matt told him.

In fact, they later found out he'd guessed correctly—the snake had tunneled into the treasury, stolen the stone, and filled the tunnel in on the way out. The palace engineers were able to plug the hole more permanently—before any human thieves could develop ideas. Prester John also made the treasury serve double duty as his mongoose breeding pen from that time on.

A cry went up. Turning to look, they saw a wedge of snake-people striding toward them across the plain, wearing only their scales. Without their robes, they seemed somehow obscene, their fronts too sickly a green, their backs too mottled, their limbs far too slender for the strength they held. Behind them marched an assortment of creatures of such ugliness and menace that half the soldiers cried out and hid their eyes. Only when their sergeants assured them that the mere sight of the monsters did not turn them to stone or burn out their sight did the quaking troopers dare look again.

With a flinten face, Prester John rode out to meet the embassy with a hundred horsemen around him.

The snake-folk came to a halt. The one at the point of the wedge grinned, tongue flicking out in insult, and said, "We meet again, O Prince of Fools."

"So it is you, the emissary," Prester John said. "Speak what you have come to say before I unleash my troops upon you."

"Only this, O King of Folly! We have your flame stone and a pride of lions caged by it. If you do not surrender at once, we shall hurl it afire into the center of your city and let it burn everything within your walls to cinders!"

Prester John paled, for he knew the power of the stone and knew it could prove as devastating as the snakeman claimed. Still he met threat with threat. "Know that we have powerful magicians to avenge such an action—and we know the name of your tyrant!"

"Only her public name. Her true name remains hidden," said the snakeman. "You may know it by this evidence—that 'Kala Nag' is a Hindu name, O Ignorant One, and the goddess is of the high steppe. Further, 'Nag' is masculine, and the goddess is very, very feminine. No, you cannot hurt her, even if your magicks were strong enough."

"A craven act indeed!" Prester John said indignantly.

The snakeman's eyes flashed with anger. "A prudent act, and you lacked such prudence yourself. We know how slow you human folk are to decide such weighty matters, so we shall give you until sunset—but when darkness falls, if you have not surrendered, your city shall light the night!"

He wheeled and stalked away. The wedge opened to let him through, then reformed behind him and arrowed through a lane that opened in the midst of the monsters. The wedge drove through, and the monsters turned to follow. The whole assemblage moved away across the plain.

Prester John turned and called, "Let all wizards appear before me!"

Balkis called for a horse and rode down to him at the gallop. Soldiers looked up, saw the white robe with the purple cloak and the golden coronet on her brows, and stepped aside, bowing as she passed.

By the time she came, half a dozen lesser wizards had assembled around Matt and Prester John. She looked around, forlorn. "Where is Anthony?"

"Yes, where is Anthony?" Matt repeated in a voice that could be heard a hundred feet away. "We need him sorely now, for your spells are far stronger with him to complete them, and if this situation doesn't call for new verses, I don't know what does!"

"He is not here," Balkis said dolefully.

"Yes, he is not here!" Matt trumpeted. "I can't blame him, actually—he isn't a subject of this land, after all. Why should he care if Maracanda burns and all of Asia and Europe are conquered by a monster, because Prester John's army is all that stands between Kala Nag and world conquest?"

The silence stretched out, broken only by Balkis' sobbing gasps as she struggled to suppress tears. Matt wondered if he had laid the guilt trip on too heavily.

A curse came from the ranks, and a soldier taller than most yanked off his helmet and shoved it and his spear into the hands of the startled trooper next to him. Then he came striding up to Matt. He bowed to Prester John and said, "Command me, Majesty! I would have preferred to fight for you like the commoner I am, but if you deem that I may defend better as a wizard, I am come!"

"Oh, Anthony!" Balkis breathed in melting tones, but he

hardened his face and kept his gaze on the emperor. Hers showed great sorrow; then she composed it and squared her shoulders, every inch a princess.

"Our course is clear," Prester John said. "We must have the firestone back before the sun sets. Who shall go to bring it?"

"I, my lord!" Prince Tashih nudged his horse forward. "I shall take our doughtiest warriors and mount a sally into the midst of their fell army! Only send me one wizard to deflect their magic!"

"I!" Anthony said instantly. "Let me accompany the prince!"

Balkis cried out in fear, and Prester John's brooding gaze rested on Anthony. "They who go to retrieve this stone shall be courting death."

"I care nothing for my own life," Anthony said stubbornly, and Balkis restrained another sobbing gasp.

Prester John only continued his weighing gaze, though, and Matt thought he understood the emperor's reasoning. Anthony was suicidal, it was true, for he was so much in love with Balkis that he didn't want to live if he couldn't be with her. He was sure that she was far above him—but he also had the frantic hope that he could prove himself worthy of the hand of a princess. Like so many young men, Anthony was after glory and was willing to die trying to gain it.

"Very well, then," Prester John said, "you shall accompany the prince."

"No!" Balkis cried, as though it were torn from her. "He wishes only to die, for he feels I have betrayed him!"

"I shall do all that I may to keep the prince safe," Anthony said stubbornly, still refusing to look at her.

"Think you this battle can be won by armed men?" Balkis cried in exasperation. "Deflect their magic! They are permeated with it, every one of them! What else could give a snake the size and form of a human? What else could support those monsters in life? If you charge into their mass, you shall all die, no matter how many wizards charge with you—and we shall still lack the stone, be even weaker with no wizards left, have to surrender all our force to that obscene goddess or watch Maracanda burn!"

Anthony's face was stone, but Matt said quietly, "She has a point."

"She has indeed." Prester John's gaze rested on his son with pride and elation. "My greatest glory is you, my son, for you are willing to risk certain death to save your people."

"But their deaths will not save the people!" Balkis said angrily. "They will only slay *me*!"

"If my elite guard cannot bring back that stone," Prince Tashih said stubbornly, "none can."

"I!" Balkis cried.

"No!" Anthony wailed. "You will sacrifice yourself!"

She turned to him, suddenly intent. "Do you care so much for a mere cat?"

"Mere!" Anthony cried. "You are the only real friend I have ever had! If I fought my brothers for you, would you not think I'd care?"

"If you care for the cat," she said, "do you care more for the woman?"

He stared at her, at a loss.

"Do unicorns and mussel shells mean nothing?" Balkis asked, her voice low.

Anthony seemed to deflate even as his face came alive. Then he seemed to swell again as he smiled, stepping closer, giving the impression of touching her even though he was afoot with his arms at his sides and she was mounted. "The cat can be only a friend," he breathed. "The woman, I would hope, could be much more." Then his eyes widened and he stepped back, horrified. "But I forget myself, forget my place. Princess, I am your humble servant! My life is yours! Command me as you will!" He dropped to one knee.

Balkis cried out in distress and leaped off her horse to kneel facing him, hands on his shoulders. "No! Not like this! I do not want you for a servant!"

Anthony looked up, eyes wide with hurt.

Matt stepped in quickly. "What's the matter, princess? I thought you did want his life with yours."

Balkis turned to him wide-eyed, then turned back to Anthony, grinning wickedly. "Very well, foolish man! You have offered me your life and I shall have it! But first, come and seize that stone with me!"

There before their eyes she dwindled and shrank, arms lengthening, hands and feet turning into paws, nose and mouth thrusting forward into a muzzle, ears moving to the top of her head and gaining points, tail sprouting and growing. There she stood, a cat like any, but with a purple back and tail, a circle of gold around her head, and a white belly.

In spite of his stubbornness, Anthony smiled fondly and reached down. "I shall never be alone again, shall I?"

"Never, silly man!" the cat meowed. "Now finish a verse for me!"

> "Like the lion's shadow, twice her size
> I shall grow and gain!
> With lion's strength and lion's might . . ."

"But not with lion's mane!" Anthony cried.

Matt winced.

It worked anyway. Even Prester John gasped with amazement as the Balkis-cat grew, swelling, until her head was on a level with Matt's and she was as large as a horse. The real horses screamed in terror and tried to bolt; their riders barely managed to hold them still. A few soldiers, more courageous than the rest, ran forward to hold their bridles.

"Come, man, and ride!" Balkis challenged as she crouched before Anthony.

Grinning, he said, "You forgot the saddle," but leaped up on her back anyway, crying, "A sword!"

Three officers leaped to offer theirs. Anthony took the first as Balkis stood up, very carefully, and in a basso meow chanted,

> "Upon the stone of blood and flame
> We shall pounce, thus to reclaim,
> Like a thief of midnight's hour . . ."

Anthony cried:

> "We'll steal back our stone of power!"

They shimmered and disappeared.

"Lord Wizard, after them!" Prester John cried in panic. "Do not let my niece face such deadly danger alone!"

"I wouldn't exactly say she's alone," Matt demurred. "In fact, I think she'll never be alone again."

"If she lives! Will you go?"

"I guess I'd better." Matt recited,

"As a fly upon the wall
I shall go to overhaul
Any spell that's gone haywire.
Take me to the stone of fire!"

The world blurred. When it cleared, he found he could see nearly three hundred sixty degrees, but it was horribly distorted. It took him a few seconds to learn to interpret the visual images, to discover what the grainy substance was beneath his feet. The spell had taken him literally; he was a fly, and the wall was the canvas side of a tent.

The snakeman had lied, of course—instead of a whole pride of lions, there were only two, standing as proudly as though they were guarding a library on either side of a pedestal which held a three-inch stone that appeared to be only polished quartz. But Anthony had faced a lion before, and materialized with a sword in his hand.

Balkis struck one lion down with a paw the size of a manhole cover even as Anthony, with the element of surprise on his side, slashed the throat of the other with a mighty blow. The beast tried to roar and charged anyway, but Balkis danced aside, and the beast collapsed, its blood spattering the stone.

Something tore the tent away, exposing them to a ring of snakemen and monsters who screamed and charged them—but Balkis was already chanting,

"To the Lord of Maracanda
We'll return and no more wander!
To the vast defending host . . ."

"We shall fly with nothing lost!" Anthony finished.

The giant cat and her rider shimmered, grew translucent, then disappeared a split second before the first monster reached them. As it did, the stone burst into flame.

Matt could feel the wave of heat. He didn't stay to watch what happened, just repeated Balkis' escape spell in his buzzing voice. The world went fuzzy; then he was falling toward a giant purple cat with a rider on her back, facing an armored man with a crown on his helmet. Matt's wings spread automatically, and he buzzed,

> "A human fly I'll be no longer,
> For my proper form is stronger
> In its hold upon my id
> Than this insect-form in which I've hid!"

To his friends, he must have seemed to appear out of thin air as he fell, landing in a crouch.

"I tell you, he did send himself after you!" Prince Tashih pointed at Matt.

"I do not doubt you, cousin." Basso Balkis blinked at Matt. "What happened to you, Lord Wizard?"

"I just decided to buzz off."

Wings boomed, horses screamed, and two dragons landed just behind the army. As sergeants and riders fought to control men and horses, Stegoman boomed, "When you call me, Matthew, be so good as to stay where you are until I arrive. It has taken us many minutes to find you."

"Sorry about that," Matt said, abashed. "They needed me in a hurry here."

"I do not doubt it. What is that bonfire out on the plain?"

"I had wondered that myself," Prester John said, staring at the fountain of flame that towered above them. They could hear screams and cries beneath its crackling. "You lit the firestone, did you not, my niece?"

"No, I did, Majesty," Anthony said, chagrined. "I had not intended—"

"It is well that you did," Prester John said.

Prince Tashih smiled. "Better here than in the midst of Maracanda, is it not?"

"Most surely," Prester John agreed.

"I saw a great number of broiling snakes as I flew over them." Stegoman wrinkled his nose. "Horrid smell, and the turbulence was abominable! There were other creatures burning like torches—there must have been a great deal of fat in them—but many more were fleeing, and thousands upon thousands of snakes streaked away across the plain."

"It is strange that many of them burst into flame as they fled," said Dimetrolas, "even though they were a thousand feet from the pyre, and more."

"Kala Nag should really learn some self-control," Matt said. "She's burning up her army in frustration."

"I fear that snakes reproduce very quickly." Prester John sighed. "And she shall have many more warriors in a year's time, or less. This conflict is not ended, Lord Wizard, only postponed."

"Well, at least we know what she's planning now," Matt said brightly. "Not the details, maybe, but enough to be on guard."

Prester John frowned at the fountain of fire. "We cannot have that torch burning forever upon the plain."

"Perhaps we can fly over it with vats of water and dump them upon it for you," Stegoman suggested.

"It is very good of you to offer, excellent beast," the emperor acknowledged, "but fire will not quench this stone."

"What will?" Stegoman asked.

Several people started to answer, then caught themselves in time.

"What?" Stegoman glowered at all the humans about him. "What is this you do not wish me to hear?"

"Understand, we're not asking anything of you," Matt said quickly, "but . . . uh . . . the only thing that will put out that fire is dragon's blood."

"N-o-o-o-o!" Stegoman roared, rearing back and contributing some fire of his own.

The humans jumped away from the jet, gibbering in terror.

Dimetrolas scowled at her fiancé. "What is this, searing serpent? Do you fear to shed a few drops in a good cause?"

Stegoman huffed, trying to find the right words, but Matt got there ahead of him. "It's a phobia of his, dragon lady—a terrible, deeply rooted fear. It goes back to the first few minutes after he kicked his way out of the egg, when a hatchling-hunter caught him."

"A hatchling-hunter! One who sought to catch small dragons, that he might sell their blood to sorcerers?"

"The very same," Matt told her.

Prester John shuddered. "I cannot blame the beast—I have an antipathy for people who want my blood, too."

"It goes with the office," Matt agreed.

"However," Prince Tashih pointed out, "that would not stop you from shedding every drop if you thought it necessary to protect your people."

"It is one thing to give of one's own blood," Dimetrolas told them, "but another to have it drained from you."

Matt blinked; he hadn't expected compassion from the acerbic Dimetrolas.

She surprised him, though. She turned to Stegoman and said, "Poor little fellow that you were! Small wonder you are horrified at the prospect of being cut! This at least I may do for you, dear drake." With that, she launched and pounded her way into the sky.

"Dimetrolas! Wait! Beware the updrafts!" Stegoman sprang into the sky right behind her.

"We should aid," the giant purple cat boomed to Matt.

"I think they've got the situation under control." Matt gazed after the flying couple. "In fact, if they come out of this all right, I think it will do wonders for their relationship . . . Would you do me a favor, princess? Change back into a woman?"

"Oh. Yes, my form is rather disconcerting." Balkis began to shrink and reshape herself. Anthony leaped off hastily.

Matt didn't bother watching the transformation; he'd seen it before. He watched the two winged forms sailing over the plain, then suddenly rocking and plunging in the updrafts from the blaze. He couldn't see exactly what happened, but the fire began to die even before the two dragons turned and came sailing back.

They landed in a booming of huge wings, and Stegoman bellowed, "Quickly! Heal her wound, wizard, for I would not have her die even as the flames do!"

Matt ran forward and caught Dimetrolas' foreleg. He winced at the sight of the ragged wound but started reciting the healing spell.

Even as he chanted, Stegoman exulted, "She is the bravest of the brave! Over the very blaze she flew and cut herself with her own claw! Through scale and leathery hide she slashed, then watched a pint of her very own fluid of life fall into the flames! They die even now—but she must not!"

"Fret not, Flame Flier," Dimetrolas said with a broad smile. She held up her foreleg to show him. "Your friend has healed me, and I am at last willing to own that humans may have their uses."

"A thousand thanks, Matthew!" Stegoman rumbled.

"I think you've already given them."

"An emperor's thanks to the gallant Dimetrolas," Prester John said.

"And a prince's," Tashih said quickly.

"It is little enough that I have done." But Dimetrolas raised shining, heavy-lidded eyes to Stegoman.

"Little? It is a pledge!" Stegoman breathed, "A blood-pledge, and I am minded to give one in return."

"Your pledge I desire, but I have no use for your blood—unless it flows through the eggs of a brood of my own."

"Do dragons marry?" Prester John asked Matt.

"They don't seem to think it necessary," Matt replied.

"Why not?" Stegoman grinned down at Dimetrolas. "I have adopted so many other human ways!"

"But I have not," she replied tartly. "Give me time, Winged Warrior—a century or two."

"I shall give you my whole life," he breathed, gaze locked on hers.

"That's the way they are." Matt turned to Prester John. "Once they mate, they're together for life. It's the nature of the breed—in the genes."

"Still, we might honor them with some small ceremony one day," Prester John said, his eyes twinkling. Then he turned to his niece. "But we must honor most of all the young woman and young man who had the fantastic courage to plunge into the heart of an army of monsters and face lions! Without them, we would all have been lost!"

Anthony reddened and became very formal again. He bowed, saying, "It has been my privilege to serve, Your Majesty." Then he turned and knelt before Balkis. "What more would you have of me, Your Highness?"

CHAPTER 33

"Oh, do not call me that!" Balkis cried, stamping her foot.

Anthony looked up, stone-faced, but Matt said, "Okay, soldier, you heard the lady. That's her next order. Anything you'd like to add to that, princess?"

Anthony looked up, taken aback.

A gleam appeared in Balkis' eye. "Yes! Anthony, you must call me only 'Balkis' henceforth!"

"If—If you command it," he said through wooden lips, "Balkis." But still he knelt.

"Any other commands come to mind?" Matt asked in as casual manner as he could.

The gleam in Balkis' eye turned hot. "Yes! Anthony, rise and take me in your arms!"

Disbelief in his eyes, Anthony came to his feet and gathered her in.

She pouted up at him and, in the tones of a petulant child, commanded, "Kiss me!"

He looked down at her for a long minute, then grinned and kissed her.

"Well, that settles that," Matt said loudly enough to break the mood.

They both jumped a little and stepped apart, blushing.

Matt went on, "We've established that he cares about you too much to let you go wandering alone, and you can't go into all the secure little nooks and crannies open to your cat shape with him along."

"But I must be free to go where my people need me," she protested.

"And I must still be your servant," Anthony insisted. "You

are a princess and I a peasant. I can never be anything more to you."

"But you are!" she protested. "You are everything!"

"Even to us, you are already a battle-hero," the prince pointed out.

Anthony looked up in surprise, then turned stubborn again.

"I think he needs a bath after all that hot exercise," Matt said. "Come on, Anthony. If you want to serve a princess, you'd better clean up."

Anthony turned to Prester John questioningly.

"Go with the Lord Wizard." The emperor's gaze was thoughtful.

Anthony turned to Balkis, but she too nodded. "He has taught me much, Anthony, though I did not wish to admit it at the time. Go with him, if you love me."

Anthony's face closed again. He bowed to her, then turned to go with Matt.

The local form of bathing involved a large tiled chamber with wooden seats, massive towels around the waist, and huge quantities of steam. Matt waited until the heat and the moisture had relaxed the boy, then said, "Balkis never told you where she came from, did she?"

"Never." Anthony tensed again. "If I had known she was a princess, I would not ever have dared court her."

"Good reason not to let you know," Matt said. "She is in love with you, you know—very deeply."

Anthony made no answer, but frowned into the curls of mist about him.

"Of course, she didn't know she was a princess until a year ago."

"What?" Anthony whirled to stare at Matt.

"It's true." Matt nodded emphatically. "She was a baby when the barbarians conquered Maracanda, but her mother managed to set her adrift in a trunk just before they caught her. Some river sprites took pity on the baby and changed her into a kitten, because a month-old cat is a lot more likely to survive than a month-old baby."

"More likely, yes," Anthony said, his gaze glued to Matt's face, "but still prey to any who wish it."

Matt nodded again. "Fortunately, the nixies turned her over to some dryads, and they raised her until she was big enough to get a job as a mouser with a caravan bound westward, out of barbarian territory. She never told you any of this, huh?"

"From this part, yes," Anthony said slowly, "that she had traveled with a caravan in cat-form. She told me what she had seen of the great cities along that route—of Susa and Novogorod, of the wide plains and the dark forest."

"But she didn't tell you that she grew up in one of those forests?"

"What!"

Matt nodded. "When she had gone far enough west to be safe and the caravan disbanded, she wandered into the woods and let the local brownies take care of her. They led her to a woodcutter's cottage and changed her back into a baby. The woodcutter and his wife were delighted—they'd always wanted children, and had never had any."

"You do not mean to tell me she grew up as a common woodcutter's daughter!"

"I mean exactly that." Matt met his eyes. "She was reared as a peasant, Anthony, just like you—but when she was grown, she found out she was something more."

"But . . . but . . . how?"

Matt turned away to stare into the mist. "She was orphaned at sixteen and had the good sense to take her chances as a cat in the forest rather than as a young girl without protection. Oh, she knew she could change into a cat, she had that much ahead of you, and enough magic had rubbed off on her that she was able to work a few tricks—but when she was left alone in the world, she went to Idris, the local wise-woman, and learned magic. Learned very quickly, too, just as you do—she'd absorbed everything Idris could teach her in a single year. So again she started her travels—Idris sent her to me for advanced training."

"And you brought her to Maracanda?"

"Yes, though I didn't know where we were going at the time," Matt said, "only that barbarians were invading from the east and I had to stop them before they reached Merovence. I didn't even know she was human until we got bushwhacked in India. Balkis helped me fight off the barbarians—saved my life a few times, too. More importantly, she helped me rescue my children when they were kidnapped." He turned to face Anthony again. "So you won't be too surprised that I came running when I heard she herself had been kidnapped."

"No, certainly not," Anthony agreed. "But when did she learn she was a princess?"

"After we'd helped Prester John win back Maracanda and sent the barbarians home to their steppes. Then he started comparing notes and found out she was his niece. He even managed to track down the nixies who had helped her survive as a baby, and they confirmed it—our peasant girl suddenly found out she was a princess."

"If she grew up as a peasant, she has learned the graces of a lady with extraordinary speed!"

"Yes, she's a quick learner," Matt said, "and Prester John tells me she has charmed the whole court. Still, though, I don't think she has a single close friend here. They all grew up in palaces, so none of them can understand what it's like to have been a peasant."

Anthony studied his toenails, frowning.

Matt waited.

"But she does know her true station now," Anthony said.

"Yes, but it took her a while to accept it—just as it's taking you."

"I am no prince!"

"No, you're a wizard, and a very courageous warrior." Matt shrugged. "Every noble house can trace their ancestry back to a commoner who was ennobled for his service to the crown and the nation. You've proved your worth by bringing Balkis safely home—"

Anthony started to protest.

Matt held up a hand to forestall him. "No, it doesn't matter that she saved your life as often as you saved hers—the fact remains that she would have died on the way if you hadn't been escorting her."

Anthony closed his mouth and turned back to studying his feet.

"Of course, you didn't stop there," Matt said. "You proved your worth in battle, too—proved yourself to have become much more than the peasant you were born, proved you're of a noble heart and noble mind, noble enough to aspire to the hand of a princess. Prester John and Prince Tashih are both eager to declare you to be a nobleman, if you'll just accept your due and let them."

"They cannot make me noble," Anthony muttered.

"No, they can only declare you to be so once you've proved it—and you have, whether you know it or not. Besides, Prince Tashih has his own reasons for liking you, whether he's stopped to think about it yet or not."

Anthony looked up, frowning. "What reason is that?"

"I told you Balkis has charmed the whole court," Matt said, "but if she marries a man who was born a peasant, she can never inherit—which she doesn't want to do, but that wouldn't stop some ambitious court faction from trying to push her into it and getting her killed in the process."

Anthony stared at him, appalled.

"In that case," Matt said, "marrying a man who was born a peasant but has proved himself to be noble might endear her to the masses, and thereby strengthen the throne even more."

Anthony went back to contemplating the steam.

"Come on," Matt said softly, "you know she isn't half the wizard she can be unless you're there to finish her verses for her. Why she has a block against end-lines, I don't know, but she does—and you have a block against starting them, but the two of you together are ten times as powerful as either of you alone. If that doesn't tell you something, nothing will."

Anthony was still silent.

"Okay, so it *won't* tell you," Matt went on, "but it has told Kala Nag. Who do you think is the other half of the pair that can block her conquest of the world? Not me, we've proved that—she can do just fine without me. But the two of you together have already beaten Kala Nag's sorcerers and army once. She knows you can do it again. She has to keep the two of you apart, and the surest way to do that is to kill Balkis."

"No!" Anthony cried, horrified.

"That's why she was so angry at Balkis' kidnapper," Matt

said relentlessly. "His plans backfired; he wound up sending her to the one person in all the world who could make her a formidable power. That's a real laugh, isn't it? That delicate little girl, a formidable wizard—but she has the heart for it, and with you, she actually does have the power."

"So the only way I can keep her alive, is to be with her?" Anthony asked.

"You got it," Matt said.

Anthony still balked. "I am only a poor peasant! A man who would marry a princess must be wealthy."

"Sure, a poor peasant with a fortune in gems in his pockets!"

Anthony stared up at Matt. "She told you that?"

"Only when I asked," Matt told him. "I saw you handing a goldsmith a nugget and a diamond in the bazaar, remember. I was worried you might have stolen them, but she set me straight."

"I do have both nuggets and jewels," Anthony admitted, "though they are now securely hidden, no longer on my person."

"Either way, you're rich enough to propose. Any more objections?"

"Objections, no," Anthony said slowly.

"But you do have questions? What?"

Anthony turned to him, eyes burning. "I have seen what barnyard animals do, but I know there must be more to it, for people. Tell me—how does a man couple with a woman and make it the ecstasy men speak of?"

Matt sighed, nerved himself to the task, and proceeded to tell Anthony what his father should have, but probably hadn't known himself. He also marveled at the excellent ruby color of Anthony's face as he told.

They were all invited to the victory banquet, of course—even Stegoman and Dimetrolas, but they didn't get the invitation; there was a full moon, and Stegoman had said something about trying a bit of night flying and about the twining of the flowers. After dinner Anthony turned to Balkis and gravely asked, "Will you come to teach me your northern stars, Balkis? I can recognize very few of the sky-pictures from my home."

"Why . . . I shall be delighted, Anthony," Balkis said, and they went out arm in arm.

Prince Tashih watched them go, frowning. "I cannot help but wonder if my cousin is safe alone with a lusty young man."

"I am delighted at such a show of brotherly feeling," Prester John said, beaming. "Still, Tashih, be not concerned—you have seen the sort of cat into which our Balkis can turn. Be assured that if Anthony misbehaves, Balkis has far stronger claws than any mortal woman I have known."

"I still mistrust the night," Tashih grumbled.

"Well, then, if it will ease your heart," Prester John sighed, "I shall stroll in the gardens myself in company with the Lord Wizard—not closely enough to spy upon them, you understand, but certainly near enough to hear her cry out, though I doubt she will."

Matt doubted it, too, very much. He went with the emperor, planning to stay only long enough to assure themselves it was just a lover's tryst.

It was more, though. Oh, they talked of idle things, carefully steering clear of their relationship. After all, Balkis had enough star-stories to last the night, and Anthony had all sorts of polite exclaiming to do about the beauty of the flowers, and many comparisons to make between their beauty and hers—always to the flowers' detriment, of course.

But little by little Balkis worked their way down to the stream.

"What a lovely prospect!" Anthony exclaimed. "Still water showing the moon her glowing face—the music of nightingales, and sweet perfumes surrounding us—but none as sweet as yours."

"I thank you, sir." Balkis batted her eyelashes at him, then grew serious. "But I cannot look upon this river without remembering that it was here my mother cast me into the waters."

"Surely you cannot remember that!" Anthony protested.

"No," Balkis said, "but there are those who can." Raising

her voice, she called out, "Spirits of the water, come to speak with me, I beg you! I have need of your counsel!"

The water seemed to swell up, then drained back, revealing two feminine forms decked in seaweed. Anthony gasped in amazement.

"I should think we would know our own magic when it calls to us, should we not, Shannai?" asked the one.

"Indeed we should, Alassair," replied the other. "What do you wish of us, river's foster?"

"Speak for this man to hear, I beg of you," Balkis said. "Was it not you who told me of my true rank?"

"We did indeed, and only a year ago," said Alassair. "Is this man so foolish as not to believe you?"

"We can change him into a carp for you," Shannai offered.

"Thank you, but I wish him landed," Balkis said.

"It is even as they say." Anthony turned away heavy-hearted. "You are a princess born."

"But not raised!" Balkis ran after him and caught his arm. "Am I not still Balkis, princess or not? Am I not still your little cat? Oh, Anthony, if you do not wish me to be a princess, I shall not be! I shall forswear my title, abdicate my station, and go off into the wilderness to live as you wish!"

"I wish you to have all the luxuries you deserve," he said, his eyes burning into hers. "You are what you are and should have naught but the best. Nothing can change that, nor would I want you to be anything less."

"Nor you," the nixie called Alassair said. "I can see, and hear, that you have been born a peasant, but I can also sense that your struggles to overcome the obstacles in your path have created nobility of spirit in you. Come hither, mortal."

Anthony stepped back in alarm, but Alassair gestured and Anthony came, steps dragging, fighting the nixies' compulsion every step of the way. "Kneel," she commanded, and his knees folded, bringing him down to her level whether he wished it or not.

The water-spirit touched his forehead, then nodded. "He has as much magical talent as she, and it comes from the greatness of his heart, from his integrity and determination. But who is this?"

Both nixies backed away, ready to dive, as Prester John came up behind the young couple. "Ah, it is the man who has decreed this garden to be built for our sport!" Alassair said. "Be assured, Majesty—this lad is indeed one of Nature's noblemen, and we who are of nature should know it better than any."

John drew a wand from his sleeve and held it over Anthony, who was still kneeling, now trembling and wide-eyed. The emperor laid the wand across the youth's right shoulder, then across his left, saying, "I pronounce you a Wizard of the Realm."

Anthony stiffened as though a current were flowing through him.

John put away the wand. "In our land that is a title of nobility, though one gained by effort and merit, not by birth. It is surely enough for you to court a princess."

Anthony rose slowly and turned to Balkis, then took her hands. They stood gazing happily into each other's eyes.

"Oh, show some pluck, mortal!" Shannai said in disgust. "She offers her lips! Take them, and her!"

Slowly, as though a wind blew him, Anthony leaned forward and covered Balkis' lips with his own.

"At last!" Alassair sighed, and with a splash, she and her sister dived beneath the surface.

Prester John and Matt smiled fondly for a while, then turned away to discuss matters of state. As they walked back to the palace, the lovers' kiss deepened, and above them a long serpentine shape drifted across the face of the moon, one that might have been two reptilian forms so thoroughly intertwined that no one could have told where one left off and the other began.